DEATH DREAM

FICTION BY BEN BOVA

* collection

DEATH DREAM

Ben Bova

BANTAM BOOKS
NEW YORK • TORONTO •
LONDON • SYDNEY • AUCKLAND

DEATH DREAM

A Bantam Spectra Book / September 1994

Spectra and the portrayal of a boxed "S" are trademarks of Bantam Books, a division of Bantam Doubleday Dell Publishing Group, Inc.

Library of Congress Cataloging-in-Publication Data

Bova, Ben, 1932–
    Death dream / Ben Bova.
      p.   cm.
    ISBN 0-553-08234-5
    I. Title.
  PS3552.084D4   1994
  813'.54—dc20   93-46463
                                             CIP

Published simultaneously in the United States and Canada

Bantam Books are published by Bantam Books, a division of Bantam Doubleday Dell Publishing Group, Inc. Its trademark, consisting of the words "Bantam Books" and the portrayal of a rooster, is Registered in U.S. Patent and Trademark Office and in other countries. Marca Registrada. Bantam Books, 1540 Broadway, New York, New York 10036.

PRINTED IN THE UNITED STATES OF AMERICA

BVG   0 9 8 7 6 5 4 3 2 1

To the "loose cannon" who is my life dream.
And to Jennifer and Lou, for eight-hundred-some reasons.

The mind is its own place, and in itself
Can make a heav'n of hell, a hell of heav'n
      —John Milton,
       Paradise Lost

When you see something that is technically sweet, you go
ahead and do it and you argue about what to do about it
only after you have had your technical success. This is
the way it was with the atomic bomb.
      —J. Robert Oppenheimer

Virtual Reality. Just who coined the phrase is uncertain. It has also been called "alternative reality" and "cyberspace." *Virtual reality* has become the catchword, the title that is most generally used to describe a computer-produced environment in which you can experience a complete electronically induced hallucination.

DEATH DREAM

CHAPTER 1

A pair of bandits, Daddy. Five o'clock high."

Jerry Adair was startled by his daughter's voice. The sonsofbitches sure know how to get my attention. Using my daughter's voice. The dirty pissing bastards.

He pulled back on the pistol-grip side stick and felt his F-22 jet fighter tilt upward into a steep climb. His right forearm rested comfortably in the cradle that protected it against the crushing g forces that would punish him in a real flight. The F-22 could pull nine g's when it was going balls-out; no human pilot could handle an ordinary up-from-the-floor, between-the-knees control stick under that kind of acceleration load. The side sticks and arm cradles were the only way to get the job done.

With the thumb of his left hand he nudged the throttle control knob and felt himself pushed deeper into his padded seat from the increasing acceleration. He knew it was actually the seat deflating, but damn! it felt real. His back even throbbed slightly where the vertebrae had been cracked years earlier in that wheels-up landing he had made in Saudi Arabia. Should never have told the bastards about that, he grumbled to himself. They use every goddamned thing against you.

Barely vocalizing the words, he murmured, "Panoramic view."

His Agile Eye IV helmet visor lit up and he saw his own fighter as a bright-yellow swept-wing symbol in the center of the universe, its nose aimed at the sky. Sure enough, a pair of red symbols were moving in swiftly after him, but far behind. Nothing else in the area. No radar locks, no missiles launched. Not yet. The ground was a rolling green carpet far below, like a cartoon or a kid's drawing, with his potential targets drawn in with big red X's painted over them.

Damn, the g suit was squeezing his guts just as if he were really flying. How do they do that? Great simulation. Physical reactions just like the real thing. Got to hand it to those double-domed sonsofbitches, they're making this ride everything you could ask for. Maybe even more.

The two bogies were diving down toward him, Adair saw. He kicked left rudder and leveled off, hoping they would overshoot him; then he would slip behind them and fire his Sidewinders at the bastards. He was surprised at how much effort it took to reach the missile-arming switches and flick them on. A small deadly black cross appeared on his helmet display. If it touched the symbols of the intruder aircraft, the missiles would launch automatically.

But the bogies were not going to overshoot him, he saw. They were slowing down, popping their air brakes to begin a high-speed yo-yo that would plant them on his tail. Cursing, puffing from exertion as if he were really flying, Adair thumbed the throttle control forward to full military power and pulled the stick back, trying to put as much distance between them and himself as he could while he clawed for altitude. The intruders immediately broke off their maneuver and hustled after him.

"They're closing in, Daddy," his daughter's voice warned, edging higher, tinged with fear.

Adair scanned the view rastering across his visor. The two red bogies were closing the gap damned fast.

"Range coordinates," he said, barely mouthing the words. The microphone in his oxygen mask caught the vocalization, and immediately the picture before his eyes was crisscrossed with a gridwork marked in kilometers. Even as he blinked his eyes, the red bandits came nearer.

Adair's mission was to strike the ground targets, not to get himself involved in a dogfight. He was alone in the sky except for the enemy fighters; he knew he would get no help. And he was a fighter pilot. His first instinct was to deal with the bandits.

The ground targets won't go away, he told himself. And the ordnance is all tucked inside the bomb bays; nothing hanging from the wings to slow me down. If I try to hit the ground targets they'll wax my tail for sure. No sense getting myself shot down before I can even start my run on them.

He kicked right rudder and turned into the bandits, who were still slightly above him. Coming at them head-on, he presented a smaller cross section to their fire-control radars and masked the heat emissions from his jet engines. Heat-seeking missiles like the Sidewinder worked best when fired from behind their target; they usually followed the jet-exhaust signature right up the engine's stovepipe.

Abruptly the two red bandits multiplied into four, two of them breaking off to Adair's right, two to the left.

"Hey, that's not fair!" he yelled aloud.

No response from the controllers at their consoles.

"You fuckin' sonsofbitches are really out to get me, huh?" he muttered, kicking in the thrust vectoring as he pulled his F-22 into a hard climbing left turn. The jet nozzles swiveled to make the climb steeper than the enemy planes could match.

But they did match it. Hell, they must have given the bastards viffing capability, too, Adair thought as he watched two of the red symbols match his climbing turn almost exactly. His chest hurt now from the continuous exertion, the g forces made his arms heavy, squeezed the breath from his body. His back throbbed with pain and the helmet felt as if it weighed six hundred pounds. How the hell do they do that? he wondered. He felt sweat beading his forehead, running into his eyes. Inside the helmet and oxygen mask he had no way to wipe the perspiration away.

Blinking and squinting, he nosed over into a split-S, but instead of completing it he turned it into a vertical dive. Two of the red bogies followed right down after him, gaining on him. The other two had disappeared from his visor's panoramic view. Maybe that was just a glitch in the program and there's only the two of them, he thought. Adair pulled up sharply, his g suit hissing and squeezing his guts to keep him from blacking out. It's not supposed to be like this, he told himself.

But it was.

Blasting along on the deck, only a few feet above the cartoon drawing of the ground, his Mach meter jittering just below Mach 1, the plane rattled and jounced, shaking his guts, jarring his eyeballs so badly it blurred his vision. The two bandits roared along behind him, inching closer.

"Radar lock!" his daughter's voice screeched.

Adair snapped the F-22 into a turn so tight that his vision grayed out despite the g suit. The bandits stayed fixed on his tail as if they had been painted there.

"Missiles launched!" she shrilled.

He popped a flare, pulled back on the control stick, and slammed the throttles to full emergency power. The overwhelming push of tremendous acceleration crushed in on his chest, flattening him against his seat, making his old back injury scream with agony. His lungs felt raw, flaming. He could feel his heart thundering in his ears.

The missiles raced past below him, chasing the bright infrared signature of the decoy flare. He saw their trails as brilliant red pencil lines darting across the green cartoon landscape. He almost gushed a sigh of relief.

But the other two bandits suddenly appeared on his visor ahead of him. "Radar lock missiles fired!" his daughter screamed all in one breath.

Adair gasped. "Shit! Punching out!"

Then the real pain hit.

The three controllers outside the mock-up cockpit were sitting at their posts in front of the simulation system's consoles, sipping coffee from Styrofoam cups and talking quietly among themselves. Twenty feet away from their desks, the sawed-off cockpit section of an F-22 tilted and shook in the grip of heavy mechanical arms that could rotate the simulator cockpit completely upside down if necessary.

The twenty feet separating the technicians from the simulator where Adair was testing the new program was festooned with cables snaking across the concrete hangar floor and coils of wire dangling from rickety support struts. The consoles had an improvised look to them, as if a dealer in used electronics hardware had just dumped a truckload of gray metal boxes on a trio of warehouse tables. Lights flickered across the faces of some of those boxes. Display screens showed graphs and cartoonlike drawings in garish colors. The three technicians—two men and a woman—paid no attention to the lights or screens.

Until the emergency buzzer began hooting, its red light glaring on and off in the middle of the main console.

"What the hell?"

The chief controller, a civilian employee wearing dingy coveralls that had once been white, yelled at the Air Force technician to his left, "Turn that damned noise off, will ya?"

The technician leaned across the rows of CRT display screens and flicked the toggle switch beneath the baleful red light. She was a young kid in neatly pressed Air Force blue fatigues with a tech sergeant's stripes on her sleeve. The alarm refused to be turned off. Its foghorn wails echoed off the hangar's metal walls. She glanced at the main controller and shrugged.

"God damn it," said the chief controller, pronouncing each word distinctly in his irritation.

All three of them got to their feet and stared at the simulator's closed cockpit.

"Why doesn't he pop the hatch?" the chief controller asked no one in particular.

The other tech, a corporal also in starched blue fatigues, pushed his little typist's chair back on its rollers and hurried across the concrete floor of the big hangar toward the F-22 simulator's cockpit. Its plastic canopy was painted a dark gray so no one could see into it or out. The simulator had stopped moving. The big mechanical arms held it tilted slightly nose-down.

"Must be the hatch release is stuck," said the woman tech. The chief controller nodded absently, but the strained expression on his pinched face as he stared at the mock-up clearly said that he did not believe it.

The corporal ducked between the embracing steel arms and clambered up the metal steps built into the side of the cockpit. He opened the hatch easily. It slid up and back smoothly, just as it would on a real plane.

"Jesus Christ," the corporal yelled over the hooting of the emergency alarm. "Call the medics, quick!"

CHAPTER 2

Susan Santorini stood in front of the kitchen range, carefully reading the instruction pamphlet clutched in her hand. Frowning with concentration, she pecked at the range's control keyboard with one finger. No lights turned on, and she noticed that her nails looked as if she had made the trip from Ohio crawling on all fours. She clucked her tongue in frustration.

"Dan," she called, her voice slightly shrill. "I can't get this stove to do *anything*."

Her twelve-year-old daughter, Angela, appeared at the open kitchen doorway. "Daddy's in the garage."

"Would you call him for me, honey?" Susan said, adding silently, Before I start climbing the wall.

Angela nodded unhappily and pushed past her mother to the door that led to the breezeway and then to the garage. Susan saw that her daughter's blond pigtails hung limp and frayed. Just the way I feel, she said to herself as she stood alone in the strange new kitchen, surrounded by unopened cardboard cartons and ultra-modern appliances that stubbornly refused to work the way the instructions said they should. On top of everything else she had to locate an orthodontist for Angie right away.

Welcome to Pine Lake Gardens, the housing development brochure had said, *the most modern community in Florida.* Susan thought she could use a little of the old-fashioned world she had left behind in Ohio. At least she had known how to turn on the stove there.

She was a slight woman in her mid-thirties, pretty enough to have been an actress in college, with a pert upturned nose, striking turquoise-blue eyes, and auburn hair that hinted at a temper. She called it spirit. Her hair was tied up and out of the way; she was in faded jeans that hugged her butt and a sweatshirt that was much too heavy for Florida despite the new house's air-conditioning—which also did not seem to be working properly. The house felt warm and much too damp to her. It was two weeks into September, but still the muggy heat outside seemed unbearable. Susan had visions of loathsome insects crawling behind the closed cabinet doors, making nests and getting into everything.

The baby woke up with a squalling cry. Susan flung the useless instruction book onto the stove top and hurried into the living room. More half-unpacked crates and cartons. At least she had cajoled the moving men into spreading the carpet for them and placing the sofa and chairs where she wanted them instead of leaving them in a jumble. Little Philip was squirming in his makeshift cradle, a colorful oversized wicker basket they had picked up on their honeymoon in Mexico a hundred years ago. The baby was wet and decidedly unhappy in these strange surroundings. Susan reached for the bag of diapers she had left on the sofa beside his basket.

"What's the matter?" Dan asked.

She turned to see her husband standing tensely in the kitchen doorway, biting his lip the way he always did when he was harried. His sports jacket was gone; his short-sleeved shirt looked wrinkled and soggy; his tie was askew. Angela stood behind him, looking worried, almost scared in all this confusion and turmoil.

"Did the car start?" Susan asked.

"Not yet. The damned battery must be shot. If we had driven from Dayton it would've been okay, probably. Recharged itself. But now it's gone."

While her hands automatically removed Phil's wet diaper, Susan said, "You'll have to find somebody who can jump it, then."

Dan shook his head. "It's not holding a charge. We're going to need a new battery."

He was not much taller than Susan, lean and dark with an artist's slender hands and delicate fingers. To her, Damon Santorini had the brooding seductive looks of an Italian film star or a male model. But Dan himself did not realize it, did not believe it even when she whispered it to him as they made love. It was as if it did not matter to him what she or anyone else thought. He went his own way, withdrawn, alone, self-contained inside his protective shell. It was the one fault she found in him. He was brilliant, but he could not see it. He was a quiet, steady, hardworking husband and father. He took his responsibilities seriously; once he decided to do something he plowed straight ahead and nothing could stop him. There had been only one real crisis in their marriage, and they had worked their way through that. It had been painful, but they had put it behind them at last. Yet somehow, somewhere in his youth, he had built a shell of armor around his inner self that only rarely could she penetrate. She knew there was pain and anger bottled up inside him, but she had never been able to shake him out of his iron self-control for longer than the time it took to make love.

"Angie said you needed me?" he asked. His voice was usually soft, gentle. But now she heard a nervous edge in it.

She could see how tense he was. Diapering the baby, she said, "I can't make anything in the kitchen work. You need an engineering degree just to get the stove to turn on."

He broke into a grin. "Don't worry about the stove. I'll take you out for dinner. I can afford a night on the town, on my new salary."

But Susan shook her head stubbornly. "I've had enough pizza this weekend. I want to cook a meal at home."

"The stove is voice activated," he said. "It's got to be programmed to recognize your voice, then it'll respond to your voice commands. You'll get the hang of it. I'll show you later." And he turned back toward the kitchen.

"Where're you going?" Susan called.

"Got to call and get somebody down here to start the car. Otherwise I'm going to miss my first day on the new job."

It was going to be a new start for them. A new job in a new company in a new community. At three times his Air Force salary. Dan had jumped at the chance; Susan had been reluctant, but she saw that this move meant so much to her husband. It scared her to move so far from everything and everyone she had known all her life, especially with the new baby, but she had taken her courage in her hands and decided that it was time for her to see if she really could stand on her own two feet, without family and lifelong friends surrounding her.

At Susan's insistence, they had flown from Dayton to their new home near Orlando on Friday so that they would have the weekend to get settled in. But the furniture and car and the rest of their belongings did not arrive until the middle of Sunday afternoon, after a dozen angry phone calls, and the moving men told them they would be charged extra for the overtime work. Now, on Monday morning, their new house was in a jumble after a weekend of fast-food deliveries and sleeping on blankets laid out on the bedroom carpeting. Nothing seemed to be working, including the car's battery.

At least Dan had set up her computer. While she and Angela had started the unpacking he had sat himself in a corner of the kitchen and put her computer system together. Some husbands watched football that weekend; Dan Santorini sat in front of his wife's computer screen Sunday afternoon and most of the night, fiddling with the programs for hours on end.

"Angie's got to get to school, too," Susan called to her husband's retreating back.

"I know," he said with a heavy sigh.

"Don't they have a school bus?" Angie asked. "I always took the school bus back home."

"This is our home now, Angel," Dan told his daughter as he brushed past her and returned to the kitchen.

Susan said, "I'm sure they have a school bus, Angel. We just don't know what time it comes. In a day or so we'll get it all settled, you'll see."

Angela gave her mother an accusing stare. She had cried for four straight days when her parents had told her they were moving to Florida. Susan knew Angie would adjust to the move faster than any of them, but at age twelve with new braces on her teeth the tears came easily and in a flood. Now she just looked angry: You've ruined my life, her stare said. You've taken me away from my home and all my friends. I'll never love you again, ever ever ever.

Trying to ignore her daughter's silent accusations and her own fears, Susan finished diapering the baby and got to her feet. Before she could start for the kitchen, the front doorbell rang.

Now what? she wondered.

She squeezed through the packing crates and reached for the doorknob just as the bell chimed again. Susan pulled the door open. Kyle Muncrief stood there in the dazzling Florida heat, a broad welcoming smile on his tanned face, looking cool and at ease in an open-necked sport shirt and whipcord slacks.

"Hello, Susan. Thought I'd drop by and see how you guys are getting along."

Muncrief was not quite handsome, but he knew how to wear clothes well and he could be elegantly charming. He was tall, wide in the shoulders, but starting to look soft in his midsection. His hands always seemed to be in motion, reaching for some invisible object, emphasizing points he wanted to make, brushing back the shock of unruly hair that constantly tumbled across his forehead. His hair was still thick and dark, but touches of silver showed at the temples. He wore it long, down to his collar. There was something restless in his hazel eyes: something urgent, demanding. His eyes did not match the charming, easygoing smile.

"Mr. Muncrief," Susan mumbled.

"Kyle. Just call me Kyle." His voice was a soft light tenor.

"Uh—come on in."

As Muncrief stepped into the chaos of the living room, Dan yelled from the kitchen, "Who was at the door?"

"Mr. Muncrief, dear," answered Susan. "Kyle's here."

Kyle Muncrief was the founder, president, and chief executive officer of ParaReality, Inc. He had personally flown to Ohio to lure Damon Santorini away from the laboratory at Wright-Patterson Air Force Base and hire him for ParaReality in the Orlando region of central Florida.

Dan popped out of the kitchen doorway like a buck private summoned by his general. "I couldn't get the car started and I don't know any gas stations to call for a jump—"

Muncrief laughed and waved Dan to silence. "I figured you'd have your hands full this morning."

"I'm sorry I'll be late."

"Not to worry. Looks like you've got plenty to keep you busy right here."

"I *hate* being late."

"It's not a problem," Muncrief said easily. "Why don't you just stay home this morning and get yourself organized a bit. Drop in at the office after lunch, okay? My personnel chief'll want to run you through the orientation routine, that's all. I'll tell her you'll be coming in this afternoon."

"And Angela's got to get to school as soon as you get the car started," said Susan.

Muncrief's eyes shifted to the twelve-year-old. She was almost as tall as her mother. "Hello, Angela. Remember me? I came to visit you back in Dayton, remember?"

Angela shied away and stood close to her mother, lips clamped tight.

"Don't be bashful," Muncrief said. "I'll drive you to school, if you'll let me."

"Would you?" Susan beamed at him.

"Sure. It's right on the way to the office. Lord, I've been there as often as I've been at my own desk. ParaReality's put more money into that school than the county has, with all the virtual-reality teaching systems I've given them."

"I certainly appreciate your help, Mr. Muncrief," said Dan.

"Kyle," he repeated. "No need to be so formal. Just call me Kyle." Pointing his finger like a pistol at Angela, he said, "Come on, Angie. I'll drive you to school. You ever been in a convertible? I've got the top down."

"It's all right, honey," Susan told her daughter. "Go wash your face and Mr. Muncrief—Kyle—will drive you to school."

"All the other kids will wonder who your boyfriend is," Muncrief joked.

Angela headed reluctantly toward the bathroom.

"Nice kid," said Muncrief.

Dan was biting his lip again. "I've got to find a gas station."

"I've got jumper cables in the trunk," Muncrief said. "I can get you started. Come on. If you need to, you can rent a car for a day or two. The company'll cover it."

Uncertainly, Dan said, "Well, if the damned battery will hold a charge long enough, I can drive Angie and get to the office."

Muncrief waved a hand at him. "Don't worry about it. You stay home this morning and help get things sorted out here. It's okay."

Susan wanted to tell Dan to go on to the office and get out of her way. She knew her husband would be much happier going to his new job than helping to straighten out the mess of their new home. But she didn't think it would be right to spurn Mr. Muncrief's offer.

Dan muttered, "Okay . . . thanks."

"Come on, let's get your car started."

The two men went outside.

Angela came back, actually smiling despite her braces. "It's a brand-new car, Mommy! I saw it through the bathroom window."

Susan realized that there were no curtains on either of the bathroom windows yet. She shook her head and took a deep breath. So much to do.

Fifteen minutes later, Dan's old Honda was growling and rattling on the driveway as Muncrief and Angela waved from his Jaguar XJS convertible. It was forest green, Susan saw from the living-room window.

Dan came back inside.

"Kyle's a thoroughly nice man," Susan said.

"Yeah. Looks that way."

"I've got to feed the baby. You want to start unpacking the stuff in here? Most of it goes in the bedrooms."

"Okay," he said absently.

"You look worried."

Dan's dark brows knit together. "Well, Jace is expecting me this morning."

"Oh, Jace!" she said. "He can wait a few hours. It won't kill him."

"I guess not."

"You could phone him and tell him you'll be in after lunch."

"Nah. He never answers the phone."

"Then he'll just have to wait for you, for a change."

Dan nodded unhappily.

Susan picked up the wicker basket with Philip in it and headed for the kitchen, knowing that it would be better if she wasn't in the same room with her husband for a while.

On the broad sunny boulevard heading toward the school, Kyle Muncrief identified the different kinds of palm trees lining the streets for Angela's benefit.

"Those over there are royal palms. See how tall and straight they are?"

"They all look the same to me," Angela said.

"Oh no, palm trees are as different as people. You'll get to recognize the differences in a little while."

"It's awful hot here in Florida."

"I think it's very nice here," Muncrief said. "It's just that you've been living in a place that's a lot colder. You'll get used to the weather here—soon you'll love it."

"I guess."

"You can swim all year round."

"I don't know how to swim."

"Don't know how to swim? Well, I can show you how to swim without even getting wet. What do you think of that?"

"That sounds weird," Angela said.

Muncrief laughed. "You'll see."

CHAPTER 3

Dan felt a twinge of surprise as he pulled his rattling old dark-blue Honda—with its new battery—into the parking lot in front of the ParaReality building at half past one in the afternoon.

For a company that's going to put Disney out of business, the place did not look like much. Just a single-story cinder-block building, painted a faded yellow. And the lot was almost empty. It's not a holiday, he told himself. He recognized Muncrief's Jag sitting in the slot closest to the front entrance, but there were only eight other cars in sight, all big four-door sedans, several of them bearing the stickers of rental or leased autos. Dan noted that Muncrief's parking space was covered by a thin roof of corrugated metal and the top of his convertible was still down. The other cars were out in the blazing sunshine.

Rank has its privileges, thought Dan as he eased his Honda into the slot next to the empty place for the handicapped. He wondered where all the other ParaReality employees were. They can't all be out at lunch. Maybe—

"How do!" called a voice from the shade of the front doorway. Dan saw a burly man in a blue security uniform limping toward him.

"Ye moughtn't be Dr. Damon Santorini, moughtn't ye?"

"Mr. Santorini," said Dan as he got out of his car. "Dan."

"How do," the security officer repeated. He had only one arm. His face was round, apple-cheeked. The cap atop his thick mop of sandy hair did not fit well; it perched up there like a kid on a haystack. He couldn't have been more than twenty-five years old.

He put out his left hand, the only one he had. "Ol' Jace tole me you was comin' today. Been lookin' out fer ye all mornin'."

Feeling inhumanly awkward, Dan took the guard's left hand in his own right. "I had a problem with my car," he mumbled.

"Joe Rucker's the name," said the guard, grinning good-naturedly. "And any friend o' Jace's is a friend o' mine."

Jason Lowrey had been Dan's partner, teammate, almost his brother when they had both worked for the Air Force in Dayton. Jace was the genius, the man with the flare for dramatic new ideas and stunning breakthroughs in the field of virtual reality. Dan was the quiet steady guy in the background, the one who made Jace's brilliant ideas work. Jace did not make friends easily, Dan knew, yet this hillbilly guard seemed to think the world of him.

"C'mon," said Joe Rucker, "I'll escort ye in."

It was barely twenty paces to the front door, and Dan could have made it faster without the limping kid at his side. But he pulled his jacket from the back seat, carefully locked the Honda, and went with Rucker.

"You and Jace are pals?" Dan asked.

"Shoot, if 'tweren't fer Jace I wouldn't even be here." He pronounced it *heah*. "Who's gonna hire a North Carolina redneck that's lost an arm an' a leg?"

"Jace got you this job?"

"He shorely did, bless his heart."

"How did you . . . get hurt?"

"Motorsickle. Some ol' grandmaw in a big camper ran rat over me. Purtty near died. I only got one lung."

They had reached the smoked-glass double doors of the front entrance. It looked cool and quiet inside.

"Well, thanks a lot, Joe," said Dan as he put on his navy-blue blazer.

The guard plucked at Dan's sleeve. "One thang ye oughtter know: all the folks workin' here hafta park their cars out back."

"Oh! I didn't know."

Before Dan could turn back toward his car, Joe said, "Dontcha worry none. I'll watch yer car for ye. T'morrow, though, ye'd best park it out back." He smiled broadly.

"Well, thanks again, Joe."

"Nothin' to it, Dr. Dan. Anythin' ye need, ye just ax me. Any friend o' Jace's is a friend o' mine."

Marveling that Jace would even say hello to a self-admitted redneck who obviously had no education, Dan hesitated a fraction of a second to check his reflection in the dark glass door. Tie straight, hair combed. Jacket looks all right. Can't see how badly the shirt's wrinkled with the jacket over it. Okay. He took a deep breath, then pushed through the tinted glass door and stepped into the air-conditioned coolness of the ParaReality lobby.

A couple of men were sitting on the couches along one side of the lobby. Salesmen, from the look of their suits. One of them was leafing through a brochure; the other puffed tensely on a cigarette even though there were no ashtrays in sight and a red No Smoking sign on the wall. The receptionist behind the curved walnut desk smiled up at him.

"I'm Dan Santorini—"

"Oh yes, Mr. Santorini. Vickie Kessel is expecting you."

Dan knew that Victoria Kessel was the head of ParaReality's personnel department. He had spoken to her a dozen times on the telephone; she had even helped them to find the house they had bought, long-distance. But he had never met her. The receptionist pointed him through the double doors behind her desk.

"Vickie's office is the first door on the left-hand side of the corridor."

Muttering his thanks, Dan pushed through the double doors. It felt odd just walking into the place without a security escort or a badge or any of the precautions that had been a way of life at the Air Force lab in Dayton. The receptionist had not asked for any identification; she had not even bothered to phone Ms. Kessel to tell her that he was on his way to see her. What if she's not in her office?

The first door on his left was wide open. The room inside made Dan wonder if he had heard the receptionist correctly. It was small but plush, and furnished more like a sitting room than a business office. There was no desk, no filing cabinet in sight. Beneath an

Oriental painting of two birds on a tree branch stood a comfortable chintz-covered wing chair. To one side of it was a small sofa, delicately curved and upholstered in some slightly fuzzy material the color of burgundy wine.

Beside the armchair was a small table that bore a simple gray keypad. There were no windows in this interior room, but a big display screen covered one of the walls, featureless smooth gray like the giant television screens that saloons put up to show sports events for their customers.

"Damon Santorini?"

Dan turned in the doorway to see a woman striding smartly down the corridor toward him. Victoria Kessel looked as if she had just stepped out of a magazine advertisement. She was wearing a stylish suit of mustard yellow, the long jacket curving around her hips almost down to the hem of her miniskirt, the color complementing her deep Florida tan. Plenty of jewelry: big earrings, several gold necklaces, and clattering bracelets.

She stuck out her hand and smiled brightly. "I'm Vickie Kessel, and you're Damon Santorini, right?"

"Dan," he said, shaking her hand. Her grip was firm, the kind that took practice.

"It's good to meet you in the flesh after all our telephone conversations. Come on into my boudoir," Vickie said, gesturing toward her office door.

He stepped back and let her go in first.

Vickie settled herself in the armchair, kicking off her high-heeled shoes and tucking her legs under her. Good legs, Dan noticed. She was not what he would call pretty—her features were too sharp and intense for his taste, her voice a little too cutting—but her face was strong and expressive and her dark hair was clipped fashionably short. He wondered how old she was; older than Sue, he was pretty sure.

"Kyle told me you had some problems with your car. I'm glad you could make it in this afternoon."

Her accent said New York to Dan, and he understood her high-voltage appearance. Vickie was the take-charge type, the kind who parlayed smarts and hustle and style into an upwardly mobile career. She pulled her keyboard over and called up Dan's personnel file. On the oversized display screen the words looked enormous, like a bigger-than-life statue of some hero. Maybe she's near-sighted, Dan thought. Vickie asked Dan to check the file over, make any corrections or additions he felt necessary. He added Philip's Social Security number to the data.

She smiled slightly. "Thinking of getting him a job soon?"

"He's only six months old."

"I know," she said. "I was only joking."

She wormed her feet back into her shoes and got up from the chair. Dan followed her down the corridor to the security office, where a guy in the same blue uniform as Joe Rucker's took his photograph and a few minutes later presented Dan with a laminated badge. Dan remembered the old joke about ID badges from his earliest days as an Air Force employee in Dayton. The photos on the badges were called holy pictures, because whenever somebody looked at one he would say, "Jesus Christ, is that you?"

But he said nothing as he accepted the badge from the security officer's hand and solemnly clipped it to the breast pocket of his blazer. This is more like it, he thought.

For the next half hour Vickie toured Dan through the building. Mostly business offices up front, all occupied by quietly aggressive men and women, making telephone calls, poring over computer screens, talking earnestly into telephones or to one another. A few good-looking young women, but most of the business staff seemed to be older. Vickie introduced him to several of the department heads—all male. Dan forgot their names as soon as he heard them.

Dan noticed that the corridors were paneled and carpeted. Everything cool and quiet. Reproductions of fine paintings and prints hung on the walls. But as Vickie led him deeper into the building the wood paneling ended and the plasterboard hallways were painted a flat pastel yellow. The floors were covered with vinyl tile here, scuffed and scratched, and the corridors wide enough to trundle sizable equipment through.

"Mostly offices for the technical staff in this area," Vickie said.

Dan heard voices yammering, a radio playing Golden Oldies, two men obviously arguing behind a closed door. It even smelled different from the quietly efficient business section. Engineers and programmers worked here; he could feel the heat of conception.

"Where are the labs?" he asked.

"Toward the rear of the building," said Vickie.

The pictures on these corridor walls were mostly group photographs of people Dan did not recognize. A few bulletin boards were scattered about with the usual clutch of notices tacked to them. There were posters proclaiming everything from Earth Day to rock concerts. Vickie pointed out the cafeteria, silent and empty, its stainless-steel counters gleaming spotlessly.

"Lavatories at the end of that hall," she said. "And down here is the Pit—the computer center."

Dan looked through the wide windows of the computer center and saw several big mainframes lined up against the walls. He could sense them humming away.

"Those are Crays," he said, feeling almost awed.

Vickie took him around a corner, then stopped in front of an unmarked door.

"And this," she announced with a dramatic flourish, "is your very own office."

Dan opened the door and stuck his head in. A bare desk, a couple of chairs, empty bookshelves. It would do.

"It has a window," Vickie pointed out.

Dan nodded absently. "Where's Jace's office?"

She seemed momentarily disappointed, but then she pointed. "Around the corner, there." Dan noticed that her fingernails were lacquered gold.

Feeling a sudden eagerness, Dan headed down the corridor without waiting for Vickie to guide him.

"He's never there," said Vickie, trailing behind him. "He's almost always in his lab. Or in Wonderland."

"Wonderland?"

"The VR simulations chamber."

"Where's that?"

"I'll show you," she said.

Dan stepped aside to let her lead the way again, impatient to get to his old friend, to start his new job, to sink his teeth into the work he had come here to do.

"That's his office," Vickie commented as they passed a closed door marked J. LOWREY. Dan saw that Jace had pasted a hand-lettered sign beneath his nameplate: *Do Not Enter! High Hazard Area! Creative Work Underway!* He grinned, remembering the nuclear-radiation sign that Jace had pilfered from one of the other Wright-Patterson labs and plastered on his office door in Dayton.

Vickie stopped in front of a blank door. This one was metal rather than wood. A red light blinked over the door frame. Dan noticed a small printed sign beneath it: *Do not enter when red light is on. Simulation in progress.* Someone had pasted other signs beside the door:

Welcome to the Emerald City
Down the rabbit hole.
Abandon all hope, ye who enter here.

Vickie tapped at the door with the back of her knuckles. The door swung outward a crack and a suspicious-faced technician peeked out at them. He was young but obese, his skin waxy and pimpled from junk food.

"This is Damon Santorini," said Vickie before the guy could say a word. "He's going to be working with Jace."

The technician grunted and pushed the door open a bit more.

"I'll leave you here," Vickie told Dan with an almost sly smile on her lips. "This is your territory now. I'm going back to my neck of the woods."

"Uh, thanks for . . . everything," Dan said to her retreating back. Then he slipped through the partially open doorway.

The control room was small, dark, cramped, and hot. Just like the ones at Wright-Patterson Air Force Base that Dan was accustomed to. It smelled of fried circuit boards and old pizzas. Two technicians were seated at consoles with their backs to him, facing a square window of one-way glass. Neither of them acknowledged Dan's presence in any way. They were hunched over their consoles, studying the display screens that flickered in the shadows. The third tech, the heavy one who had opened the door for Dan, pulled it shut and took the only other chair in the narrow, sweaty chamber.

Dan wormed his arms out of his jacket. There was no place to put it, so he folded it over one arm. Pulling his tie loose and unbuttoning his collar, Dan leaned in between the other two technicians seated at their consoles and peered through the tinted window. Beyond the one-way glass stood his friend, his colleague and partner, Jason Lowrey.

The room in which Lowrey stood was spacious, although its

ceiling was almost oppressively low. The chamber was utterly empty: walls totally blank, not a stick of furniture, floor bare gray vinyl tile. Jace was crouched slightly, hands on knees, as if winded from exertion. He wore a heavy-looking bulbous black helmet with a darkened visor pulled down over his face. Metallic gloves on both hands. Barely visible wires trailed from the helmet and gloves toward the window where Dan was watching.

"What's he doing in there?" Dan asked in a whisper.

One of the young men at the consoles glanced up at him. "Baseball," he said.

Jace straightened up and started running backward. Dan saw that he was on a treadmill. Jace reached up with his right hand and clutched at something invisible. Then he grabbed it with his left and threw it with a sweeping overhand motion.

"How long's he going to be in there?" Dan asked.

The technician looked up at him again. He looked like an Asian-American, and he seemed very young to Dan. He made a tight smile. "Who knows? He might decide to play the whole World Series."

Dan nodded ruefully. That was Jace, all right. He did things his own way, and everybody else had to wait on him.

After several minutes of watching a pantomime of baseball, though, Dan grew impatient.

"Can't you call him out of there?"

"Not me!" said the Asian. "He doesn't like being disturbed."

"Then let me." Dan reached for the microphone on the console.

"I've got a better idea," said the young man. He pushed his chair back and got to his feet. "Let me show you some of the other things going on around here. Jace will let us know when he's ready to see you."

The executive offices of ParaReality were in the front of the single-story yellow brick building, where their long windows faced the carefully nurtured lawn of Bermuda grass and the nodding palms and flowering hibiscus bushes that bordered the nearly empty parking lot.

Kyle Muncrief had prevailed upon United Telephone of Florida

to construct a videoconference center in his building for the private use of ParaReality, Inc. He had it installed in a windowless
interior room next to his own office, with a connecting doorway
linking the two rooms.

Now he sat at the head of the long polished table and spoke in
conference with three of his key investors, each of them a life-size
image on the high-definition screens that filled three of the room's
walls. The room was otherwise empty, except for Victoria Kessel,
sitting at the foot of the table, out of the view of the three men in
teleconference with Muncrief.

"The baseball game is coming along extremely well," Muncrief
was saying, with a big salesman's smile. His hands unconsciously
clasped around a nonexistent Louisville Slugger as he added,
"You'll be able to play against anybody who ever appeared in the
major leagues. And pick your own teammates, too!"

"The major leagues of the United States, I presume?" said
Hideki Toshimura. His pinched, puffy-eyed face was not smiling.

Muncrief conceded the point with a slight dip of his chin. "It'll
be a simple matter to program the players of the Japanese leagues
into the game. As long as you have the statistics, we can produce
the player. Imagine Sadaharu Oh socking home runs again!"

Lars Swenson, who happened to be in Zurich at the moment,
asked, "Can the program be adapted to other games? Football, for
instance?"

"Certainly, certainly," Muncrief said easily, making a mental
note to check with Lowrey if that might be possible.

"He means soccer, Kyle," said Maxwell Glass, from New York.

"Any game you like—virtually." Muncrief laughed at his pun.
The others did not.

"May I point out," Toshimura said, "that the development effort is more than four months behind schedule? And"—he
glanced down briefly—"six and a quarter million dollars over budget."

Muncrief brushed at the lock of hair that fell boyishly across his
forehead. "Look, friends, we're talking about cutting-edge research here. Breakthroughs like you've never seen before! You
can't expect these things to follow a schedule, for God's sake!"

Swenson said, "*You* can't expect an unending flow of money,
Muncrief."

"We'll open Cyber World on time," Muncrief said.

"In seven months?" Glass looked utterly unconvinced. "That's what the schedule calls for: April first."

Squirming slightly in his chair, Muncrief replied, "In seven months. That's right. The construction's already underway and—"

"That's only brick and mortar," said Swenson.

"And about half the games are in the can, ready to go," Muncrief continued. "This isn't like Disneyland, you know. We don't need elaborate structures and all those clanking mechanical nightmares. All we need are a few simple buildings and the electronics."

"Half the games, you said?" Toshimura prompted.

Ticking his fingers, Muncrief said, "We've got the Moonwalk—which can be converted to a Mars walk fast as you can blink an eye. And the undersea adventure. And the trip through the human body. And the creation of the universe!"

"But not the baseball."

"Not yet. Soon. Very soon." Muncrief's jaunty grin returned. "And remember, these games aren't passive. You don't just walk through the human body. You can change it! You can go right into the brain and make the body speak and move! And you haven't seen the Space Race game yet! Virtual reality is an *experience;* you interact with the environment you're in."

"But the conflict games are giving you trouble," Swenson half-guessed, half-accused.

Muncrief's grin froze on his face. "The conflict games call for two or more people to share the simulation at the same time. Naturally, that's a bit more complex than a simulation where one person runs everything by himself. Or herself."

"The conflict games will be the big attraction," said Glass. "That's the one thing Cyber World will have that nobody else can do. Take part in the gunfight at the O.K. Corral. I was looking forward to that one myself."

"To pitch against Babe Ruth while one's friend sees himself batting against Nolan Ryan." Toshimura's face was expressionless, but his voice had a slightly dreamy ring to it.

Muncrief held up his hands. "The conflict games will be there, I promise you. They just need a little more time." His investors waited, and sure enough Muncrief added, "And a little more money."

"How much more money?" Toshimura asked.

Pushing his hair back again, Muncrief replied, "Enough to keep the team working at the problem until it's solved. That runs to roughly four, five hundred thousand a month. It's not so much."

"For how many months?" Swenson asked.

"Until it's perfected."

"You want us to make an open-ended commitment?" Glass looked startled at the idea.

Muncrief said, "I wish I could give you a schedule, but we're dealing with very creative people working at the cutting edge of the technology. Lord, they don't know how long it will take. How on earth can I know?"

"But the conflict games must be ready when Cyber World opens!" Toshimura insisted. "Otherwise there is no point to opening the park."

"Oh, they'll be ready by then," Muncrief promised. "Lord, that's seven months away."

"Two point eight to three point five million dollars," muttered Swenson.

"Call it three mil and let it go at that." Muncrief spread his hands and tried to smile at them.

"After we have already invested so many millions," Toshimura said.

"It's necessary," Muncrief said, almost apologetically. "I told you at the outset that we'd probably need more funding. Our original budget was based on the proposition that we wouldn't hit any serious snags."

"You're saying you've hit a serious snag?" Glass snapped, frowning.

Muncrief put up his hands as if to shield himself from a blow. "No! Not really. It's not serious in the technical sense. It's just that we're running closer to the deadline than I thought we would, and more money would allow us to put more people on the problem."

"Three million dollars more," Toshimura repeated.

"It's small change." Muncrief glanced from one face to another.

"It's blackmail," said Swenson. "Or extortion, at the least."

"It can't be done," said Glass sternly.

Waggling one hand, Muncrief replied, "Aw, come on! We're so close to success, you can't throw in the towel now."

"It isn't a matter of giving up, Kyle," Glass said. "You're over budget and we're overcommitted."

"What's another three mil?" Muncrief pleaded.

"We do not have an unending supply of funds," said Swenson. "We would have to go out and raise that three million from other sources."

"What other sources?"

"Sony has expressed an interest," Toshimura said. "And, I am told, there has also been an expression of interest from the Disney people."

"Oh no!" Muncrief almost leaped out of his seat. "No you don't! I didn't start this company to sell it out to Disney, goddammit! Or Sony, either."

"A partnership would make sense," Swenson said.

"No!" Muncrief slammed a hand on the table. "No partners. I told you that when we started this venture."

"You were not over budget then."

"No partners. No selling out."

"In that case," Swenson barely suppressed a bitter smile, "no additional funding."

"But—"

"Kyle, you can't have your cake and eat it too," said Max Glass. "If you want the additional three million, you've got to let Disney or Sony or one of the other big boys buy into Cyber World."

"And lose control of my own company."

"There is an alternative," said Toshimura.

Muncrief looked into his image on the life-size screen, sitting in his office in Tokyo.

"You could finish your work without additional funding," Toshimura said. "You could open Cyber World on schedule—and within the budget you now have available to you."

Muncrief began to shake his head. "I just told you that—"

"It's either that or open up this venture to a partnership," said Swenson.

Muncrief looked toward Glass.

"That's the long and short of it, Kyle. You can't have it both ways."

Gritting his teeth, Muncrief said, "Okay. Okay. You want to play hardball, we'll play hardball. I'll open Cyber World on schedule—with the baseball game. If I have to lay off three-quarters of the staff here, if I have to hock my balls, I'll get it done."

Toshimura gave him a thin smile.

"That's the spirit," said Glass.

"April first," Swenson repeated.

Once the three wall screens had gone opaque, Muncrief mopped his face with a handful of Kleenex. Victoria Kessel, who had been sitting at the far end of the conference table, unseen by the investors, arched a brow at her boss.

"Do you really intend to hock your balls?" she asked.

"If I have to," Muncrief said, pushing his chair back from the table.

"I've got a better solution."

"Vickie, I've told you before, I'm not interested in a government contract."

"We need the cushion, Kyle. We can't operate on this shoestring for much longer."

"I don't want a government contract!" he snapped. "Take money from the blasted government and they tie you up with all their everlasting red tape."

"This wouldn't be an ordinary kind of government procurement. It would come straight from the White House," Vickie said. "Believe me, Kyle, they don't want to get wrapped up in red tape, either."

"Yeah, sure."

"Kyle, they don't want anybody outside the White House to get a whiff of this. Not even the Congress. It's discretionary money, straight out of the Oval Office. Nobody will be looking over your shoulder."

He tried to scowl at her, but it didn't work.

"They'll pay well, and the work shouldn't be all that difficult. It could be the cushion you need."

"I don't want to deal with the government," he said. Weakly.

Vickie allowed herself to smile slightly. "Just talk to them, Kyle. It won't hurt you to talk, will it?"

He grumbled something too low for her to hear.

"It's either that or sell out to Disney," said Vickie. She knew that would get him to do what she wanted. Muncrief had no intention of letting any other company get its hands on ParaReality.

Vickie was not sure that he could keep his independence. The competition was already sniffing around ParaReality, trying to make deals with some of the employees for inside information. Industrial espionage, it was called.

Victoria Kessel knew all about industrial espionage. She was already involved in it.

CHAPTER 4

Angela had desperately wanted her father to take her to school on this first day, but Daddy had stayed home to help unpack. And Mommy had been busy with Phil, as she almost always was. Angela loved her baby brother, of course, but ever since he had been born Mommy had less and less time for her.

Her only friend was Amanda, the thumb-size doll that her grandmother Emerson had made for her out of knitting yarn when she had been just a little girl, back in Dayton. Amanda was faded and frayed, but Angie had slipped her into the pocket of her jeans. She needed a friend with her this first day in a strange new school.

Mr. Muncrief had been nice, though. His car was totally hot, and he walked her all the way into the school building and right to her classroom. It made her feel important, because all the teachers and grown-ups in the school seemed to know Mr. Muncrief. He was an important man.

Her teacher, Mrs. O'Connell, made Angela feel pretty much at home right away.

"This is a brand-new school," she explained to Angela, "so everyone here is a newcomer."

She brought Angela to the front of the classroom and introduced her. "Angela has come to us from Dayton, Ohio," she explained. "Is that the farthest any of us have come from?"

The kids buzzed among themselves for a moment, then several hands shot up eagerly. After a few minutes the class decided that the one who had come the farthest distance was a blond, good-looking boy from Santa Barbara, California. His name was Gary Rusic.

Angela did not have to say anything more than "Hello" to them all, and when she smiled she kept her lips closed so nobody could see the braces on her teeth. She wormed her hand into the pocket of her jeans and felt Amanda there, comforting and familiar. Then she noticed that several of the girls wore braces, and she felt a little better.

"This is a different kind of school," Mrs. O'Connell told the class once Angela had taken the seat assigned to her. The students' desks were scattered around the room, not lined up in rigid rows the way they had been back in Ohio.

Pointing to the six doors at the rear of the room, Mrs. O'Connell said, "We're going to be using virtual-reality programs and games quite a bit. I know you're going to like them, because instead of listening to me tell you things or reading things out of a book, the virtual-reality system will allow you to *go* places and *do* things so that you'll *be* in the places you're supposed to be learning about."

Angela felt a little confused about that. Daddy worked on virtual-reality stuff, she knew that. But she could not imagine how the things he did could be used here in school.

She quickly found out.

There were only eighteen students in the class, and Mrs. O'Connell divided them into three groups. Angela was in the second group. She read from a brand-new textbook about how the Native Americans lived before Columbus discovered the New World. But she kept one eye on the back of the room, where Mrs. O'Connell was helping the first six kids into the booths back there.

After a while, the teacher returned to the front of the room and started talking with the children about life in America before the Europeans arrived. Angela paid attention with only half her mind, wondering what the kids were doing in those booths.

Half an hour later, the first group came out of the booths, smiling happily as if they had been to a movie or a party or something. Angela felt a little excited as Mrs. O'Connell got them settled back at the desks and then called for the next six to go to the booths.

It was dark inside. Small as a telephone booth, but instead of a phone there was a little bench to sit on and a shelf with a plastic helmet resting on it. Like a biker's helmet; only, a set of wires came out of it. The wires were wrapped in coils of metal, just like the telephone wire in a public booth. Mrs. O'Connell helped Angela put on the helmet and wriggle her fingers into the fuzzy gloves that had been inside it.

"It will get completely dark for a few moments," she said as she slid the visor down over Angela's eyes. Her voice was muffled by the helmet's padding. "You're not frightened of the dark, are you?"

"A little," Angela confessed.

"It will only be for a moment or two."

It got *very* dark. Pitch black. Angela heard the door of the booth click shut. She reached out with her gloved hands and touched the walls of the booth. She felt scared.

"It's all right," she whispered to Amanda. "Don't be afraid."

Then she saw colors. Like a sunset; only, these colors shifted and swirled around and then . . .

She was in a forest. Big trees rising all around her, their leafy canopies almost blotting out the sun. The sweet smell of grass and pine. Flowering bushes everywhere. Birds calling back and forth, flicking in and out among the trees in darting flashes of brilliant color. It wasn't like watching a movie. She was *in* the forest. She walked among the trees, eyes goggling. The mossy ground felt soft and a little springy beneath her feet. A deer peeked at her from between some bushes, its big brown eyes limpid, its ears twitching. It was beautiful.

"This is the forest home of the Iroquois," said a man's voice, "as it existed more than five hundred years ago."

The voice spoke about the Native Americans for a few more minutes. Then suddenly Angela was lifted off her feet, rising through the trees, soaring above them. She was flying! Flying above the swaying tops of the trees, racing along in the sun-warmed air like a bird, an eagle, high above the ground.

"And this," said the voice, "is the home of another tribe of Native Americans: the Aztecs."

From her high eagle's vantage Angela saw a mighty city built on islands in a huge lake. Streets and houses and temples built atop steep stone pyramids.

"Mexico City," said the voice. "The largest city in the world. The year is A.D. fifteen hundred. Would you like to explore this city?"

"Yes!" Angela answered. She wanted to shout, but she was so excited that all she could do was whisper. "Yes!"

"My name's Gary Chan," said the Asian-American after he and Dan had slipped out of the dank, hot control room.

Dan shook his hand as he asked, "You work for Jace?"

Chan grinned. "Who doesn't? When he needs somebody to run the board for him or some other errands, he rubs his lamp and we obey."

They were standing in the hallway outside the control room. Dan studied the youngster's face. Not quite as inscrutable as the proverbial Oriental. Dan recognized the eager look in his eyes.

"You said you wanted to show me something."

Trying to sound casual, Chan said, "While we're waiting for Jace, I thought I might as well show you some of the stuff I've been doing."

"Okay. Good." Dan followed him down the hallway.

"Jace's doing the conflict games," Chan said. "The rest of us have been putting together the simpler stuff." He was still trying to appear nonchalant, but the excitement in his voice showed through.

Dan knew that ParaReality's main business was to create an amusement park using VR instead of the mechanical games and rides of older parks like Disney World.

"Conflict games?" Dan asked.

"Like the baseball sim," Chan replied, opening a door. "Two people can play against one another."

"They've been doing that for years in video arcades."

Chan almost scowled. "Yeah, and they call that simpleminded junk virtual reality. It's as crude as cave paintings compared to what we're doing. Have you ever tried one?"

Dan nodded. The kid was right. The so-called VR systems he

had seen at arcades were little more than video games, primitive and boring.

The door Chan opened led into another control booth. Smaller. Simpler. The VR chamber beyond the one-way glass was also smaller than the one Jace was using.

"I've been doing the travel sims," Chan explained as he slipped into the only chair in the narrow booth and powered up the console. "Want to try one?"

Dan wanted to see Jace. But he replied, "Sure, why not?"

Chan smiled boyishly. "There's a helmet and gloves over on the shelf. You know how to hook yourself up, don't you?"

"Sure."

In a few minutes, Dan was sitting in the chair placed in the middle of the otherwise empty VR chamber. The gloves felt stiff as he flexed his fingers; the helmet slightly unbalanced, as if it wanted to slide forward on his head. He saw his own reflection in the one-way glass, looking tight-lipped and slightly suspicious. He loosened his tie some more and waited.

"You can slide the visor down now." He heard Chan's voice in the helmet earphones. "This sim is called 'Space Race.' "

"Okay." Dan pulled the dark visor over his eyes. "I'm ready."

All at once he was sitting at the controls of a futuristic spacecraft. Beyond its windows he saw a field of stars and several other spacecraft hovering in the dark emptiness.

"Seven . . . six . . . five . . ." intoned a voice. Dan saw the displays on the console in front of him light up like a Christmas tree. Shit, he thought. Another goddamned cockpit simulation.

"Two . . . one . . . BLAST OFF!"

The lurch of acceleration caught him unawares and slammed him back into the cushions of his chair. All the other spacecraft sprouted dazzling flame from their rocket nozzles and streaked out of his view.

"Malfunction! Malfunction!" his ship's computer blared. "Main thrusters have misfired. We are on a collision course with Space Station Alpha."

Dan saw the space station rushing toward him, its spindle shape revolving slowly like the hands of a clock as his ship gyrated wildly. He *felt* the jerks and shudders of his ship in the pit of his stomach.

"Manual override!" the computer voice urged. "Manual override!"

Dan grabbed the two control sticks as the space station loomed bigger and bigger. He knew this was a game, a simulation. Yet his hands were sweaty and his stomach was hollow, queasy.

The station hurtled toward him, close enough to see the ribbing on its solar panels and a pair of space-suited astronauts flailing their arms at him. His earphones sizzled with radio voices screaming warnings. He yanked both control sticks all the way back and the station flashed past below him, leaving nothing but serene stars in his view.

"You have avoided a collision," said the computer voice, calmer now, "but your maneuver has taken you far off course."

My maneuver? Dan argued silently.

"At present velocity, you will leave the Earth-Moon system entirely and drift into interplanetary space."

Dan scanned the controls. Not a hint as to what to do.

"Your only chance of survival is to alter course and attempt a landing at lunar base Copernicus."

"How do I do that?" he asked.

The main display screen in the center of his control console showed a graph with a red curving line on it. A swept-wing symbol indicated the position of his spacecraft.

"I get it," Dan muttered. "I've got to keep the ship on the indicated trajectory. Looks simple enough."

It was not. More malfunctions dogged his attempts to follow the trajectory. A meteor shower strafed the ship, puncturing several compartments and knocking it farther off course. A pirate spacecraft began chasing Dan, firing laser beams at him, forcing him to take evasive action.

Dan almost enjoyed it all. Part of his mind kept telling him this was a kid's game, meant to entertain twelve-year-olds no matter what their calendar age. But another part of him marveled at how realistic the simulation was, how detailed the graphics, how he felt viscerally every jolt and lurch of the ship.

And there's no time lag, he realized. They've beaten the time-lag problem! In all the simulations he had been involved in, there was always a slight but noticeable delay between the moment you moved your head or hands and the moment the simulation moved in reaction. Only a fraction of a second, but enough to make you realize you were in a simulation, not the real world. Here there was no time lag at all: Dan moved and the world around him responded instantly.

By the time he settled the spacecraft down to a safe landing at Copernicus Base on the Moon, Dan's shirt was sticking sweatily to his back and his hands ached from gripping the imaginary control sticks.

"Touchdown," said the computer voice. "Welcome to Copernicus Base."

"You made it!" came Chan's voice through the helmet earphones. "Good going! I thought you were going to buy the farm a couple of times."

Wearily Dan slid his helmet visor up and saw that he was once again in the empty VR chamber. No spacecraft, no console, no control sticks. Nothing but the bare room and the chair he was sitting on. His hands were trembling slightly.

"That's a helluva ride," he said as he lifted the helmet off his head. His hair felt damp, matted.

"You can take a tour of Copernicus Base if you like." Chan's voice came through the speaker in the wall below the one-way window.

"Uh, not right now, okay?"

Chan opened the control-booth door and crossed the VR chamber in three swift strides. "Are you all right? You look a little green."

Dan saw that the kid was grinning at him. "It's a damned good game," he said, pushing himself to his feet.

"Thanks." Chan seemed genuinely pleased.

"How the hell do you get the physical sensations? I actually felt the accelerations and the maneuvers. Thought I was going to puke a couple of times."

"Visual cues," Chan said, grinning widely now. "The information you get from your eyes almost overpowers all your other senses. When they conflict, you start to feel queasy. Your eyes tell your brain that you're bouncing all over the place, while your inner ear and your tactile senses tell you that you're sitting still in a chair—"

"Like space sickness, only in reverse."

Chan nodded enthusiastically. "Sort of, yeah. In fact, I've been wondering if we couldn't work with NASA to train astronauts."

"What happens if the player messes up? Like, if he hits the space station?"

Leading the way back to the booth and then to the hallway outside, Chan explained, "Oh, we don't let that happen. The ship will miss the station and get away from the pirates and land safely at Copernicus no matter how lousy the player is."

"How lousy was I?" Dan asked.

Chan laughed. "You got through it safe, didn't you?"

"That bad, huh?"

"Come on," Chan said. "Jace ought to be about finished by now."

CHAPTER 5

Jason Lowrey worked the palm of his bare hand into the well-oiled pocket of his outfielder's glove. Nervous? You bet. Who wouldn't be with the game hanging by one run, runners on first and second, and Babe Ruth up there at the plate.

The crowd had gone silent. Jace could hear the flags whipping on their masts up along the roof of the grandstand. A plane droned somewhere in the brilliant blue sky. The wind was blowing out, as if the Babe needed any help. Still, Jace backed up a cautious few steps on the outfield grass.

Lefty Grove was pitching against the Yankees. Ty Cobb was in right field, alongside Jace, with Ted Williams on his other side in left. Two men on base. And if Grove walked the Babe, Lou Gehrig would come to bat with the bases loaded. Jace knew that Gehrig hit more grand-slam home runs than anybody in the history of the game.

He could see the Babe standing at the plate in his odd pigeon-toed stance. He faded out a little, then his image stabilized, but it still looked too much like a cartoon, with those pipestem legs propping that big balloon of a body. Gehrig, kneeling in the on-deck circle, was only a vague blur. No definition at all. And the crowd in the grandstand was an undefined gray smear with splotches of red and yellow daubed here and there. A peanut vendor was hawking his wares loud and clear, but there was no way to see him in the flat background that represented the crowd.

At least Grove looked clear and convincing, scowling at the Babe. He checked the base runners, then threw a wicked low fastball. Ruth golfed it, a massive uppercut swing with all the power of that big torso behind it. The ball popped high into the air, over second base, a dying quail looping into short center field.

Jace raced in as hard as he could but saw he'd never catch the ball on the fly; he'd been playing too far back. Joe Morgan, the second baseman, was racing out, but Jace knew he would never make it either. He yelled for the ball, and Morgan dutifully turned away. The runners were moving. Jace let the ball bounce once in front of him, then grabbed it and threw with every ounce of his strength to Campanella at the plate.

"JACE?" a voice boomed through the stadium loudspeakers. "COME ON OUT OF THERE, JACE. IT'S ME, DAN."

Jace hunched, hands on knees, to watch the play at the plate. Campy tagged the runner out! The inning was over! The fans erupted into wild cheers, throwing a blizzard of straw hats and scorecards out onto the field in celebration.

"COME ON, JACE. COME OUT AND SAY HELLO. I'VE BEEN WAITING FOR DAMNED NEAR AN HOUR."

"Terminate," said Jason Lowrey.

The baseball stadium disappeared. He lifted the visor of his helmet. He was standing alone in the low-ceilinged VR chamber of blank walls, wearing a plastic visored helmet and a pair of metallic gloves, all of them connected by a tangle of hair-thin optical fibers to an assembly of gray electronics boxes mounted on a table beneath the one-way window in the otherwise bare room. The helmet seemed very heavy all of a sudden. He lifted it off and shook out his long, tangled hair. He felt tired, let down, annoyed at having to come back into what people called the real world.

Jason Lowrey was a genius. Everyone knew it, and if anyone doubted it Jace would immediately set him straight. He looked the part and dressed it. Tall and lean to the point of looking gaunt, he always wore faded old blue jeans and T-shirts. And Indian moccasins. A heavy Navaho belt buckle of silver and turquoise clasped a decrepit old leather belt around his thin waist. His sandy-blond hair was unclipped, uncombed, and often unwashed. His pinched face looked emaciated, all angular cheekbones and stubborn jaw and prominent patrician nose, with big yellowed teeth like old ivory tombstones. His skin was pasty pale from a lifetime spent first in childhood video parlors and then in front of increasingly more sophisticated computers.

Dan waited patiently for Lowrey in the cramped narrow control booth of the simulations lab, his blazer hanging from his arm, his conservatively striped rep tie pulled loose from his collar. The two technicians who had been monitoring Jace's run in the chamber got up and left, mumbling their greetings to the new employee.

"I'll leave you two guys alone," said Gary Chan. Before Dan could object, he, too, slipped out into the hallway and let the door click shut behind him. Dan got the feeling that Chan was afraid of Jace, or at least fearful that Jace would be pissed about Dan's calling him out of the simulation.

The solid metal door to the simulations chamber opened and Lowrey stepped through. Dan saw the motto on Jace's T-shirt: *Reality Is a Crutch for the Unimaginative.*

For a moment the two men simply stood facing each other. Then Jace burst into a huge smile and flung his skinny arms around Dan's neck.

"You're here! You're here!" he sang, prancing around in the narrow control booth as if he were dancing with Dan.

"I'm here," Dan said, grinning at his partner. "It's really me, not a simulation."

"It's great! Why the hell didn't you call me out earlier? You said you've been waiting a friggin' hour?"

"Well, you were busy, and the technicians—"

"They should've called me out of the sim. Shit, you coulda come in with me. Those fart-brains!"

Jace brushed past Dan and leaned over one of the consoles, pecking at its keyboard.

"We're gonna do great things here, Danno. Terrific things. These dumb games are just the beginning."

"That's what I'm here for," said Dan.

"We got a lotta work to do, though," Jace muttered, typing with two lean fingers. "Nothing around here works right. Got the best friggin' equipment money can buy, but still it's not doing the job."

His words had an edge to them that Dan did not recall from earlier days. Jace's voice had always been rasping, almost hoarse. He could be nasty, biting. But never with Dan. Now he seemed wired, clanked up.

"What's wrong?" Dan asked.

"Every frigging thing. That's why I told Muncrief I had to have you here. Just like at Dayton: I dream up the programs and you make 'em work. Right? Right!"

Dan shrugged resignedly. Jace's attitude had not changed much in the year since he had last seen him. He was like a precocious brat who had never grown up. Working with Jace was like trying to work with Mozart: frustrating, exasperating, and—every now and then—exalting beyond words.

"Come on in," Jace said, jerking a thumb toward the chamber door. "Lemme show you what I've been doing."

"Not now . . ."

"Come on, come on, come on!" Jace tugged at Dan's shirt-sleeve like a little boy urging his daddy to buy him candy. "Only a coupla minutes. You gotta see this. You gotta!"

"I just spent half an hour playing space pilot."

"Charlie Chan's game? Kid stuff! Wait'll you see what I'm doing here!"

With a mixture of reluctance and anticipation, Dan draped his blazer on the back of a chair and took off his tie altogether, while Jace paged his technicians over the phone on the console desktop. The two techs showed up; Chan did not. Within minutes, Dan was outfitted with a helmet and gloves. He followed Jace through the metal hatch into the simulation chamber.

"I haven't even sat down in my own office yet," he complained.

"We'll just play one inning. You pitch, I'll bat."

"We play against one another?"

"Yep." Jace's grin was smug. "I call 'em conflict games. Nothing like it anywhere. You'll see."

Jace walked over to the far corner of the chamber in long-legged strides. Dan closed the heavy metal door firmly, then started connecting his helmet and gloves to the color-coded hair-thin optical fibers that plugged into the electronics. He saw that Jace had already finished his connections and was waiting impatiently for him, arms crossed over his narrow chest. Dan nodded an apology and pulled down the visor of his helmet. Utter darkness. Like being blind.

"Okay, you guys," he heard Jace's impatient voice in the helmet earphones. "We're waiting. Make it pronto, Tonto."

Lights flickered before Dan's eyes and swiftly coalesced into a recognizable scene. Dan saw he was in a baseball stadium, three tiers packed with a restlessly murmuring crowd, bright blue sky above. The crowd was flat, lacking detail, but he could hear the bullfrog voice of a vendor hawking peanuts.

He was standing on the pitching mound, wearing a regular baseball uniform, complete down to his spiked shoes. Jace stood in the batter's box, batting left-handed, grinning at him with those big yellow teeth of his from under the bill of an Oakland A's cap. The catcher was flashing signals, the umpire crouching behind him. Dan felt the baseball in his right hand. He looked down at it: real to the tiniest detail, even the signature of the league president. The stitches felt slightly rough in his hand. The ball had the proper weight and solidity. Great stuff, he said to himself.

Jace was waving his bat, waiting for the pitch. He's probably loaded the game in his favor, Dan thought, knowing Jace. He doesn't like to lose. Well, what the hell, Dan thought. It's only a game.

Taking a deep breath, Dan swung his arms over his head, kicked his left leg high, and threw as hard as he could.

The crack of the bat sounded like a pistol shot. The ball rifled past Dan's ear, a solid hit into center field. Jace pulled up grinning at first base as the fielders got the ball back to Dan. And another Jace came up to the plate, bat in hand, an identical toothy grin on his long angular face.

After four Jaces had batted, three hits and a long fly ball that resulted in two runs scored, Dan let the ball drop out of his hand.

"That's enough," he called down to Jace.

"Don't you want a turn at bat?"

"At this rate, I won't get to bat until Christmas."

"Okay, okay! You bat, I'll pitch."

Dan envisioned Jace pitching against him, saw himself striking out ignominiously. He felt the slightest tendril of an asthmatic wheeze in his chest, as if somebody had run a sheet of sandpaper along the inside of his lungs.

"I've had enough," he said.

"Come on," Jace called from the batter's box. "We're just getting started."

"I'm having trouble breathing," Dan half-lied. "My damned asthma's starting up." It was an excuse and he hated it, but he also knew it always worked.

Jace scowled, narrow-eyed, but said, "Terminate."

Dan lifted his helmet visor. They were standing in the bare chamber again.

"You just don't have the competitive instinct, do you?" Jace said.

Dan shrugged. "You've got enough for both of us."

They carried the helmets and gloves back into the control booth.

"You can see what I'm up against," Jace said as he squeezed past the technicians in the narrow booth and opened the door to the hallway outside. "If I get good definition on the players, the background goes flat. Try to sharpen up the background, and the players get fuzzy."

Following him, Dan asked, "What're you using?"

"Got a pair of Cray Y-XMPs and a brand-new Toshiba Seventy-seven Hundred that's supposed to put the Crays to shame. But I think you gotta talk Japanese to the friggin' Toshiba to get it to do what you want."

"That was a Toshiba I saw in the computer center?"

"They're not in the Pit," Jace snapped. "I've got 'em in my lab, out back. I don't share my machines with the rest of the slobs."

"Oh."

"We don't lack for equipment, Danno. It's not like the friggin' Air Force. Muncrief bitches and complains about the cost, but he comes through for me. Anything I want, just about. That's how I got you, pal. But he's been getting antsy lately. Keeps moanin' about the money."

Dan had worked with Jace for nearly ten years at the Air Force laboratory in Dayton, the quiet guy in the shadow of Jace's brilliance. No one noticed Dan, except their boss, Dr. Appleton. Dan had been just another electronics technician, a civilian working for government pay, when Appleton had teamed him with the wildly eccentric Jason Lowrey. Their task: to make flight simulations as realistic as actual combat missions. To train fighter pilots to fly and fight under brutally vivid lifelike conditions—in the safety of a laboratory on the ground.

The answer was virtual reality: simulations that are as utterly lifelike as human ingenuity and high technology can make them.

"I wanna create worlds where you can't tell the difference from reality," Jason Lowrey had proclaimed to anyone who would listen. "I wanna build whole universes out of nothing more than electrical impulses fed into your nervous system. I wanna be God!"

Jace didn't look much like God, Dan thought as he followed his old buddy down the corridor to his cubbyhole of an office. Didn't smell much like God, either.

"Jace, when's the last time you took a shower?"

Lowrey interrupted his monologue of problems to look down at Dan. He frowned, then quickly broke into a sheepish grin.

"That's another reason I wanted you here," he said. "You always were a mother hen to me."

His office was a certified disaster area. It looked as if a tornado had struck a library: papers strewn everywhere. Dan could make out the shape of a small desk and a pair of cheap plastic chairs beneath snowdrifts of loose papers. Bookshelves on every wall stuffed with reports and journals. No decorations of any kind; or if there were, they were buried beneath the papers. One window, which Jace had painted black. Dan saw that Jace must have painted it over himself; the paint was streaked and lumpy, the work of a man who had no time or interest in careful workmanship.

"Lemme tell you, Danno," said Jace as he pushed papers off his desk chair and plopped down on it, "we got the chance here to do great stuff. Really great stuff."

"That's what you told me in Dayton. That's why I came down here."

As if he hadn't heard Dan, Jace went on, "Muncrief's got the kind of vision I need, pal. Thinks big. We're gonna put Disney out of business, you watch."

Dan grinned at his partner and tossed his rumpled blazer onto one of the paper piles. "Good. Maybe I can work the glitches out of my symphony-orchestra program."

"The conflict games are the quantum leap, Danno," Jace rattled on. "Get two people to share a simulation, share a world together. This baseball stuff is just the beginning, pal. Just the beginning."

"I'd still like to develop the symphony-orchestra program," Dan said, raising his voice slightly.

Jace glared at him. "Don't start that again! Let me do the creative stuff; you handle the details."

"I can do it on my own time," Dan said. "It won't get in the way."

But Jace was already off on another tangent. "Two people sharing the same dream, that's gonna be *powerful*, man. You can fight duels, settle court cases—and sex! Better than real life! Better than anything you ever imagined!"

Same old Jace, thought Dan. His mind races ahead of everybody else and he leaves me to make his ideas work. But inwardly he was grinning with anticipation.

"Hey," he said, interrupting Jace's monologue. "Why don't you come over for dinner?"

"Huh?" Jace blinked at him like a man suddenly awakened from a nap. "When?"

"Tonight. Now."

Jace had been such a frequent dinner guest back in Dayton that Susan had called him "my oldest child."

"Uh . . . I don't know . . ." Jace hesitated.

"Come on. Sue hasn't seen you in more than a year. And you haven't seen Phil yet, have you? And Angie! You wouldn't recognize her, she's grown so tall."

"Angie," said Jace, his eyes shifting away from Dan's. "Angie. Yeah."

CHAPTER 6

The heavy traffic surprised Dan.

Glancing at the dashboard digital clock, he complained to Jace, "Jeez, look at all these cars."

Jace shrugged. "Orlando's a big city, pal."

Then Dan remembered that he had driven to work in the middle of the afternoon. Still, it was damned near eight o'clock and the broad, palm-lined avenues were choked with cars inching along from one stoplight to the next. He saw a highway overpass where the traffic was zooming by at a good clip, but there were huge semitrailer rigs roaring by up there, spurting black diesel smoke and running up the back of anyone doing less than seventy.

"Does the highway go past Pine Lake Gardens?" he asked Jace.

"Damned if I know. I'm on the other side of town."

Dan was stuck with the crowded streets. I'll have to find the best route, he told himself. Must be side streets and cutoffs I can use, once I get to know the area.

It was hot. He had rolled all the Honda's windows down, but inching along like this brought no cooling wind. A sleek red hatchback pulled up beside him, radio blaring raucous rock music with a bass thumping so loud Dan could feel his sinuses spasming. He glanced over. A pretty young blonde wearing wraparound sunglasses and lipstick the same fire-engine red as her car. Her windows were up, her air-conditioning on, and still her radio was giving him a headache.

"Hope she doesn't live on my block," Dan said.

"Who?"

Dan jerked a thumb toward the hatchback. Jace looked, then turned back to Dan with a puzzled look. "Why not?"

Grinning, Dan said, "Forget it."

The traffic crawled along. Dan stared absently at the big Buick in front of him with a driver so tiny that her wispy white hair barely came up to the steering wheel. The car bore a bumper sticker: *Welcome to Florida. Now go home!*

Jace was strangely silent. He got moody sometimes, Dan remembered. Most of the time you couldn't shut him up; he talked nonstop and brooked no interruptions. But then he would go quiet and you could hardly get two words out of him. Usually when he had a problem to solve or he was working on some new idea that hadn't gelled yet.

"You've really made a lot of progress in one year," said Dan.

"Yeah, but we got a long way to go, kiddo."

"That baseball game—it's going to be a dream come true for every guy who ever went to a game or bought a baseball card. All those couch potatoes who never got picked when the kids chose up teams. They'll all be able to play with Reggie Jackson and Roger Clemens."

Jace's lantern-jawed face broke into a wide toothy grin. "And that's just the beginning, Danno. Just the beginning. I been thinkin' about these conflict sims. Got a lot of ideas about 'em."

That was all it took to break Jace out of his daydream, whatever it was. He started spouting ideas and concepts while Dan laughed inwardly and told himself, *It's going to be like old times. It really is. Just like old times.*

Yet a faint tendril of worry nagged at the back of his mind. *Jace had to make me play against him. Why did he do that? It's as if he had to show me he's the top dog. As if I cared. Damned games are only games. Must be important to him, though. I guess he needs to feel that he can beat me, beat anybody. He needs to feel he's king of the hill.*

He's right about one thing, though. These games are only the beginning. We can do great things with VR.

"I'll do my symphony-orchestra simulation," Dan said.

Jace huffed at him. "Yeah, sure. There's lots of applications for teaching. Muncrief's had me working on games for the local school half the time."

"The school Angie's going to?"

"Watch your driving," Jace said.

Dan was hardly doing any driving, just inching along the crowded street from one stop sign to the next.

"What else have you been thinking about?" Dan asked.

"Besides teaching?" Jace frowned in concentration. "What about microsurgery? We can put the surgeon inside the patient's body and let him see and feel what's going on in there while he's operating."

"Yeah."

"And entertainment. We can make a guy dance like—what the hell's that guy's name?"

"Fred Astaire?"

"Yeah, the one from those old videos."

Dan almost missed the turn onto his own street. He was unfamiliar with the neighborhood, and all the bright new houses looked virtually alike to him. But finally he drove the dark-blue Honda up onto the driveway and into the cool shadows of the garage. I've got to watch out for rust, he thought as he got out of the car. In this humidity she'll rust out fast if I let it go.

Susan was in the kitchen, red hair tied up in a bandanna, wearing shorts and a blouse that hung loosely about her hips. Two pots were on the stove, one of them steaming.

"Jace!" she said, putting down the spoon she was holding to fling her arms around his neck. "How's my oldest child?"

Jace grinned and hugged her.

"How about your lord and master?" Dan demanded.

"Hello, darling." Susan pecked at his lips. "How was your first day?"

"Not bad," said Dan.

"I got the stove working," Susan said proudly. "Tonight we eat spaghetti à la Susan."

"Great," said Jace.

"Sauce from a jar, though. Haven't had time to make it from scratch. And I couldn't carry that much from the supermarket, on foot."

"Uncle Jace!"

A blond blur whizzed into the kitchen and threw herself into Jace's arms. Dan smiled, thinking of Dorothy and the Scarecrow. Jace hauled Angela off her feet and swung her around, nearly knocking her feet into the pots on the stove.

"My gosh, Angie," he said as he put her down, "you've grown a foot! Here it is on top of your head!" And he mussed her hair with his knuckles.

"You're silly," Angela said, laughing. Jace scooped her up again and carried her, giggling and wriggling, into the living room.

Dan followed them into the living room, then went out to the master bedroom. He tossed his blazer on the bed. It was wrinkled and limp; just the way he himself suddenly felt. Tired. A little disappointed. The excitement of seeing Jace again was wearing off. Like a kid who waited all year for his birthday party and now it's over. Back on the job. It all came flooding back to him, all the memories of the old days at Wright-Patterson with Jace. It was as if the two of them had never been separated. Jace was happy to see him again, sure, but he just took it for granted that Dan would be there when he wanted him. As if he had just been off on vacation or sick leave for a while. This wasn't a new start for Dan, it was just a continuation of his life as Jace's partner.

Well, what the hell. You couldn't do what Jace does, Dan told himself. The sonofabitch is brilliant. Who the hell else could produce a simulation that two people can share completely? These conflict games are his baby. Two people sharing a dream together. Or a nightmare. Nobody else has even come close to what Jace has accomplished. He's jumped light-years ahead of anything that anybody else is doing. A quantum leap.

As he sat down to take off his shoes, Angela came bouncing in.

"Mommy says dinner will be ready in five minutes and I can sit with you and Uncle Jace even though I've already had my dinner." She seemed quite pleased with her announcement, almost smug.

"That's fine, Angel," he said. "How was your first day at school?"

"It was real neat," his daughter replied, getting up on the bed and tucking her bare feet under her to sit cross-legged.

"You liked it."

"Yeah! I went to Mexico City and saw the Aztecs. It was terrific!

They wore costumes made of bird feathers and they had these big tall pyramids and marketplaces and ball courts where they played a kind of soccer and—"

"You used a VR system."

Angela nodded so hard her pigtails bounced. "It's awesome, Daddy. I was really there! With Mr. Muncrief."

"Huh?"

"Did you make that VR, Daddy? Is the one about the Aztecs one of the VRs you made?"

"No, not that one, honey," Dan replied. "What did you say about Mr. Muncrief?"

Her blue eyes were shining with happiness. "He was there, too. I saw him. He was one of the priests. He climbed all the way up the biggest pyramid, to the temple up at the top."

"Mr. Muncrief?"

"Uh-huh."

"It couldn't have been."

"I saw him. He was there, all dressed up in feathers and everything. He looked kinda funny."

Dan tickled his daughter's chin. "You just thought you saw him, sweetie. He drove you to school and there was a priest in the simulation that looked something like him, and you thought it was him."

"It *was* him, Daddy! He even waved to me!"

Dan smiled at his daughter. Twelve-year-olds and their imaginations, he thought. But inwardly he wondered if twelve-year-olds might be too young for VR simulations.

"Come on," he said, "let's see what Phil's doing."

He padded in his socks into the baby's room, Angela trailing behind him, still chattering about school and Muncrief. His son was already asleep. Dan smiled down at Philip. Things will get down to normal pretty quick, he thought. For some reason, it made Dan feel almost depressed. The same furniture, the same routine. He realized that he had looked forward to Florida as a bright new beginning, and the sameness he saw all around him made him feel as if nothing had changed. Nothing that was really important.

At dinner, Angela rattled on about Indians and Aztecs and her first VR experience.

"Hey," said Jace, "that's a game I cooked up, Angie. Did you like it?"

Nodding, Angela told Jace, "I saw Mr. Muncrief in it!"

"You did, huh?" Jace glanced at Dan.

"Muncrief isn't in that sim," Dan said. Then he added, "Is he?"

Very seriously, Jace asked Angela, "Are you sure it was Muncrief? Not just somebody who kinda looks like him?"

"I'm . . ." Angela hesitated, "pretty sure."

"Pretty sure?" Jace asked, grinning. "Or kinda pretty sure?"

"Kinda pretty sure."

"Kinda pretty sure, or maybe sort of kinda pretty sure?"

Angela laughed. "You're talking silly."

Jace laughed, too. "Yeah. I'm a silly person. Didn't you know that?" And he stuck out his tongue at her.

Angela did likewise. Susan said, "That will be enough from both of you. Angela, you can go brush your teeth now. Jace, finish your salad."

"Yes, ma'am," Jace said sheepishly. But the ghost of a smile still curled his lips; he gave Angela a sly wink.

After Jace left and Angela had gone to bed and the dinner dishes had been stacked in the ultraquiet dishwasher, Dan slouched in their old sofa, Susan beside him, blearily watching television.

"Did your computer work okay?" he asked, eyes on the flickering screen.

"Fine. Thanks for setting it up for me."

"And the fax board?"

"I haven't had a chance to try it yet," Susan replied. "Tomorrow I'll send out reminders about my Florida phone numbers to all my old clients."

"Good."

"I'll drive you to the office tomorrow," she said. "I need the car."

"Uh-huh."

"We can shop for my car Saturday, okay?"

"I guess."

"Or Sunday. Whichever you prefer."

He let his chin sink onto his chest. The TV show was something about a woman lawyer dealing with sexual harassment in her office. Dan thought about flipping to a different channel, but Sue seemed interested in it.

"I'll probably go to the lab Saturday. Got a lot of catching up to do."

Susan did not reply.

"Jace has jumped a million miles ahead of where we were at Wright-Patt. Even the *simple* games I saw today are way out. The imagery is fantastic. Not like the cartoony stuff we were doing for the Air Force. I mean, you can't tell the difference from the real world, it's that good. They've beaten the time-lag problem, Sue. Hell, even the kids on the staff are light-years ahead of me."

"You'll catch up to them in a week," Susan said.

"I don't know. You ought to see what they're doing. Jace is developing conflict games, games that two people can play in, against each other."

"That's what he was talking about! I couldn't quite figure out what he meant by 'conflict games,' and he was rattling on about it so fast. He's really excited about it, isn't he?"

"There's a lot to be excited about, Sue. It's fantastic."

"Angie said the same thing about the VR in her classroom."

"Yeah, she told me about it."

"How much about the Aztecs do they show the kids?" Susan's voice sounded troubled. "I mean, they did human sacrifices, didn't they? Do you think they're going to show that to the children? Cutting out the heart and all that?"

"I doubt it. What do you think about her seeing Kyle Muncrief in the sim?"

"I don't know what to think."

Dan tried to make light of it. "Imagine Muncrief dressed up as one of the Aztec priests, in all those feathers and stuff."

"How could that be?"

"Just her imagination. Muncrief must've made a big impression on her."

"Do you think that maybe she's too young to use VR?" Real worry etched Susan's voice.

"No," he said flatly, hiding his own concern.

"I wonder," she said.

"The school wouldn't let the kids use them if they thought

there would be any problems." Listening to his own words, he almost convinced himself of it.

Susan murmured something that Dan could not make out. He turned his attention back to the TV screen, although he had lost whatever interest he had originally had in the drama. His mind was picturing an Aztec priest cutting the heart out of a sacrificial victim. The priest looked like Muncrief.

"Jace seems happy here."

He felt his brows rise. "Yep. Just the same as always. I don't think he's even changed his shirt."

Susan laughed. "That's Jace."

"Yeah." Dan did not crack a smile. He knew that he had not told his wife the exact truth. Jace was different, somehow. The difference was subtle, only one of degree. But it was there. Dan tried to shrug it off. *Just the first day; we'll get back to normal in a day or so.*

A commercial came on, showing a gleaming silver little convertible hotfooting along a winding mountain road.

"Now that's some car," Dan said.

"Not for us," said Susan. "I'm going to get myself something much more practical."

"I can dream, can't I?"

"I only meant," she said, worming an arm around his waist, "that convertibles don't make sense here. The sun's too hot almost all year long."

"Muncrief doesn't seem to mind the sun," Dan muttered.

"He doesn't have two children to think of. And a wife with fair skin."

He turned toward her. "Fair? Your skin's better than fair. I think your skin's terrific." Dan traced a finger along the curve of her jaw, then tapped the end of her pert nose. "Wouldn't want that cute little proboscis to get sunburned."

She heaved an exaggerated sigh. "I love it when you talk scientific."

He broke into a grin. Leaning closer, he whispered into her ear, "Testosterone. Estrogen. Penis. Coitus."

Susan whispered back, "More! More!"

"Fellatio. Cunnilingus."

"Oh God!"

He scooped her up in his arms and marched off to the bedroom.

The first time they had made love, Dan had surprised her with his fiercely single-minded intensity. Susan had known a soft-spoken, reserved, gentle man who had taken her to dinners and movies and picnics. Many nights they had talked for hours, usually in his car, often until the sun came up. Dan had told her all about his childhood in Youngstown, his work at Wright-Patterson, how much he owed to Dr. Appleton. Susan had fallen in love with an earnest, shy, hardworking man who was almost a nerd in comparison to some of the men she had dated.

Yet there was something beneath the surface, a smoldering drive that she sensed from the very first. When at last she decided to go to bed with him, Susan found that she had been more right than she had dreamed. In bed Dan turned into a different person altogether. All the inhibitions, all the cautions and modesty and self-effacements disappeared once he had his hands on her naked flesh. She saw the passion that he hid from everyone else, even from himself. It almost frightened her, at first, but then she realized that Dan was much more than the uptight engineer she had first imagined him to be. What she had taken to be shyness was actually something close to fear; Dan was not bashful so much as wary, always on guard, as if to protect himself against being hurt by the people around him. She began to see him as a coiled panther, every muscle tensed, every nerve straining against the dangers of the world.

Except in bed. There he was a fiery, passionate Italian who swept away all her doubts and inhibitions. It was as if the rest of the world disappeared and there were only the two of them with Dan concentrating every facet of his attention, every molecule of his existence on her and her alone. God knew what fantasies might be boiling through his mind; she did not care and did not want to know. It did not matter to her. He never said a word while making love; he did not have to. His hands on her, his tongue on her, his body hot and eager, inflamed her more than any words he could have spoken.

Now, as they thrashed together on their creaking old springs and mattress in their new air-conditioned house, Susan remembered all over again how important sex was to Dan. It was his only release, his only moment to unleash all the tensions and angers and fears that he carried inside him. In a way it was a sadistic game they played: the more frustration and anger that built up in him during the day, the more passion he unleashed at night.

Only once had Susan forgotten how vital sex was to him, and it had almost shattered their marriage. She had never made that mistake again. Susan loved Dan Santorini, and she knew he loved her. But it had taken long years of careful, deliberate consideration, day by day, to rebuild the trust in each other that they had almost thrown away.

He could forget everything while making love; she could not. Even so, he could excite her to a pitch of arousal that made her wish there were nothing to remember. He responded to her whispered urgings and she responded to his touch, his lips on her throat, her nipples, her clitoris until they both came and she had to turn her head away to bite her pillow so she would not scream and wake the children.

Then Susan lay on the bed, sheets twisted and sticky-wet, body sweaty and shining in the faint red glow of the digital clock on the night table, panting as if she had just run ten miles. Dan lay beside her. She could feel him retreating into his shell again. He got embarrassed afterward, and the more Susan told him how wonderful he had been the more flustered he became.

"Another triumph for modern science," she whispered, half giggling.

Dan's only reply was a grunt. Because he was ashamed. While making love to his wife, a vision of Vickie Kessel's face had flashed through his imagination. And then he found himself fantasizing about Dorothy. After all these years, he still thought about Dorothy.

He loathed himself for that.

CHAPTER 7

The door was always open, so it was difficult to see the nameplate on it, which read: DR. WILLIAM R. APPLETON —CHIEF, ADVANCED SIMULATIONS SYSTEMS.

Despite the hefty title the office was small, almost threadbare. Dr. Appleton's desk was standard government-issue steel, painted olive drab, scuffed and dented from years of use. The two chairs in front of the desk were also old, steel frames with olive-drab plastic cushions that were so hard they felt like concrete. The only other furniture in the office were rickety metal bookshelves packed with reports and journals and folders that threatened to spill onto the floor any minute, and a tablette behind the desk chair on which sat a personal computer and a small row of hardbound textbooks. There was one window, off to the side, the only wall space that was not covered with shelving. It looked out on a concrete building that was almost identical to the one that held this office.

Three men sat in Dr. Appleton's office. Appleton himself was behind the desk on the creaking swivel chair, slim, slope-shouldered, paunchy, his receding hairline halfway up his scalp. He was in shirtsleeves, fiddling nervously with an unlit black briar pipe. His eyes were icy blue, and behind the rimless glasses he wore they looked like a pair of pale moons gazing at the world.

Lieutenant Colonel Ralph Martinez was also in shirtsleeves, starched and ironed so crisply that their creases looked razor-sharp. His blue Air Force jacket hung neatly from the back of the chair on which he sat. Martinez was a fighter pilot, a veteran of air combat in the Middle East, a commander of men. He was built like a welterweight contender, compact and solid, with square shoulders and a flat midsection. His face was square, too, the blunt plain swarthy face of a man whose ancestors had toiled in the sun for generations before him. His eyes were the rich brown of the earth, steady and reliable. His lips were set in a tight, belligerent line. Yet there were lines around his eyes and mouth that showed he knew how to laugh.

The third man in the office was a physician and neurophysiologist, Chandra Narlikar. He looked extremely uncomfortable.

"But according to your own records, Chandra," Appleton was saying, "Jerry was in perfect health."

"Not perfect. I never said perfect. Not that."

Martinez said, "He was certified for flight duty, wasn't he?"

"Yes, of course," Narlikar said hurriedly. "He had a slightly high blood pressure, but it was not sufficient cause to ground him."

"And he died of a stroke." Appleton made it half a statement, half a question. His voice was soft, almost a whisper.

"Yes, indeed. A massive cerebral hemorrhage. A stroke, poor fellow."

"And there was nothing to indicate that he was at risk?" Martinez asked impatiently. Almost angrily.

"Nothing at all," said Narlikar.

"His high blood pressure?" Appleton suggested.

The physician shrugged his slim shoulders. "It was well within normal range. Not as high as the colonel's, here, in fact."

Martinez snorted. His blood pressure had led the medical staff to take him off active flight duty, a fact that infuriated him—and drove his pressure higher.

"So let me see if I can put all this together," Appleton said slowly, leaning his elbows on his cluttered desktop and steepling his fingers. "Jerry had no significant health problems. He flew the new simulation and suffered a stroke that might have happened to him anyway. Is that right?"

Narlikar nodded unhappily. "It could have happened in his home, at his desk, anywhere. Many stroke victims are felled early in the morning in their own homes. Nine A.M. is the time when strokes occur most frequently."

"You're saying the simulation had nothing to do with it."

Narlikar started to reply, then hesitated. At last he said, "I cannot rule out that factor. You must understand that there is a great difference between a diagnosis and an explanation for the causative factor. He suffered a massive cerebral hemorrhage; that we know. What caused his stroke is unknown. We have no way of knowing."

Martinez looked at Appleton. "No way of knowing," he repeated, more than a hint of disgust in his voice.

Dr. Appleton said, "I don't see what else we can do about this. There's nothing new to add to what's already been reported. Jerry Adair suffered a stroke while he was flying the new simulation, and we have no idea if the simulation played a part in causing the stroke."

"It wasn't the simulation," Martinez insisted. "It couldn't have been. How the hell could a simulation give the guy a goddamned stroke?"

Appleton shrugged.

Turning to the physician so abruptly that Narlikar actually flinched, the colonel demanded, "Do you think that a simulation could scare a veteran pilot to death?"

"I—I am told it is a very realistic simulation," Narlikar said.

"But it's only a damned simulation!" Martinez insisted. "Jerry's flown *real* combat missions. He's been a test pilot, for chrissakes. He wouldn't be scared in a lousy sim. He knew it wasn't real."

Appleton said mildly, "We tried to simulate all the physical stresses, remember. You insisted on that, Ralph."

"Yeah, yeah. So we made the g suit squeeze and we tilted the simulator and rolled it around in response to the pilot's control forces. So what? We couldn't put in the real g loads that you'd get in actual flight. The simulator doesn't give you the accelerations, doesn't punish you the way a real flight would."

"I doubt that the physical stresses of the simulation were sufficient to cause Captain Adair's stroke," said Narlikar, with the slightest of stresses on the word *physical*.

"Then what did?"

Silence. The physician had no answer. He stared at Lt. Col. Martinez for a moment with his big liquid brown eyes, then looked away.

Finally Dr. Appleton got up from his chair and, leaning across his desk, extended a bony arm to Narlikar. "Thank you, Chandra. You've been very helpful."

Narlikar rose to his feet and took Appleton's hand gratefully. "I'm afraid I have been of very little help, actually. But stroke cases are often puzzling, you know."

"Thanks," Appleton repeated.

Martinez got up grudgingly and shook the physician's hand also. Once Narlikar had left the tiny office, the colonel stared at the closed door as he grumbled, "About as much help as a box of Kleenex."

Appleton sank back into his creaking swivel chair. "Oh, I don't know. In a situation like this, Ralph, a negative report can be almost as helpful as a positive one."

"What's that supposed to mean?" Martinez fished a cigarette pack from his shirt pocket as he sat down again.

Reaching for his pipe, Appleton said, "Safety regulations forced us to shut down the simulation until we come up with a definite reason for Jerry's death, right?"

"And after three weeks of investigation, all that Narlikar and his needle-pushers can tell us is that Jerry died of a stroke. Which we knew two hours after it happened."

"Okay," said Appleton. "What Narlikar is telling us is that the simulation probably didn't have anything to do with Jerry's stroke."

"Probably."

"You've been over the tapes. Do you see anything that could've killed Jerry?"

"It was a rough mission," Martinez said, lighting his cigarette with a disposable Bic. "We piled it on him. We were trying to see how realistic we could make the sim, remember?"

Appleton looked into the colonel's steady brown eyes. Not a flicker of remorse. If he feels any responsibility for making the simulation too realistic, he certainly isn't showing it, Appleton thought.

"Well, then," he said aloud, "if we're both convinced that the simulation had nothing to do with Jerry's death, we can recommend to the safety board that we resume our program."

"Uh-huh."

"Do you see any reason to keep it shut down?"

Martinez hesitated. He had been a flier all his adult life. He had seen men killed in stupid accidents, killed by the weather and by enemy action. Flying always had some element of danger in it, and military flying was the most dangerous of all. You had to be able to fly at night and in bad weather and in situations where a sane pilot would stay on the ground. You had to be able to face missiles and guns and enemy pilots who maybe were just as good as you were. Maybe. That was the biggest risk of all, and the biggest kick. Man to man, pilot to pilot, who's going to win? Who's going to die?

Appleton's a civilian, Martinez told himself. The Doc's a good guy, but he's a civilian. Not even a pilot. He flies a desk. He's a scientist. What does he know about how the adrenaline jolts through you when you see a bogie on your six? Maybe he can read numbers off a page, but he's never felt the real thing, the real blast that goes through you when you wax some bastard's tail and knock him out of the sky. How could he? The only flying he's ever done has been as a passenger.

For long moments the two men sat looking at each other, their thoughts spinning. Maybe I made the sim too tough, Martinez admitted silently. But dammit, it's *got* to be tough. I can't send kids out into combat situations without making their training as tough and as realistic as it can be. Civilians don't understand. Every time one of my kids climbs into a cockpit and straps that plane onto his back, he's putting his life on the line. I want them to be ready, to know what it's like, to have as much experience as we can jam into their skulls. And that means the most realistic simulations we can get these scientists to produce. Maybe it killed Jerry. Maybe it did. And maybe Jerry would have killed himself the next time he took a real plane up.

"Do you see any reason to keep the simulation shut down?" Appleton repeated.

Martinez realized what was bothering him. "What if the program was deliberately tampered with?"

Appleton's pale-blue eyes widened.

"We had that Russian here, remember? The exchange guy: Yevshenko."

"Yuri?" Appleton's voice nearly cracked. "Ralph, surely you don't think—"

"I know the Cold War's over and we're all lovey-dovey with the Russians and trying to help them become good democratic capitalists. But . . ." Martinez let the idea dangle between them.

"Why would Yuri want to sabotage the program?" Appleton asked softly. "How could he do it?"

"Why? To keep their air force from falling too far behind ours, maybe. Maybe they figure that someday they might have to fight us, and they don't want us to be so far ahead of them that they'll be completely outclassed."

"I can't believe that."

"I can."

"But even so, how could Yuri—how could *anybody* tamper with the simulation so deeply that it killed Jerry?"

Martinez shook his head slowly. "I don't know. That's your department. I'm just a fighter jock. You're the scientist."

"Well, then, I know what I'd like to do."

"What?"

"I'd like to get Jace and Dan back here."

Martinez blew smoke through his nose. "Fat chance."

"They designed the simulation, originally. I'd like to get them to take a look at it, see if we're missing something. See if somebody's tinkered with it."

"They're not working for us anymore."

"I think they'd come back if I asked them to. Just for a week or so, just to check the program over. Dan would, I'm sure. Jace—" Appleton waggled one hand in the air.

"I've got a better idea," Martinez said. "One that'll work without going crawling to those two turncoats."

Appleton's pale eyebrows rose.

"I'll fly the simulation myself. I'll check it out from the user's perspective."

"But you've been redlined."

"For actual flight," Martinez snapped. "This is a sim. I won't leave the ground."

Appleton sank back in his chair, fiddling with the unlit pipe. "But if you think it's been sabotaged . . ."

"The fastest way to find out is to try it again."

"As you yourself pointed out, Ralph, this is a rough simulation.

Even if nobody's messed it up. You purposely made it as rough as you could."

"Yeah. I did. So I ought to be the one to try it next."

"I don't know . . ."

Martinez put on a grim smile. "Listen, Doc. If a grounded old geezer like me can fly that simulation without trouble, then we've proved it didn't kill Jerry. Right? And we'll have proved it hasn't been buggered."

"I suppose so."

"Then let's do it!"

"We'll have to take the simulator apart first and check it out thoroughly."

"That could take weeks!" argued Martinez. "Months!"

With a nod, Appleton said, "Still, it's got to be done. Standard practice after an accident. You know that."

The colonel fumed, but muttered, "Yeah. I know."

"I'd still like to see if I can get Jace and Dan back here first."

"To hell with them! We don't need them!"

Appleton lifted his thin shoulders in a small shrug, but privately decided he would at least call Dan Santorini before he allowed the colonel or anyone else to fly the simulator again. He could not believe that one rather shy, inoffensive Russian who had been at the lab for only a few months had deliberately sabotaged their simulation. How could he? How could anyone?

CHAPTER 8

A ngela Santorini bit her lip in concentration. All around her swam colored spheres the size of tennis balls. But they were really atoms. Each different kind of atom had its own distinctive color. Hydrogen was red. Oxygen was blue. Nitrogen was yellow. Carbon was sooty black. Gold was—well, gold, of course. Then there were some strange ones: shimmery pink helium and bright green neon. And some others she couldn't remember. They all looked beautiful, though, floating around in the deep blackness.

"What is water made of?" asked the instructor's voice in her headphones. "Can you put the atoms together to make a molecule of water?"

The voice was a recording and the whole chemistry simulation was an interactive VR program. Angela was actually sitting in one of the telephone-booth-size compartments in the rear of her class-room. She wore a helmet with a visor that covered her eyes and instrumented data gloves on her hands. On the inside of the visor a pair of miniature TV screens played stereoscopic images into her eyes.

If Angela got things right, the program automatically went on to a more difficult problem. When she stumbled, the program gently counseled her and helped her to correct her mistake.

"Water," Angela murmured to herself, "is made of one hydrogen and two oxygens."

"Is it?" said the voice. "Try it and see if you're right."

Angela reached out and grasped a hydrogen atom as it passed by. It felt slightly spongy in her fingers. "Stay there," she said, and the red sphere held its place in front of her. Then she grabbed a blue atom of oxygen. It was noticeably larger than the hydrogen. As she brought it close to the hydrogen atom, the red sphere seemed to jump toward the blue and attach itself to it.

Now I need another oxygen, Angela thought. She picked one out of the stream flowing past, but it stubbornly refused to stick to her red-and-blue combination. Each time she tried to force them together they pushed back, rebounding away from one another.

For a few moments Angela sat there, frowning in puzzlement.

"What is the water molecule made of, Angela?" her instructor's voice asked. She noticed just the slightest difference in tone between the way her own name was pronounced and the rest of the question. As if her name had been stuck in at the last minute.

"Aitch-two-oh," Angela replied. Then she clapped her hands in sudden understanding. "*One* oxygen and *two* hydrogens!"

"Why don't you try it that way?" the voice prompted.

Angela did, and the water molecule fit together easily. She felt thrilled. Suddenly she was surrounded by water molecules that all merged together and became an ocean complete with beautifully colored fish swimming past.

But they disappeared quickly and she was back in the stream of flowing colored spheres. At the instructor's cues, Angela built molecules of carbon dioxide, methane, and ammonia. All without a hitch.

"You've done so well," the instructor's voice said, "that you have time to play a game. Would you like to play?"

"Yes!" said Angela.

"Good." There was a moment's hesitation, barely long enough for Angela to notice it. But in that brief moment, the VR program automatically sent a signal to the supercomputer in the ParaReality building to switch from the chemistry lesson to the game. It inserted Angela's name into the program and recorded her name, the date and time, and the name of the game in the central log kept in Victoria Kessel's files. It also, unrecorded, alerted a satellite system in Kyle Muncrief's office.

Angela found herself deep in the ocean, surrounded by beautifully colored fish that darted swiftly before her delighted eyes. Sunlight filtered down from the surface into a world of brilliant blue. A different voice, a man's, said, "This game is called 'Neptune's Kingdom.'"

Angela thought she had heard that man's voice before. A gaily colored fish swam up to her and said, in the same man's voice:

"Hello, Angela. I'm an angelfish. I'm your guide to Neptune's Kingdom."

It sounded like Mr. Muncrief's voice, Angela thought. "Is that you, Mr. Muncrief?" she asked. Her daddy's boss had driven her to school several times over the past three weeks in his shining open convertible. He seemed to show up at their house at least once each week early in the morning before the school bus arrived, saying that he was on his way to the office and he thought Angela might like a ride.

"I'm an angelfish. My name is nearly the same as yours, isn't it?"

The fish was almost a foot long, its body flat and triangular in shape, like an arrowhead except for its prominent fins that fluttered before Angela's face. It was electric blue in color, with vivid stripes. Its big round eye seemed to look straight at Angela.

"*Tolocanthus bermudensis* is my official name," said Mr. Muncrief's voice. "But everyone knows me as an angelfish."

"You're too big to be an angelfish," Angela said. "I had angelfish in my aquarium back home in Dayton, and they were a lot smaller than you. Prettier, too."

"Those were freshwater angelfish. I'm an ocean-water angelfish. I can grow almost as big as you."

Angela saw that the fish had a tiny mouth, but it was filled with sharp little teeth.

"Would you like to see Neptune's Kingdom and meet the mermaid princess?" it asked.

"Yes, I would."

"Then just follow me," said the fish. And it darted deeper into the darkening waters.

Angela did not feel as if she was moving. Instead, the undersea world seemed to flow past her, without her getting wet at all. All around her a wonderland of deep-sea life flowed, fish and coral and swaying green fronds of plants. The angelfish named each new form of living thing and even showed Angela the tiny coral polyps, almost microscopically small, when it stopped briefly to nibble on some.

"Delicious," said the fish.

"That's what you eat? Ugh!"

"To me they taste delicious, Angela. All animals have to eat something; I eat tiny little things. Some of the bigger fish like to eat fish like me. Life is a chain," said her guide, "and it all starts here in the sea."

Angela thought that maybe this wasn't a game at all, that somehow this fish was trying to teach her about—what did they call it? Biology. That was it. But it was fascinating to see all the different things in the ocean, all the different kinds of beautiful living creatures.

A shark glided by, sleek and deadly-looking. Angela shivered, especially when it opened its wide mouth and showed rows and rows of sharp white teeth.

"There's nothing to be afraid of," said her angelfish. "Nothing can hurt you here in Neptune's Kingdom." But she thought her angelfish moved a lot closer to her as the shark swam past.

"Most sharks are *predators*, Angela. They eat other fish. We may not like that, but it's the way life is. Can you think of any predators that live on land?"

"Lions?" Angela replied.

"Very good! And tigers and wolves. Even dogs and house cats were once wild predators, before people tamed them and turned them into pets."

"I had a little cat, but my baby brother was allergic to her and my mother gave her away."

"That's a shame," said the fish.

"I don't like sharks."

"They're part of nature, just like lions and tigers and wolves."

"I still don't like them," she said, quite firmly.

"You know, Angela, there's a kind of shark that is sometimes called an angelfish. It doesn't ever hurt people. Would you stop liking me if I were an angel shark?"

"I like you the way you are," Angela said.

"But suppose I was a big old ugly angel shark," asked Mr.

Muncrief's voice. "Would you still like me, even though I looked different?"

"You wouldn't bite me?"

"I would never hurt you, Angela. I'm your friend, no matter what I look like."

"I suppose," said Angela. "But I like you better just the way you are. You're kind of pretty."

"Thank you."

And too small to scare anybody, she added silently.

Deeper and deeper into the ocean they moved. The water grew darker. Angela saw fish that had lights on their sides, long snake-like eels that glowed like an airplane at night. She was starting to get bored, though.

"Where is the mermaid princess?" she demanded. "You promised."

"Just a few moments more," said the angelfish, not showing the slightest displeasure or impatience. It still spoke with Mr. Muncrief's voice.

They seemed to swim past a flattopped mountain, and there, down on the very bottom of the sea, was a fairy city of golden spires and alabaster rooftops. It glowed softly in the deep dark water, pulsating almost like a thing alive.

"It's beautiful!" said Angela.

But as they flowed down onto the broad main avenue of the underwater city, the glowing light seemed to dim. One by one, the golden mansions that lined the avenue went dark until there was only a single light shining from the topmost tower of the great palace made of coral and pearl, up at the head of the long stately avenue.

"Where are the people?" Angela asked as she followed her guide along the dead and empty avenue.

"There is a great sadness in Neptune's Kingdom today, Angela," said the fish. "A very great sadness."

"What is it? What happened?"

"You'll see."

The palace's silver gates were wide open, and they swam right through. They could see no one in the courtyard, no one in the great halls or long corridors or lofty-ceilinged chambers as they made their way through the palace. The palace seemed completely empty, but all through it Angela could hear a soft moaning sound, almost like someone sobbing. It frightened her.

Up into the tower they swam, up and up until they reached its topmost chamber.

"Here is the mermaid princess," said the angelfish somberly.

The princess was sitting beside a long dark table, her emerald-green-scaled tail curled beneath her, her long golden hair swaying in the gentle currents of the water. She was crying softly.

The princess looked familiar to Angela. Almost like her mother, yet— She looks like me! Angela realized.

There was a long black box atop the table. The mermaid princess ran her hand along its smooth edge. Angela swam up to it and looked inside.

There, lying with his eyes closed and his arms folded over his chest, was the mermaid's father. He was dead. He looked just like Angela's own daddy.

She screamed, and everything went black.

"Nothing at all is coming up on your screen?" Susan asked anxiously. She was sitting at her computer, speaking into the pin-head microphone of the headset she had clamped over her red curls. Her display screen showed a long list of legal mumbo-jumbo scrolling by.

"Nothing at all," said her client, a lawyer in Cincinnati who had a phobia against using computers.

Susan thought swiftly. "Is your computer switched on?"

A pause, then the man answered, "Of course it is!" rather irritably.

"Is the *screen* on?"

"Uh— Oh. For gosh sakes. That's a separate button, isn't it? Yep, here's your material coming through. My mistake, Susie. It's coming through fine now."

Susan did not like to be called Susie, but she kept her mouth shut. This lawyer was one of her oldest clients. As long as he paid so well to have Susan do the computer searches that he could have hired a law student to do, she was not going to correct his misuse of her name.

Susan had been a reference librarian in the Dayton Public Li-

brary system when she had first met Damon Santorini, nearly fifteen years earlier. When Angela had been born and she took an
extended maternity leave, Dan had helped her learn how to use a
home computer to "plug into" the growing number of reference
services that were available through the telephone lines. It took
quite a bit of arguing and cajoling, but her boss at the library
finally allowed Susan to work part-time from her home—after she
hotly insisted that they either give her this opportunity or have the
story blurted to the news media that the library was discriminating
against motherhood.

She built up a clientele across much of Ohio, but still worked as
a part-time employee of the library system. Gradually people from
further afield heard of her service through friends or their local
librarians. Gradually Susan became an entrepreneur, working on
her own, charging fees directly for looking up anything from ob-
scure book titles to arcane scientific references. She even helped
Dan several times in his work; he got the Air Force lab to pay her a
regular consulting fee. She settled bets over the telephone from
late-night barroom arguers, although she soon enough learned to
put the phone on an answering machine once they went to bed.

When Dan received the offer from ParaReality, it meant that
they would have to move to the Orlando region.

"Doesn't matter much where you are," Dan told her when
Susan worried about her business. "As long as you've got a telephone, you'll be okay."

Then Dan learned that the house Vickie Kessel had helped them
to find was being wired with fiber-optic cables. The entire Pine
Lake Gardens development was a "fiber-optic community," as the
advertising brochure put it.

"Is that good?" Susan had asked her husband.

"Better than good, honey. With fiber-optic lines direct to the
house, you can plug straight into the NREN."

She was accustomed to his speaking in jargon. The National
Research and Education Network linked thousands of universities
and research laboratories with the Library of Congress and other
data banks all across the country. It even had international
branches, connected by fiber-optic cables across the oceans or by
satellites hovering in orbit. Susan could access the world's libraries
without stirring from her new home.

So she sent notices to everyone whose address or phone number she had in her computerized database and left their new Florida number with Ohio Bell. Within a week of their arrival in their new home, Susan was doing nearly as much business as she had in Dayton. Within three weeks, her business had almost doubled.

Now she was sitting at her tiny desk in the alcove off the kitchen that had been designed to be a breakfast nook, sending a massive file of legal references to the lawyer back in Cincinnati who was too intimidated by computers to do his own searches.

"Is it coming through okay?" she asked into her headset mike.

"Yep, fine. I just hope this danged machine is really storing all this material and not losing it like it did the last time."

The last time, Susan knew, he had dumped the file by turning off his computer before saving the incoming data in its hard-disk memory. Susan had to get Dan to write an idiot-proof subprogram for him that automatically saved everything she sent to him.

The file was almost at its end, she saw from the notation on her screen. The data scrolled past almost too fast even for her trained eye to follow. Then the machine beeped twice and began transmitting facsimile pictures of actual patents, straight from the files of the U.S. Patent Office in Washington.

"Wow," she heard the lawyer gasp in her earphone. "The drawings and everything! Just like that! If I tried to get this stuff out of Washington by mail, it'd take a month."

"Fiber optics," Susan murmured, knowing it would impress him. "I can send you faxes, photographs, even videos if you ever need it."

She heard him chuckle. "How about a picture of yourself, Susie? I have no idea what you look like."

Her chin went up a notch. "I'm not a photographer's model," she snapped, then immediately hoped it did not sound as harsh to him as it had to her.

He went silent. The computer finished its run, beeped once, and then automatically transmitted the bill: the telephone time charges plus Susan's fee. The lawyer had not paid for the earlier transmission that he had lost, even though it had been his own fault.

Almost every cent Susan had made all year had gone into buying a teal-blue Subaru Legacy wagon. In Dayton, with Mother and her sisters nearby, she had always had a lift when she needed one. Baby-sitters, too. But here in this new housing tract of Pine Lake Gardens, surrounded by strangers, she needed a car of her own. Proudly, Susan emptied her bank account to buy the little station wagon that could carry all of the kids' paraphernalia and still give her good gas mileage.

Little Philip was sitting in his playpen by the big sunny windows. Thank God his asthma hasn't bothered him so much here, Susan thought. So far, that was the one unequivocally good thing to come from this move to the humid heat of Florida: the baby would escape a winter of asthma and bronchitis. Her neighbors all seemed friendly, maybe too friendly. They liked to pop in for coffee and gossip at any time of the day. Susan had explained firmly that she worked at home and could not be bothered during business hours. The neighbors had become quite frosty after the first week or so.

So what? Susan asked herself. Who needs a bunch of hens clucking around? Half of them are old enough to be my grandmother; they've got nothing to talk about except their golf games and their husbands' heart ailments. But she knew she was kidding herself. She was lonely. She missed her mother and her sisters, all back in Dayton, all safely tucked in the old neighborhood that they had known since childhood.

Dan has his work; as long as he can tinker sixty or seventy hours a week with his machines and work with Jace, he's happy. What happens here at home he barely notices. Angela's gotten her first period and he's more embarrassed than interested. He loves us, but all he really comes home for is food and sleep. And sex, of course.

Something's bothering Angie. She hasn't been the same since we moved here. She seems to be doing okay at school, but she's not adjusting to the new environment very well at all. Maybe it's just her period, on top of the move and the new neighborhood and all that. But what if it's something else?

Susan had phoned her mother about Angela's sulky unhappiness. Mother had laughed. "I raised the four of you girls, and all four of you cried every day from the time you were twelve until seventeen or so."

"I don't remember—"

"I do!" Mother had said cheerily. "Cried every day, each one of you. I think it's puberty. It hits your tear glands along with all the other glands."

"But Angela seems really unhappy, and she won't tell me what's wrong."

"Just like her father."

"Well, yes, I suppose," Susan said.

During those terrible weeks when their marriage had nearly broken up, Susan had told her mother how uncommunicative Dan could be. When he had a problem that troubled him, he would keep it bottled up inside him until he nearly shattered. Sex helped to release his tensions, but he could never tell Susan what the problem was. Air Force security, he would claim. He would fret and frown and gnaw on his lip with the pressure building every day, until he'd explode with an outburst of anger over some trivial thing at home. He was always sorry afterward, apologetic, ashamed. But the tension was still there twisting inside him until he found the solution to whatever it was that had been bothering him. Then he was fine. Until the next problem arose.

"Dear little Angie probably doesn't even know what's bothering her," Susan's mother said. "All she knows is that she's unhappy."

"There must be *something* bothering her."

Mother said, "Why don't you send her up here over the Thanksgiving holiday? We'd love to have her. Love to have all of you. This will be the first Thanksgiving without all four of my babies sitting around the table."

That had turned the conversation into a long apology for leaving Ohio and an explanation of how expensive it is to travel with two children for just a few days and besides the weather might not be so good for Phil and Dan probably will be working right through the holiday anyway and—

The wall phone rang. Startled, Susan saw that the computer screen showed her bill and the words TRANSMISSION FINISHED blinking at her.

Pulling off the headset, she turned in her little swivel chair and reached for the telephone on the wall above the kitchen counter. The computer hummed to itself and continued to blink.

"Hello," Susan said.

"Mrs. Santorini?"

"Yes."

"This is Eleanor O'Connell—Angela's teacher."

Susan went rigid. "What's happened?"

"Nothing serious, Mrs. Santorini. Please don't be alarmed. But if you can, I'd appreciate it if you could drive over here and pick Angela up."

"What's happened?" Susan fairly screamed into the phone.

"She's had a little fainting spell, that's all. She's in the doctor's office now. She seems perfectly all right, but she did faint in class a few minutes ago."

CHAPTER 9

Jason Lowrey did not seem to be sitting so much as leaning his long, lanky body against the chair like a wooden pole slanting across it or a case of rigor mortis. His chin was pushed down on his narrow chest, his fists jammed into the pockets of his tattered jeans, his scuffed-up alligator boots poked out from the jeans' frayed bottoms. He almost seemed to be asleep or hypnotized into rigidity, like some stooge for a stage magician.

Dan knew better.

"We're wasting time here," he said.

"I'm thinking," said Jace, without opening his eyes.

"Sure you are."

Dan got up from the molded plastic chair in which he had been sitting and started to pace the lab, unconsciously gnawing on his lip. As usual, he had come to work in a short-sleeved white shirt, neatly pressed slacks, and a sports jacket. He had quit wearing ties after a couple of weeks on the job, when he realized that no one wore a tie anywhere in Florida, except bankers and dark-suited missionaries. Now his jacket was hanging from a peg behind the door and his shirt looked rumpled and sweaty despite the frigid air-conditioning.

This simulations lab was Jace's real office, his real home: a long narrow windowless room of bare gray cinder block jammed with computers of every type and description, from the refrigerator-tall Crays and the glistening new Toshiba 7700 to gray desktop models that had been worked so hard their keyboards looked grimy.

If a neat, orderly, well-scrubbed laboratory was a sign that no creative work was being done, then Jace's simulations lab looked like a whirlwind of innovation. Computers hummed. Their screens glowed with long streams of alphanumeric symbols that seemed gibberish to everyone—even most of the ParaReality staff—except Jace and Dan. Cables and connecting wires coiled across the desks and tables, snaked along the floor, hung from jury-rigged ceiling supports like dark pythons waiting to ensnare the unwary traveler in this electronic jungle.

Dan stopped in front of the largest of the display screens. It was fully six feet tall, from its floor mount to its top, slanting slightly backward like a full-length mirror. An intricately detailed picture of Babe Ruth showed frozen on the screen, grinning at Dan out of his wide fleshy face, gripping a heavy baseball bat in both his big hands and resting it against his left shoulder. Dan could see the nubbing on the Babe's sweatshirt sleeves, beneath the short-sleeved Yankee pinstripes. The wood grain of his massive Louisville Slugger was clear and beautiful. He could read the label on the bat.

He turned back to Jace, still rigidly aslant the chair, eyes closed, chin on chest.

"Well, it's not the graphics," Dan said, heading back toward the inert scarecrow.

"Tell me something I don't know."

"We just need more brute power," Dan said. "That's all there is to it. Otherwise the imagery's going to keep looking fuzzy."

"What're we up to now?" Jace mumbled.

"Five and a half gigaflops." Five billion five hundred million floating point operations per second. Dan had paralleled both the Crays and the new Toshiba to achieve that much computing power. And still the background images in the baseball simulation looked fuzzy, cartoonlike, not even close to the crisp, realistic imagery that Jace was insisting on.

"And Muncrief said no more hardware?"

Kyle Muncrief had almost screamed at Dan earlier that morning.

In the three weeks Dan had been working for ParaReality, Dan had seen Muncrief, strangely enough, only at his own home when Kyle popped in a few times at breakfast and offered to drive Angela to school. Angie loved the attention, and had even started calling the man Uncle Kyle.

That morning, though, after deciding with Jace that the baseball simulation needed more computing power, Dan had gone up to the quiet paneled offices in the front of the building and asked Kyle if he had a few minutes.

Muncrief was on the phone, but he waved Dan into his office and pointed a finger like a pistol at one of the upholstered chairs in front of his broad cherrywood desk.

Dan sat as Muncrief said suavely into the phone, "That's right. The Pine Lake Middle School. It's the only one in the country. . . . Sure, we could arrange a visit for you. I think you'll be very impressed. And the teachers love it! They don't need any special training, either. A day's orientation at the beginning of the school year is all it takes."

Dan's eyes wandered to the architect's rendering on the wall behind Muncrief: a low, windowless building of pure white with a tall slender tower by its entrance, almost like a minaret. Over the front door was emblazoned CYBER WORLD in computer-style letters.

Muncrief smiled at Dan as he continued. "That's fine. Great. I'll have my assistant set up a visit for you. Her name's Victoria Kessel. Hang on, I'll transfer you. . . ."

He punched buttons on the phone console like a man whacking at mosquitoes. "Vickie? Got the superintendent of schools from St. Louis on the phone. She wants to visit Pine Lake. Set it up, okay?"

He banged the phone back into its cradle. "Those school people! They're so unbelievably slow to move, you could starve to death before they start to say hello."

Dan wanted to talk about buying more hardware, not the shortcomings of school administrators.

"We've got the best thing to hit education since lead pencils, and all they do is pussyfoot around and come to visit and tell me how tight their blasted budgets are."

"Well, maybe—"

"You know how much that school is costing me? A good-size fortune, every month. But I keep it going because one of these days VR is going to be the *only* way those people will build their schools. The only way to go."

"We've got a problem," Dan blurted.

Muncrief raised his eyebrows. Dan began to explain that they needed more hardware to make the baseball simulation completely realistic. Muncrief's usually smiling face got tauter and tauter as Dan talked, and he realized that Jace had sent him in here because he didn't want to face the boss's ire.

"Another Toshiba!" Muncrief exploded. "Do you know what they cost?"

"We'll only need one—"

"The hell you do! You listen to me, Dan. I hired you to keep Jace happy, not to come running to me asking for money. If Jace can solve his problems with more hardware, what do we need you for? He's already got a Toshiba and two Crays and God knows what else. That's it! The piggy bank is busted! Now get back there and tell that big genius to get his brain in gear and make that baseball game work!"

Dan clenched his teeth so hard, his jaw hurt. He pushed himself up from the chair and headed for the door.

"Hey, Dan, wait a minute," Muncrief called.

Dan turned back toward him.

The suave smile was back in place. "I didn't mean to yell at you. I know you're doing your best. It's just that we're running tight, financially, you know. I don't have the capital for major new equipment buys. Jace told me he had enough hardware when he asked me to hire you. There just isn't enough money in the company to buy anything big. Our cash flow is negative."

Dan nodded, tight-lipped, not trusting himself to say anything.

"And besides," Muncrief added, pointing to his blank computer screen, "every additional dollar we spend on computer power for the simulation increases the ticket price we'll have to charge the customers. The accountants tell me we're already up against the limit that we can reasonably charge. We've got to be competitive with Disney and the other amusement parks, especially at the beginning."

Dan nodded. "I understand."

"You guys have to solve your problems without more hardware."

"I'll see what we can do."

Dan got as far as the door.

"Another thing," Muncrief said.

Turning, Dan saw that Muncrief was standing behind his desk, his face deadly serious.

"The media's gotten wind of what we're doing. We've been getting calls; reporters are starting to sniff around."

"So?"

"All media contacts must be handled by the front office. Understand that? I don't want *any* of the staff talking to reporters on their own. Somebody calls you, somebody starts pumping you at the local bar, somebody bumps into you at the supermarket—you tell 'em to talk to me. And you tell me or Vickie right away. We can't have leaks to the media! I don't want to wake up some morning and see a scare story about us on *Good Morning, America*."

"I carried a Top Secret clearance most of the time I worked for the Air Force," Dan said, barely keeping the anger out of his voice. "I know how to keep my mouth shut."

"Good," said Muncrief.

As he walked down the corridor toward the simulations lab, where Jace waited, Dan did not wonder why Muncrief was so afraid of the media. His mind kept echoing Muncrief's words: *I hired you to keep Jace happy.* He hired me because I'm cheaper than a supercomputer. I'm cheaper than buying new hardware.

"No more hardware," Dan answered Jace, who was still slanted rigidly across the wooden chair. "I thought he'd have a stroke right there in his office, he got so worked up."

"Maybe he'd leave us enough in his will to buy the extra machine."

Dan grinned, despite himself. "Intel's working on a teraflop machine," he mused.

"Yeah, the Paragon XP/T," Jace muttered. "Probably cost a mint and have more bugs in it than Guatemala."

"It's not ready yet, anyway," said Dan.

Jace opened both eyes and lifted his chin a little. "Muncrief must be really strapped for cash. He's always bought me whatever I asked for."

"Like buying me," Dan said.

Jace ignored the thrust. "You're just gonna have to come up with something brilliant, Danno."

"Hey, you're the genius. I'm just a glorified technician."

It was a standing joke between them, sometimes a bitter joke. Dan had been surprised and hurt when Jace had left him behind in Dayton; his comfortable view of their partnership and his own worth had crumbled. His work deteriorated; he had been hell to live with and he knew it. Dr. Appleton tried to straighten him out; Susan tried to be understanding. But then Jace had phoned and asked Dan to come to Florida with him, and Dan's world bloomed into spring.

Until he realized that he would be leaving Dr. Appleton, the man who had given him his chance, his career. The man who had been better than a father to him.

"I'll be able to develop VR systems for teaching," Dan had said to Appleton. "Medical systems for surgery, systems for operating spacecraft remotely—all the things we've dreamed about."

Appleton had nodded understandingly. "You might as well go with Jace, Dan. You haven't been much good to us or yourself since he went away."

Dan straddled the plastic chair backward and leaned his chin on his forearms. "Why don't we just let the background details fuzz out? We can make the individual batter stand out when you're in the field, and the infielders and the pitcher when you're at bat. The details of the stadium and the crowd don't matter that much, do they?"

"The hell they don't!" Jace sat up in his chair, both eyes snapped fully open.

"But—"

"This is supposed to be an *experience,* buster. A full friggin' three-dimensional experience with sight and sound and feeling. The background is important. Vital. I don't want the user to think he's in some friggin' video arcade! I want him to *be* there! Yankee Stadium or Wrigley Field or whatever, he's got to be there with full detailed sights and sounds. Even smells."

"The smells are easy," Dan said. "We can just pipe some vapor into the VR chamber."

"That's cheating."

"But it would work."

"Yeah. Maybe. It's the friggin' visual details we've gotta sharpen up. We can't go brute force if Muncrief won't spring for another Toshiba."

"It would make the price of the game a lot higher than Cyber World wants it to be, that's for sure."

"So we've gotta go smart instead of brute force. And we gotta do it pronto, Tonto. How can we get more detail without more computer power?"

Dan puffed out a breath. "Good question."

Jace went back to his rigid posture.

"What is this, yoga or something?" Dan asked. "I never saw you do this before."

"Shut up and lemme think." Jace closed his eyes and folded his arms across his scrawny chest.

With a shake of his head, Dan got up from his chair and started pacing the length of the lab again. There's got to be some way to put more of our existing power into the visual details, he told himself. Without sacrificing the background details. Got to be.

But another part of his mind argued, You can't get something for nothing. If you put more MIPS into the close-up details, you're going to have to take bytes away from something else. That's all there is to it.

Dan started to agree with himself, but suddenly a new thought struck him. The persistence of vision. He had read the phrase somewhere, something about the earliest attempts to make motion pictures, a century or more ago.

The persistence of vision. What is there—

The phone rang.

Jace's chair was two feet from the desk where the phone sat, but he remained fixed in his rigid closed-eyed position. Dan hurried toward the desk as the phone rang again. It was starting its third ring when he picked it up and snapped, "What is it?"

Susan's voice answered, "Dan, I'm sorry to bother you at the lab—"

"What's wrong? What's happened?"

"Nothing too terrible," Susan said. Her voice sounded steady and almost calm. Dan thought he heard a slight tremor in it.

"I'm at the school. Angie's had a fainting spell. The doctor thinks it was just from excitement. She was using one of the VR games when it happened and she just seems to have screamed and fainted, but there's nothing physically wrong and she seems okay now."

Dan knew that if Susan really believed Angie was okay she wouldn't have called him.

"Are you taking her home?" he asked.

"Yes. Mrs. O'Connell and the doctor both think it's best to take her home and let her rest for the remainder of the day."

"Mrs. O'Connell?"

"Eleanor O'Connell. Angie's teacher."

"Oh."

"I'm going to drive her home now."

"I'll come right home. Is Angie really okay? Can she talk on the phone?"

"You can talk to her when you get home."

"Yeah. Sure. Okay, I'm on my way."

He hung up the phone and found that Jace was sitting up, peering narrow-eyed at him.

"What's wrong?" Jace asked.

"Angie fainted in school."

"Fainted?"

"While she was in one of the VR games."

Jace's face contorted into a frown. "How can she faint in a VR game? That doesn't make sense."

With a shake of his head, Dan reached for his jacket. "I'm finding out that twelve-year-old girls don't make sense very often."

"I told you not to have kids!" Jace called after him as he headed down the corridor toward the back parking lot, his jacket flung over his shoulder.

Vickie Kessel was on the telephone, promising the principal of the Pine Lake Middle School that she would send a technician to check out the VR equipment ParaReality had installed in the classrooms. A student had fainted while using the equipment, and the principal insisted on a thorough check.

"Of course," Vickie soothed. "I'll have a team over there in less than an hour, and they'll work all night if they have to. We want that equipment to operate properly just as much as you do."

As she hung up the phone she saw Jace storm past the open

door of her office, his lantern-jawed face set into an angry grimace. There could only be one person the company's resident genius was heading for. Curious, Vickie got up from her chair and went out into the corridor.

Sure enough, Jace ducked through the doorway to Kyle Muncrief's office and slammed the door behind him. She heard Jace's voice, but it was too muffled for her to make out his words. Then Kyle said something, loud and impatient.

Glancing both ways along the corridor to make sure that she was alone, Vickie tiptoed to Muncrief's videoconference room and closed its door softly. Through the door that connected to Kyle's office she could hear the two men arguing. She went to the door and pressed her ear against it.

"What did you do?" Jace's voice.

"I just manipulated the game a little. That's all."

"You went too friggin' far!"

"Nonsense."

"Don't bullshit me, man. She's just a kid!"

"I didn't hurt her. How could I possibly hurt her?"

"She passed out, for chrissakes! You musta scared the crap outta her."

"We needed to get her reaction, didn't we?" Muncrief said, his voice high, defensive. "Okay, so we got it."

"Not so friggin' soon! She's just a kid. You shoulda worked up to it one step at a time."

"I didn't think it would hit her so hard. I don't want to hurt her; that's the last thing I want."

"She's just a kid," Jace repeated.

"Look, it's over and done with. She'll be okay and we've got the reaction we wanted. Right here on the laser disc."

"I oughtta quit," Jace said, sounding furious. "I should never have let you talk me into this. It's crazy. He's my best friend, for chrissakes."

"He'll never know. Unless you tell him."

"Why the hell did you hafta pick *his* daughter? There must be twenty kids in the friggin' class!"

"I didn't want it to be this way." Muncrief's voice turned almost desperate, pleading. "I *need* her. She's the one I need."

"I oughtta just walk out that friggin' door and never come back."

"You can't do that! You'll never find another company that'll give you a free hand to develop what you like, somebody who'll go to the edge of Chapter Eleven to buy you all that fancy hardware and get you the assistants that you want. You know that."

"You shouldn't have scared her so bad." Jace's voice was so low that Vickie barely could hear it through the door.

"I didn't mean to scare her. It won't happen again, I swear," Muncrief said, smoothly reasonable. "We needed her reaction and now we've got it. I'll make it up to her. Now I can be nice to her."

Their voices dropped lower, and Vickie heard nothing more. She waited in the conference room, her thoughts whirling. They were talking about the student who fainted. Kyle's interfering with the VR games at the school. She realized that the girl they were talking about must be Dan Santorini's daughter. That's not smart, Vickie said to herself. Definitely not smart.

When Dan came through the breezeway door into the kitchen, he could hear the TV: some stupid kids' cartoon show, from the sound of it. There was Angie in the living room, sitting on the sofa with her bare feet tucked up under her, her little Amanda doll grasped in her right hand, staring rigidly at the screen but otherwise looking completely normal. Susan must be in the baby's room.

Angie seemed transfixed by the cartoons, seeing or hearing nothing else.

"Hi, Angel," Dan said as brightly as he could manage. "How are you?"

She glanced up at him, then swiftly returned her gaze to the TV. "Okay, I guess."

Dan tossed his jacket onto one of the armchairs, thinking that their Dayton furniture looked dull and heavy and totally out of place in this Florida house.

"Where's Mom?" he asked.

Angela shrugged.

At a loss, Dan went back toward the bedrooms. Sure enough, Susan was standing in the doorway of the baby's room, watching little Philip sleeping in his crib.

"I thought I heard him wheeze," she whispered.

Dan stared hard at the baby. He had spent many painful nights in Dayton helplessly watching his son struggling to breathe, his tiny shoulders hunched, his frail little chest heaving. Dan knew what the baby was going through. He knew what it was like when you couldn't lift your chest to get air into your lungs. Watching Phil suffer made him feel worse than having an asthma attack himself.

"He looks okay to me," he whispered back.

"I had to take him with me to the school. I thought maybe it bothered his breathing."

Nearly a month we've been in this heat, and she still thinks like we're in Ohio in the middle of the winter, Dan groused to himself.

"He's okay," he said.

"Yes, I think he is," Susan said with some relief.

"What happened to Angie?"

Susan's face was tight with worry. "Her teacher called me and said she had passed out while she was in one of the VR booths."

"Fainted."

"Eleanor said she heard Angie scream, and by the time she opened the booth door Angie had fallen off the bench and was on the floor, unconscious."

"Electric shock?" Dan wondered aloud. "Could there have been a short in the circuitry?"

"The school doctor didn't find any physical signs of anything."

"I'll tell Kyle to send a technician over to check that—"

"It's already been done. Eleanor got the principal to call Vickie Kessel before I left the school with Angie."

"Eleanor?"

"Mrs. O'Connell," Susan said, with just an edge of impatience in her voice. "Angie's teacher. You've met her."

"Oh. Yeah."

"They couldn't find anything physically wrong with Angie. It must have been something in the VR game she was playing."

"What's she doing playing a game in school?" Dan asked.

Susan huffed, "I wish you'd paid more attention at the PTA meeting. They allow the students to play games if they finish their lessons ahead of schedule."

"Oh."

"Angie did very well in her chemistry lesson, so she was allowed to play Neptune's Kingdom—which is really a biology/ecology lesson, not just a game."

"Yeah, I remember now."

He turned away from his wife, who looked as if she wanted to scream rather than whisper. "I'll go talk to her," Dan muttered.

Back in the living room, he sat beside his daughter on the sofa and said as cheerfully as he could, "So you had some excitement in school, huh?"

Angie kept her eyes on the TV screen. Phil Donahue held a microphone in one hand and was pointing to someone off-camera with the other.

Dan picked the remote control from the end table. "Do you mind if we shut this off and talk for a while, Angel?"

Angela nodded glumly.

Clicking off the TV, Dan asked, "What happened to you this afternoon, honey?"

"I don't know," Angela said.

"You fainted."

"Uh-huh."

Susan came into the living room and sat on the armchair facing the sofa, looking drawn with anxiety.

"Can you tell me about it? You were playing a VR game, weren't you?"

"Uh-huh."

"Which one? Do you remember?"

"Neptune's Kingdom. It was all about fish and the ocean and stuff like that."

"Your teacher said you screamed. What made you scream?"

Angela's lip began to tremble. Her eyes filled with tears.

"Honey," Dan began, "whatever it is that's bothering you, we—"

"I saw you dead!" she wailed. "I saw you in a coffin and you were dead!" The child broke into heavy, terrified sobs.

Dan stared at his wife. Susan sat openmouthed, round-eyed with stunned surprise. Angela cried as if her world had come to an end and buried her face against her father's chest.

"But that's silly, Angel," Dan said as soothingly as he knew how. He wrapped his arms around her. "I'm not dead, you can see that. I'm right here."

"But I saw you!" Her voice was muffled, tear-filled. "You were in a coffin and your face was all gray and cold and your arms were folded over your chest and the mermaid princess was crying for you and she was me! The princess was me and her father was you and you were dead!"

Dan held his daughter tightly and rocked slowly back and forth with her. Susan, white with shock, came from her chair and sat on the floor at his feet. She, too, enfolded Angela in her arms and laid her head against the child's sob-racked body.

"It's all right, baby," she murmured. "It's all right."

For several minutes the three of them sat there entangled in Angela's fear and grief. Dan felt increasingly uncomfortable. This is all a mistake, he said to himself. If we can just calm her down enough to talk logically to her, I can show her that it's all a mistake.

Slowly Angela's sobs subsided. Susan whisked a wad of facial tissue out of nowhere and helped the child dry her eyes and blow her reddened nose.

Dan took her gently under the chin and lifted her face up to look at him. Angela's eyes were swollen from crying.

"I'm right here, Angel," he said. "See? I'm really alive." He wiggled his eyebrows. She smiled weakly.

Susan got up from the floor and sat on the sofa next to her daughter. "There must be something wrong with that VR game," she said.

A flash of anger blazed in Dan's gut. There's nothing wrong with the damned game! he snarled inwardly. But he suppressed his anger.

To Angela he said, "When you're in that game it seems like you're really in the ocean, doesn't it?"

"Yes." She sniffled slightly.

"You know, we make those VR games to feel as realistic as possible. We work very hard to make them seem real."

Angela said nothing. Susan was giving him a doubtful look.

Dan went on. "Sometimes they can be so real, you imagine things that aren't actually in the game."

Susan's expression was going from doubt to anger.

"Like your game today, Angel. It seemed so real to you that you thought you saw yourself as the mermaid princess, didn't you?"

She sniffled again and nodded.

"But that's not you in the game, honey. It's just a picture that an artist drew. It's very realistic, but it's not a picture of you."

"It *was* me," Angela said, her voice barely audible.

"No, it wasn't," Dan insisted. "It wasn't you, and the mermaid's father wasn't me."

"But—"

"It really wasn't, Angel. Believe me."

"But I saw it!"

"You thought you saw it."

Susan said, "Dan, really! If that's what Angie saw—"

"Listen," he said. "Once, when I was a kid in Youngstown, I was sneaking through the alleys behind the houses on our street. I forget why; maybe I was trying to get home without running into any of the tough kids on the block. Anyway, there I was, going down this narrow alley. It had big tall wooden fences on both sides of it."

Angela was looking up into his face, fascinated that her father was telling her a story about himself. Susan was watching, too.

"All of a sudden a big dog starts barking and running down the alley after me. I was scared to death! I looked over my shoulder and there was this dog! He looked as big as a lion, and he had horns on his head! Like a bull! Honest, that's what I saw, big black sharp horns on his head. I can still see that dog and his horns, right now."

"Dogs don't have horns," Angela said weakly.

"I know. I even knew it then. But I was so scared, I *thought* I saw horns. And when I think about that dog even today, my mind still shows me that same picture, with the horns."

"Did the dog catch you?"

"No, honey. I ran faster than I ever had in my whole life and got to the door in the fence of our own house and went inside and locked that door tight!" He looked up at Susan. "Then I came down with an asthma attack that kept me in bed for a week, almost."

Angela seemed to perk up after that. Dan stayed with her, telling stories and even breaking out an old jigsaw puzzle that they spent the rest of the afternoon on. Susan ignored the messages piling up on her phone machine and took care of things around the house that she had been putting off for days. The baby woke up, and for almost a whole hour the four of them played together on the sun-warmed floor of the living room, almost like a family in a television commercial.

By suppertime Angela seemed to be behaving normally, her

trauma forgotten. But after the children were put to bed and Dan was stretched out on the sofa watching the local weather forecaster talking gloomily about the drought affecting Florida, Susan came out of the kitchen, drying her hands on a towel.

"Can we talk about it now?"

Dan swung his feet to the floor and sat upright, clicking off the TV with the remote control. "About what?"

"Angie."

He made a wry face. "Those VR games can be very realistic. She just got carried away."

"Maybe they're too realistic. For children."

"Aw, hell, honey. How many kids in that school have used the games and how many have been affected the way Angie was?"

"I don't know."

He blinked at her. "You mean you think other kids might have been affected, too? No, that can't be. The school would've shut the games down. They'd be yelling bloody murder at us."

"Maybe."

"No maybe about it."

Susan asked, "Do you think she really saw you in the game?"

"Couldn't have," he said gruffly. "You think we paint in every kid's picture and run their own special version of the game? Get real!"

"But she seemed so certain," Susan said. "I mean, it scared her so much, she fainted!"

Dan looked up at the ceiling, his way of signaling that he thought his wife was being ridiculous. "Okay, look. Tell you what I'll do. I'll check out the game myself. We've got all the laser discs at the office, so I'll just run through that one during my lunch hour tomorrow. Okay?"

"All the games are kept at the office?"

"Sure. The VR booths in the school are just the output sites. We keep all the computer hardware and software at the office. They pipe the programming to the school over a dedicated phone line. A fiber-optic line. Didn't you know that?"

"No." Susan's brow furrowed slightly. "So all the games are actually run from your office, then."

"From Vickie Kessel's office," Dan said. "Vickie's in charge of the school programs."

CHAPTER 10

t was full dark when Jason Lowrey finally left the ParaReality building. Other employees left by the rear entrance, through the double metal doors that bore the company's logo in stylish gold lettering. Other employees walked out into the parking lot and got into their cars and drove home.

Not Jace. He went back through the storerooms and workshops to the loading dock, where he kept his battered old ten-speed bike leaning against the wall beneath the overhang so it wouldn't get rained on. In spite of that, the bike was blotched with ugly patches of rust; Jace laughingly called it eczema whenever someone told him he should clean it up or get a new bicycle. In the humid Florida air the gearshift had rusted, too. He had not used the gears since he had arrived in this flat land around Orlando; there was no need to.

Jace flung one long lanky leg over the saddle seat and pushed away from the wall, coasting down the loading ramp and out onto the back driveway, heading for the little bungalow that other people called his home. Back in Dayton, Dan—always the worrywart —had bought him a chain and padlock to protect his bike while it was parked outside the Wright-Patterson lab during the day. Jace had laughed his head off.

"Who the hell would steal my eczema special?" he asked Dan. "Anybody needs a bike so bad they're willing to steal my junker, they're welcome to it."

Jason Lowrey was the only son of a university professor of mathematics and a San Francisco socialite who had been beautiful enough to be a fashion model. Not that his mother chose to work; she regarded a job as beneath her station in life. But she did pose for photographers now and then in connection with charity drives to raise money for the homeless or other good causes. Jace's father doted on his mother, but, with his teacher's income, he could not afford to show his love in any material form, like jewelry or a fine home or even a ski condo up in the Sierras. She bought those things for herself, constantly reminding her husband that he was not enough of a man to provide for her in the manner she expected.

As Jace grew up he began to realize that love meant pain. Not physical pain, perhaps, but constant mental and emotional torture. His mother seemed a coldly unattainable goddess: distant, haughty, demanding, often stern, occasionally brutal, never willing to give the warmth and affection he craved. Jace watched his father grovel before his beautiful, demanding mother. As he grew older, he wondered why his father would behave so. Then Jace discovered sex, and his sudden understanding of the true reason behind his father's slavery stunned and disgusted him.

When Jace was little, his father virtually ignored him. "You're not a human being until you can hold an intelligent conversation with me," Jace remembered his father telling him. Even when Jace was rushed to the hospital with acute appendicitis, his father went ahead with his trip to some conference on education. "I can't do anything to help the boy," he had said. "No reason for me to miss my conference."

Once Jace started going to school his father became an unbending tyrant, demanding that his son be the brightest, best-behaved, most-honored student in his class. Jace rebelled in little ways. School was so easy that he could not help but get good grades. But he played pranks on his teachers and got into fights with the other kids. He became a discipline problem. And he learned that he could play his mother against his father, get her to blame him for his difficulties in "adjusting to his peer group" while he blamed his wife for "spoiling the child rotten."

Jace's earliest friend was his TV set. His first memories were of Bugs Bunny and the Road Runner. He laughed with childish glee whenever Bugs outslicked Yosemite Sam or the cloddish Elmer Fudd. Later he graduated to superheroes who righted wrongs and won the world's admiration while wearing wonderful costumes with masks and capes. The only effective way his parents had to discipline him was to turn off his TV. Later they had to physically remove the set from his room. By the time he was a teenager, he kept his cartoon addiction a secret from the few acne-faced friends he possessed, but the Teenaged Mutant Ninja Turtles were his companions every Saturday morning.

By then he had discovered video games. Every nickel and dime he could lay his hands on went into video arcades. He pestered his parents for games that he could play on his home computer and even bribed them by promising to behave himself in school. They found it easier to placate their son than to fight against his insatiable thirst for increasingly complex games.

When Jace was ready for college, he looked like the stereotypical nerd: a tall, gangly, pock-faced kid with unruly hair, squinting narrow eyes, and nervous mumbling voice. He knew that love meant pain and sex meant subjugation. Yet he was not so much afraid of other people as uncertain of how to make friends—or even of the need to have friends. He was almost totally self-contained.

But he was a genius. That became clear as he breezed his way through his first year at Berkeley, where his father taught mathematics. Triumphantly, Jace transferred to the California Institute of Technology. "Do him good," Jace overheard his father say to his mother. "He thinks he's such a hotshot, wait till he gets to Cal Tech and finds that there are hundreds of other kids just as bright as he is. And even brighter. That'll take him down a peg or two."

There was no one at Cal Tech brighter than Jace. At least, no one that he would admit was brighter. On a campus renowned for brilliance and a certain easiness when it came to discipline, Jace began truly to shine. Even his pranks won campus-wide admiration. He blossomed socially. He made friends, almost all of them fellow male students. He avoided most of the women on campus. Love meant pain. Sex meant subjugation. He substituted the worlds he could create inside computers. He longed to make those worlds real, alive.

After three years his despairing faculty adviser warned, "You've got to settle down to *some* curriculum, Jace! You're picking classes here and there and making no progress toward a degree."

Jace had no interest in a degree. He had no desire ever to leave Cal Tech. He loved his life there. He attended classes when he chose to, passing them all with ease. He lived alone in a series of one-room apartments, always thrown out sooner or later by a landlord or landlady who could no longer stand his indifference to cleanliness. One irate woman got the FBI to search his room, certain that all the electronic gadgetry Jace had accumulated could only be the tools of a high-tech terrorist or a madman.

Cal Tech shelters its geniuses only up to a point. After six years the administration made it clear that Jace either had to buckle down to a stiffly regulated curriculum that would lead to a degree and graduation, or they would throw him out unceremoniously forthwith. Jace might have eventually gotten his degree if it had not been for Ralph Martinez.

Martinez was a captain then, just returned from a combat tour of the Persian Gulf and, much to his disgust, assigned to a public-relations swing through the nation's leading universities. He gave his perfunctory little illustrated speech in one of the Cal Tech lecture halls, then—as ordered—"met informally with interested members of the student body."

Barely a dozen and a half students showed up at the student lounge to talk with Martinez. One of them was Jace. Most of the students were interested in the supersonic airplanes and high-tech weaponry that Martinez had shown in his slides. Jace's only interest was in being the star of the group, and that meant he had to bait the hardedged captain unmercifully.

"You enjoy killing Iraqis?" Jace asked, a big-toothed grin on his gaunt, angular face.

Martinez's eyes flashed like flint struck with steel, but he said nothing. They stood facing each other, the tall lean scarecrow with his hair pulled back in a ragged ponytail and the stocky, square-shouldered captain in Air Force blue. The other students, all male except for one buxom young woman with a loud voice, seemed to move back as if they were getting out of the way of a shoot-out.

"Don't mind him," said the young woman disdainfully. "He's subhuman."

Jace's smile widened. Without taking his eyes off Martinez, he said, "I mean, does it give you a kick to drop bombs on helpless women and children?"

"We bombed military targets," Martinez snapped.

"Then who the hell bombed all those women and children we saw in the news?"

The young woman stepped in front of Jace, as if trying to separate him from the captain. "What is this, Lowrey? Now you're a political agitator?"

"I just wanna know what it's like to kill people," Jace replied. "I never met a killer before."

Obviously seething, Martinez repeated, "We bombed military targets. Not every bomb hit its intended target, though. There was some unintended collateral damage—"

"Like that civilian shelter," Jace said. "How many people did you kill in there? A hundred? Two hundred?"

Martinez said, "That was a military command post. We didn't know they had brought the civilians into it."

"I thought you were using smart bombs," Jace sneered. "They sound pretty stupid to me."

"Then make them smarter, wiseass."

That stung. "Me?"

"That's right: you. Do you think we're a bunch of homicidal maniacs? Do you think we *enjoy* risking our butts and dropping bombs on people?"

"Yeah, I think you do."

"Then think again, asshole. I love to fly. Nothing in the world beats the thrill of flying a high-performance jet. But combat is something else. I've been there. I can do without it, believe me."

Jace shook his head in distrust.

"And if you're so fucking worried that we're killing civilians by mistake," Martinez went on, "then come and help us build smarter weapons."

"Not me!"

"Sure, not you. You'd rather sit back and make wisecracks about us. But you won't help us to do our jobs better. You're too fucking chicken to put your brain in gear and tackle the toughest problems you'll ever face."

Jace gave the captain a studied grin and a one-finger salute, then left the room. Martinez had clearly won the exchange.

Two months later, Jace showed up at Martinez's new office in Wright-Patterson Air Force Base.

"What the hell are you doing here?" Martinez had demanded. On his shoulders were the bright golden oak leaves of a brand-new major.

"You're a hard guy to find," Jace said, standing in front of Martinez's desk like a tall shabby scarecrow. His T-shirt proclaimed, *Split Atoms, Not Logs*.

"I've just been assigned here."

"Well, you said something about tackling the toughest problems I'll ever face. Okay, I'm willing to take a look at your problems."

Martinez stared at him for a long silent moment. What Jace had not revealed was that he was fleeing from Cal Tech's determined effort to get him to graduate. And that he had neither forgotten Martinez's besting of him nor forgiven him for it.

"I got to reading about what you guys are doing," Jace said. "I don't wanna work on any weapons; I'm not gonna help you kill anybody. But there was some pretty interesting stuff about cockpit simulations—building better simulators. I got some ideas about that."

Martinez eyed Jace warily, then reached for the telephone on his desk. "I'll ask Bill Appleton to talk to you." To himself he added, If anybody can put this kook in harness, Appleton's the one to do it.

Before the week was out, Jace was happily working in Appleton's simulations laboratory. He sent a picture postcard to his parents in California. It showed an aerial view of the city of Dayton. Jace did not put a return address on the card.

Eventually he phoned his mother, just to hear her voice, just to tell her he was okay and doing well and maybe hear her say she was pleased that he called. Instead she told him that his father was in the hospital dying of cancer.

"I can't do anything to help the boy," Jace said, echoing his father's remark from twenty years earlier. "No reason for me to miss my conference."

He did not even bother to send a card when he moved to Florida; he had merely left his forwarding address with the post office. His mother had not written to him in the fourteen months since he had moved.

Jace bicycled up to his bungalow in the yellowish light of the street lamps out on the avenue. The bungalow was tucked away behind the houses that fronted on the street. Ghostly blue flickers from TV screens lit most of the windows he passed. The gravel driveway was dark, but Jace knew every bump of it. Somebody was barbecuing ribs; burning them, from the smell of it, Jace thought.

He leaned the bike against the bungalow wall next to the front door, then pecked out the elaborate security code on the keypad he had installed in the doorjamb. It beeped and winked green lights at him, and the door popped open with a sigh and a puff of air like the airlock of a contamination-proof biology lab or an aerospace clean room.

The track lights he had installed along the ceiling came on automatically as Jace stepped into the room and kicked the door shut behind him. He had carefully opaqued all the windows and knocked down all the partitions, turning the bungalow into a single room that never saw sunlight. It was filled with television sets, computer boxes, display screens, keyboards, dull-black remote-control units scattered everywhere, green circuit boards lying on the floor, on the bed, on the long worktables that were the main items of furniture in the one room. Microchips lay everywhere like a fine high-tech dust. There was not a book, not a magazine or a journal or a report anywhere; not even a newspaper or a TV listing.

There was one chair in the room, a jet-black curved recliner that looked like an astronaut's acceleration couch. Jace stretched out on it, his booted feet hanging past its end, cranked it down almost to a prone position, and reached for the TV remote controls on the floor where he had left them. He turned on three of the TV sets lined against the wall, each of them showing a different channel, each of them muted to absolute silence.

There was no refrigerator in the house, no stove or microwave oven. Jace had removed the entire kitchen and covered the sawed-off pipes with cabinets that held videotapes. He ate at the lab and, lately, had been taking his infrequent showers there, too. His own bathroom was too filthy even for him to feel comfortable in it.

Got to clean out that mess one of these days, he told himself as he stretched out on the couch, watching all three television screens at once. He knew he should be working on Muncrief's special project; he had the laser disc Muncrief had recorded from his special run of the Neptune's Kingdom game. But what Muncrief wanted bothered Jace down at a level of conscience that he seldom felt. There's nothing wrong with it, he told himself. He's not hurting the kid. Still, he felt uneasy, almost afraid. Muncrief's a weirdo; I should never have gotten tied up with him.

Except—except he gives you a free hand to do what the hell ever you like. He's right about that. Nobody else'd give me that kind of latitude. As long as I can keep him happy about his special project, I can do whatever else I want.

Aw, to hell with him, Jace told himself. So I'll make him the program he wants. So what if it's Dan's kid he's got the hots for. It won't hurt her, and Dan'll never know about it. The kid herself will never know about it. And now that Dan's here, we can polish off this friggin' baseball program and go on to some really neat stuff.

With a snort he pushed himself up from the couch and went to the table where he kept his helmet and data gloves. He slid a disc into the CD player that was hooked up to a series of computers that he had wired together, then slipped on the helmet and gloves. Trailing their wires, he went back to the couch and stretched out his lean, lanky body. Now he was in a world of his own making, a world of enslaved robots and hordes of slimy, evil alien soldiers ruled by a viciously beautiful goddess who looked very much like his mother.

His object was to wipe out the evil alien armies, liberate the robots, and capture the goddess queen for his own pleasure.

CHAPTER 11

Bput she's got to use the VR booths," said Eleanor O'Connell. "The school's entire teaching methodology is based on the virtual-reality systems."

Susan frowned worriedly. "Angie seems to be afraid of them."

"I can understand that, but we've got to work together to help her overcome this bad experience."

The two women were sitting in a corner of the teachers' lounge of the Pine Lake Middle School. Susan was impressed with the luxury of the lounge's carpeted floor and cushioned chairs. There were neat little tables in front of a row of gleaming machines that dispensed snack foods and cold drinks. A coffee maker burbled next to the sink where someone had left a white cardboard box filled with doughnuts. A couple of other teachers were relaxing on the sofas by the windows on the other side of the room. One of the women was smoking; Susan's nose wrinkled at the smell.

"Angie's been such a good one in class," O'Connell was saying, "we can't let this little incident stop her."

"But she seems afraid of the very idea of getting into one of those booths again," Susan said.

O'Connell leaned forward slightly and touched Susan's knee. "If Angela can't use the VR systems, she can't remain in this school. We're not set up to teach with the old-fashioned methods. This is a very special school, the only one in the state—I think it might be the only one in the country."

Susan saw that the teacher was not making a threat; O'Connell seemed genuinely upset by the idea that Angela might have to go to an ordinary school.

"I tried to explain to her last night that what happened was a freak . . . well, accident, I guess."

"She had an emotional experience that she wasn't prepared for," said O'Connell.

"Her father's tried to explain it to her, too."

"The school psychologist talked with her this morning," said the teacher. "She told me Angela seems a little frightened, but otherwise reasonably all right."

"She was really scared yesterday," Susan said.

"I truly don't think it would be good for Angela to allow her to run away from this disturbing experience. She's got to face it down."

Susan nodded, but she felt terribly uncertain. "Have any of the other children had similar experiences?"

"No," O'Connell said slowly, drawing out the word. Then she added, "One of the boys got into a bit of trouble last semester because he liked the VR games so much he didn't want to come out of the booth. He even sneaked into school over one weekend and tried to use the booth, but of course it wasn't working on the weekend."

"A boy sneaking *into* school?"

O'Connell laughed. "Yes. Strange, isn't it?" She had a hearty laugh that made the teachers across the lounge look over their way.

"That was our first semester, of course," she went on. "We were all new at the VR systems. We had ParaReality technicians in here every morning, it seemed. The equipment was always breaking down in one way or another."

Susan clutched at that morsel. "Could what happened to Angie have been an equipment failure of some sort?"

O'Connell shook her head. "Believe me, the equipment has been checked out. There was a ParaReality team here half the night; they couldn't find anything wrong. Even your husband looked it over."

"He did?" Susan was jolted with surprise.

"He was in here first thing this morning, before classes started. Before anyone else showed up. The janitor let him in, from what I heard."

"Oh."

"Listen," O'Connell said. "I have an idea that may help. Why don't you go through the game that Angela was playing? You can see for yourself what it's like."

"I've never used a virtual-reality simulation," Susan heard herself say. She was still wondering about Dan. He had promised to check the VR program at his office, but he said nothing about stopping at the school to check the equipment. He should have told me, she said to herself. Maybe he didn't think of coming to the school until he was on his way to work; the school's on the way to his lab. But no, that's not like Dan. He thought about it all night and left early this morning to come here and check out the system. Without mentioning a word of it to me. *That's* like Dan. Just like him.

"There's nothing to be afraid of," O'Connell said, misreading Susan's silence.

"I know," she said. "You're right, it is a good idea. Can we do it right now?" Phil was at her next-door neighbor's house, and Susan did not want to impose on the woman for a minute longer than necessary. Already she feared that the neighbor would take up the rest of the afternoon chatting with her once she returned and she would be unable to break away without seeming ungrateful.

O'Connell glanced at her wristwatch. "Lunch period is almost half over, but I think we can squeeze in the game before the children come back to class."

The two women walked to the classroom that Susan had seen at the PTA meeting a few weeks earlier. Now she overlooked the desks scattered irregularly across the floor and the posters tacked up to the wallboards. O'Connell took her straight to the row of six booths at the back of the room. They looked dark, confining, like confessionals in a church. Taking a breath, as if she were about to plunge into deep cold water, Susan stepped inside the nearest booth and sat down on its curved padded chair. It felt slightly small to her. On a bench next to the seat rested a pair of data gloves and a light-blue plastic sensory helmet decorated with stick-on stars of red and gold. The helmet was nicked and scuffed from hard use.

"I'll set up the game from my desk," O'Connell said as Susan wormed her hands into the metallic data gloves.

"You control it from your desk?"

"It's controlled from the ParaReality offices. I phone their computer and tell it what I want by touching keys on the phone pad. It's all automatic, actually."

She closed the door of the booth softly, leaving Susan in nearly complete darkness. Susan flexed her fingers inside the gloves. They felt slightly stiff and a bit small for her. Each glove trailed a thick wire to electronic boxes beneath the bench. Feeling slightly nervous, she reached over and picked up the helmet. It looked like something a biker would wear, smoothly curved plastic with a visor that came down over the face. But the visor was opaque. Susan knew there were two small TV screens on the visor's inner surface, one for each eye. They presented stereoscopic images to the wearer's eyes, producing a fully three-dimensional picture.

She slid the helmet over her hair. It fit snugly. There was no chin strap. Despite its bulk the helmet felt feathery light. But she was in total darkness now, like being blindfolded. Scary.

"Can you hear me, Mrs. Santorini?" O'Connell's voice startled Susan, even though it sounded soft in the helmet's earphones, far away.

"Yes," said Susan.

"I'm starting the game now."

"Okay." She felt shaky, as if she were stepping out onto a steep stairway in total darkness with no safety rail.

"This game is called 'Neptune's Kingdom,' " said a voice. It sounded warm and friendly, but Susan could not tell if it was a man's voice or a woman's. It's a computer synthesizer, she told herself.

The darkness remained for several moments, long enough for Susan to wonder if something had gone wrong. Then slowly it faded into a midnight blue that seemed to pulse rhythmically, almost hypnotically. Her hands tingled, but not uncomfortably so. The confining press of the helmet seemed to disappear. Susan felt herself relaxing, easing back on the padded seat. Her breathing slowed.

The world around her became somewhat brighter, then brighter still, until she was floating in warmly sunlit water like a skin diver in the crystal ocean of the Bahamas. Myriads of beautiful fish were swimming past, all the colors of the rainbow, and beyond their streaming schools Susan could see a coral reef shimmering in the deep currents of the sea. Her breath caught in her throat. She was not merely watching a video, she was surrounded by the ocean, she was living in this breathtakingly beautiful underwater world.

A gaily colored fish swam up to her and said, in the same androgynous voice of the computer: "Hello, there. I'm an angelfish. I'm your guide to Neptune's Kingdom."

An angelfish, thought Susan. Was that a coincidence? Do they use the same kind of fish for everyone who plays the game, or do they try to pick out fish that have some special relevance to each individual child? Maybe the game is still set for Angela.

Susan remembered that this so-called game was actually a biology/ecology lesson for the schoolchildren.

A shark glided by, sleek and deadly-looking. Susan watched, fascinated, as it opened its wide mouth and showed row upon row of sharp white teeth.

"There's nothing to be afraid of," said her angelfish. "Nothing can hurt you here in Neptune's Kingdom." But Susan saw that the angelfish moved a lot closer to her until the shark swam past.

"Most sharks are *predators*. They eat other fish. We may not like that, but it's the way life is. Can you think of any predators that live on land?"

"Lawyers," Susan snapped.

"No. Try again."

Susan grinned to herself. She was enjoying this. Let's see, she thought, predators. "Lions," she said.

"Very good! And tigers and wolves. Even dogs and house cats were once wild predators, before people tamed them and turned them into pets."

Susan said nothing, and they moved deeper and deeper into the ocean. It became quite dark, but Susan felt no cold. Down at this shadowy depth she saw fish that had lights on their sides, long snakelike eels that glowed like an airplane at night.

They seemed to swim past a flattopped mountain, and there,

down on the very bottom of the sea, was a fairy city of golden spires and alabaster rooftops. It glowed softly in the deep dark water, pulsating almost like a thing alive.

Susan gasped. "It's beautiful!" she said.

As they flowed down onto the broad main avenue of the underwater city, the glowing light seemed to grow brighter. The golden mansions that lined the avenue were thronged with beautiful mermaids and handsome muscular mermen, the scales of their fish tails glittering like green and blue jewels, their faces smiling in welcome. Susan noticed that the mermaids were demurely clad in scallop-shell bras. Everyone seemed happy and carefree, swimming along and waving to Susan as her angelfish guide led her toward the great palace of coral and pearl up at the head of the long stately avenue.

The palace's silver gates were wide open, and they swam right through. They could see no one in the courtyard, no one in the great halls or long corridors or lofty-ceilinged chambers as they made their way through the palace. The palace seemed completely empty, but all through it Susan could hear a faint tinkling music, almost like wind chimes heard from afar.

"This is a very special day in Neptune's Kingdom," said the angelfish. "A special day indeed."

"Why? What day is it?"

"You'll see."

Up into the tower they swam, up and up until they reached its topmost chamber. The walls gleamed with precious stones. The musical tinkling grew louder.

Then they entered what seemed to be a great hall, filled to its walls with smiling, bowing mermaids and mermen. Myriads of brightly colored fish hovered all around Susan. A broad aisle led from the entrance where she stood to a jewel-encrusted dais at the far end of the room, where a white-bearded merman and charming mermaid sat on golden thrones, their emerald-green tails flicking gently, their faces warm with loving smiles.

"Today Neptune's Kingdom welcomes its new princess," said the guide fish.

"Who is it?" Susan asked.

"Why, it's you, Susan," the angelfish answered. "You are the new princess of this kingdom."

Everything went black. Susan jerked with shock, as if she had been slapped in the face.

"That's the point where your daughter fainted," O'Connell's voice said in her earphones.

She was in darkness again. She could feel the weight of the helmet on her head and the slight stiffness of the data gloves. The small of Susan's back felt slightly cramped, as if she had been sitting frozen in one position for too long.

"Can't we go on to the end of the game?" she called out into the darkness.

A pause. Then O'Connell said, "I'm afraid my students are due back from their lunch period in just a few minutes. You've been in there nearly half an hour."

"Half an hour?" Susan felt as if she'd been in the booth only a few moments. Reluctantly she pulled the helmet off and shook her hair loose. She was peeling off the gloves when O'Connell opened the booth's door. The early-afternoon sunlight streaming in from the classroom windows made Susan wince and squint.

"Did you learn anything?" the teacher asked as she walked Susan to the door of her classroom.

Shaking her head, Susan replied, "Some biology about ocean life, I guess. Nothing that seemed frightening or scary."

O'Connell's round face looked troubled. "Angela's got to be able to use the VR booths."

"But something upset her so . . ."

"I'll restrict her to regular class work. None of the games. Not for a while."

"Until she feels better about this," Susan agreed.

"If I were you," O'Connell said, "I wouldn't hound her about this. Drop the subject. Take the weekend off, do you know what I mean?"

"Maybe we could all take a little trip tomorrow or Sunday. We haven't been to the beach yet."

O'Connell made a slight smile. "That's a good idea. Get her mind off it. By Monday she'll have forgotten all about it. We'll still be worried half sick and she'll be wanting to stay in the booths all day long."

Susan smiled back, but she felt completely unconvinced.

CHAPTER 12

I just don't understand it," Dan said to Vickie Kessel. "There's nothing wrong with the equipment at all."

She nodded agreement. "I had Bernie and her technical crew spend half the night checking out the system."

"And I was over at the school this morning," Dan said. "Everything seems to be perfectly all right." He gnawed at his lip.

They were in Vickie's plush little office. She was sitting in the comfortable chintz-covered wing chair; it seemed to fold protectively about her. She looked tiny in the chair, with her legs tucked up beneath her. Dan could see her high-heeled shoes lying carelessly on the carpet. Dan had perched himself nervously on the front two inches of the love seat.

The wall-size display screen showed a security camera's view of the front parking lot, just as if Vickie's office had its own big window. He could see Joe Rucker lumbering across the lot, guarding the four cars parked there as if they were armored trucks holding fortunes.

"Of course, it was a long time ago," Vickie said, smiling archly, "but I seem to remember my teen years as a time of terrific emotional turbulence."

Dan looked at her. "You think the trouble's with Angie?"

Vickie shrugged. "If there's nothing wrong with the equipment . . ."

"It could be the program itself," Dan muttered, as much to himself as to her. "Maybe the simulation's too powerful for a child."

"Dozens of kids have used that game, Dan. Kids in Angela's own class, too. Nobody else has had trouble with it."

"I know, but—"

"But you want to run through it yourself, just to make sure. Right?"

"Yeah." He nodded wearily. "I guess so."

Vickie untucked her feet and sat up straight. Dan saw that her stockinged feet barely reached to the carpeting. The stockings were patterned, pale green.

"Dan, there are only so many hours in the day," she said in a voice that was suddenly stern, demanding. "I know you're upset about what's happened to your daughter, but we have a big job to finish here and a deadline staring down our throats."

"I know that."

"I hate to be the one who cracks the whip, Dan, but we need you and Jace to finish up that baseball simulation. Every hour counts!"

"Come on, Vickie," he countered. "I waited until my lunch break to come and talk with you about this."

"You left the lab early yesterday afternoon and you didn't come in this morning until half past nine."

Anger flared in him. "You want me to punch a time clock?"

"No, not at all." She was instantly soothing, her voice softer. "It's just that the future of this whole company is hanging on that baseball simulation, and the work isn't moving ahead."

"Yeah. I know." Dan's head drooped.

"But you want to run the Neptune's Kingdom game just so you can see for yourself what might have happened to your daughter."

"I could run it tonight."

With a slight shake of her head and an understanding little smile, Vickie said, "Do it now. Spend the rest of the lunch hour on it. You won't be any good to us all afternoon otherwise, will you?"

He bolted up from the love seat. "Thanks, Vickie! Thanks!"

Before he could get to the door, Vickie said, "And, Dan—I'd like you to look in on Gary Chan after you're through. Would you, please?"

"Gary?"

"Kyle wants him to juice up the Moonwalk game a bit, and I think he's run into some problems. He could use your advice."

"Yeah, okay. Sure."

Victoria Kessel leaned back in her wing chair and watched Dan race out of her office. Like a schoolboy set loose from classes, she thought. No, she corrected herself immediately. Like a father who's worried about his child. Mustn't think of him as a vigorous young male; he's married and has two children. And he's too important to this company to mess around with. She smiled at the door he had left open in his haste. At least you shouldn't mess around with him until he's finished the baseball simulation, she told herself.

Her smile faded. She glanced at the Louis XIV clock hanging on the wall by the office door. Inside its gilt frame was a Japanese battery-powered quartz works. Kyle should be landing at National Airport in another few minutes; he had finally bowed to necessity and flown to Washington. Vickie wondered for the hundredth time that day what she should do about Kyle. Of all the children in that school, why is he messing around with Dan Santorini's? He'll ruin everything if he's getting himself involved with Dan's daughter.

Her phone rang, snapping her attention to the here and now. Instead of picking up the handset, Vickie touched the speaker button.

"Victoria Kessel," she said.

"Hello, Vickie."

A stab of surprised fear jolted her. She grabbed the handset and whispered into it, "I don't want you calling me here!"

"Just a quick question: Why'd Muncrief fly to Washington?"

The man's name was Luke Peterson. He was a paunchy, balding, middle-aged former engineer who had contacted Vickie months earlier with an offer of ten thousand dollars in exchange for information about ParaReality. Vickie had taken the money, telling herself that if Peterson was an industrial spy, it would be best for her to seem to be working with him. Otherwise he would find another employee to corrupt.

At first she thought of herself as a counterspy, trying to find out who Peterson was working for. But her contacts with him were neither glamorous nor exotic. Peterson was a drab little man engaged in a dirty business; gradually Vickie realized that it could become a dangerous business. But in the back of her mind she thought that if anything went wrong with ParaReality, if Kyle Muncrief cracked under the pressure and self-destructed, a contact with the competition would be to her advantage. It could be my fallback position, she told herself.

Yet she still did not know who Peterson was working for. The man did not trust her any more than she trusted him.

"He's got friends in Washington," Vickie temporized. "He went to try to raise funding from them."

"Friends in the government?" Peterson asked.

"In the investment community, I think," she lied.

"Really?" Peterson sounded unconvinced.

"You shouldn't be calling me here."

"Then meet me tonight and we'll talk about it more."

"Not tonight. I'm busy."

"Tonight."

She hesitated a moment. "All right. After dinner. Around eleven."

"I'll be in the parking lot of your condo building."

"All right."

Peterson drove a beat-up old Cutlass; Vickie knew it well. Most of their meetings had taken place in his car. He seemed to live in it.

She put the phone back in its cradle, her hand trembling slightly. She was determined to keep the government connection a secret from Peterson and everyone else for as long as she could. That's my other fallback option, she told herself. If Kyle actually goes through with the government work, then I won't need Peterson or the corporation he's working for.

But she knew that she could not trust Kyle Muncrief to make a successful contact with the government. He went to Washington reluctantly and he'll screw it all up, she felt certain.

Kyle Muncrief felt wet, chilled, miserable, and terribly uneasy as he entered the Air and Space Museum.

Why pick this place as the spot for our meeting? he asked himself. But he already knew the answer. Hide in plain sight. These guys don't want anyone to know what they're up to. What better place to meet, then, than in the midst of the biggest crowds in Washington?

It had been a rough ride from Orlando. A massive early-autumn storm was moving up the East Coast from Cape Hatteras, making even the high-flying jet airliner shudder and bump in its turbulence. The flight had come in to Washington National nearly an hour late. It was pouring a hard, wind-driven rain, cold and miserable compared to Florida. Taxis had been scarce at the airport, and Muncrief had been forced to wait in line with other soggy, disgruntled passengers nearly another hour before the dispatcher pushed him into a broken-down cab. At that, he had to share his ride with three other trench-coated men. They all complained every inch of the way into town about the weather, the airport, the taxi service, and anything else they could think of.

The cabdriver, an elderly silent unsmiling black man, had calmly charged each of them twenty-five dollars for their ten-minute ride. On an impulse, Muncrief had added a five-dollar tip. The driver looked surprised.

"For putting up with those bozos," Muncrief said as he ducked out of the taxi.

As he hurried up the steps to the Air and Space Museum's front entrance, the driving rain soaked his light sports jacket. He had not bothered to bring a raincoat, and he did not own an umbrella. Inside the entryway, he stopped to catch his breath while the streams of incoming tourists flowed past him.

Then he looked up.

Above his head hung the Wright brothers' original Flier. The first airplane to truly fly. Next to it, suspended from the high ceiling, was Lindbergh's *Spirit of St. Louis,* gleaming aluminum contrasting to the Wrights' fabric and wood. And directly in front of him, set on the floor like a miniature temple of adoration, stood the *Apollo 11* command module: the spacecraft that had carried the first astronauts to the Moon and back.

Muncrief blinked, looked up and around, then blinked again. Half a century from first flight to Moon flight. In front of the spacecraft was a small stand with a sliver of stone embedded in its wooden surface. A rock from the Moon. Muncrief stared at it in wonder. This isn't a simulation, he realized. They actually brought this back from the Moon with them. It's real. Like all the other tourists, Muncrief reached out and touched the Moon rock with the tips of his outstretched fingers.

"Impressive, isn't it?"

The man standing beside Muncrief looked perfectly ordinary at first glance. He was on the short side, barely topping Muncrief's shoulder. Wore a gray suit with a white shirt and a conservative dark blue tie. His hair was a sandy brown, the kind that had been blond in youth but was now darkening. Cut short, carefully combed. A lightweight plastic raincoat was hanging from his arm.

Muncrief, in his damp sea-green sports coat, tieless, wrinkled, felt at first that this kid was some errand boy sent to fetch him for the people he was supposed to meet. But then he looked again.

The younger man's face was taut, tight-lipped. It was a squarish face, hard stubborn jaw and pugnacious button nose. His eyes were cobalt blue, penetrating, like a cop's.

Muncrief felt his insides tremble.

"You're almost an hour late," said the younger man in a clear tenor voice just loud enough for Muncrief to understand him over the babble of the crowd. Then he started walking slowly into the main section of the museum.

Following him, Muncrief mumbled, "My plane was an hour late. I still would've made it on time, except there weren't any taxis."

Despite the chatter and laughter all around them, the man seemed to hear Muncrief perfectly. "Sure. The important thing is you're here now."

Summoning up some courage, Muncrief demanded, "What's your name?"

"What difference does it make?" The younger man kept walking, slowly, flowing with the crowd heading for the escalator.

"I don't like doing business with people I don't know."

"Look, Dad!" a kid shouted from a few steps above them on the moving stairway. "There's the Skylab!"

The young man cast Muncrief a sidelong glance. "What makes you think you're going to be doing business with anybody?"

Exasperation overtook Muncrief's fears. "Look, you guys called me. You asked me to come up here. Now what's this all about, or do I go back to Orlando and forget the whole blasted thing?"

His companion made a grudging smile; almost a smirk. "My name's Smith."

"Yeah, sure," said Muncrief. "And I'm Pocahontas."

The guy actually laughed. "You asked for a name, and I gave you one."

They had reached the museum's upper level. Muncrief was tall enough to see over the heads of most of the crowd. They were heading past the IMAX theater and into the area where old rockets and spacecraft were on exhibit, standing on the ground floor and thrusting their sleek noses up toward the high ceiling.

"What's this all about?" he demanded of Smith. "What do you people want?"

Smith gestured with one hand toward the curving metal bulk of the Skylab space station, big as a ten-room house. "That piece of hardware was built to go into space, not to sit here as an exhibit."

Muncrief said nothing.

Pointing again, Smith added, "Take a look at these rockets. Look at those Saturn V engines. That's what lifted our astronauts off to the Moon. And that little guy there, that's a Minuteman missile."

"So what—"

"It's an ICBM. They called it Minuteman because it stood ready to protect our nation at an instant's notice."

"Protect? You mean it carried a hydrogen bomb and was aimed at some Russian city."

"Several hydrogen bombs," said Smith tightly. "Each one carried three warheads. Now we're dismantling them. Breaking up the last of the missiles and destroying the bombs."

"Thank God."

Smith leaned casually against the railing and smiled coldly at Muncrief. "I thought that would be your reaction. You're not into defending your country, are you?"

The dread that Muncrief had felt just below the surface of his consciousness ever since Vickie had talked him into this journey to Washington now broke into the open. Muncrief knew now what he feared.

Smith's smile was like a snake's. "When your country called on you, back in 1969, you ran off to Canada, didn't you?"

"That was more than thirty years ago, for God's sake!"

"You're a draft dodger, Muncrief."

"That's all over and done with. Carter granted all of us amnesty, remember?"

"I remember very well. My older brother was killed in Nam. He left college to volunteer for the Marines. He got killed while you shacked up with some Canadian broad in Toronto."

How much does he really know? Muncrief felt his heart thudding, his armpits dampening with the cold sweat of fear. But he leaned close to Smith's coldly angry face so that no one in the passing crowd could hear him.

"Vietnam was a crock," he said. "I'm sorry your brother got killed, but it was all for nothing and you know it."

"Do I? I know a lot of things, but I don't know that."

Muncrief stepped back and waited for the other shoe to fall.

"I want to give you the opportunity to do something for your country, Mr. Muncrief," Smith said with murderous calm. "I'm giving you the chance to atone for running away during the Vietnam period."

Muncrief blinked at him. Holy God, does he know or doesn't he? Could it be that the government really doesn't know about me?

Kyle Muncrief had been born of a woman who had mistakenly believed that a son would force the man she was living with to marry her. It was the second time she had tried to gain such a hold on him; she already had a two-year-old daughter.

Even though she named the boy after his father, the man left her and the two children, fled from Baltimore altogether for parts unknown. Somehow she blamed Kyle for that. His earliest memories were of her beating him, screaming that he was no damned good, that he was a mistake, a failure.

His sister took care of him while their mother was away from their one-room flat and even while she was home. Not much more than a baby herself, his sister Crystal fed and clothed him, bathed him in the kitchen sink, and showed him the only love he knew.

Kyle's mother had run away from her stern Baptist parents in Georgia, who had written her off the family rolls as if she had died. She knew she could not go back to them. She did not want to, in any event. She had no skills to speak of; she wandered through a succession of menial jobs, either quitting or getting herself fired within a week or so. She began to augment the welfare checks she received from the state with occasional liaisons with other men, seeking with deepening despair someone who could end her poverty and loneliness.

She did not realize she was a prostitute until a pair of hard-faced men pushed their way into their shabby flat one afternoon and told her that from now on she would turn over half her earnings to them. In return they would protect her from the police. And from violence. Then they showed her a taste of the violence. Afterward they took turns raping her.

Kyle was six years old, sitting terrified on the surplus army cot that was his bed, clinging to his eight-year-old sister, while the men beat and raped his mother. His sister threw a blanket over them both, but nothing could muffle their mother's screams and cries.

For four years he lived in hell. His mother turned into a zombie, dazed on drugs most of the time, bringing home men who laughed and drank and took off their clothes and did things to his mother, who also laughed and drank and took off all her clothes. After the men left, his mother always crouched naked on her sagging bed, bent over almost double, rocking back and forth for what seemed like hours. Then she would go to the filth-encrusted toilet in the bathroom they shared with the woman next door and vomit as if she were trying to empty herself completely.

He was under strict orders to stay in his cot under his thin blanket whenever his mother brought a man to the room. His sister always stayed there with him, frozen numb as a statue, holding him so tightly sometimes he thought he would die from lack of air.

Kyle watched, terrified, from under the covers of his cot the night that one drunken sailor insisted that his sister join him and his mother in bed.

"It's all right, Crystal dear," his mother had said, almost as drunk as the sailor on the bottle of vodka he had brought with him. "Come on here next to Mommy."

Kyle could feel his sister trembling, but she let go of him and got off the cot and climbed onto the bed with her mother and the strange, grinning man. Crystal began crying as the sailor and her mother took off her clothes, her whimpers of fear growing to terrified wails until her mother smacked her sharply across her bare buttocks and snapped, "Behave yourself!"

Even with the blanket pulled tightly over his head, Kyle knew they were hurting her. Crystal screamed when the sailor penetrated her, and Kyle could stand it no longer. He leaped out of the bed and flung himself at the naked sailor. Drunk as he was, the sailor easily fended off the skinny ten-year-old's ineffectual blows and knocked him spinning off the bed. He laughed as Kyle climbed slowly to his feet, rubbing the side of his head, standing in his T-shirt with his stubby bare legs and hairless genitals exposed.

"You jealous, kid?" the sailor asked. "So maybe you wanna get fucked too, hah?"

Kyle ran to the drawer beside the sink where the knives were.

"Don't you dare!" his mother yelled as Kyle pulled the bread knife from the drawer. The sailor, grinning lopsidedly, got up from the bed. His softening penis was dark with Crystal's blood. He walked slowly across the bare floorboards, long hairy tattooed arms dangling at his sides.

"Better put the knife down, kid, before you get yerself hurt."

Kyle wavered.

"Put it down!" his mother commanded. "Crystal's not hurt. She's all right."

Confused, scared, his anger turning to fear, Kyle put the knife down on the countertop. The instant he did, the sailor grabbed the front of his T-shirt and yanked him up off his feet. "Gonna slice me up, huh?" He smacked Kyle across the face, hard, once, twice, three times, then threw him across the room to bang onto his cot so hard that it collapsed.

His mother got out of bed as the sailor pulled on his clothing, talking softly to him, begging him not to go. "Come on, you can have both of us. We'll have a party." But the sailor buttoned up his pants and left. "I don't like wiseass kids with knives," he snarled.

When he shut the door behind him, Kyle's mother staggered over to his collapsed cot and pulled him from its tangled blanket. "You little bastard!" she screeched. "You little troublemaking bastard!"

She beat him with the leather strap she kept hanging on the closet door. Because the sailor had left without paying.

Stiff and sore as he was the next morning, Kyle made his way through the cold damp wind coming off the harbor down the long blocks of row houses to school. School was a refuge for Kyle, a safe place where he could escape the reality of his hellish existence. If the teachers knew of his mother's business, they never mentioned it. The kids teased him, but it was no worse than the teasing they subjected all the other kids to. Kyle took their teasing good-naturedly; he was willing to accept it to have friends. Teasing was nothing; only kids who liked you bothered to tease you.

At school Kyle could escape. He was a good student, not the brightest in class, but he did his homework faithfully and always came to class prepared—no matter how late he had to stay up at night.

But on this day Kyle's mind was not on the classroom lessons. He knew he could not go home after school. He knew he could not face his mother or watch his sister do what his mother did. And he heard that sailor's drunken, leering, terrifying "So maybe you wanna get fucked too, hah?"

That night he slept in a cardboard carton, part of a small mountain of discarded cartons and crates piled up by one of the dock-side warehouses. It was cold and wet, the kind of chill that penetrates to the bone. But it was better than going home. He dreamed of his mother—sometimes she was Crystal—but no matter who she was she was angry at him, furious, slashing at him with that leather strap and screaming wildly.

In the earliest light of morning he made his way to the nearest dock, furtive as one of the rats that dwelled in the old warehouses, and crapped into the harbor's scummy water. His stomach ached with hunger, and he wondered how he could get something to eat. He washed as best he could in a rain-filled oil barrel that he found leaning against a warehouse wall, then put his books under his arm and made his way to school.

He lived like that for nearly five weeks, sleeping in the trash piles outside the warehouses, scrounging food from other kids at school or stealing their lunch bags when hunger pressed so hard he did not care if they caught him. His teacher, a wrinkle-faced spinster who always looked unhappy, noticed that he was losing weight, dirty-faced, coughing. But he remained quiet and obedient in class despite the increasing filthiness of his clothes.

Each night Kyle avoided the occasional shadowy figures he saw along the docks. He wanted no part of those older men, even though he saw that sometimes they lit fires and cooked food for themselves. He stayed to himself despite the steamy aromas of their cooking that made his stomach growl impatiently. And all through those weeks, neither his mother nor his sister made the slightest attempt to find him. At first he had expected his mother to appear at the school, demanding that he return home. Or maybe his sister might hang around outside the school, trying to catch a glimpse of him. One evening he snuck back to the corner of the street where their flat was. He saw Crystal walking up the street toward him, her face smeared with heavy makeup. She was wearing one of her mother's dresses; it looked stupid on her, but still some guys across the street whistled at her. Kyle ran away, unable to face his own sister.

He felt guilty about that. He wanted to protect Crystal, wanted to take her away on one of the ships he saw in the harbor. But he knew that was a dream, a fantasy so far removed from him that he might as well ask her to fly to the Moon with him.

Kyle did not know he had caught pneumonia. He was lucky, though. The night he collapsed, body flaming with fever, one of the homeless winos eking out a living among the docks stumbled across his unconscious form and dragged him out to the front of a warehouse, where even the laziest and most obtuse night watchman would inevitably spot him.

When he woke up in the hospital, Kyle had the good sense not to give his name. He did not want his mother to find him. He could not face returning home to her and Crystal. He steadfastly refused to say a word about his family or background, even to the police officers who were brought in to question him.

"They'll put you in an orphanage, kid," said one of the policemen, half angry at Kyle's stubbornness, half worried at the life ahead for this scrawny boy.

"You won't like the orphanage," warned the other cop.

His first view of the orphanage was through the windows of a police van. Under a bleak gray winter sky the buildings looked even bleaker and grayer, like a prison. Inside, the walls were cold and bare, the floors worn smooth by generations of boys passing through.

They brought him to a small office and sat him down in front of a desk. Behind the desk sat a young woman, a social worker, with a long paper form to be filled out. The first question on it was "Name?"

"I don't remember my name," said Kyle.

The woman did not believe him. The guard standing behind him cuffed him lightly on the ear to encourage his memory. The woman frowned up at the guard.

"You have to have a name," she said to Kyle. "If you won't give us one, or can't give us one, I'll make one up for you."

That was how he came to be called Kyle Muncrief. It was the name of a handsome leading man in a soap opera that the social worker watched every afternoon.

Kyle did not like the orphanage, true enough. But it was better than home. He tolerated the half-spoiled food and intolerant staff workers who treated the boys like diseased cattle. He did not mind the gray barracks of the living quarters; his cot was actually better than the old one he had slept on at home, its scratchy army-surplus blanket thicker and warmer. He survived the brutal hazings and bullying of the other guys. He made friends easily enough, but he took no part in their gangs and tribal wars. When the guards handed out physical punishment to everybody because some wise guy did something and they could not determine who the culprit was, Kyle took his beating without saying a word.

The one thing that Kyle resisted was the attempts some of the boys made to sodomize him. "I'm straight," he insisted, even though he had never had sex with anyone. When three boys laughingly tried to pin him down, he fought them until they were all bloody. The guards had to break up the battle. Kyle spent a week in solitary detention because the other three all blamed him for the fight. He took his punishment, and when he came back to the barracks no one bothered him again.

There was a school that took up most of his waking hours. Gradually the other guys left him alone, knowing that he was not a partisan of any gang and that he could be trusted to keep silent about their doings. Eventually they even came to him for help with their own schoolwork or, pathetically, help with writing the letters that they hoped would spring them free of the orphanage.

He became good at writing. He learned that books allowed him to escape into different worlds and leave the orphanage far behind. Thanks to his reading and the determination of his favorite teacher, he developed a vocabulary that was almost refined, compared to the other boys'. His teacher made Kyle promise that he would never sound the way they did, never debase his language with their filthy four-letter words.

"If you want to get somewhere in the world out there," the man repeated endlessly to Kyle, "you should sound like a gentleman, not a gutter rat."

Every boy learned a trade at the orphanage. Kyle learned bookkeeping. In his teens he was offered an opportunity to take correspondence courses that would lead to a CPA certification. He leaped at the chance, knowing that it was a sure road to the real world outside the institution's walls.

When he was finally released from the orphanage, he had an accountant's degree in his hand and a job in Baltimore arranged by the social worker who had handled his case from the very beginning. She had grown fond of Kyle over the years, and predicted that of all the boys leaving the orphanage that year he would go the farthest.

He went to Canada. Six months after he began working for the accounting firm in Baltimore, he received his draft notice. Even in the orphanage Kyle had watched news reports from Vietnam almost every evening. He had no intention of being killed in some senseless jungle ten thousand miles away. He fled to Toronto.

First, though, he snuck back to his old neighborhood one evening, searching for Crystal. He had dreamed of taking her with him, off to Canada or South America or Xanadu, anywhere to be away from the life her mother had forced on her. But there was no trace of his mother or Crystal. No one he questioned admitted even to remembering them. They had disappeared. Or died.

He went to Toronto alone then, and took the first job he could find, as a delivery boy for an office-supply firm. He rode in a pickup truck through the downtown business district and lugged heavy cartons of papers into plush offices where the carpeting was thick and the air was hushed with the quiet urgency of big money. He spent most of his salary on clothes. After years of living in hand-me-downs or institutional uniforms, Kyle became a fashion plate. He wore the latest styles, and he wore them handsomely.

He knew how to make friends, and even began dating some of the filing clerks and secretaries he met on his delivery rounds. But when he dreamed, he dreamed of his sister Crystal, the twelve-year-old that he had failed to protect. Even when he finally summoned up the courage to take a young redheaded typist to bed, he fantasized about his sister while he clumsily made love to her.

Within little more than a year, Kyle was working as an accountant in one of the business offices he had delivered supplies to. He rose quickly, despite some sneers from his fellow workers about "the eager-beaver Yank with the flashy wardrobe."

Then he met Nancy. She was the daughter of one of the firm's vice presidents. She had a pretty face but an overweight, heavy-legged body. She was intelligent, gentle, and shy, but beneath it all there was a good sense of humor and a trace of mischievousness. Her father was wealthy.

They met at a company picnic. Kyle recognized the opportunity she represented. Her physical appearance did not matter much to him; he was not driven sexually—or so he told himself. Nancy's parents were at first alarmed that their daughter was attracted to such an upstart. But as they began to see how happy he made Nancy, they began to regard him as a diamond in the rough, and told each other that he was honest, hardworking, and undoubtedly a good catch.

By the time President Carter granted amnesty to most of the Vietnam draft evaders, Kyle was engaged to Nancy and on his way to a vice presidency of his own. He had no intention of ever returning to the States. But to his horror he found himself helplessly attracted to Nancy's sister, Judith, who was fourteen.

For almost a year he struggled against his growing obsession as each night he dreamed of Crystal and each day he tried to avoid seeing nubile, laughing Judith. That summer she lolled around the family's lakeside cottage in nothing more than a T-shirt and underpants, or ran off for a swim in the cold lake wearing a skimpy bikini. Local boys seemed to rise up out of the ground wherever she appeared, and she was enjoying her first experience of sexual power.

Kyle never touched her, never allowed himself to be in the same room alone with her. But he knew it was only a matter of time until his self-control crumbled. He could not see Nancy without seeing Judith. And he could not take his eyes off her. In his dreams she became his sister, his lost, lovely, loving Crystal. Crystal was the one he wanted, and he began to loathe dull, overweight Nancy.

Kyle fled once again. He left Nancy without a word of explanation and went back to the States. Once again Kyle Muncrief found himself starting a new life. He worked his way into a position with a small Wall Street investment firm that specialized in finding start-up money for new high-tech companies. He met dozens of scientists, most of them wildly impractical when it came to business. But even from the most unrealistic of them he learned important hints of what was possible, what could be developed in the reasonably near future.

He swore to himself that he would never even look at an underage girl again, but it took every ounce of his willpower to keep that oath. The pressure within him built relentlessly, night after night. He needed Crystal; she was the only person in the world he could trust, the only one who loved him, the only one he could love. He began prowling the seamy night streets searching for Crystal, staring at the preteen girls being offered on dark corners, knowing that Crystal was much older now, fearing that he was going insane.

He worked out at gyms, he went on religious retreats, he saw psychiatrists. He denied it all night after night after night. But inevitably, inexorably, he would find himself searching for the sister he had lost. He began to think about suicide.

He worried about his secretary, a sharp-minded woman named Victoria Kessel. Soon enough she learned that he was visiting psychiatrists. The thought of Victoria finding out about Crystal filled him with fear. But Vickie made it clear that she sympathized with her boss. Whatever demons were driving him, she made no judgments. But she wanted responsibility, authority. She wanted power.

Shaken, Kyle realized that he had found someone he could depend on. He *had* to trust Vickie; even in the swinging world of Wall Street, where cocaine was commonplace and sex a tool of power, mental illness was beyond the pale. Kyle reinforced Vickie's loyalty by giving her the kinds of additional responsibilities she craved. With her added responsibilities, of course, came added salary, and bonuses, and perks. And his added dependency on her.

Kyle first learned about virtual reality from a magazine article that Vickie pointed out to him. He was intrigued. Could a man create a long-lost sister in the electronic world of virtual reality? He visited several university laboratories, tracked down the best minds working on VR. He decided that he could not risk having some scientist or engineer develop what he wanted for him. Not unless he could be absolutely certain that the man (it would have to be a man, he was convinced) would never reveal his desires.

But there was more to it than that. Virtual reality could be a money-maker, a big one. Kyle saw that the technology capable of producing private fantasies could be sold to the public as entertainment.

He searched the nation for the key technical expert, the man he would build his company around, and found him at Wright-Patterson Air Force Base. Everyone who knew anything about virtual reality agreed that Jason Lowrey was the brightest, most innovative, most daring specialist in the field. "But he's a madman," Kyle was told time and again. "He's hell to work with. A total flake."

Kyle flew to Dayton and met Jace Lowrey. He sat in a simulator cockpit and experienced a virtual-reality dogfight. That night, trembling with fear and anticipation, he asked Lowrey if VR could be used for personal fantasies.

Jace seemed neither surprised nor disapproving. "Oh, sure," he answered easily. "I've already done that for one of the blue-suiters here. I could put all the whorehouses in the world outta business if I wanted to."

Muncrief hired Jace on the spot, left his investment firm in New York and founded ParaReality Corporation, bringing Victoria Kessel with him to be vice president.

One by one he found Hideki Toshimura, Lars Swenson, and Maxwell Glass, each of them eager for the profits they foresaw from Muncrief's vision of Cyber World. Then he set up shop in the Orlando area, only a few miles from Disney World, and started building a technical staff around Jason Lowrey. He gave Jace two priorities: First, develop the conflict games that would make Cyber World unique. Second, give him his dearest heart's desire: give him Crystal.

And now, as he flew home from Washington, he knew that a branch of the U.S. government was going to force its way into his company whether he liked it or not. He only hoped that they did not know about his obsession and his sessions with the psychiatrists in New York. And that they would not find out.

In Jason Lowrey he had at last found the man who could construct the fantasy that haunted his dreams. As long as Jace got what he wanted, he seemed perfectly content to create a virtual-reality simulation of Crystal—and to keep silent about it. Kyle knew that this gave Lowrey a hold over him, but the antisocial, introspective genius appeared to have no interest in pressuring Kyle for anything more than additional equipment and assistants so that he could further his own virtual-reality dreams. Still, Kyle worried. If his investors found out about it, if Glass and Toshimura and that self-righteous prig Swenson knew, it would bring the roof down on his head.

That's why I've got to play along with this Smith character and whoever he's working for, Muncrief told himself as the USAir flight approached Orlando. I don't know how much the bastards know, and I can't afford to take the chance that they know everything. Maybe it'll be okay after we get Cyber World up and running. Once the money starts pouring in, maybe then it won't matter. But until then I've got to play along with them.

CHAPTER 13

an stood encased in a bulky space suit on the surface of the Moon, staring at Tranquility Base. It looked like a high-tech junkyard, abandoned equipment strewn across the bare, barren ground around the spraddle-legged base of the landing module *Eagle*. The American flag that Armstrong and Aldrin had unfurled still stood stiffly in the airless silence.

Picking his way carefully through the scattered equipment, awkward in the clumsy suit and thick boots, he slowly approached the landing module. Welded to its side was a stainless-steel plaque, still polished and gleaming after all the years.

HERE MEN FROM THE PLANET EARTH
FIRST SET FOOT UPON THE MOON
JULY 1969, A.D.
WE CAME IN PEACE FOR ALL MANKIND

He was surprised at the lump in his throat. It was only a simulation, he knew, yet still . . .

Turning slowly away from the lander, Dan saw that the bare dusty pockmarked lunar surface stretched to the hard uncompromising slash of the horizon. Beyond the horizon was the black emptiness of space. The only sounds he could hear were his own breathing and the suit's air-circulation fans whining like distant mosquitoes. He turned again slightly, and his breath caught in his throat.

Hanging there in the dark sky was the glorious beckoning crescent of Earth, glowing brilliantly, rich deep blue streaked with perfect white swirls of clouds, shining down on the empty rocky wasteland of the Moon, a haven of life and beauty in a vast and cold universe.

"It's awesome," Dan whispered into his helmet microphone.

Gary Chan replied, "Yeah, isn't it?" Even through his earphones Dan could hear the smile in the younger man's voice.

"So what's your problem?"

"Gravity," Chan answered. "Everything's supposed to weigh one-sixth of what it does on Earth."

"Uh-huh."

"Try lifting your arms."

Dan raised both arms. "Feels okay to me."

"That's just the problem. It feels normal. Just like on Earth."

"Oh."

"Try jumping."

Dan hopped several times, almost landing on one of the abandoned instruments littering the ground. It was nothing like the films he remembered seeing of astronauts floating across the lunar landscape. This was more like jumping in a gym or your own living room. It made him realize that, despite what his eyes were showing him, he was standing in a simulations chamber a quarter-million miles away from the Moon.

"I see what you mean," he said.

Chan's voice was somber. "I can make anything you pick up feel like it should on the Moon, but I can't make your own body feel lighter. It ruins the illusion that you're really walking or jumping on the Moon."

The kid's done a good job, Dan thought, but if he can't get the gravity right the whole simulation's a bust. Muncrief wanted the Moonwalk to be absolutely authentic, of course. Gary had spent weeks studying NASA photographs, and Vickie had even found a retired astronaut living in Arkansas to serve as a consultant.

His space suit weighed nothing, because it existed only as a set of instructions in the electronics of the VR system's computers. But to Dan it seemed completely real. He lifted his gloved hand and touched the smooth curved plastic of the fishbowl. It felt reassuringly solid. But raising his arms, moving his legs to walk, it all took just as much effort as it did on Earth.

"I don't know what to do," Chan said. "I've run into a blank wall on this."

"Maybe we're being too sophisticated about it," Dan said. "Or not sophisticated enough."

"What do you mean?"

"Well . . ." Dan pumped his arms up and down once, twice, then said, "Why don't you try ignoring the user's weight? There's nothing you can do about it anyway."

"But—"

"But make the environment around him react as if it's all in one-sixth gravity."

"I don't understand."

Dan picked up a fist-sized rock and threw it. In the airless light gravity it soared out toward the horizon until he could not see it anymore against the dark sky.

"You've got all the objects around the user behaving in one-sixth g. When the guy moves—when he walks or jumps or whatever—program the environment around him to react as if he really weighs only one-sixth of his normal weight."

"Program the environment?"

With a nod, Dan explained, "Set up everything to move as far as it would if the user really was one-sixth his Earth weight. If you can't raise the bridge, lower the water."

"Man, that would take a thousand hours of calculations! Maybe more. And he'd still feel his own internal weight, anyway."

"He'd still feel his weight, yeah, but remember that his internal sense of his own weight feels completely normal to him. If he sees that world around him moving *as if* he weighed one-sixth, he'd believe what his eyes are telling him and forget about his inner sense of weight."

"You think so?"

"Just like your Space Race game makes people feel motion sickness."

"Yeah, but the calculations I'd have to do."

"That's why we've got computers, Gary. I think I can dig up a program that'll let you take a few shortcuts."

"Really?" There was eagerness in the younger man's voice now. Excitement.

"Yeah. If I remember right, there's a—"

"Uh, wait a minute," said Chan, sounding suddenly flustered.

"Hey, Dan," Jace's unmistakable raspy voice came through Dan's earphones. "Come on outta there. I got something to show you that'll knock your ass off!"

Jace was almost dancing with excitement as he led Dan along the hallway toward his lab at the back of the building.

"Vickie asked me to help the kid out," Dan was saying. It sounded apologetic, even to himself. "He's having a problem with his Moonwalk sim."

"Aw, let Charlie Chan find his own answers," Jace said, grinning. "This is a helluva lot better than anything he can do."

"You've made a change in the baseball sim?"

"Not quite." Jace's toothy grin got even bigger.

He stopped at the metal door to Wonderland, the simulations chamber that he claimed for his own exclusive use.

"Is this going to take long?" Dan asked as they stepped into the narrow control booth.

"You got a hot date?"

"It's almost seven. If we're going to be a while, I want to call Susan and let her know."

Jace shook his head. "Five, ten minutes. Half hour at the most." Jace took a helmet-and-glove set from the rack on the side wall and handed them to Dan.

"What is it?" Dan asked.

"Go on in." Jace's grin was almost malicious. "You'll see."

Puzzled but curious, Dan stepped through the hatch into the simulations chamber. He put on the scuffed plastic helmet and tugged on the data gloves, then connected them to the optical-fiber wires.

As he looked up, Jace came into the chamber, already wearing helmet and gloves.

"Who's running the board?" Dan asked.

Jace pointed to the remote-control box clipped to his old leather belt. "It's on automatic."

"Automatic? How—"

"I can start the run and stop it from here. Otherwise it chugs along to the end all by itself."

"When did you work that out?"

Jace shrugged carelessly. "You think I been sittin' around doing nothing all these weeks?"

You're supposed to be figuring out how to perfect the baseball game, Dan said to himself.

Jace hooked up his wires and slid the visor over his face. He was still grinning in anticipation. Wondering what was coming up, Dan pulled his visor down.

A moment of darkness and then Dan found himself standing in the middle of a dirt street in a town of the Old West. The sun was high and hot. The street was lined with covered wooden walks. Saloon, bank, general store: they all had a cartoony look to them. Nothing else in sight. Not another person anywhere. Nothing moving on the hot dusty street.

Dan looked down at himself and saw that he was wearing boots, jeans, a checkered shirt, and a leather vest with a sheriff's star pinned to it. And a Colt revolver in a leather holster at his hip. The gun felt solid, heavy.

"Jace," he called. "Where are you?"

"Right behind you, Sheriff."

Dan whirled and saw Jace standing a dozen paces away, in a black gunfighter's suit, broad-brimmed hat pulled low over his narrow eyes, two guns at his hips.

"I'll give you a fightin' chance, Sheriff," drawled gunfighter Jace. He crossed his arms over his chest. "You go for your gun."

"What is this, the gunfight at the O.K. Corral?"

"Draw, you yellow polecat!"

Feeling as though he had been tricked into playing a child's game, Dan reached for his pistol. Jace's hands dropped to his guns and he pulled them both smoothly out of their holsters. Dan had time to think that Jace must have been practicing his quick draw for weeks.

The guns roared, and the bullets slammed into Dan's chest and knocked him to the ground. He felt no pain at first, only stunned surprise as the cartoon world faded into darkness. Then the pain hit: flaming agonizing pain that roared through his chest and engulfed him entirely. Jesus Christ, Dan thought. He's killed me!

It wasn't until Jace lifted the helmet off Dan's head that he realized he was lying on the floor of the simulations chamber. He felt confused, helpless, frightened at a deep inner core of his being. He killed me, Dan kept repeating to himself. He shot me down and killed me.

"Hey, buddy, you okay?" Jace was leaning over him, his face serious.

"I . . . think so."

"You sure you're okay? You want a doctor or something?"

"You shot me."

"That's what the game's all about, Danno."

"But I—you killed me. I felt the bullets hit me."

"Yeah!" The concern on Jace's face melted into a delighted grin. "Wasn't it terrific?"

"How did you do that?" Dan heard his own voice; it was almost whining, high and trembling with fright.

Jace was squatting on his heels, still wearing the fuzzy data gloves. "I've figured out a lot of things in the past year or so, pal. How about that? *Bam!* You're dead."

Dan's mind was spinning. How could he get such a realistic physical sensation into the simulation? I felt the bullets hit me. Knocked me over backwards. Everything went black, like I really died.

"You look kinda pasty, Danno."

"That's too damned powerful to turn loose on the public."

"Aw, don't worry. I'll tone it down for Cyber World. But wait'll Muncrief tries it! He'll go apeshit."

Dan tried to get to his feet. He needed Jace's help. His legs were shaky.

"It really hits hard, eh?" Jace was glowing.

"I've got to get home" was all that Dan could say.

"Sure. Sure. I just wanted to show you what I was doing. Better than Charlie Chan's lousy Moonwalk, huh?"

Dan nodded weakly and headed for the door. He went to his office, legs rubbery, plopped down onto his desk chair, and phoned Susan.

"Are you all right?" she asked. "You sound funny."

Dan pulled in a deep breath. "I'm okay. I'll tell you about it when I get home."

Still, he sat behind the wheel of his Honda for nearly half an hour in the evening darkness before he felt strong enough to turn on the ignition and start the car rolling.

Luke Peterson had a blandly unimpressive appearance: middle-aged, balding, squarish face going jowly. The normal expression on his otherwise forgettable face was an abstracted smile that seemed painted on, like a clown's. Except for that absurd smile he looked more like a high-school principal than an industrial spy.

He had started his career as a NASA engineer, but was caught in the layoffs that followed the end of the Apollo moon shots. Like so many others unable to find steady employment, he became a consultant. The last refuge of a failed engineer, he said to himself. All he needed was a briefcase, a decent suit, and a car. He spent most of his waking hours in his car.

Slowly it dawned on him that he could win more consulting hours by telling Martin Marietta what was going on inside Lockheed. Or vice versa. But that was small potatoes compared to the curiosity that commercial electronics firms had about one another. Or toy manufacturers! There was money to be had, far more than an engineer could hope to earn. Money for a handsome house trailer to live in and women to visit in it from time to time. Money to put in the bank and save up for the sailing sloop that he was going to retire to when he was sixty.

Good old country-boy Luke, with that easygoing smile plastered on his face, took out a private investigator's license so that he had a legal reason for carrying all the photographic and electronic gear that his profession required. He bought a handgun, a compact Beretta, and took the required training course at the police pistol range. God forbid he should ever have to use it. He kept it stashed under the driver's seat of his car.

Over the years, industrial espionage evolved into a major international profession. Even the CIA was involved in it nowadays. For once in his life, Luke Peterson had gotten into a growth industry. The only drawback was that he often had to deal with men who frightened him, men with foreign accents and cold remorse-less demands. But every year brought him closer to that yacht and the life he was going to lead at sea, far from all of his past. The world could go its own way then; Luke Peterson would be happily retired.

His office was his automobile, an elderly green four-door Cutlass just as undistinguished as he was. He had equipped the car with a cellular phone and a notebook computer that ran off the cigarette lighter; all the cameras and electronic gear he needed were either on the back seat or stowed in the trunk. That was why he always drove old, lackluster cars. No temptation to kids who like to snatch the fancy new models, nor to the professionals who go for cars that bring a good return from the chop shops.

He was a businessman, not an adventurer. Although on occasion he had been forced to hightail it from a darkened laboratory or office building, he had never been stopped by the law for anything more than a broken taillight cover. He had no criminal record, and the credit cards he used had names different from his own. Industrial espionage was not ordinarily a high-risk business, but it paid to be careful.

So he drove at the speed limit from his motor home to Orlando International Airport. Slowly he tooled the Cutlass up and down the rows of cars in the short-term parking lot until he found the gray Mercedes four-door with the proper license-plate number. Peterson parked as close to it as he could, then locked his Cutlass and walked to the Mercedes. It looked brand-new, its finish gleaming under the parking lot's tall fluorescent lamps. He laughed inwardly. Most of his corporate contacts drove prestige cars, ego cars. Mercedeses were so commonplace in executive parking lots that they were called Florida Fords.

He tapped on the sedan's heavily tinted window and heard the door lock click. Swiftly he pulled the door open and slipped into the right-hand seat.

"Well?" asked the man behind the wheel. He was lean, angular, his face almost ascetic with deep-set eyes and thin bloodless lips. He spoke with a slight accent that Peterson had never been able to identify, even though he had worked with this man off and on for several years. The man reminded him of a priest he had seen once in a film about the Spanish Inquisition: a gaunt, austere celibate with burning eyes who put his prisoners on the rack and tortured them until they were willing to confess to anything. Peterson called him the Inquisitor—to himself.

Peterson concisely described his latest conversation with Victoria Kessel. The Inquisitor lit a cigarette but otherwise did not react to Peterson's report. Peterson coughed and waved at the smoke. The other man gave no indication that it mattered.

"Well," he said when Peterson finished, "what do you think?"

"I think she hasn't really made up her mind," Peterson said.

"She has some ambition, though, doesn't she?"

"Yeah, that's true. She may be trying to counterspy on us. But I think she's really scared that ParaReality's going to go under and leave her stranded."

"That's not enough to hold her, though."

"No. Underneath it all, she's scared of dealing with us."

"Frightened of you?" The lean-faced Inquisitor turned slightly toward Peterson, a ghost of a smile on his gaunt lips.

"I don't think we can make her go along with us if she doesn't want to."

"She's taken the money. That means she's committed to us."

"Maybe."

"You think we need something stronger?"

"She's very skittish. But strong, underneath it all. She might just decide to dump us, money or no."

"That could have unfortunate consequences. Is she aware of that?"

"Not yet."

"Then you must impress her with that information."

Peterson shook his head. "I think that if we come on too strong she'll just run away."

"What do you know about her? What can we use to keep her with us?"

Waving at the smoke again, Peterson answered, "There's not much. She's single. No immediate family. No major vices. Just a clean, hardworking, ambitious woman."

"A liberated female," said the Inquisitor. "A Jew with ambition."

Peterson coughed.

The Inquisitor took the cigarette from his lips and held it vertically between his thumb and forefinger, its glowing end less than a centimeter from his fingertip.

"Perhaps we should look at this from a different point of view," he said.

"What do you mean?"

"Our real objective is to prevent ParaReality from opening their Cyber World park."

"And getting our hands on the VR technology they're developing," Peterson added.

"Yes, of course. But if they fail to open Cyber World on schedule, Muncrief will go bankrupt. His investors will abandon him, his company will dissolve, and all the lovely technology he's developed will be on the auction block."

"Oh. I see."

"So our primary purpose is to prevent ParaReality from opening Cyber World."

"And how do we do that?"

The lean-faced man moved his shoulders slightly in what might have been a shrug. "Perhaps we can convince one of their key people to work with us."

"Like Vickie Kessel."

"Perhaps her, although she knows next to nothing about the technical work. Perhaps we can reach someone else in ParaReality through her."

"Who?"

"The easiest people to get an angle on," he said slowly, calmly, "are those with a family or debts or something in their background that they want to keep secret."

"She certainly doesn't fit any of those criteria."

"Then who does?"

Peterson ran a hand over his bald scalp. "Let's see, now. There's Muncrief; about the only trouble he's ever had was dodging the draft during the Vietnam War."

"Hardly the kind of thing we could use on him."

"Jason Lowrey—he's a complete kook. No ties to anybody, no loyalties except to his work."

The other man said nothing.

"There's Lowrey's assistant, Damon Santorini. He has a wife

and two kids. Just bought a new house here and a new car for his wife."

The Inquisitor took a final drag on his cigarette and stubbed it out in the dashboard ashtray. "Can you get to him?"

Peterson shrugged. "I don't know."

"Think about it. Watch him. I want a contingency plan along those lines. We may not need it, but—who knows?"

Peterson agreed swiftly and got out of the car. He took a deep double lungful of night air. He did not like the idea of pressuring people, but he knew that sometimes it was necessary. He hoped it would not be necessary in this case.

an's office was one of the few for the technical staff that had a window. It looked out on the asphalt driveway that led to the rear parking lot. All Dan ever saw through his precious window was an occasional car passing by and, every now and then, one-armed Joe Rucker plodding by on his daily rounds. He hardly noticed the oleander bushes lining the driveway with colorful flowers.

Dan's attention was usually focused inward. In the two months he had been working at ParaReality, he had added one extra piece of furniture to his office's polished new wooden desk, its row of bookshelves that were mostly bare, and its two light-blue molded-plastic chairs: an incongruously long black leather couch that took up one whole wall. The couch was for Jace, whose own cluttered office was too bizarre for Dan to feel comfortable in. So when they were not in the lab or in the Wonderland simulations chamber, Jace would stretch out on the couch while he spewed ideas and directions to Dan.

Except for the couch, which was already sagging and scuffed, the office was as neat as a furniture showroom. Dan's desk bore a telephone console that contained a built-in answering machine and tape recorder. Alongside it was a trio of snapshots of Susan and the kids. Otherwise the desktop was bare. On a credenza attached to the desk like a wing there sat a personal computer that linked Dan with the company's mainframe back in the Pit and the supercomputers in Jace's lab that they used for their simulations.

Dan sat disconsolately at his desk, tilting back in the padded swivel chair and staring at the ceiling. He had not slept well, had not been sleeping well for the past several weeks. Susan told him that he moaned in his sleep and ground his teeth. The pressure of his job had never bothered his sleep before, but now—Dan knew it was more than the pressure. He was having bad dreams, dreams that left him sweating and shaken when he awoke. But he could not remember what he dreamed; only that the dreams were making him dread falling asleep.

Now there was something more. The message screen on his phone stated in glowing red LCD alphanumerics: DR. APPLETON— 513-990-4547—3:26 P.M. THU. Dan tried to ignore yesterday's message from his former boss. It nagged at him, though, while he tried to concentrate on the problems he faced. Jace was goofing off, chasing some mysterious ideas that he refused to talk about and letting the baseball simulation gather dust. And there was nothing Dan could do about it. It had been hard enough keeping Jace even halfway in line back in the old days at Wright-Patt, but now he was becoming totally impossible.

Could it be that gunfight sim? Dan asked himself for the thousandth time in the past few weeks. Ever since Jace had gunned him down—ever since he had felt the impact of those bullets in his chest, ever since he had died—Dan had felt unable to cope with Jace, unable to rein him in the way he used to. It's as if he's got the power of life and death over me, Dan thought. But then he would shake his head and tell himself that he was being melodramatic. It's just Jace. The same old wild man. I can't let him get away with all this goofing off.

But try as he might, there seemed to be no way that Dan could get Jace to stick to the problem Muncrief wanted them to solve.

At least things had settled down at home. Angie was doing okay now. Better than okay; she seemed fine. No repeats of her problem with the VR games. Plays them all the time now, from what she tells us. Loves them. That's a relief. She's doing fine at school, and Phil is doing great, no asthma attacks, no allergy problems. Susan's business is going so well, she'll be making more than I do in another year or two. Everything's in good shape at home.

Dan's eyes inadvertently strayed to the phone screen. I ought to return Dr. Appleton's call, he told himself. Doc wouldn't call unless it was something important. He doesn't make social chitchat, not over the phone.

Jace barged into the office, banging the door open and plopping down on the couch, his head resting on one arm, his cowboy boots on the other.

"So what's happening?" he asked, locking his fingers behind his head. "How we makin' out?"

"What've you been doing all morning?" Dan asked, already knowing the answer.

"Thinking deep thoughts."

"You've been playing VR games with Joe Rucker, that's what you've been doing!"

"So? I think deep thoughts while I'm playing with the hillbilly."

"You're supposed to be working on the baseball game."

"Yeah, yeah. I am. Foolin' around with Joe frees up my subconscious mind, lets me come up with new ideas."

"So what new ideas have you come up with?"

Jace grinned at him but said nothing.

For more than six weeks Dan had been trying to hammer out some way of getting more visual detail into the baseball simulation. Every one of his attempts had run into a dead end.

"And what've you been doin' all morning?" Jace asked.

"You weren't available, so I looked in on Gary Chan and his dinosaur hunt."

"Charlie Chan? That kid?"

"His name's Gary, not Charlie."

"Don't be so obtuse. Everybody calls him Charlie Chan."

"Well, whatever his name is, that kid has done some very neat work," said Dan. "And I think he's making progress on his Moonwalk, too. And have you seen the medical sim that Hurst and his people are developing?"

"Yeah, yeah." Jace dismissed the subject with a flap of one hand. "Muncrief's gonna be pissed as hell if we don't show some progress real soon."

"We? You haven't even looked—"

"I hear he's talking to people in Washington, trying to raise more money."

"Jace, Muncrief's been breathing down my neck while you're off playing games with Joe Rucker."

"So what have you done about it?"

Dan sank back in his chair.

"Come on, Danno, we need something slick. Elegant."

"You're the genius."

"Yeah, but this is a hardware problem. That's your department."

All the tough problems are my department, Dan thought. You come up with the brilliant ideas and then I've got to make them work.

"So?" Jace urged. "You wanna be a genius, too? Solve our problem!"

Dan hesitated only a fraction of a moment. "Have you ever heard of the persistence of vision?"

Cocking a brow at him, Jace said, "Yeah, sure. From the movies. You show one still picture and the brain registers it as a still picture. Show a series of stills at the right speed and the brain overlaps 'em, makes you think you're seeing motion."

"What I'm thinking about," Dan said slowly, "is that maybe we can split the time the computers spend on each image projection. Like time-sharing—"

Jace sat bolt upright. "Half the time on the foreground and half the time on the background! Yeah!"

"We could give the computer's full power to each segment of the image, but only part time. Before the eye and the brain can register that a piece of the image is missing, it'll be back on again. To the user it'll seem like a continuous image, just like a motion picture does."

"That effectively doubles our computing power!"

"Right."

Scratching at his two-day beard, Jace asked, "Can the hardware switch back and forth fast enough?"

"The machines operate in nanoseconds, don't they? That ought to be plenty. Movie projectors run something like twenty-four frames per second, I think. Or is it forty-eight?"

"What's the difference? That's dead slow compared to nanoseconds!"

To a nanosecond computer, a twenty-fourth of a second would seem like years. The machines could easily switch back and forth a million times before the human eye–brain system would notice even a flicker.

"It could work, I think," Dan said.

"Sure it'll work!" Jace said, jumping to his feet. "You'll make it work!"

"Well, I don't know—"

"Do you realize what I can do with this?" Jace started pacing the office with long-legged strides, brimming with excitement. "We can get a thousand times the detail we've ever had before! They'll be able to read the print on the friggin' scorecards!"

"I'm not certain it'll work," Dan said.

"Sure it will. It's been done before, for different applications. All you have to do is write the program and debug it."

"That could take months."

Jace halted and whirled toward Dan. "We don't have months. Not many, anyway. Doesn't anybody else have a program we could use? Borrow it, copy it, steal it—anything!"

Dan looked up at his partner. Jace looked as if he had not been sleeping either. His face was unshaved, scruffy. His eyes bleary and red. His hair a tangled mess. Yet he was almost trembling with excitement. His eyes were glowing, bloodshot and all. Dan had dangled a new possibility before him, a new opportunity to build even more complexity into his simulations, a new toy bright and shining, almost within his grasp.

"I don't know—" Dan began.

"What about Bob Frankel?" Jace prompted. "Wasn't he working on something like that for his shitfaced SDI architecture?"

"I thought you had no use for 'Star Wars.' "

Jace twitched his shoulders in a bony shrug. "Shit, man, if he's got something we can use, who the fuck cares where it comes from? Maybe something good can come out of all the trillions they're spending on that crap."

Robert Frankel had been one of the brightest mathematicians on Dr. Appleton's staff. But he and Jace fought each other from the day they met. Two oversized egos, like a pair of network anchormen. When Frankel finally quit Dayton and went to work for the Strategic Defense Initiative Office in Washington, Jace's only comment was "I never realized he was a friggin' fascist."

"The work he's doing must be classified Top Secret," Dan objected.

"Give him a call," said Jace. "They can't classify mathematics, for crap sake."

"He can't talk about what he's working on."

Jace leaned over the desk until his face was so close that Dan could smell his breath. "Look, Danno old buddy, I know you hate to admit you need anybody's help. But give Frankel a call. Can't hurt, and you might learn something. Do it! Pronto, Tonto."

Dan scowled. "What the hell's this pronto Tonto crap? You think you're the Lone Ranger?"

Grinning crookedly, Jace said, "You don't know what *tonto* means in Spanish, huh?" Then he spun around and practically loped out of the office.

Dan sat at his desk for several minutes, staring at the closed door Jace had left behind him. He knew Jace was right, he knew he should phone Bob Frankel, yet Dan felt all the old reluctance hanging on to him like a deadweight. All his life Damon Santorini had worked out his own problems by himself. If Dan had one flaw, it was his aversion to seeking help from others. He would gnaw on a problem for months rather than ask for assistance. He usually solved the problem, but its eventual solution brought him little joy. By then he was already worrying about the next problem confronting him. And the one after that.

It took a conscious effort of will for Dan to reach out and activate the smart phone on his desk. But Jace had told him to do it, and Dan knew that Jace was right.

"Robert Frankel," he said aloud. "Department of Defense in the Washington, D.C., area."

The phone was programmed to understand Dan's voice. Even so, he had to be careful to speak slowly and distinctly to it. Its "search" light began blinking yellow. Connected to the company's mainframe computer, the phone was accessing the District of Columbia telephone directories, searching for Robert Frankel at the Pentagon. Dan half hoped it would not find him.

But within seconds he heard the beeping tones of the phone calling a number, then a ring, two rings, and:

"You have reached Dr. Robert Frankel's phone. I'm not available at the moment, but if you leave your name and number—

including the extension, if applicable—I will get back to you as soon as I can."

Dan felt almost relieved as the answering machine emitted its long beep of a cue.

"Bob, it's Dan Santorini," he said. "I need to talk to you about time-sharing. Please call me as soon as you can." Then he touched the phone's Off button; the machine would automatically add his number to the tape that Frankel's machine was recording.

Leaning back in his chair, Dan almost succeeded in ignoring the message still glowing on the phone's LCD screen. Pronto, Tonto, he thought. What the hell does *tonto* mean?

Finally his sense of duty overcame his reluctance. He reached out again and touched the keypad. "Return the call in memory." His instinct was to add "please," but he felt foolish being polite to a box of microchips.

Maybe Doc will be out of his office, Dan said to himself, glancing at his wristwatch. After all, it's Friday afternoon and—

"Appleton," came the familiar soft voice from the phone's amplifier.

Dan picked up the handset. "Hello, Doc. It's Dan Santorini."

"Dan! I'm glad to hear from you."

"Sorry I couldn't return your call sooner."

"Oh, I know you must be very busy down there. How's everything going?"

"Pretty well."

"How's Jace?"

Dan hesitated, then replied, "Jace is Jace."

Appleton chuckled. "Yes, I guess it was a foolish question."

For a moment neither man said anything. Then Dan asked, "What's happening with you?"

"We have sort of a problem here, Dan." Appleton's voice dropped a notch, became guarded.

"Problem?"

"I need to talk to you over a secure line."

Dan felt his brow knitting into a frown. "A secure line?"

"I can set up a call from Patrick Air Force Base."

"That's over at Cape Canaveral."

"Could you drive over there tonight?" Appleton's voice sounded strained, urgent. "Or tomorrow morning?"

"Tomorrow's Saturday . . ." Dan muttered.

"I know it's an imposition, son, but I really need to talk this thing over with you."

Two dozen excuses ran through Dan's mind. The only time he had to spend with his kids was the weekend. There was a mountain of work to do here at ParaReality. Susan expected him to help her over the weekend. He hadn't seen Phil awake since last Sunday.

He heard himself say, "Eleven o'clock tomorrow morning. Will that be okay?"

"Fine," said Appleton. "Let me give you directions and the name of the officer who'll take care of you there."

CHAPTER 15

Dan blinked and tried to remember how he got here. He was walking down his old street in his old neighborhood in Youngstown. He recognized the kids playing on the sidewalks, and they stopped their games to wave at him.

But they'd all be grown-ups now, he said to himself, just like me.

Then he smiled and realized what was happening. This is a simulation. And a damned good one. How the hell did Jace learn so much about my old neighborhood?

He passed the tobacco store where the kids all bought their comic books. Fat old Mr. Stein waved to him from the doorway. But how did I get into this sim? Dan asked himself. I don't remember . . .

Then he saw Doc Appleton standing by the street lamp on the corner.

"What're you doing here, Doc?" Dan asked.

Doc's form shifted, and suddenly he was Jace in that black gunfighter's outfit.

Jace grinned at him. "Draw, Danno."

"But I don't have a gun. I'm not in your gunfight sim, Jace, this is—"

Jace pulled both revolvers from their holsters and fired point-blank. Dan felt the bullets slam into his chest and knock him over backward into pain and pain and more pain.

He sat bolt upright in bed, soaked with sweat, his chest flaming raw.

"Dan, what's the matter?" Susan reached for the lamp on her night table and turned it on.

Dan was wheezing so hard, he could barely speak.

"Oh, my God," said Susan. "Where's your inhalator?"

"Dream," Dan gasped. "I was . . . back . . ."

"Don't try to talk." Susan got out of the bed and went around to Dan's side. She rummaged in his night-table drawer until she came up with the inhalator. Dan had not had to use it since they had come to Florida.

He fumbled with the little plastic cap, then got the mouthpiece between his teeth and squirted a long acrid spray of epinephrine down his throat. Susan put her own pillow atop his and plumped them up for him.

"You've never had an asthma attack in your sleep before," she said, sounding worried. Looking worried, too, even in the nude.

Dan sagged back against the pillows. "I had a dream," he croaked. "A nightmare."

She got back in bed and pulled the sheet over them both. Resting her head on the pillows next to his, she stroked his chest lightly as she murmured, "It's all right, Dan. It was only a dream. You're all right now."

She turned out the lights, and they waited in the darkness for his breathing to return to normal. Susan fell asleep before Dan did, her head on his bare shoulder. It was that damned gunfight, Dan grumbled to himself. Jace's damned gunfight. That's what I've been dreaming about all these weeks.

The next afternoon, Dan squinted into the blaze of the setting sun as he drove along the Beeline Expressway back toward Orlando.

Traffic was lighter than usual this Saturday, mostly trucks and semi rigs barreling along at more than seventy miles per hour despite the posted speed limits. Dan glanced down at his daughter slumped asleep on the bucket seat beside him, her braided hair blowing in the warm wind coming through the car's half-open windows. Her safety belt had slipped over her slim shoulder; he wanted to adjust it and tighten it up, but he would have to pull over and stop the car to do that. A double trailer rig whooshed past the old Honda, making it shudder in its turbulent wake. Dan decided to keep on going. *The sooner we get home, the better. I'll fix it at the next tollbooth.*

It had been a long afternoon of walking and gawking at the Kennedy Space Center. Despite her early indifference, Angela had stared wide-eyed at the immensity of the Saturn V rocket booster lying on its side. "It's bigger than a whale!" she had said. "Bigger than a whole lot of whales!" And the Vertical Assembly Building was so huge that the space-shuttle orbiter standing inside it looked almost like a toy until they got up close to it. "The world's biggest building," Dan had told his daughter over the hubbub of the other tourists. "It's so big that sometimes clouds form up near the ceiling and it rains in here."

Angela did not quite believe that, but she seemed to enjoy seeing the space hardware. She clicked away with her little camera, the bursts of its flash quickly lost in the immensity of the cavernous VAB.

If Angie was still bothered by her experience in the VR game at school, she showed no signs of it. She talked with her father on the way over to Cape Canaveral about Mrs. O'Connell, her teacher, and the other kids in class, and whether or not they could put up a Christmas tree next month even though Florida didn't look very Christmasy with no snow and even the pine trees along the highway didn't look like the kind of trees you could use for a Christmas tree. She never even mentioned the VR games, not once all during the drive to the Cape.

It was his conversation with Dr. Appleton that kept preying on Dan's mind as he drove his sleeping daughter home. He had brought Angela to the communications center at Patrick Air Force Base, a pastel pink case full of magazines and hand-size video games under her arm, and asked the Officer of the Day if there was someone who could take care of the twelve-year-old while he conducted his videophone call. The lieutenant's gold bars looked shining new on her shoulders. She had smiled and assured Dan that she would set up Angela at her own desk and personally keep an eye on her.

The videoconference room was small and stuffy. Dan was surprised to see that its windowless walls were covered with faded photographs of Air Force planes and rocket launchings. He had expected wall-size display screens, as Muncrief had installed at the lab. Instead there was a bank of ordinary television monitors lining one wall and a row of scruffy student-type chairs with writing arms attached to them facing the TV screens.

Dan slid into the chair that the tech sergeant pointed out for him, feeling as uneasy as if he had suddenly been thrown back into school. The screen in front of him brightened and then broke into a swirling pattern of colors that weaved and flickered nauseatingly. It took more than fifteen minutes for the link to Dayton to be descrambled so that Dan could see Dr. Appleton's face.

The older man looked serious, almost grim. He was in his shirt-sleeves, tie loosened from his collar as usual. Dan remembered that deep-blue tie; he and Susan had given it to Doc many Christmases ago. But Appleton seemed much older than Dan remembered him: what was left of his receding hair was very gray, and there were lines in his long narrow face that Dan had never noticed before.

"Good morning, Dan," said Appleton.

"Good to see you, Doc."

"I'm sorry to disrupt your weekend," Appleton said, "but we have a problem here and I need your help."

"What is it?"

Appleton hesitated a heartbeat, then, "Do you remember Jerry Adair?"

"Adair?"

"Fighter jock. A captain. Real towhead; his hair looked almost white."

Dan nodded. "Yes, I think so. What about him?"

The reluctance showed on Appleton's face. Dan saw that it was more than reluctance. Doc looked absolutely miserable.

"He's dead," Appleton blurted at last. "Died while flying the F-22 simulation."

Dan froze. *Doc's telling me a fighter jock died while flying our simulation.*

"You think that something in the simulation affected him physically?"

"We don't know," said Appleton.

"The simulation might have killed him? Our simulation?"

A shrug of the older man's bony shoulders.

"That's not possible, Doc. You know that. It's only a simulation. We couldn't even put in the g forces that the pilot would feel in actual flight. The guy just sits in the cockpit and reacts to the program. How could that hurt anybody?"

"We've gone through the program a hundred times in the two months since it's happened," Appleton said. "There doesn't seem to be anything unusual about it."

"Has anybody else been affected? Physically, I mean."

"Nobody's used it since Adair's death. We've spent the past two months checking and rechecking it."

"What'd he die of?"

"A stroke."

Dan snorted disdainfully. "Come on, Doc! The damned simulation couldn't give anybody a stroke—except maybe the poor slobs who have to program it."

Strangely, Appleton smiled. "You still feel possessive about it, don't you? Like a father feels about his child."

"That simulation couldn't hurt anybody," Dan insisted.

"Martinez wants to fly it himself, check it out."

"Ralph? I thought he was redlined."

Appleton nodded. "But flying the simulation isn't the same as flying for real. You said so yourself: the simulation can't hurt anybody."

"He's still got the blood-pressure problem?" Dan asked.

"Yes."

Dan fell silent, telling himself that just because one pilot happened to die while flying the simulation didn't mean a goddamned thing and there was no reason Ralph shouldn't fly it, high blood pressure notwithstanding.

But he heard himself asking, "The guy died of a stroke?"

"That's right."

"It *can't* be the simulation," he said again. "It must have been a coincidence."

"I was wondering," Appleton said slowly, "if you could find the time to come up here—maybe next weekend—look the program over, make sure we haven't missed anything."

Dan's heart sank. Inwardly he had feared that his old boss would ask for a favor like that.

"Doc, I really can't. I would if I could, but the work load here is so tremendous I hardly get to see my kids anymore. We're under tremendous pressure . . ." His voice trailed off.

Appleton nodded grimly. "I should have guessed. I'm sorry, Dan. I didn't mean to lay this on you."

But you did it just the same, Dan replied silently.

"It's not your responsibility," Appleton said, and Dan heard his real meaning, just the opposite. He and Jace had created the F-22 sim, but for almost a whole year after Jace had left for ParaReality, Dan had worked on it alone, improving it, putting in new wrinkles while Ralph Martinez constantly prodded him to make it tougher, more realistic.

"I had to bring Angie here with me just so I'd have a chance to be with her," Dan said.

"I could send an Air Force jet down there to get you. Fly up here Friday night and be back by Sunday night."

Dan realized he was gripping the little desk extension to his chair with both hands, hard enough to hurt. "I can't, Doc. I just can't."

"Okay," said Appleton, his grim expression unchanged. "I understand."

"There's just too much in my lap right now. Maybe after April things'll ease off."

"Ralph wants to fly the simulation this coming week."

"Maybe that's the best thing to do. If he flies it and nothing happens, then you'll know the other guy's death was just a freak accident."

Appleton's shoulders moved, then he brought his blackened old pipe to his mouth. Teeth clamped hard on its well-bitten stem, he asked, "How's Jace doing?"

"Up to his armpits in snakes, as usual."

Appleton made a wry smile. "Dan, could you do me one favor?"

"Sure! What is it?"

"Talk over this situation here with Jace. See if he has any ideas that might help us."

"Yeah, okay. I can do that."

"I'd appreciate it."

"Sure. No sweat."

"Maybe you can give me a call early in the week, before Ralph gets into the simulator."

"Yeah. Right."

"Thanks, Dan."

"Look, Doc—I'm really sorry I can't come up there like you want me to."

"It's all right. I understand."

"It's not that I don't want to help you."

Appleton took the pipe from his mouth. "I understand, Dan. And you're probably right, the simulation is probably perfectly okay."

"I'll talk to Jace and call you Monday."

"Good. Thanks."

The blast of an air horn jolted Dan out of his reverie. God-damned semi rig was inches away from his rear bumper, crawling right up his back. Dan flicked a glance at his speedometer: sixty-eight. He was in the right lane. Why doesn't the sonofabitch pass me?

He pushed down on the accelerator and watched the speedometer's needle crawl past seventy. Another huge double trailer roared past him on the left and then the rig behind him pulled out and passed, shaking the Honda so hard that Dan almost went onto the shoulder of the road.

Those fighter jocks ought to try driving around here, he said to himself. If they don't get a stroke here they'll never have to worry about flying jets in combat.

CHAPTER 16

Indian summer in Ohio. The trees were bare, the gold and red and auburn leaves of autumn long since raked up and carted away. On the suburban Dayton street where the Martinezes lived, only the gnarled old oaks on a few of the front lawns still bore some of their withered brown leaves. But the sky was deep blue, the sun warm. Indian summer: the last good weather before the gray cold of winter.

The Martinez house looked perfectly ordinary, a white saltbox with charcoal shutters and trim. A middle-American home, it might have belonged to a junior corporate executive or a skilled factory worker, as did the houses on either side of it. Ralph Martinez was reclining on a folding lounge chair on the wooden deck he had built behind his house, wearing ragged cutoff shorts and a dark-blue sweatshirt, but he was far from relaxed. The Cleveland Browns were on the screen of the portable TV he had brought outside with him; getting trounced by the Philadelphia Eagles. In one hand he gripped the remote-control box for the little electric lawn mower that was faithfully humming up and down the still-green backyard. His other held the portable phone to his ear.

"I didn't think you'd get any help from him," Martinez was saying into the phone.

Dr. Appleton's voice replied, "Don't be so sure, Ralph. Dan

takes a while, but he generally gets there. He'll think this over and call me back in a few days, you wait and see."

"A phone call won't solve our problem."

"Maybe he'll get Jace to think about it," Appleton said hopefully.

"That flake! He doesn't give a shit about anything but himself. He's not going to help us."

"I wouldn't write him off altogether."

"He's a jerkoff. We can't sit around waiting for him. Or for Dan, either."

"You really want to fly the simulation yourself, then?"

Cleveland's quarterback disappeared under a ferocious green tide of Eagles linemen. Martinez winced. "Yeah," he said into the phone. "I want to get the equipment cranked up tomorrow morning."

"It'll take a few days to run through everything, check it all out."

"I want to be in the cockpit no later than Wednesday."

"Why the rush?"

Martinez knew that if he said Wednesday, maybe by the end of the week the simulator would be ready for him. But he said to Appleton, "Every day we wait is a day lost. That simulator was built to train fighter pilots, not sit idle and soak up tax money."

He heard Appleton chuckle softly. "All right. All right. We'll have it ready for you by Wednesday, even if we have to work overtime."

"Good," said the colonel. "Do it."

"Have a nice weekend. What's left of it."

"You too, Doc."

As he put the phone down on the wooden planking, Dorothy pushed the back door open, carrying a tray of snacks and two bottles of beer.

"How's the game going?"

"Don't ask."

"That bad?"

"Worse."

She put the tray down on the table at her husband's elbow and pulled up the other recliner. Dorothy Aguilera had been the prettiest secretary in the lab when Martinez had first arrived at Wright-Patterson Air Force Base, a smoldering raven-haired Latin beauty with big flashing eyes and a warm sparkling smile. Every man on the base was after her; even many of the married men tried to chase her down. Now, more than a dozen years later, she was still a feast for the eyes in suede jeans and a scoop-necked cotton T-shirt that clung to her deliciously. She dressed to please her husband, and she was very successful at it.

"The mower's heading for my flower bed," she said as she handed him one of the beers.

"It'll turn around in time," said Martinez. "I checked the program this morning."

Dorothy looked doubtful. When Ralph had first brought the little robot home it had thoroughly chewed up the impatiens and marigolds that edged the front lawn.

"Who was on the phone?" she asked.

"Doc."

"Did I hear you say you were going to fly the simulation yourself?"

"Yeah." He turned away from her and watched the lawn mower. It stopped short of the flower bed, executed a precise ninety-degree turn, and began cutting the grass along the edge of the bed, just as he had programmed it to do.

But Dorothy was no longer worried about her flowers. "Why do you have to fly it? Why can't—"

"It's just a simulator. It's on the ground. I won't really be flying."

"Jerry was killed in it, wasn't he?"

Martinez tried to concentrate on the football game. The Eagles had fumbled the ball away; a break for Cleveland, at last.

"Wasn't he?" Dorothy insisted, her voice rising.

Martinez turned back toward his wife. Her eyes were fiery.

"Look," he said. "I'm supposed to be the leader of this group. We've got a problem, and it's up to me to find the answer. That's my job. That's what I get paid to do."

She reached out and touched his arm, stroking it gently as she said, "*Querido,* there must be dozens of pilots who can fly the simulator."

He tried to control his temper. I shouldn't get angry at her, he told himself. She loves me. She's just trying to protect me. But dammit, she doesn't understand! After all these years, she still doesn't understand anything at all.

"There isn't any real danger," he mumbled.

"Then let one of the others do it."

"No!" he snapped. "It's my responsibility. I'll do it myself."

Dorothy knew her husband's limits. She knew how angry he was that he'd been grounded by the medics. She knew how worried he was that he would be passed over for promotion to full colonel and forced to retire from the Air Force.

"It's bad enough they won't let me fly until this damned blood pressure comes down," he said. "If it looks like I'm scared even to get into a goddamned simulator, what'll they think of me?"

She leaned across the distance between them and brought her lips close enough to kiss him. "Anyone," she whispered, "who thinks that my husband is afraid of anything is a damned idiot."

But she was afraid. And he could feel her trembling for him.

As he drove to work Monday morning, his mind churning over his phone conversation with Dr. Appleton, Dan could not help but think back to his daughter's bad experience that first week of school. Angie seemed normal enough now. She had not had any more problems with the VR games. Yet she had fainted. And an Air Force pilot had died. In VR simulations.

There can't be anything in the simulation that would kill a pilot, he told himself. The worst physical stress we can put into the simulator is to tilt the cockpit and slew it around to give the guy inside a feeling of the plane's motion. We can't duplicate the g's he'd be pulling in a real flight.

But when he arrived at ParaReality he went straight to Jace's office. Miraculously, it had been cleaned up. Most of the papers that had littered the chairs and floor were gone. Dan could see that Jace had even cleared off his desk. He was bent over the keyboard of his computer terminal, long slim fingers flashing like a concert pianist's. They looked boneless, like snakes, they were moving so fast.

Dan sat wordlessly in one of the plastic chairs in front of the desk. Jace did not seem to notice him; his eyes were focused entirely on the computer screen.

After a few minutes, Dan said, "Jace?" Then louder, "Hey, Jace!"

"Not yet," Jace mumbled, still bent over his keyboard.

"Might as well get a cup of coffee," Dan said, and he started to get up from the chair.

"Don't go," said Jace, still without looking up. "Hang on a minute."

Dan let himself drop back into the chair. It squeaked. Then the only sound in the room was Jace's click-click-clicking on the computer keys.

"Right!" Jace said at last. "Got it!" He lifted his hands triumphantly and turned, grinning, toward Dan. "That oughtta do it."

"Do what?" Dan asked.

"Fill in the background details of the baseball simulation. Now all you've gotta do is get that time-sharing program from Frankel and we're ready to knock Muncrief's socks off."

Dan's gut tightened. "I phoned Frankel—"

"Yeah, yeah. He returned your call last night. Message is on your machine."

"Last night? Sunday?"

"He said to call him this morning at ten sharp. He'll be waiting for your call."

"Oh."

"So how'd you spend your weekend?" Jace leaned so far back in his chair, Dan feared it would tip over. He locked his hands behind his head, planted his boots on the desktop, and stretched so hard that Dan could hear his vertebrae pop.

"Doc's got a problem."

"Appleton?"

"One of the fighter pilots died in our simulation," Dan said.

Jace's eyes narrowed. "Who? Martinez?"

"No. A guy named Adair."

"Never heard of him."

"Doc says he had a stroke while he was flying the simulator."

Jace shrugged. "Tough."

"Doc's worried that maybe something in the simulation affected him."

"Bullshit! How could anything in the simulation hurt anybody? Doc's going off the deep end without his snorkel."

"Still—"

Jace swung his legs off the desk and jumped to his feet. "Come on, we've got our own fish to fry. I wanna try this new background graphics before you call Frankel."

He pushed past Dan and went out the door, heading for their lab. Shaking his head, Dan got up and followed him.

The background was damned good, Dan saw. Better than good. He stood up close to the six-foot display screen and studied the details carefully. Yankee Stadium, crowded to the topmost tier. He could see individual people sitting in their seats, walking up and down the concrete steps between sections, munching hot dogs, making a wave.

"Damn, it looks great," he called to Jace across the cluttered lab. "Details as crisp as they can be."

Jace was worming a data glove onto his left hand. "I'm gonna try it out on the system. You get back to your office and call Frankel. We need his time-sharing program!"

"What if he can't talk about it?" Dan asked.

"Then we'll have to get Muncrief to put the squeeze on him."

"Muncrief?"

"The big boss has lots of friends in high places. Frankel might not want to help me, the little shit, but Muncrief can get people in Washington to put pressure on him."

"I don't think so, Jace," said Dan. "After all, we're talking about programs that're probably classified."

"Classified, my ass! Haven't you heard, the Cold War is over. They got Russians working side by side with them in the Star Wars offices now. They got no right to keep anything from us. Not a simple little time-sharing program, at least."

Simple little time-sharing program, Dan thought. If it's so damned simple, why don't we work it out for ourselves instead of begging Bob Frankel for help?

But he went back to his own office, fidgeted nervously for six minutes, and then at thirty seconds before ten he told his phone to get Frankel.

"Frankel here." His voice came from the phone's built-in speaker.

Dan picked up the handpiece. "Hello, Bob. It's Dan Santorini."

"Hello, Dan. Haven't heard from you in a long while." Frankel's voice sounded tight to Dan, not suspicious, exactly, but not brimming with good cheer either.

"I'm working at ParaReality now. In Orlando."

"With Jace, huh?"

"Yeah."

"How is the big jerk?"

"He's fine. We're doing some interesting things here."

"Yeah? Like what?"

As Dan described their work on the interactive games, the tension between the two men began to ease. The personality clashes between Frankel and Jace faded as the intrigue and excitement of technical challenges pushed it away.

"This is all proprietary stuff, by the way," Dan was saying. "I'm trusting you to keep it to yourself until the park opens."

"Who's the head of your outfit?"

"Kyle Muncrief."

"Never heard of him."

"He's not a technical guy. He's a businessman."

"Oh."

Dan had gone as far as he could. He had run out of chat. Frankel had not asked why he had called, so he had to bring up the subject himself.

Very reluctantly Dan said, "Bob, I wonder if you could help me with a problem we've run into."

"Me? Help you? You mean help the boy genius, don't you? The guy who wants to be God?"

"I know you and Jace didn't get along—"

"That's putting it mildly."

"But it's really me who needs the help."

"If you're working with Jace, then he's the one who needs the help and he's too big of an asshole to ask me for it himself. He's using you as an errand boy."

Grimacing, Dan asked, "Don't you even want to hear what the problem is?"

A long silence from the other end of the connection, broken only by Frankel's breathing.

Finally, "All right, what is it?"

Dan described his idea of splitting the computers' time between the foreground images and the background.

"Sure, we've done things like that here. Hell, we've got to keep track of ten thousand objects at once, all of them flying at hypersonic speeds, all in real-time. The only way to do it is with stuttering."

"Stuttering?"

"That's what it's called. Jumping the sensors from one object to another in nanosecond time frames. Or less. Stuttering."

"Is it classified?"

"The particular programs we use sure as hell are. But the technique isn't. It's been published in at least one of the math journals."

Bingo! Dan said to himself. Trying to keep his voice from showing too much excitement, he asked, "Do you remember which one?"

"Not offhand. And I'm not going to look it up for you, either. Find it for yourself. That's what NREN and CompuServe and all those other electronic databases are for."

"Okay, right. I'll look it up."

Another hesitation. Then, "I've got a paper coming out on the subject. It'll be in the *Journal of Applied Mathematics* in January or February."

"Could you fax me a copy of it?"

"So you can help Jace get rich?"

The idea of money had never entered Dan's head. But he swiftly replied, "I think I could get Muncrief to hire you as a consultant. How does that strike you?"

Frankel actually laughed. "Have you forgotten everything they drummed into your skull when you worked for the Air Force? Remember the conflict-of-interest regulations?"

"Oh. Yeah."

"If this stuff about stuttering helps you, get me a lifetime pass to your Cyber World."

"Okay. Sure. I can do that."

"And tell Jace I still think he's a horse's ass. In spades. Tell him that."

CHAPTER 17

Victoria Kessel leaned back in her chintz-covered armchair and said to the speakerphone, "If you've used the game yourself, Sue, then you must have seen that there's nothing in it to cause any harm to anyone."

Coming over the phone's speaker, Susan Santorini's voice sounded strained and implacable. "But it's not just that one game. It's almost all of them! The games that Angela describes to me all seem to be tailor-made just for her. There are differences—"

"The differences are in your daughter's perception of her experience," Victoria said, trying to keep patient.

Susan could hear the growing edge in Vickie's voice. She was sitting in her kitchen alcove, her morning's work pushed aside as she tried to track down what was happening to Angela. Every time she asked her daughter about the VR games at school, Angela told her how wonderful they were.

"There's always people in them that I know," she told her mother. "You and Daddy and even Uncle Kyle sometimes."

The child seemed happy with the games, but Susan checked with Eleanor O'Connell and found that what Angela was reporting was not programmed into the games.

"How could they program each child's friends and relatives into each game?" O'Connell asked Susan. "That wouldn't make any sense, would it?"

Instead of being afraid of the games, Angie now looked forward to them so much that Susan was beginning to fear she might be getting addicted to them.

"It's as if the games are made specifically for her," Susan said into the phone. "The differences are small, but they're there."

"That's just not possible," said Vickie.

"I've talked with Angie in some detail about it," Susan explained. "What she's experiencing is different from the other kids."

The edge in Victoria's voice grew sharper. "That's exactly what I've been trying to get across to you, Susan dear. Her *perceptions* of the game are different. It's like two people looking at the same painting; they can see entirely different things."

"No," Susan insisted. "This is more than—"

"Didn't Dan go through that game she played? Neptune's Kingdom? What did he experience?"

That brought Susan up short. Dan had told her next to nothing about his run through the game. Only that he didn't see anything harmful and couldn't understand what had bothered Angie so badly. In the two months since then, Susan had mentioned her growing worries about Angie a couple of times, only to have her husband mutter that there was nothing wrong with the VR games.

"Dan saw the same game that I did," she replied.

Victoria sensed the slight sullenness in Susan's tone. She glanced sharply at the phone's little speaker grille, as if she could see Susan's face in it.

"There. You see? You and Dan went through the same game. Dozens of schoolchildren use the games every day without any problems at all. If your daughter is seeing things in those games that the other children don't see, the problem is with her, Sue. I know it's hard to face up to that fact, but we really don't keep separate disks on hand for individual students."

It was a lie, and Victoria knew it. But it was one more hold she had acquired on Kyle Muncrief.

Susan hung up, still obviously unconvinced. Victoria sat tensely in her chair. She knew that she was going to have more trouble with Susan Santorini. Something would have to be done.

In the meantime, though, she had to follow up on Kyle's dealings with Washington. She got up from her chair, checked her hair and makeup in the Venetian mirror hanging on the opposite wall of her cozy office. She worked hard to keep looking good. Her silk blazer was a hot fuchsia color, set off with a heavy gold necklace and gold bangle bracelets and earrings. Just a hint of décolletage, enough to keep some of the younger guys interested. Satisfied with her appearance, she started down the corridor to Muncrief's office.

Thanks to modern electronics and Victoria's insistence, there were no secretaries at ParaReality. One young woman served the top six of the corporate executive group. Her title was Executive Assistant to the President. All told, there were four other "executive assistants" in the company, two of them male. Almost all the typing, filing, telephoning, and other secretarial services were done by computerized machines. Even the coffeepots were automatic. Joe Rucker emptied and scrubbed them each night; he broke quite a few because he had only one hand to work with, but Jace Lowrey—of all people—insisted that Joe not be embarrassed by giving the chore to someone else. The executive assistants took turns filling them each morning.

So there was no secretary guarding Kyle Muncrief's privacy when Victoria opened his door and stepped into his office. Muncrief was on the phone with a man who was obviously Japanese. It was not Hideki Toshimura in the desktop phone screen, but one of his underlings. A bad sign, Victoria thought as she perched herself on the leather couch next to the door, out of range of the telephone's TV camera.

"Let me explain it one more time," Muncrief was saying, smiling his most cordial smile into the screen. "The programs that we develop and all the other technical data are the property of ParaReality, Inc. The investors do not own that material."

The man's face seemed as immobile as stone. "It is highly unusual, is it not, for one to own shares in a company and yet not own a share of the company's assets."

"The investors own shares of Cyber World, not ParaReality. Cyber World, Inc., provides the funding for ParaReality but does not own any of it. ParaReality is privately held. By me. That is the agreement that Mr. Toshimura signed," Muncrief said with strained patience.

"That is not our understanding of the agreement."

"Very well, then. Have your lawyers talk to my lawyers. There's no sense in our going around this again."

The Japanese flushed visibly, then dipped his chin slightly. "I am sorry to have taken up your very important time, Mr. Muncrief."

Muncrief smiled even more widely. "Think nothing of it. Tell Mr. Toshimura for me that I'm sorry this misunderstanding has come up. I'm sure our lawyers can iron it out."

The image on Muncrief's desktop phone screen winked off. He glared across the room at Victoria. "Toshimura thinks he can steal everything we're developing here and set up his own version of Cyber World in Tokyo."

"That's what he's after?" Victoria asked as she took one of the chairs in front of Muncrief's desk.

"What else?"

"But in our agreement it says we'll set up a Cyber World in Japan after the Orlando park is up and running."

"Sure. But if he can get his greedy little hands on our programs, Toshimura can dump us and go off and do it himself. Or make a deal with Sony or MGM or one of the other biggies."

"What about Swenson?" Victoria asked. "Does he want to steal everything, too, and set himself up in Europe?"

Muncrief's whole body seemed to sag. "I hadn't even thought of that! Lord, these guys are supposed to be investors, not competitors."

"You're swimming with sharks, Kyle."

"Tell me about it."

"All the more reason to get some protection from Washington."

He glowered at her.

"How is the Washington deal going?" Victoria asked, crossing her legs primly.

Muncrief barely glanced at her legs. He huffed and brushed his hair back from his forehead. "How's it going? Smith wants a particular program. Won't tell me what he wants it for, but he says it's got to be developed and delivered before February first."

"Why then?"

"Who knows?" With a shrug.

"Can we do it?"

"If we can get the blasted baseball game going we can do it. From what he's telling me, we'll get the basic visual and audio material from Smith himself. All we have to do is to program it into an interactive system."

"What kind of audiovisual material?"

Muncrief fluttered his beefy hands. "Sounds like news footage, mostly. Videotapes from CNN and other news services. Stuff like that."

"And what do they want to do with it?"

"Use it as the basis for interactive scenarios. You know, what'll happen in the Middle East if somebody knocks off the prime minister of Israel or there's another revolution in Iran—that sort of thing."

"Scenario building."

"Yeah. It'll need the best possible graphics program; and it's got to be interactive. When I told Smith about the conflict games we're developing, his eyes lit up like a Christmas tree."

Victoria leaned back in her chair, fascinated. When Esther Cahan, an old friend from Victoria's college days, had first contacted her about this all she had said was that somebody in the government was interested in virtual reality. Slowly, over weeks that lengthened into months, she would phone Victoria and ask roundabout questions about what ParaReality was doing. Victoria was equally roundabout, fearing at first some subtle kind of government investigation might be underway.

Gradually the two former college friends began to trust one another. It turned out that Esther was working in the White House; well, not actually *in* it, but in the Executive Office Building next door that housed most of the White House's ever-growing staff. And someone who really *did* work in the White House itself was intrigued by certain possibilities of virtual reality.

As she watched Muncrief struggle to keep his investors happy while maintaining the ever-increasing flow of development money he needed, Victoria realized that a connection with the power—and funding—of the White House would not be a bad idea. It had taken much more work than she had expected to convince Muncrief of that. He was afraid that Washington might uncover his past. But at last her boss, in desperation, had bitten the apple.

It's my chance, she thought. My fallback position. Even if Kyle goes wacko and screws up the Cyber World deal, I can still take our expertise and make an exclusive deal with Washington. I won't need that slob Peterson and whoever he's working for. I can work for the White House instead.

"Can you deliver what they want on time," she asked Muncrief, "without jeopardizing the Cyber World work?"

"That's the big question, Vickie. I've got everybody working flat out to deliver the Cyber World games. How can we fit this blasted extra work in?"

"Jace Lowrey could do it, if it interested him enough."

"Oh no!" Muncrief snapped. "Not Jace. He'd drop the conflict game work he's supposed to be doing and play with this new program."

"But isn't this a conflict game, too?"

"Could be, maybe. Jace's done enough of the basic work. We don't need a genius for this. Especially not a crazy one like Jace."

Victoria smiled and nodded reluctant agreement.

"Besides, this project is supposed to be very hush-hush. Tell that to Jace and he'll be blabbing to the *Washington Post* before the sun goes down."

"Who, then?"

Muncrief shook his head.

"What about Dan?" Vickie suggested. "He's a solid citizen. Quiet and dependable."

"Dan," Muncrief muttered.

"Can he do the work? Would it be too deep for him? He's really just a glorified technician, isn't he?"

"It shouldn't be that tough. Like I said, Jace's already done the hardest part. Yeah, I think maybe Dan could handle it."

"Then you'll pull him away from Jace?"

"No, no! I'll just get him to do this on overtime. Nights, weekends. He's a workaholic anyway."

Victoria thought that "workaholic" was not the most accurate description of Damon Santorini. Serious, yes. Very sensitive to his responsibilities. Very dedicated, with a strong sense of commitment.

"He has a family," Victoria murmured.

"I know that. I'll give him a nice fat incentive bonus for doing this extra work. Start a trust fund for his kids' college education. How's that?"

"It might work."

"He'll do it. He doesn't have the guts to say no to me."

"I wouldn't put it exactly that way," Victoria said. She hesitated long enough to draw in a breath, then asked, "What about his daughter?"

Muncrief looked startled. A silence stretched between them, electrical, crackling.

"Well, what about his daughter?" he asked warily, his hands fluttering nervously across the desktop.

Victoria thought out her words very carefully. "Kyle, you're tampering with the VR games at the school when she plays them."

He did not deny it. He just stared at her, eyes burning, face reddening.

"And Jace is helping you."

"The kid isn't being hurt," he mumbled.

"She fainted."

"That was two months ago! She loves the games now."

"And she likes you a lot, too, doesn't she? She even calls you Uncle Kyle."

"So what?" Truculently.

Victoria said, "Kyle, what you do in your private life doesn't concern me. But if Dan finds out about why you're interested in his daughter, it could wreck this company."

"He won't find out."

"Dan would kill you, you know. He's the quiet, soft-spoken kind who goes berserk. He'd pick up that lamp and smash your skull in with it."

Muncrief inadvertently glanced at the heavy brass lamp on the corner of his desk.

"I'm not hurting his daughter," he muttered.

"That won't matter to him."

With an angry scowl, Muncrief said, "Well, he won't find out unless somebody tells him." And he pointed his finger like a pistol at Vickie's chest.

"I won't tell him, you know that. But if Jace knows about it, how long will it stay a secret?"

Mrs. O'Connell had almost stopped worrying about Angela. Whatever had bothered the child two months ago in the VR booth seemed to have blown away. Angela loved the VR games now. She used the booths for her weekly reading-skills demonstration, for her science lessons and her history lessons. And for games.

The day's work had gone smoothly, so that by the final half hour O'Connell allowed the children a free period of independent study.

"Can we use the booths for a music program?" asked Mary Mackie. O'Connell saw that she wanted to share the program with a girlfriend.

Three of the booths at the back of the classroom were unused at the moment.

"Angela," she called, "would you like to try the concert, too?"

Angela looked up from the computer screen she had been studying. The display screen showed a map of Florida.

"You do enjoy music, don't you, Angela?"

"I guess."

O'Connell directed Angela, Mary, and another girl to the empty booths. While they were pulling on the data gloves and slipping the helmets over their heads, she went to her desk at the front of the classroom and tapped out the number of the program to be shown and the names of the children in each booth. The information went over fiber-optic lines, fast as light, to the mainframe computer at the ParaReality laboratory.

As soon as Mrs. O'Connell closed the door to the VR booth, Angela pulled frayed old Amanda out of her pocket and sat the little doll on her lap.

"This is going to be fun," she said softly to Amanda. "You're going to enjoy this."

Once she put on the helmet, it blocked out all light and muffled the sounds from the classroom. She barely heard Mrs. O'Connell's footsteps, her murmured "Everything is connected properly. Very good." With the data gloves on, Angela could not caress Amanda the way she wanted to, but it felt good to know she was there with her.

The darkness slowly brightened into a soft glow, and a voice said gently, "The symphony orchestra is one of humankind's greatest achievements." Angela saw that she was sitting in the middle of a big orchestra, surrounded by men and women tuning up their violins and trombones and flutes and other instruments she did not know the names of. The noise was pleasantly chaotic; everybody seemed to be playing his or her own tune.

"Which instrument would you like to play, Angela?" asked the voice. It was a man's voice, but not Uncle Kyle's, as she had half expected.

Angela looked around the orchestra. All the other players stopped their tune-ups and turned smiling toward her. Angela twisted around in her chair, looking first one way, then the other.

"Is there a piano?" she asked.

"I'm afraid not," said the man's voice. "How about a violin? Or maybe you'd like to play the timpani."

"Timpani? What's that?"

After a few moments of discussion, she settled for a piccolo. It looked small and easy to handle. The voice told her to move to the woodwind section. A chair appeared there for her, with a piccolo resting on its seat. Wondering if the other girls were going through the same routine, Angela sat down. She realized that she was now wearing a long black gown that rustled when she moved.

"Beethoven's Sixth Symphony is called 'The Pastorale,'" the voice began explaining. Angela fidgeted on her chair. She wanted to play music, or at least listen to some. She saw Mary Mackie sitting up in the first row of violins. She started to turn around to find the other girl, but just then the orchestra conductor walked out onto the stage and Angela realized there was an audience out in the darkened theater beyond the stage lights. She heard them applauding. The conductor stepped up onto his podium, bowed to the audience, then turned to the orchestra and raised his baton.

Angela picked up her piccolo, wondering which fingers were supposed to go over which holes along the slim metal tube. "Don't worry about a thing," the man's voice whispered into her ear. "Just put the mouthpiece to your lips and have fun."

The conductor swept his baton down gracefully, and the orchestra began to play. Including Angela. She did not know how to move her fingers properly, and she blew awkwardly into the piccolo's mouthpiece. But the instrument sounded sweet and clear whenever its turn came to play.

Angela did not know whether to be pleased or annoyed. She was playing in the orchestra, true enough, but she knew it was not really herself playing the instrument.

And then, as the beautiful music soared and swept onward, the orchestra slowly faded away and Angela found herself in a soft green meadow under a bright blue sky dotted with scattered cotton-white clouds. Her piccolo was gone and she was wearing shorts and a loose shirt. The sun was warm, and she saw that the meadow sloped down gently toward a meandering brook where horses and smaller animals were drinking.

The music followed her as she walked slowly toward the stream, barefoot in the warm grass. Birds fluttered overhead, and from the trees not far away she could hear melodious singing.

Everything in this pastoral scene seemed to move in rhythm to the music, even the clouds floating by. Angela smiled, then laughed aloud as she approached the stream's bank. Rabbits and deer were gathered there, so tame that she could pet them. A mare and her foal bent their graceful necks to drink from the brook, then turned their soulful brown eyes toward Angela.

She had never ridden a horse before, but it seemed so easy to climb up on the mare's back, and suddenly she was racing across the greenery, splashing into the brook and up the other bank, off into the woods with the foal running easily alongside in rhythm to the music.

It was glorious. Angela clung tightly to the mare's back and leaned forward, gripping her mane with both hands. They broke clear of the woods, and Angela saw an endless plain stretching out beyond the horizon where vast herds of horses galloped free and happy, raising great plumes of yellow-gray dust.

The mare turned back, though, and they were among the trees once again, the brilliant sun winking in and out of the high leafy canopies. At last they returned to the brook, and the mare trotted slowly along its bank, then stopped.

And Angela found herself sitting in the orchestra again, back in her long black gown, her fingers tight around the piccolo, her eyes on the conductor. The man's face seemed to shift as he led the orchestra with graceful gestures; his features seemed to go into shadow and change slightly, much as a distant landscape changes as drifting clouds throw their shadows across it.

At one instant the conductor seemed like someone Angela knew, someone she had seen before. His face almost looked like Daddy's, and Angela drew in her breath in surprise and sudden delight, but the face shifted again, changed even as she stared at it. It became, just for a moment, the face of Kyle Muncrief, smiling and happy. Uncle Kyle nodded at Angela as he led the orchestra and gave her a big wink. Then his face changed again and he was a stranger once more.

The music ended. A voice said, "Session over. Please take off your helmet and gloves."

Feeling more puzzled than alarmed, Angela wondered how Uncle Kyle almost always managed to get into her games.

CHAPTER 18

S tuttering," said Dan.

Susan almost laughed at him. "S-s-stuttering?"

They were sitting on the sofa, drinking coffee and watching an old Steve McQueen movie on a satellite TV channel. The kids were asleep, and Dan was telling his wife about his conversation with Bob Frankel.

"That's the key word," Dan replied, utterly serious. "Bob wouldn't tell me much. He didn't like the idea of helping Jace."

"He wouldn't tell you the name of the journal or the title of the report?" Susan asked.

Dan shook his head. "Said I could look it up for myself. Can you find it for me?"

Susan felt surprised, delighted, that her husband was confiding in her. He so seldom did. Dan had not mentioned a word about his talk with Dr. Appleton on Saturday. She knew that much of what went on at the Air Force lab was secret, but Dan had ground his teeth horribly in his sleep for the past three nights.

He needs my help, Susan said to herself. He really needs my help. Then a new thought struck her.

"You wait right here," she said, getting up from the sofa. "Watch the movie. I'll see what I can find."

"Now?"

Susan grinned at him. "The computers never sleep," she said as melodramatically as she could. "And they obey my every command."

With that she swept out of the living room, heading for her tiny office in the kitchen alcove.

"While you're at it," he called to her, "can you find out what the word *tonto* means in Spanish?"

"I don't need the computer for that. It means stupid."

"Stupid?"

"Don't you know that old joke? The Lone Ranger calls his faithful Indian companion Tonto, but he doesn't know what kee-mo-sabey means."

Stupid. Dan sank back on the sofa, not knowing whether to be angry at Jace or himself. Pronto, Tonto.

He picked up the cups and saucers and went back to the kitchen. As he rinsed them and placed them in the dishwasher, he cocked an eye at his wife. Susan was sitting in front of her computer in the tiny alcove, telephone headset clamped over her red hair. Dan could see the glow of the computer screen on her face. It made her eyes shine. The tip of her tongue was peeking between her lips.

Susan's mind was racing as fast as the lists of titles scrolling along her computer screen. If I can get Dan to make me a consultant, then maybe I can get into the computer system in his lab and take a really good look at the games they pipe into Angie's school. I don't care what Vickie Kessel says, something's not right with those games. Angie keeps seeing people she knows in them.

The scrolling stopped, and the screen showed a single title.

"Got it!" Susan yelped. " 'Applications of Nanosecond Switching in Parallel Processors.' By Armbruster, Bernoff, and six other guys. All from MIT."

Dan went around the counter and leaned over beside Susan to peer at the screen. "It doesn't say stuttering," he muttered.

Susan pecked at the Page Down key a few times and Dan saw a footnote: "This technique has acquired the popular name of 'stuttering.' It seems an inelegant description of the technique, but frequently barbarous usages find their way into scientific jargon. Witness 'quasar' and 'flop.' "

"Holy cow, you did it!" Dan exclaimed.

Susan pressed another key and the printer on the floor under her little table began chugging. Then she tapped the keyboard again. The screen showed an invoice.

"You owe me a dollar seventy-five for the telephone charges," she said triumphantly. "And a hundred dollars for my fee."

"A hundred dollars?"

"That's my minimum fee," she said, grinning.

Dan pursed his lips. "That's an awful lot for just a few minutes at the computer."

She raised an eyebrow. "It's my minimum fee," she repeated.

"For just"—he squinted at the computer screen—"six minutes' work?"

Susan pursed her lips. "I suppose I could throw in a bonus."

Dan asked, "What kind of a bonus?"

"What would you like?"

He took her by the shoulders and helped her out of the chair. They kissed and headed for the bedroom, his arm around her waist, her head on his shoulder, while the printer continued to buzz and churn out pages of the MIT paper.

Much later, as they lay warm and sticky next to each other, Susan murmured, "Dan?"

He was already half asleep. "Hnnh?"

"Dan, do you think you could hire me as a consultant?"

"Consultant?" His voice was muffled by his pillow.

"Like I was for your lab at Wright-Patt," Susan said. "I could do all your searches for you on a regular basis. For the whole company!"

Dan turned over and looked blearily at her. "I guess I could ask Vickie about it."

"Does *everything* have to go through Vickie?"

"I thought you liked her."

"I don't dislike her," Susan said. "But she seems to be at the center of everything that goes on at the lab."

"Yep, she sure is."

Vickie must know that there's something wrong with Angie's games, Susan thought. Then it hit her. If someone was altering the games Angie plays, then Vickie must know all about it.

•   •   •

Dan's office door banged open the next morning while he was reading the MIT paper and Jace slouched in, bleary and unshaven. His clothes looked as if he had slept in them for a week. His grimy T-shirt read, *Curiouser and Curiouser*. He flopped onto the couch.

"So?" he asked, his voice a croak.

"What's happening to you, Jace?" Dan asked, feeling a surge of worry. "You're falling apart, for Pete's sake."

"I'm okay. Been working nights, that's all."

"Working? On what?"

Jace's eyes shifted away from Dan. "Something special," he said evasively. "My own business. Private stuff."

"You going into business on your own behind Muncrief's back?" Dan tried to make it sound light, joking, but inwardly he was surprised that Jace was working on something that he obviously did not want to share with him. Surprised and hurt.

Jace gave him a red-eyed stare. "That'll be the day," he mumbled.

"I found out what *tonto* means, by the way."

Jace grinned at him.

"I don't like being called stupid."

"It's just a joke."

"I still don't like it."

"Don't be a sorehead."

An uncomfortable silence grew between them. Dan could feel it, like a palpable force. It bothered him. Dan felt torn, uncertain of what he should do or say.

He picked up the MIT paper in one hand. "I got the goods from Frankel," he said. "A group at MIT did it. They call it stuttering."

Jace snapped wide awake. He sat upright, almost quivering. "Stuttering? That's what we need?"

Dan nodded.

"How quick can you put it into our program?"

"A couple of weeks, maybe three," said Dan. "Then I'll have to debug it. That might take another three, four weeks. Maybe a little more."

"That's no problem," Jace said, hopping to his feet. "We can get Charlie Chan or one of the other slobs to do the debugging."

"Gary's got his own work to do," Dan said.

"Then we can automate the friggin' debugging."

"Oh, no! We can't let some half-ass AI program debug this; it's too damned important to let a computer screw it up."

"Don't be an old lady," Jace countered. "We can use the same AI program we've used to debug the program so far."

"I don't trust it. This is too important to mess around with."

"You're just being possessive," Jace said, with a lopsided grin. "I know you, Danno. You're the kind who can't bear to see anybody else touch his precious program, not even an AI system."

"It can make mistakes. And it did, when we started using it on the graphics program. Remember?"

"And we fixed the mistake. Remember? It'll never make that mistake again."

"No, it'll figure out new ones."

They argued the point back and forth for nearly half an hour, then settled on a two-track approach. Dan would develop the stutter program and make two copies of it. One he would debug himself; the other would be debugged by the lab's AI program.

"I'll bet you anything you want that the AI program finishes the job before you do," Jace taunted.

"Finishes it right? Without errors?"

"Yah."

Dan gnawed on his lip for a moment. "Okay. If I win, you have to buy a whole new set of clothes. I'm tired of looking at your rags."

With a reflexive glance down at his T-shirt and faded jeans, Jace said, "Okay. You're on."

"Wait a minute. What do you want if you win?"

Grinning at him, Jace replied, "Just the look on your face will be enough, pal."

"Yeah, well—"

Gary Chan stuck his head through the open doorway.

"Hey, Dan," he said, looking slightly worried, "Muncrief's looking for you. He said he's been trying to get you on the phone for the past half hour."

Startled, Dan replied, "I've had the answering machine on."

Chan said, "You better get down to his office. He told me to find you right away and bring you in, dead or alive!"

Jace laughed as Dan scrambled from behind his desk. "Remember what they say, Danno: Artificial intelligence will never be a match for natural stupidity."

As Dan headed for the door, he added, "Tonto."

Hurrying along the corridor toward the front of the building, Dan wondered if Muncrief knew about the stuttering technique already. Of course not. He couldn't know about it. I just told Jace about it two minutes ago. Muncrief couldn't know unless he's got my office bugged.

Dan waved to Vickie Kessel as he passed the open door of her office. She was talking on the phone but she smiled at Dan and returned his wave.

Muncrief was at his desk when Dan arrived at his open doorway. "You wanted to see me, Kyle?"

Muncrief looked up, almost startled, as if some private reverie had been rudely interrupted.

"Oh, Dan. Yeah. Come on in, pull up a chair." Getting up from his broad desk, he gestured toward the round conference table in the far corner of his office.

"How's it going?" he asked as Dan sat down at the little table. Muncrief took the chair next to him. He did not look upset in the slightest. Dan realized that Gary Chan had exaggerated the boss's call.

"I think we've made the breakthrough," Dan said, wondering how much Muncrief already knew.

"Oh?"

"The baseball game ought to be ready by the middle of February, maybe earlier. It'll be a knockout, so detailed you won't be able to tell it's not real."

Muncrief broke into a wide smile. "No kidding?"

"No kidding," Dan said. "We've found a technique that'll allow us to effectively double or triple our computer power. Maybe even better, but I want to play it safe until we're thoroughly familiar with how to use this new technique."

"That's great!" Muncrief said, unconsciously brushing at his hair. "That's terrific! By mid-February, you say? Wait'll I tell Toshimura and the others that!"

Impulsively, Muncrief reached out and clasped Dan's shoulder. "By God, if you guys can deliver the baseball game by mid-Febru-

ary, we'll still have six weeks to develop variants of it for other
sports. I can farm that out to the rest of the technical staff and get
you and Jace to go on to the next challenge."

"What will that be?"

Muncrief laughed. "How in the world should I know? That's
for Jace to figure out. He's the genius!"

Dan felt his lips press tight. He wanted to suggest his symphony-orchestra simulation or an idea he had about teaching music, but before he could struggle the first words out, Muncrief said:

"Now there's something else I need you to do for me, Dan.
Something extra. I need you to find time for it, maybe nights,
maybe weekends. It's not a really difficult job, I don't think, but I
need a man of your skills to do it for me."

"An extra job?" Dan echoed. "But I'm going to have to debug
this stuttering program and install—"

"I'll get you all the help you need on the baseball problem. This
job is kind of simple, but it's got to be done quick and it's got to
be kept just between you and me. I don't want Jace or anybody
else to know about it, understand me?"

"What are you talking about?"

Muncrief ran a hand over his chin and glanced around, as if
afraid of being overheard. "Listen, Dan," he said, lowering his
voice and hunching close, leaning one elbow on the little round
conference table. "This has nothing to do with Cyber World.
Understand? It's a special job. I don't want a single word of it
to leak out to anybody. It's just you and me on this one. Nobody else."

Dan could see from the seriousness of Muncrief's expression
and the almost conspiratorial tone of his hushed voice that he was
not going to be allowed to say no to his boss.

So he asked, "What's it all about?"

"I'm not going to even try to give you a briefing on it," Muncrief replied, still almost whispering. "The guy we're going to be
doing this for is coming in from Washington this afternoon. I'll
get the two of you together towards the end of the day. Okay?"

A welter of feelings swirled through Dan: resentment at having
this extra task dumped on him, curiosity about what it might be,
anxiety, and then a sudden realization that this was an opportunity
for him to demand a favor in return.

"Okay, Kyle," he began, "I'll be glad to do whatever I can for you. But there's something I'd like you to do for me."

Muncrief pulled away from him slightly, his face going hard. "What?"

"My wife's been a big help to me."

"Susan?"

"She runs her own information search service, you know," Dan said. "She's the one who found the background paper we needed to make this breakthrough for the baseball game."

"I didn't know she had her own business."

"Would you consider giving her a consulting contract? It doesn't have to be very big, but I think she can help us a lot and save me in particular a lot of time tracking down information that I need."

Muncrief stared at Dan for a long moment, the way a used-car dealer might stare at a man who was trying to palm off a clunker on him. Then he broke into an easy, warm smile.

"Sure, why not," he said, waving his hands as if brushing away a problem. Then he leaned forward again until his face was mere inches away from Dan's. "But you can't tell her anything about this special job you're going to do for me. Understand that? You can't tell her or Jace or anybody. Not a word!"

Dan nodded solemnly.

"Okay, good. The guy from Washington will be here later today. He'll fill you in on the details. You'll have to do this work at night and over weekends. And you can't slow down your work on the baseball game; Jace'll get suspicious."

Nights and weekends, Dan repeated silently. And I can't explain to Sue what it's about. That's going to be just great.

"Just how long will this job take?" he asked.

"It's got to be finished by February first."

Ten weeks, Dan calculated. Without slowing down on the baseball game.

Muncrief got up from the little conference table and went toward his desk.

Getting to his feet, Dan asked, "Uh, about the consulting agreement for my wife . . ."

Muncrief glanced up and gestured toward the door with one hand. "Sure, sure. Get Vickie to set it up. Tell her I said it's okay."

• • •

Vickie's office always seemed more like a boudoir to Dan than a business office, with the pastel prints on the walls and the delicate feminine furniture. Although Vickie was in slacks, her denim outfit clung to the curves of her body disturbingly. Dan saw that she wore no blouse beneath its jacket. When she shifted in her chair he could see a hint of hot red lace.

"You know, Dan," she was saying, "if we were under contract to the Department of Defense what you want would be an illegal conflict of interest."

Dan felt a flash of surprise. "But we're not under any Defense contracts."

Vickie made a strained smile. "No, that's true."

"Anyway," Dan countered, "Sue did some consulting for my lab back in Dayton. Nobody said anything about conflict of interest."

"That was an Air Force laboratory. The government has one set of rules for its own organizations and another, much more stringent set for private companies that it contracts for work."

Why is she putting me through this? Dan asked himself. "Well, Kyle said it was okay," he repeated stubbornly.

"Yes, I know." She drummed her manicured fingers on the arm of her chair. "It's just that we've never entered into a contractual agreement with an employee's spouse before."

"There's nothing wrong with it. Sue's already given me a lot of help."

"I'm sure," Vickie murmured.

Dan sensed her hostility. It was blatant enough for a blind man to see. Is it because Kyle okayed it without talking to her first? Or is she just sore because it's an employee's wife? Or maybe because it's Sue! Maybe she doesn't like Sue.

While he was trying to sort out these possibilities in his mind, Victoria swung the swiveled arm of her computer keyboard toward her and tapped on the keys. A few seconds later, the printer in the corner of the room hummed to life. A single sheet of paper rolled into its output bin.

Vickie got up and brought the paper to the cushioned love seat. Sitting next to Dan, she leaned toward him, almost pressing against his shoulder. Dan avoided looking at anything but the paper in her hand. Still, he could not avoid the scent of her perfume: softly feminine, gently pleasant. Dan realized that he had not noticed any perfume at all on Susan in a long, long time.

"This is our standard consulting agreement," she said. With a red fingernail she pointed. "Have Susan fill in her Social Security number here and sign here. I've set the contract for a minimum of thirty days' consulting over the next twelve months. That means even if she doesn't do a single thing more for us, she'll get thirty days' worth of consulting fees."

Dan saw that the space where the fee was entered remained blank.

"What will the fee be?" he asked.

Vickie smiled again, still strained. "That's for Susan and me to negotiate. She'll have to phone me tomorrow."

"Okay," said Dan. Suddenly he was anxious to get out of Vickie's office, away from this woman who was obviously angry at something yet leaning close to him seductively. He had to almost push her aside as he got up from the love seat.

"Thanks, Vickie. I hope this hasn't caused you too much trouble."

"Not really," she said, following him to the door. "Only, next time you want something, Dan, don't bother Kyle about it. Come straight to me. I'll take care of any problems you might have."

He thanked her again and practically bolted from the office.

This Washington deal has got to work out, Vickie told herself as she headed for the parking lot to pick up Mr. Smith from the airport. We need the cash flow and the protection. She had been stringing Peterson along, telling the ever-smiling little man next to nothing about what was really going on inside ParaReality. But she had the uncomfortable feeling that Peterson could see right through her and was merely biding his time, giving her enough rope to hang herself, before he snapped shut the trap on her. He still hasn't told me who he's representing, Vickie said to herself. Until he does, until I get to meet the people he works for, I'm not giving him anything valuable. And if this Washington deal works out, maybe I won't have to give him anything at all.

But as she drove down Interstate 4 heading for the Beeline Expressway, Vickie realized all over again what a power Disney and the other amusement companies were. This multilane highway lined with hotels would not exist if the Disney people had not decided to turn a few thousand acres of scrub and swamp into Disney World. And now she and Kyle were challenging such power. She almost laughed as she maneuvered her shiny maroon Mustang past campers and semi rigs: a nervous wreck and a horny bitch from the Bronx taking on the biggest entertainment corporations in the world.

When she reached the airport she parked the Mustang and walked from the warm Florida sunshine into the air-conditioned chill of the terminal. It was relatively quiet inside. The big Thanksgiving rush had not started yet. She saw that the Washington flight was on time for a change and went to the security gate to wait for Mr. Smith.

Esther Cahan had told her only that Smith was young, ambitious, and bound to move ahead through the jungles of Washington's insider politics. Vickie had spoken to him on the phone twice since Kyle had met with him in Washington. His voice sounded crisply assured. "Don't worry about what I look like," he had said. "I'll spot you."

A trickle of arriving passengers was coming down the corridor, she saw. The Washington plane must have landed. Vickie looked the passengers over, trying to figure out which one Smith might be. Most of them were elderly, or at least older than Vickie herself. A few younger people, but mostly couples. Smith would be traveling alone.

Then she saw him and smiled. Kyle said he looked like an FBI agent, and here was this square-shouldered guy with his sandy hair cropped down almost to a crew cut striding along the corridor like a toy soldier, one hand clasping a garment bag, free arm swinging as if he were whistling a Sousa march to himself.

She stood unmoving, even turning her gaze farther up the corridor, just to see if he really would spot her. At least he's not wearing sunglasses, Vickie said to herself, almost with a giggle.

"Victoria Kessel," said Smith, stopping an arm's length in front of her.

She smiled and nodded. "Quenton Wayne Smith the Third, I presume?"

He stuck out his hand. She took it and noticed that his grip was just right: not too hard, but certainly not flabby.

"Do you have any other luggage?" she asked.

"Nope. Just this."

"I arranged for a rental car to be waiting for you at your hotel," Vickie said, starting for the doors.

"Good. But I want to go to your office first. Somebody can drop me off at the hotel later."

"If that's what you want."

"Right. Let's get started; the sooner the better."

CHAPTER 19

I still think we ought to go straight to the mission that Jerry flew," said Ralph Martinez. He was pulling on the equipment vest over his g suit, feeling slightly silly about decking himself out in parachute, survival kit, and even a pistol when he was never going to leave the ground.

But the set of rules that he himself had signed into ironbound regulations required that all pilots and/or crew members must wear exactly the same equipment for each simulation as they would in an actual flight mission. The only exception was that on this simulation mission Martinez also wore a fine mesh data net of microminiaturized medical sensors next to his skin, beneath his flight suit. Without puncturing his skin, the sensor net would monitor his physical condition moment by moment throughout his simulated flight: heartbeat, respiration rate, skin temperature, blood pressure, even the amount of perspiration he was exuding and the galvanic charge on his skin.

So Lt. Col. Martinez stood in front of Dr. Appleton like a twenty-first-century knight, clad in flame-retardant flight coveralls, a g suit of rubberized tubes that looked as if it had been taken from the Michelin Man, parachute pack, and equipment vest that carried everything from a jungle knife to whoopie bags.

"We need a baseline," Appleton said. "We'll get to the mission Jerry flew in a couple days."

Martinez grunted and headed for the locker-room door, trailing dangling wires and tubes that would plug into the cockpit's systems. Appleton followed slightly behind him in his tweed jacket and rumpled slacks.

No smoking was allowed in the hangar, even though there was no aviation fuel or any other flammables stored there. Appleton had not lit his pipe anyway, but now he stuffed it into his jacket's side pocket. Martinez's boots clunked against the concrete floor of the hangar like some Hollywood monster plodding toward its doom.

The technicians were already at their consoles alongside the F-22 cockpit. Accustomed to easy informality during these simulation missions, they did not quite snap to attention as Martinez and Appleton walked up, but they were all on their feet. Appleton knew that it was not him they were scared of, even though he was director of the simulations division. Martinez wormed on his data gloves and accepted the Agile Eye IV helmet from the female tech.

"This the same helmet Jerry wore?" he asked.

The young tech sergeant looked startled. "No, sir," she said. "Uh—his size is a little smaller than yours."

Turning to Appleton, the colonel growled, "I thought everything was supposed to be exactly the same. That means *exactly*."

Appleton raised one hand placatingly while he unconsciously fished for his pipe with the other. "It's all right for this mission, Ralph. By the time we get to the air-to-air combat, we'll have adjusted his old helmet to fit you."

Martinez muttered something under his breath and pulled the helmet on. No one made the slightest smile or even thought about a joke involving head size. To a tech sergeant, lieutenant colonels sometimes seem telepathic.

Ten minutes later Martinez was buckled into the cockpit, oxygen mask covering the bottom half of his face, all the electrical and radio and oxygen lines connected properly. He almost believed that he was really flying. The simulator tilted up and down and slewed around in response to his movements of the side stick and rudder pedals. There were no noticeable g forces, of course, although his suit actually did hiss and squeeze when g forces would have assailed him in a real flight.

This mission was a night bombing raid, using the F-22's speed and stealth to sneak through enemy ground defenses and strike at targets before the enemy even knew an attack was underway. Then the problem was to get out, through all the antiaircraft fire and surface-to-air missiles the bad guys would throw up. No enemy fighters on this mission, but the ground fire would be intense.

Martinez was going through his fence check, the detailed checkout of all the aircraft's systems just before leaving friendly territory and penetrating into enemy airspace. He smiled grimly when he saw that the programmers had left his wingtip lights on: all the stealth technology in the world wasn't worth a damn if you flew with your lights on.

He turned off the running lights. Inside the cockpit the only lights came from the dimly glowing displays on the control panel. Martinez pulled down the visor of his helmet, and for an instant even that dim glow disappeared. Then the visor display lit up and he saw the world around him in the weird greenish glow of the passive infrared display. The bare rocky desert below rolled by swiftly. The night sky was empty of opposing aircraft.

He changed his heading every few seconds, zigzagging toward his target so that even if an enemy radar got a slight glint off his plane it would blink away before they realized they were seeing anything real. Fuel check okay. Bombs armed.

As he neared his first target—a hardened bunker that was supposed to house an enemy communications center—Martinez lifted his visor briefly and manually switched his computer system from navigation mode to weapons-delivery mode. Then he pulled his visor down again. That would be the last manual control change he made until he was well back into friendly airspace.

In the stereo display on the visor he saw the bunker, half buried in sand and camouflaged a desert dun brown. "Target acquisition," he said in a throaty near-whisper. The view changed, showing the bunker far off near the horizon and the yellow dotted line of his approach path leading to it.

He licked his lips. It was only his imagination, he knew, but he thought he could feel his heart pulsing against his ribs. As he nosed the plane into its attack attitude, he noted that his stereo display showed several radar sites, looking like feeble pinkish eyes glowing against the desert sands. If any of them locked onto him, they would turn fire-engine red and a warning voice would alert him. But the radars remained harmless, tracking randomly.

"Open bomb doors." He heard the electric motor whine. The plane shook slightly in the airstream's buffeting. His infrared sensors were picking up parked trucks next to the bunker and an unpaved road that apparently led to a town off beyond his horizon.

Now his stereo display showed crosshairs in one corner, creeping up on the bunker as he flew toward it. "Automatic release," he said. The brilliant thin red line of a laser beam reached out to the exact center of the bunker's roof. The laser actually emitted an invisible infrared beam, but in Martinez's helmet display it looked like a Christmas light. When the crosshairs centered on the spot illuminated by the laser, Martinez heard a *clunk* that represented one bomb being released. The plane's controls bucked in his hands just as they would in a real flight when a two-thousand-pounder is suddenly let go.

He pulled the plane's nose up sharply and banked hard to the right, the safety harness straps cutting into his shoulders. His visor display continued to show the bunker. The smart bomb, guided to the laser-lit spot, smashed directly into the center of the bunker's roof. For an instant nothing happened, then Martinez saw the bunker's doors blow off. Smoke billowed out. The roof fell in and the entire area was smothered with heavy boiling smoke.

Martinez pushed the throttles forward and felt the plane surge higher into the sky. The radars were skewing about wildly now, and a volcano of antiaircraft tracers lit up the night. He was quickly above the small-arms fire, but now there were large-caliber cannon pumping shells up at random, blindly seeking him.

He could feel his blood thundering in his ears now. In the bright helmet display he had to remind himself that for the enemy it was midnight-black out there. They could not see him. They could not even find him with radar.

He saw the whooshing flash of a trio of SAMs lighting off. No active radars on them, or at least none that his display revealed. Probably guided by infrared sensors, looking for the heat from my engines. The stealth design reduced the F-22's infrared signature, but if those missiles were advanced enough to have IR-guided upper stages, one of them might find him in the dark and fly right up his stovepipe.

But they failed to track him. Martinez banked away from the frenzied defenders and their destroyed comm bunker, heading for his next target. This time the defense would know there was a bogie sneaking through their airspace. They'll be firing at a fucking bat if it happens to flap by.

Suddenly his helmet display went black. Martinez felt his breath catch in his throat. Then he heard in his earphones, "MISSION ABORTED. SIMULATION ENDED."

He sank back in his seat and realized he was soaked with sweat. Fucking simulation got me so clanked up I might as well have pissed myself, he snarled inwardly as he slid his visor up. He banged the switch that raised the canopy and was starting to unbuckle his harness when the two junior techs clambered up and began to help him.

"Who the hell aborted the simulation?" Martinez yelled at the chief tech, down by the console. His voice echoed across the big hangar like a roar of doom.

Appleton was still there, standing beside the chief technician. "The program is set to abort automatically, Ralph," he called back, his voice maddeningly calm, "when the pilot's pulse rate hits one-forty."

"That's a goddamned crock of shit!" Martinez pulled himself free of the loosened harness and clambered out of the cockpit past the two young techs.

"It's part of our safety regulations," said Appleton, moving between the colonel and the chief technician.

"Since when?"

Appleton gave him a disappointed look. "Since you insisted on flying the simulation yourself. I don't want you popping an artery in there."

Martinez glared pure fury. "A pilot's pulse rate *always* goes way up during a mission, dammit! What the hell do you think they're doing in there, playing hopscotch?"

"Ralph, it's for your own protection."

"Goddammit, let *me* worry about my own protection! I don't want any artificial cutoffs on the simulation! Understand me?"

Technically, Appleton was the man in charge of all simulations. But he was a civilian, and Martinez was a lieutenant colonel who was enraged at anything that might prevent him from being promoted—or from feeling like a man.

Putting a hand on Martinez's stocky shoulder, Appleton suggested mildly, "Let's take a break, Ralph. It's almost dinnertime. We ought to discuss this calmly and—"

"No break," Martinez snapped. "And no automatic cutoffs. Got that?" He turned on the chief technician. "Crank it up again. And take that stupid pulse-rate cutoff out of the loop."

The chief technician was a civilian. His two assistants were Air Force noncoms. The chief looked to Appleton.

Reluctantly, Appleton said, "Set it up for the same mission profile—without the medical subroutine."

Then he turned back to the colonel. "But let's take a break anyway, Ralph. You need to cool down and they need some time to refigure the program."

CHAPTER 20

t was at the end of the normal working day when Muncrief phoned Dan to tell him that "this guy from Washington" was here. Dan put aside his work on the stuttering program and headed for Muncrief's office, his mind in a turmoil, wondering what this special job was all about and why he was going to have to spend his nights and weekends working on it when he should be putting every moment into the stuttering program.

And in the back of his mind he still felt that he was letting Dr. Appleton down. I should have at least phoned him, he thought.

People were already coming down the corridor, heading for the parking lot out back and evenings of relaxation at home or restaurants or entertainment. But the red light was blinking over the door to Wonderland; Jace was in there fooling around with something.

"How do, Dr. Dan!"

Startled, Dan saw Joe Rucker lumbering down the corridor toward him.

"Joe," he said. "On your way home?"

The one-armed guard was in his street clothes, a checkered shirt and faded jeans.

"Nope. Gonna play another game or two with ol' Jace," said Rucker cheerfully. "We play jes 'bout every night."

"You do?"

"Surely do." Rucker's lopsided grin showed all his uneven teeth. "Why, inside that-there game Jace rigs fer me, I got two whole arms and two whole legs! We play till I'm plumb tuckered out."

Dan did not quite know how to respond. "Well," he said weakly, "have a good time."

"You bet!"

Rucker opened the heavy steel door with his one hand while Dan hurried up the corridor, guiltily hoping that Joe would not mention to Jace that he had bumped into him.

Dan was surprised to see Muncrief alone in his office with the stranger. Somehow he had expected Vickie would be in on this, as she was on everything else. But she was not there. Only Muncrief standing behind his desk as if it were a defensive barricade, and the man from Washington, also on his feet in the middle of the room.

He introduced himself as Quentin Smith. "I know Mr. Muncrief here doesn't believe it, but that's my name, so help me." Smith raised his right hand as if taking an oath.

Dan saw that Smith was about his own height, but much more solid in his build. Sandy-blond hair, conservative gray suit and dark tie, broad shoulders: he reminded Dan of the kind of actor who always plays FBI agents. Smith looked young, and he was smiling pleasantly. But his blue eyes were hard as agate. He had a blocky square-jawed face with a silly little button nose in the middle of it. There was an air of tension about him, an aura almost electrical, as if he were ready to spring at the slightest stimulus.

Muncrief ushered them to his round conference table and took the seat in the corner for himself, his back to the wall.

"Mr. Muncrief was good enough to send me your personnel file," Smith said to Dan, "so I know your professional qualifications."

Dan twitched inside but said nothing.

"What we're trying to do," he went on, "is extremely important. It's got to be done quickly, but it's got to be done right. The first time. We don't have time for screwing around."

Dan glanced at Muncrief. His normally affable face was radiating something close to anger. He doesn't like this guy, Dan realized. He doesn't like him *a lot*. So why is he helping him?

"What's the job entail?" Dan asked. "And why does it have to be so quickly?"

Smith smiled tightly. "The schedule is fixed. There's nothing I can do about that."

"Why? What's this for?"

Instead of answering, Smith said, "We need a VR system that can show various scenarios. Instead of reading a report or watching a video, I want a VR system that will allow the user to manipulate a scenario; make changes in it and see how they work out. Can you do that?"

"Within limits," Dan said.

"What limits?"

Glancing again at Muncrief, Dan replied, "That depends on how complex your scenarios are and how much time we have to develop the system."

"It's got to be ready by February first."

"I know."

"That's a solid date," said Smith. "If you can't have it done by then, tell me now and I'll go elsewhere."

"There isn't anyplace else," Muncrief said in a low rumble.

"There's Chapel Hill. And MIT."

"Universities," Muncrief snorted. "You'd get along *swell* with university types, wouldn't you?"

"NASA and the Air Force have been heavily involved," Smith countered.

"Then why didn't you go to them in the first place? Or Silicon Valley, for that matter?"

Smith let his teeth show. "Look, we're here," he said. "We need to have this job done by February first." Turning to Dan, "Can you do it?"

"I've got to know the size of the job," Dan answered. "It all depends on how complex these scenarios are; how complex a simulation you need."

The man from Washington looked into Dan's eyes for a long moment. Then he turned in his chair to face Muncrief. "We don't need you in on this. The fewer people who know the details, the better."

Muncrief threw up his hands. "Fine by me! I've got plenty of other things to do with my time, believe me."

"Why don't we go down to my office, then," Dan suggested.

They walked down the emptied, half-darkened corridors, past Wonderland where the red light still blinked steadily, their footsteps echoing off the silent walls. Dan gestured Smith through his office doorway, then stepped in himself and closed the door softly behind him.

Smith looked around the neatly kept little office and took a flat oblong black box from his inside jacket pocket. He swept it through the air, along the desktop and phone console, across the bookshelves as if he were dusting them with a hand-size vacuum cleaner.

"You think the room's bugged?" Dan asked.

"It's all right, it's not." Smith took the plastic chair in front of the desk. "But you never know."

Dan felt relieved as he went behind his desk and sat in the swivel chair. "You're doing a good job of making me curious as hell," he said. "Now just what is this all about?"

Smith seemed to relax half an inch. "People in high places have to make important decisions. Those decisions are based on the information they receive from their staffs. But the information gets more complex every year, and the time scale gets shorter, too. They've got to make their decisions *quick*, and they've got to be the right decisions, too. If you can produce a VR system that helps certain people make better decisions—well, you'll have done your nation an important service."

"People in high places," Dan echoed.

Smith leaned forward in his chair and laid one powerful arm on the edge of the desk. "Get this, Santorini: *the quality of the decision can only be as good as the quality of the information input.* Understand that? When a man has to make a decision about going to war in the Middle East, he has to juggle a thousand factors: the price of oil, the reaction of ethnic groups here at home, the readiness of the armed services, the number of bases available in the proposed area of conflict, the reaction of our allies, the possibilities of other nations joining the country we're going to fight, the United Nations, the international banking system—a thousand other details. He's got to make a decision *fast,* and he's got to consider all those interacting factors."

"This is for the President, then," Dan guessed. "You're working for the President of the United States."

Smith actually laughed. He leaned back in his chair and broke into a sharp barking laughter. Dan thought of a hyena.

"What's so funny?"

Smith shook his head and pulled out a Kleenex to dab at his eyes. "I'm sorry. I shouldn't laugh at you. People who aren't in the loop always think that the President makes all the big decisions."

"He doesn't?"

"Oh, sure, of course he does." Smith's face went sober again. "He makes the ultimate decision. But by the time a problem gets to the Oval Office, a lot of other people have worked it over. They make their decisions before the President ever sees the problem."

Dan thought that over for a moment. "You're saying that the President's just a puppet? His staff people make all the real decisions?"

"Hell no! Nothing like that! The Man in the Oval Office makes all the final decisions, that's for sure. Most of the time the staff's split seventeen different ways on any really tough issue, and the Man has to decide which way to go."

"So you want a VR system that can show certain scenarios—"

"And play them out to their logical end," Smith said. "We want to use VR to show the user what will happen if certain kinds of decisions are taken."

"Give me an example," Dan said, feeling an old thrill of excitement edging up his spine.

Smith looked excited, too. He had dropped his suspicious, cloak-and-dagger attitude. Dan wondered if Smith was some kind of engineer or technician. Maybe he's from the President's scientific staff, Dan surmised.

"Okay," Smith said, "let's go back to the example of a war in the Middle East. We do a VR scenario that shows what will happen if we don't go to war; just let things happen without us getting involved. That leads to one conclusion. We see what happens to the price of oil. What happens to Israel, to Saudi Arabia, to the Moslem Republics on Russia's southern flank. All that kind of stuff."

Dan nodded.

"Then we can run another scenario that shows what would happen if we went to war, but all by ourselves. Without any allies, not even Israel. How we fight the war. How many casualties. All the factors I mentioned in the first scenario, of course. We can change our military tactics, see which approach works best. Then we see how it would go if we went in with allies, or under a UN authorization—you get the picture now?"

"Yeah. But I see a problem."

"Problem?"

"GIGO."

Smith's face went hard again. "Garbage in, garbage out."

"Right," said Dan. "These scenarios will only be as good as the data that's fed into them. A VR system isn't a magic wand. Just because you experience a certain scenario in a virtual-reality simulation doesn't mean that the scenario is any better or more accurate or apt to turn out right in the real world."

"That's my problem, not yours," Smith said tightly. "All you've got to worry about is making the system work. I'll provide the inputs."

"The garbage?" Dan joked.

Smith did not laugh.

"It's going to be a pretty big job, then," Dan said.

Smith leaned back in the creaking plastic chair. "Yeah, I know. We've got a lot of work to do between now and February first."

"We?"

"We," he said with a sigh. "I'm stuck here in this tropical paradise until the job is finished."

"You're staying in Orlando?"

The man looked decidedly unhappy. "For the duration. Dammit."

When Dan finally arrived home that evening, the kids had already had their dinner. He gave Philip his nightly bath in the sink of the second bathroom while Angela watched, already in her pajamas. The baby splashed them both with warm sudsy water.

"How's it going with you, Angel?" Dan asked his daughter as he toweled off the baby.

"Okay," she said.

"Everything all right in school?"

"I guess."

Dan sighed inwardly. Angela either babbled so much he could not stop her, or she was as incommunicative as a clam. There did not seem to be any in-between with her these days. And she's not even a teenager yet, he told himself.

Finally Dan settled onto the living-room sofa with Susan, both children tucked safely in their beds. The local weather channel was showing a special about the continuing drought. Dan saw that the water district was imposing limits on watering lawns and washing cars.

"I don't care what Vickie says," Susan muttered, frowning, "there's something weird going on with those VR games."

Dan had been waiting to tell her about Muncrief's "special" job. He felt his own brows knitting.

"Not that again," he grumbled.

"Vickie keeps saying there's nothing wrong, but Angie says she's seeing people she knows in those games. This afternoon it was Phil—he was in a game she was playing about baby-sitting."

"I think Angie's just very impressionable," Dan said. "Maybe too impressionable."

Susan shook her head.

"Maybe we should just tell her teacher not to let her play any of the games."

"And what will she do when all the other kids are playing games?" Susan snapped.

Dan shrugged. "She could read a book, I guess. Wouldn't hurt her."

"She'd be the class oddball."

"She could still use the teaching programs. They haven't bothered her any, have they?"

"No, apparently not."

"It's just the games, then. She gets wrapped up in them too much."

Susan shook her head stubbornly. "It's not Angie. It's the games themselves."

"But none of the other kids have had a problem with them."

Susan did not reply. Dan studied her face. He saw doubt there, worry, and a simmering anger. Time to change the subject, he thought.

Forcing a grin, he said, "I've got good news and bad news."

Susan's eyes lit up. "Give me the good news first!"

"I have a consulting contract for you in my briefcase. You'll get a minimum of thirty days over the next twelve months, guaranteed."

"Great!" She clapped her hands. Then, "At what fee?"

"You're supposed to phone Vickie tomorrow and settle the fee with her."

"Oh."

He saw the disappointment darkening her face. "What's the matter? Don't you like Vickie?"

Looking troubled, Susan replied, "I don't know. She seems— cold. Maybe it's because I've been bugging her about Angie's reaction to the games, but I get the feeling she doesn't really like me. At all."

Dan had gotten the same feeling, although he had never thought of Vickie as cold.

"She's okay," he said. "She didn't give me any trouble over giving you a contract. Give her a call and work out your fee."

But Susan looked dubious. "That's the good news?"

He nodded. "The bad news is that Muncrief's got a super special job he wants me to do, and I'll have to work overtime on it because I can't take the time away from the work I'm doing with Jace."

"Overtime?"

"Nights," Dan said. Then he added weakly, "Weekends, too, I guess."

"Nights *and* weekends." Susan frowned. "Dan, you're already working fifty or sixty hours a week. You're not sleeping well, either. You've been grinding your teeth every night for the past several weeks."

"At least I haven't had another asthma attack," he countered weakly.

"Are you still having nightmares?"

"No," he half-lied. His dreams were disturbing, frightening, but he had willed himself to forget them when he woke up. All he recalled was a vague feeling of dread, a kind of terror buried so deeply in his subconscious that he barely recognized it. But he knew it was there, like the asthma, always lurking and ready to pounce on him.

Susan asked, "Will Jace be working nights and weekends, too?"

"Jace always works nights and weekends. But he won't be working on this project."

"He won't?"

"Too hush-hush. I'm supposed to do it completely alone and not tell anybody about it, not even you."

Strangely, Susan almost smiled. "You mean Kyle has asked you to do a special job by yourself? Without Jace?"

"Yeah."

She seemed actually happy about it. "He's recognizing your value, Dan! He knows you're reliable; he knows you'll get the job done for him, whatever it is."

"At night and over weekends," he reminded her.

"How long will it take?"

"Got to be done by February first."

"Ten weeks."

"Ten weekends," he said, thinking, The rest of the football season, right through the goddamned Super Bowl.

"Yes, but it'll be *your* job. Your accomplishment."

"I guess."

Susan hopped off the sofa and headed toward the kitchen. "Well, I'm going to make some fresh coffee!" she announced cheerfully. "Want a cup?"

"Okay," he called after her, baffled by her sudden chipper attitude.

As he sat alone in the living room, sniffing the aroma of perking coffee, Dan wondered how his wife's mind worked. To her it's more important that Muncrief respects me than my being home weekends. But Angie needs me, the kid needs her father. Sue's drummed that home often enough. Maybe if I spent more time at home, Angie wouldn't have so many problems.

He shook his head. I guess I just don't understand her priorities, he told himself.

Even though he was smiling as usual, Luke Peterson was unhappy and sweating inside the stuffy phone booth. He could feel his shirt sticking damply to his back as he said into the phone,

"ParaReality's in real trouble, financially. There's even talk that Muncrief's backers are going to make a deal with Disney or maybe a Japanese outfit."

The Inquisitor asked, "Did the Kessel woman tell you that?"

"Not in so many words. She's very cagey about what she tells me. But that's the sense I make of it."

"Yes, that is what I have heard, as well."

Peterson felt relieved. The Inquisitor was working for a European consortium of corporations that wanted ParaReality stopped. They must be thinking about buying out Muncrief's investors. If that was in the wind, then he wouldn't have to pressure Vickie or Santorini.

But the Inquisitor said, "Do you think you could get Santorini to spend a weekend with us?"

"What?"

"I have come to the conclusion that I would like to tap Santorini's brain for forty-eight hours or so. To find out what he knows about their technical accomplishments."

"But I thought your people are going to buy out Muncrief's investors."

He could sense the Inquisitor's chilling smile. "Why buy what you can steal?"

"You want Santorini? He won't come willingly; he's got a very strong sense of loyalty, from all I've been able to find out about him. Why not try the other one, Lowrey? He's the really creative one."

"No," said the Inquisitor. "Lowrey is *too* creative. He wouldn't cooperate, and there's no telling what he would do under drugs or physical pressure. Santorini has a wife and family to think of. He'll be much more amenable to talking to me."

"I don't like it. Why don't we use the Kessel woman to—"

"Forget the woman. And you don't have to like it. The money will be worth the risk, I guarantee it. Deliver Santorini to me and you can retire for life."

Peterson hesitated, uncertain of what to say.

"Deliver Santorini to me," the Inquisitor repeated. Peterson heard the unvoiced "or else" in his coldly menacing tone.

CHAPTER 21

Saturday morning. Ralph Martinez snapped awake and sat bolt upright in bed. The digital clock on the TV said 7:07.

"What is it?" Dorothy mumbled sleepily.

"Got to get up."

He felt his wife's warm hand slide across his thigh, reaching for his groin.

"Feels like you're already up," Dorothy said. Even in the shadows of the curtained bedroom he could see her smile.

"Got to get to the base."

"It's Saturday!"

"The Doc's people screwed up the simulator yesterday so bad we couldn't fly the mission. We're going to do it this morning."

"On Saturday?"

He knew he should be getting out of bed, but he had not budged since Dorothy's hand had closed around his penis. "Yes," he said with a sad sigh, "on Saturday."

"What time is the mission scheduled for?"

"Nine sharp."

Dorothy raised her head slightly and squinted at the TV clock. "You've got plenty of time, *querido*."

Martinez leaned across and pulled the covers from his wife's naked body. "Yes," he murmured, smiling at her beauty, "you're right."

By 8:45, Martinez was striding across the concrete floor of the simulator hangar, decked out in flight coveralls, g suit, equipment vest, sidearm, and parachute. Appleton and the three technicians stood by the F-22 cockpit, waiting for him. The one item of equipment that the lieutenant colonel had not put on was the medical sensor net.

The real reason that they had not run his mission the day before was that Martinez and the usually soft-spoken Appleton had gotten themselves into a knock-down battle over the medical sensors. Martinez had refused to wear the net. Appleton had refused to run the mission without his wearing it.

"It's for your own safety," Appleton had insisted.

"Fuck it!" Martinez had snapped. "I'm not going to let a pack of transistors terminate my mission again. We've already lost damned near the whole week."

They were in the locker room, but already their voices were loud enough for the techs outside to hear.

"But, Ralph, you wrote those safety regs yourself!"

"The hell I did! You and those clowns in the medical staff wrote them and then you got me to sign off on it."

"They are the rules by which we run these simulations," Appleton shouted. "You can't scratch them out just because you feel like it."

"I'm in charge of this group, and I'll do whatever the hell I think is necessary!"

"I won't permit it!"

"You don't have the authority to override me!" Martinez had roared. "You're just a goddamned civilian! I'm the one who's putting his ass on the line."

"That's exactly my point, Ralph." Appleton's voice lowered a bit; he tried to placate his angry friend and colleague. "You're taking a medical risk. We need the sensors to warn us if you're getting into real trouble."

"Bullshit! What trouble can I get into in a fucking simulation?"

Appleton sighed and almost whispered, "You know as well as I do, Ralph. Your blood pressure. Jerry died of a stroke in there. You're in much greater danger of a stroke than Jerry ever was."

They talked around the subject for another two hours, Martinez insisting and Appleton just as stubbornly refusing. But at least they were talking, not screaming at one another. In the end, Appleton bent to the lieutenant colonel's inflexible will. Martinez dictated and signed a memorandum stating that he was overriding the medical regulations for this one simulation in the interests of testing the program to its fullest capacity.

"Test to destruction," he muttered grimly as he signed the memo in Appleton's office. Doc knew what he meant: to find the absolute limits of a piece of equipment, you tested it with more and more strain on it until it finally shattered. Then you knew how far you could push it in the real world.

"We're talking about people in these tests," he reminded Martinez.

"I know it," said the colonel.

"Your life."

"I know!"

Now, as Martinez strode toward the simulator, Appleton looked embarrassed, sorrowful, worried. The technicians managed to busy themselves with their consoles so they would not have to look at either one of the men.

"I'm ready," Martinez said.

Appleton, fiddling with his unlit pipe, asked, "You're sure you want to go ahead with this, Ralph?"

"Yep. One hundred percent."

Appleton put the pipe in his mouth and clamped his teeth hard on it. "All right, then. Let's get it over with."

Martinez climbed up and swung one leg over the sill of the cockpit like a cowboy mounting his horse. He settled down in the seat as the male corporal climbed up after him and handed him the data gloves and helmet.

"This Jerry's helmet?" Martinez called down.

Appleton turned to the chief technician, who nodded. "Yes," he shouted up to the pilot. "We adjusted it for your head size."

Martinez pulled the helmet over his close-cropped hair, keeping the visor up. It felt snug to him, but not uncomfortably so. He put on the gloves, then wiggled his fingers inside them as the two young techs checked all the connections between his equipment and the cockpit: gloves and helmet lines, electricity for his g suit, oxygen, radio.

The female tech sergeant gave him a thumbs-up. "All plugged in, sir."

Martinez nodded. "Clear the aircraft."

They clambered down to the hangar floor as he leaned on the button that closed the canopy. Its little electrical motor whined and the plastic teardrop settled over the cockpit, closing Martinez into an opaque gray world separated from everyone and everything else outside his cockpit.

He went through the engine start-up and taxied to the runway, the sound effects and vibrations of the simulator as realistic as they could be. In his earphones Martinez heard the crackling instructions of the nonexistent traffic controllers. He set his flaps and ran the throttles up to full takeoff power. The simulator roared and shook nicely.

Pulling the helmet visor down in front of his eyes, Martinez saw the runway stretching out ahead of him.

"Flight oh-oh-one," said the controller's electronic voice, "cleared for takeoff."

"Rog."

His hands moved automatically. The runway slid past, and Martinez saw the ground fall away below him as he arrowed the F-22 into the sky.

This was a daylight mission and there would be enemy fighters meeting him, he knew. Stealth was not as important for this mission as speed, maneuverability, and the pilot's skill at air-to-air fighting. Martinez licked his lips in anticipation. He felt almost like a kid going into an ice-cream parlor with a blank check. I can't lose, he told himself. I'll knock down anything they throw against me, and even if they get me, it's only a sim. Even if I crash and burn, I'll just get up and walk out and have lunch with Doc.

He laughed to himself. How in the hell could he have thought even for an instant that a piece of cake like this might give Jerry a stroke? Bullshit.

He went through his fence check as he approached the line that marked the border of enemy airspace. All systems working smoothly except for the radio, which was being jammed. No matter. He was a lone eagle on this mission, and he was supposed to maintain radio silence anyway.

That is why he felt a distinct shock of surprise when a voice said in his earphones, "A pair of bandits, Daddy. Five o'clock high."

Ralph Martinez was startled by the little girl's voice. Then he remembered Doc telling him they were going to experiment with using familiar voices to warn the pilot of emergencies, rather than warning buzzers or flashing lights or even a computer-synthesized voice. That was Jerry's daughter, Martinez realized. How in hell did Doc get her voice on tape?

Even as he wondered about that, he pulled back on the pistol-grip side stick and felt his fighter tilt upward into a steep climb. Strangely, his arm felt heavy as the plane nosed upward, almost as if he were really experiencing the g forces that an actual maneuver would put him through. It's just your imagination, he told himself. Damned simulation's so good, your mind is filling in the missing details. Still, both his arms felt heavy and his g suit was hissing air pressure against his midsection and thighs.

With his thumb he nudged the throttles on the knob of the control stick, and he felt himself pushed deeper into his padded seat from the increasing acceleration. He knew it was actually the seat deflating, but damn! it felt real. Even his neck was feeling the g forces now; the helmet felt heavy on his head.

He called for a panoramic view. His Agile Eye IV helmet visor lit up and he saw his own fighter as a bright yellow swept-wing symbol in the center of the universe, its nose aimed at the sky. Sure enough, a pair of red symbols were moving in swiftly after him, but far behind him. Nothing else in the area. No radar locks, no missiles launched. Not yet. The ground was a rolling green carpet far below, like a cartoon or a kid's drawing, with his potential targets drawn in with big red X's painted over them.

The g suit was squeezing his guts just as if he were really flying. Got to hand it to Doc and his brain boys. Physical reactions just like the real thing. Almost.

The two bogies were diving down toward him, Martinez saw. He kicked left rudder and leveled off, hoping they would over-shoot him; then he would slip behind them and fire his Sidewinders at the bastards. He was surprised at how much effort it took to reach the missile-arming switches and flick them on. We ought to put that on vocal command, along with everything else, Martinez told himself. Too much effort at this g loading to reach over and hit the switches physically.

He realized he was panting. A small deadly black cross appeared on his helmet display. If it touched the symbol of either one of the intruder aircraft, one of his missiles would launch automatically.

But the bogies were not going to overshoot him, he saw. They were slowing down, popping their air brakes to begin a high-speed yo-yo that would plant them on his tail. Cursing, puffing from exertion as if he were really flying, Martinez thumbed the throttle control forward to full military power and pulled the stick back, trying to put as much distance between them and himself as he could while he clawed for altitude. The intruders immediately broke off their maneuver and hustled after him.

"They're closing in, Daddy," Adair's daughter's voice warned, edging higher, sounding frightened.

Martinez scanned the view rastering across his visor. The two red bogies sure did seem closer.

"Range coordinates," he said, barely mouthing the words. The microphone in his oxygen mask caught the vocalization, and immediately the picture before his eyes was crisscrossed with a gridwork marked in kilometers. Even as he blinked his eyes, the red bandits came nearer.

Martinez was alone in the sky except for the enemy fighters; he knew he would get no help. And he was a fighter pilot. His first instinct was to deal with the bandits. The ground targets won't go away, he told himself. No sense getting myself shot down before I can even start my run on them.

He kicked right rudder and turned into the bandits, who were still slightly above him. Coming at them head-on, he presented a smaller cross section to their fire-control radars and masked the heat emissions from his jet engines somewhat.

Abruptly the two red bandits multiplied into four, two of them breaking off to Martinez's right, two to the left.

"What the hell?"

No response from the controllers at their consoles.

Martinez began to realize that this simulation was really strenuous. Doc and his people had loaded the dice on this one. He kicked in the thrust vectoring as he pulled his F-22 into a hard climbing left turn. The jet nozzles swiveled to make the climb steeper than the enemy planes could match.

But they did match it. Hell, they must have given the bastards viffing capability, too, Martinez thought as he watched two of the red symbols match his climb almost exactly. His chest hurt now from the continuous exertion, the g forces making his arms heavy, squeezing the breath from his body. His neck ached, and the helmet felt as if it weighed six hundred pounds. It's all your imagination, he snarled at himself. You're sitting in a fucking chair on the ground; you're not really pulling nine g's. Yet he felt sweat beading his forehead, running into his eyes.

Blinking and squinting, he nosed over into a split-S, but instead of completing it he turned it into a vertical dive. Two of the red bogies followed right down after him, gaining on him. The other two had disappeared from his visor's panoramic view. Martinez pulled up sharply, his g suit hissing and squeezing his guts to keep him from blacking out.

He was blasting along on the deck, only a few feet above the cartoon drawing of the ground, his Mach meter jittering at Mach 1. The plane rattled and jounced, shaking his guts. The two bandits roared along behind him, inching closer.

"Radar lock!" the little girl's voice screeched.

Martinez snapped the F-22 into a turn so tight that his vision grayed out despite the g suit. The bandits stayed fixed on his tail as if they had been painted there.

"Missiles launched!" she shrilled.

He popped a flare, pulled back on the control stick, and slammed the throttles to full emergency power. The overwhelming push of tremendous acceleration crushed in on his chest, flattening him against his seat, making his pulse thunder in his ears. Someone was shoving a red-hot needle behind his eyes; the pain was screamingly intense.

The missiles raced past below him, chasing the bright infrared signature of the decoy flare. He saw their trails as brilliant red pencil lines darting across the green cartoon landscape. *"Gracias a Dios,"* he gasped despite himself.

But then the other two bandits appeared on his visor ahead of him. "Radar lock missiles fired!" Jerry's daughter screamed all in one breath.

Martinez yelled, "Fuck it! Gotta punch out!"

But he could not move. His arms were plastered to their rests as if cemented in place. His chest was aflame with agony. His head felt as if it would explode.

Eyes bursting from their sockets, he watched the two deadly missiles race straight into him and explode into a hellish fireball. He could not even scream. Everything went black. The last thing he sensed was somebody laughing, someone so far away he could barely hear him laughing with evil triumphant glee.

CHAPTER 22

Dan spent all day Saturday digging into the stuttering concept and writing the first few lines of programming to apply the technique to the baseball game. Jace had hovered over his shoulder, constantly reminding him of their bet about using the AI system to debug Dan's program once it was finished.

He went home for a quick dinner, then drove back to the lab in the dark, happy to see that Jace's rusted old bicycle was not at its usual spot on the loading dock. The building was empty and dark, except for the night guard who opened the back door after nearly ten minutes of Dan's leaning on the buzzer.

He felt guilty, sneaking around Jace like this, but he forgot about that once he settled himself at his desk and started working on Smith's project. It wasn't particularly difficult, Dan realized very quickly. It just took a lot of time to set up the program properly. Probably that's why Muncrief asked me to do it, he thought. They don't need a genius, just somebody who knows what he's doing and won't go blabbing about it to anybody.

Dan was startled by the clear lilting song of a bird chirping outside his window. He looked up from his computer screen and saw that the sky was already a pearly gray. Christ, the sun's coming up!

Susan was half awake by the time he got home. He grabbed a couple of hours' sleep, mumbled through a late breakfast with the kids, and drove bleary-eyed back to the office.

Jace's bike was there, he saw. The only other car in the back lot was Joe Rucker's battered old Thunderbird, with the handicapped license plate in its rusting frame. Dan literally tiptoed past Wonderland, wondering what games Jace was playing with Joe in there. He closed the door to his office and buried himself in his work.

Of course, he could not avoid Jace forever. Dan bumped into him at the cafeteria. They were not serving any food on Sunday; Dan had brought a sandwich he had put together for himself while Sue had made breakfast. The coffee and cold-drink dispensers were working, though. So were the junk-food vending machines, which is where he saw Jace, peering at one of the machines as if trying to hypnotize it, his long skinny frame adorned in the usual shabby jeans with a T-shirt hanging loose over his belt, proclaiming on its back *Lead, follow, or get out of the way.*

"I thought that was your car in the parking lot," Jace said, barely glancing at Dan.

"Hi," said Dan, feeling flustered.

"What're you doing in here today?" Jace asked.

"Uh, putting some time into the debugging—"

"Oh? Tryin' to beat the AI system, huh?"

Feeling miserable about lying, Dan admitted, "I'm doing an extra job for Muncrief, actually."

"Yeah? What? Need any help?"

Shaking his head, Dan replied, "No, it's pretty simple, really. Just needs some time put into it."

Jace gripped the vending machine with both hands and jiggled it like a kid working a pinball machine. "So you're working on Sunday?" he asked over his shoulder.

"Yep." Dan headed for one of the tables. They were all empty. Nobody else in the lab, as far as he could tell. No telling where Rucker was; maybe he had left already.

"What about the family?" Jace whacked the machine smartly with one open palm and a bag of chips fell into its tray. He tore it open and started munching on them as he walked to the table.

As he put his lunch bag on the table and pulled out a chair, Dan asked, "Don't you intend to pay for that?"

"Why should I?" Jace looked truly surprised at the question. "Isn't that stealing?"

Jace shrugged. "Think of it as a contest of skill: man against machine."

Dan shook his head in disapproval as he sat down.

"How's your wife feel about this?"

"About what?"

"Working Sunday."

"How can you eat that crap?" Dan tried to evade his interrogation. "It's pure grease."

"I'm on a high-cholesterol diet," Jace said, grinning. He swung a lanky leg over a chair back and sat down. "I thought Sue wanted you home on the weekends. That's what you told me when I asked you to come in a couple Sundays ago, remember?"

"You just wanted company."

"I'm a lonely creative genius," Jace said, only mildly kidding.

"Sure you are."

Jace shrugged and grinned and munched chips, all at the same time.

"I've been thinking," Dan said, trying to get the subject off his working on Sunday.

"That's what you get paid for," Jace mumbled, his mouth full of chips.

"About my symphony-orchestra simulation."

Jace made a sour face.

"No, this is different," said Dan. "I was thinking—what if we put together a system that'd teach kids how to play musical instruments."

Jace's eyebrows rose.

"I mean, do you think we could jigger the data gloves to move the user's fingers? Make the kid's hands play the instrument properly and burn the information into the kid's nervous system that way?"

Jace stared at Dan.

"We'd have to attach servomotors to the gloves, I guess. Like those power-amplified gloves the astronauts use, or the waldoes they use at remote-manipulation labs. I could kludge something like that together and we could see how it works."

"Get a real musician," Jace said, his voice low as if he were talking to himself rather than Dan. "Track the motions his hands make. Track his whole friggin' breathing system, from his diaphragm to his lips, if he's playing a wind instrument—"

"And then play it back to a kid who's learning to play that same instrument. Yeah!"

"Cripes," said Jace, his eyes starting to glow.

"We could start the kid on simple scales and easy things like that, while her nervous system learns the moves she's supposed to make."

"Screw music," Jace snapped. "What about sports? You could train athletes like that! Jesus! We could corner the market for training Olympics teams!"

"You think it's possible?"

"Damn right!"

"It'd be a major change, feeding physical motions *into* the user instead of having the system react to her motions."

Jace's eyes widened slightly, as if he had just thought of something else. His excited grin faded.

Dan went on, oblivious in his growing enthusiasm. "I mean, we could train a user's nervous system instead of just feeding his senses with sensory input. But you think we could do it?"

The look in Jace's narrow eyes had become wary. "I don't know. It's something to think about, I guess."

"It's a whole new approach—"

"Eat your lunch," Jace said. "Don't get yourself into an uproar."

"But this could be even bigger than the games we're doing!"

"Maybe. We gotta finish this friggin' baseball sim before we start anything new, y'know."

"We'll have that locked up in a month or two," Dan said, then added, "If we don't hit any bumps."

"Yeah. Lemme think about it." But Jace's voice, his face, had lost all the eagerness of a few moments earlier.

"I'll tell Muncrief about it. The company can make a fortune out of this."

Jace waggled a bony finger. "Uh-uh. No sense telling Muncrief until we're ready to. He'll just get pissed and think we're not going balls-out on the baseball sim."

"But—"

"Besides"—Jace's sallow face went crafty—"why should we make Muncrief any richer than he's gonna be from Cyber World, huh? With an idea like this, we can walk away and start our own outfit."

Dan stared at his partner. The last thing in the world he had expected from Jace was entrepreneurship.

"But this could be big enough—"

"Forget about it!" Jace snapped. Then he added, "For now, anyway."

Dan felt confused. He had never known Jace to put off a good new idea.

Hunching closer, leaning his scrawny arms on the table, Jace asked, "Okay, so what's so important to Muncrief that you gotta come in on Sunday, huh?"

Wishing he were a thousand miles away, Dan tried to evade his friend's curiosity. "It's nothing important enough to bother you with."

Jace eyed Dan closely. Dan unwrapped the sandwich he had made for himself and took a bite. It was dry and flavorless. Somehow Sue always made better sandwiches, even when they used the same ingredients.

"You're not gonna tell me?" Jace said.

"It's not important. Forget it."

"I wanna know!"

Dan could feel his chest constricting the way it always did when he was under pressure.

"Look," he said, thinking as he spoke, "Muncrief asked me not to bother you with this. He doesn't want you distracted from the baseball game."

"You can just tell me what it is, for chrissakes."

Feeling awful inside, Dan said, "He made me promise not to tell anybody."

"Even me?"

"Even you."

"And you're not gonna tell me?"

"I can't. I promised."

Jace's eyes were blazing. "You're really not gonna tell me?"

Dan said nothing. He just gripped his cardboard sandwich tightly enough to squeeze half the cold-cut slices out of it. They fell with a messy *plop* onto his plastic bag spread out on the table.

Jace grabbed his tattered bag of chips and pushed himself up from his chair. He stalked to the door of the cafeteria, furious.

"Okay, keep your friggin' mouth shut," he shouted from the doorway, his voice echoing off the bare walls and silent counters. "I got secrets, too! Stuff I don't tell you!"

Dan looked down at the shambles of his sandwich.

"I'm doin' a special job for Muncrief, too, y'know," Jace yelled. "That's what's been keepin' me up nights. Weekends, too."

Sure you are, Dan replied silently.

"It'd make your goddamn eyes pop if you knew what Muncrief wanted me to do for him!"

Dan stayed silent.

"And I'm doin' it!" Jace bellowed. Then he spun around and left the cafeteria. Dan could hear his boots clomping down the hallway.

Dan was startled when Gary Chan tapped at the open door to his office later that afternoon.

"What're you doing in here on Sunday?" he asked.

Chan stepped into the office, a happy grin on his face. "Got a minute?" he asked.

Not really, Dan thought, but he felt himself smile back at the younger man as he said, "I guess. How's it going?"

"I think I've got it."

"The Moonwalk sim?"

"Yes. Want to see?"

"Uh, Gary . . . I'm pretty busy here."

"Oh." Chan looked crestfallen. "Sure, I understand. Sorry I bothered you." He retreated toward the door.

"Wait up, Gary," Dan said to him. "I can squeeze a couple minutes in." And he got up from his desk, wondering how much of Chan's politeness and self-effacement was a ploy for maneuvering the people around him.

Five minutes later, the two of them stood side by side on the dusty surface of the Moon.

"It took a lot of calculation," Chan's voice came through earphones in Dan's helmet, "but that program you tipped me about saved me weeks of work."

They were both in space suits, big bulky cumbersome suits with thick-soled boots and clear plastic fishbowl helmets. As they walked across the lunar surface, their boots kicked up dust that fell in dreamlike slow motion back to the ground. Dan could see their boot prints clearly, bright against the dark lunar soil. All around him the barren, crater-pocked emptiness of the Moon stretched off to a horizon that seemed disturbingly close. Worn-down old mountains slumped across the horizon, and beyond them the stars shone with hard, brilliant intensity.

"Okay," Chan's voice said in his earphones, "now try to jump."

Dan nodded. He trotted a couple of steps and then jumped toward a big dark boulder some fifty yards away.

"Holy cow!" Dan soared across the rock-strewn ground as if he were flying and landed, staggering, almost halfway between the boulder and the spot where Chan was still standing.

"How's that?" Chan asked eagerly.

"Terrific!"

Dan jumped back, again gliding across the barren ground. He had time almost to count the tiny craterlets pockmarking the ground before he landed again at Chan's side.

"It works just the way you said it would, Dan. I can't eliminate your inner feeling of weight," Chan said proudly, "but I can make your body behave as if you were really in the Moon's one-sixth gravity."

"This is great, Gary. Simply great!"

"And it's pretty simple to refigure the program for the Mars sim."

"You've done a marvelous job."

"Want to see Mars?"

For a few moments Dan had been able to forget his own work, his own responsibilities. But it all came back to him.

"I'd love to, Gary, but I can't. I'm really loaded with a lot of stuff."

He sensed Chan nodding inside his helmet. "I understand. I just want to thank you, Dan. You've saved my butt. If there's anything I can do for you, anything at all, just let me know."

Dan's only thought was, Just let me get back to my own work, kid.

Thank God it's a new house, Susan said to herself as she tucked the sheets under the mattress. It doesn't need the fixing and painting that our place in Dayton did. Good thing, if Dan's going to be working weekends now. He never was much help with housework, but he did take care of the heavy jobs.

The big chore was shopping. Susan had it all worked out: she would shop for the week on Sundays, when Dan was home to keep an eye on the kids. But now Dan was at the lab seven days a week and she would have to take Angie and little Phil to the supermarket with her. It was not something to look forward to.

She finished the bed and went into Philip's room to start dressing the baby, trying to get socks onto him while the baby was gurgling happily and kicking his feet in the air like a pair of tiny windmills. Ordinarily Susan would have laughed and played with him, but at this particular moment she was feeling harried and exasperated.

Angela came in and sat on the edge of the bed.

"Did you make your bed?" Susan asked.

"Uh-huh." Glumly.

"No smile for me, angel face?"

Angela forced a tight smile.

"What's wrong, sweetheart?"

Angela looked down at Philip, wriggling and grinning with his one tooth.

"Daddy likes Phil better than me," she said.

"He loves you, honey," said Susan.

"He likes Phil better."

"Men get a little silly about their sons, for a while," said Susan. "But Daddy loves you, Angie. You know that."

"I guess."

"Fathers get closer and closer to their daughters as the years go by," Susan said, remembering her own father. "They have fights with their sons, sooner or later."

Angela did not seem mollified at all.

Susan looked at her fair-haired daughter, wondering how much more she could tell her. Maybe Dan does have some ancient Italian thing about his son. Maybe he blames Angie unconsciously for the trouble we had between us when I was carrying her. What can I say? What can I tell her?

The doorbell chimed.

Placing the little cotton sock down on the table next to Philip's crib, Susan asked her daughter, "Angie, could you try to get his socks on?"

As Susan headed for the front door, she realized that she herself was not spending enough time with her daughter these days. Susan promised herself to have a long talk with Angela, a real heart-to-heart to find out how she was doing and how things were going at school. But between her own work and taking care of the baby and Dan's longer and longer days at the lab and the house and everything, she just hadn't gotten around to it yet.

The bell chimed again.

Pushing her vague feelings of guilt away, Susan went to the front door and opened it.

Kyle Muncrief stood there, smiling in a slightly embarrassed way. In a pair of crisply creased slacks and a starched white short-sleeved shirt, he looked like a fashion model.

"Hello, Susan."

"Kyle." Susan stepped back from the door, an invitation for Muncrief to come into the house.

He looked a little flustered, almost embarrassed. "I, uh, thought that since I've . . . well, since I've asked Dan to work weekends for a while . . ." He cleared his throat. "Well, I thought maybe I could offer you whatever help I can give you. Baby-sit or go to the store for you, whatever."

Susan felt flabbergasted. "Why, Kyle, that's awfully nice of you."

"Well, it's my fault your husband's going to be away so much. It's the least I can do."

"I *do* have to do the week's grocery shopping," Susan said, leading him back toward Philip's nursery.

"I could stay with the kids," Muncrief suggested. "I don't know much about babies, though."

"Angie, look who's here," said Susan as they entered the blue-papered nursery.

Angela smiled happily. "Uncle Kyle!"

"Hi, Angie."

Susan said, "Angie, Uncle Kyle's going to stay with you while I do the shopping. You can take care of Phil for an hour or so, can't you, sweetheart?"

Without taking her eyes from Muncrief, Angela said, "I guess."

"I'll set him up in his playpen in the living room," said Susan. "Angie, would you bring some of his toys?"

In ten minutes, the baby was happily batting at a colorful mobile attached to the rim of the playpen. Angela sat on the floor next to her brother while Muncrief sat on the sofa, the TV remote-control box at his side.

"I'll only be an hour or so," Susan said. "Maybe less."

"Take your time," said Muncrief. "We'll be okay here. Right, Angela?"

"Sure!"

Susan hurried out to her Subaru wagon. Angela was capable of minding her brother for an hour or so as long as there was an adult on hand to watch over her. Kyle may not know anything about babies, she told herself, but he'll keep Angie from being frightened at being alone with Phil.

Angela sat on the living-room carpet, watching her baby brother amusing himself, glancing shyly now and then at Uncle Kyle sitting comfortably on the sofa where Daddy usually sat.

"Cat got your tongue?" Muncrief asked, smiling.

"What?"

"That's what you say when the person you're with isn't saying anything," Muncrief explained. "Does the cat have your tongue? That means, aren't you going to talk to me?"

Angela thought that over for a moment, then said, "Can I watch TV?"

"Don't you want to talk to me, Angie?"

"I guess."

"Don't you like me, Angie?"

"Oh, sure."

"Do you like driving to school in my convertible?"

"Uh-huh. But the kids tease me when I don't go with them on the school bus."

"Does that bother you?"

"I saw you leading the orchestra," she said.

"Oh?"

"My father says I was imagining it, but I saw you."

"Maybe it was just because you like me so much that you wanted to see me."

Angela shook her head with the stubborn certainty of youth. "I saw you."

"Have you seen anybody else you know in your VR games?" Muncrief asked.

"Oh, sure. I saw my brother, and some of the other kids from class."

"Did you ever see your mother or father?"

A cold hand gripped Angela's heart. She remembered seeing her father lying in the coffin in the mermaid's city beneath the sea.

"I thought I saw my daddy once," she said uncertainly.

Muncrief heard the quaver in her voice. "Maybe we ought to watch some TV now." Patting the sofa cushion beside him, he said, "Come on up here and sit beside me."

Angela wished that Amanda were with her, instead of on the night table in her bedroom. But she slowly got up and sat on the sofa, at its end, as far from Muncrief as she could get. He picked up the remote unit but did not click the TV on.

"Do you have any boyfriends?" he asked.

Angela shook her head.

"None at all?" Muncrief probed, smiling wider. "I would think a pretty girl like you would have lots of boyfriends."

"Well," she said slowly, "there's Gary Rusic. He's nice. But he's not really my boyfriend."

"I could be your boyfriend, Angela."

Very seriously Angela replied, "But you're too old, Uncle Kyle!"

Muncrief sank back on the sofa and turned on the TV, trying to keep the disappointment he felt out of his flushed face.

Dan was half asleep on the living-room sofa waiting for the eleven-o'clock TV news to get to the weather report. In the back of his groggy mind he thought that the local weather forecasters here in Florida always predicted warm temperatures and plenty of sunshine, no matter what was really on its way.

Susan had told him over supper that Kyle Muncrief had come

over and sat with the kids while she went shopping. Dan said nothing, but thought, That sonofabitch makes me work all day, while he comes over and plays with my kids.

"How is it going?" Susan asked from the armchair on the other side of the end table.

"Not bad," he said. "It's a big job, but it's not all that complex. Nothing new needs inventing; just a lot of work to get done by February first."

"What's so important about February first?" she wondered.

"Damned if I know."

"Who is this man you're dealing with? What do you know about him?"

"Not much," Dan said, yawning. And whatever I find out, I'm not supposed to tell anybody, he added silently. Not even you.

But Susan's question echoed in his mind. What's so important about February first? Smith is from Washington; apparently from the White House itself or someplace damned close to it. Why is February first such an important date to him?

He realized he had missed the weather forecast. The sports guy was blathering about the Dolphins game.

"What'd he say about the weather?"

Susan said, "You were staring right at the screen."

"My mind was someplace else."

"It's going to be fair and warm, plenty of sunshine." Then she grinned mischievously. "If it doesn't rain."

"Thanks a lot."

"What do you care? You're going to be in the lab all day, aren't you?"

He looked at her. She didn't look angry, but her words had a sting behind them.

Before he could say anything, the phone rang.

"Who in hell could be calling at this time of night?" Dan grumbled, swinging his legs off the sofa.

"Jace," Susan guessed.

"One of your customers," he countered as he headed for the kitchen.

"They don't have our home number, and the business phone is on the answering machine. I think. Check it while you're there, will you?" Susan called after him.

Dan picked up the wall phone on its fourth ring.

"Dan, it's Bill Appleton."

He could hear from the Doc's ashen voice that something terrible had happened.

"What is it, Doc?"

"Ralph. He's in intensive care."

"Ralph Martinez?" Dan's voice ran an octave higher than usual.

"Yesterday he flew the same simulation run that Jerry did. And had a massive stroke. His whole left side is paralyzed. He can't even talk. . . ." Appleton's voice choked off.

"Jesus Christ," Dan muttered.

"We need you here, Dan. I need you here. Something's gone haywire with the simulation—"

"I'll be there," Dan said. "Soon as I can get a flight to Dayton."

"I can send a military plane for you."

"Okay. Phone me tomorrow morning with the details."

"Thanks, Dan."

"I'll be there," said Dan.

The line clicked off. Dan hung up the phone on its wall rack, then realized that Susan was standing beside him.

"Ralph Martinez." Dan choked out the words. "He had a stroke. In the simulator."

"But that's not your fault," Susan said. "It's not your problem."

"I've got to go back there tomorrow, try to find out what's wrong."

"No!" Susan snapped, her lips white, her eyes burning. "You're not going back to *that woman*!"

CHAPTER 23

She had hit the simulations lab at Wright-Patterson like a bombshell. Barely twenty, her dark skin exotic, her dazzling smile inviting, Dorothy Aguilera had the men ogling openly and the women whispering to one another over what to do about her.

At first she was considered merely a "twofer": a Hispanic female who accounted for two slots in the Air Force's affirmative-action program. But within a week it became apparent that this young Latina with the thickly tumbling hair of midnight black and the big beautiful eyes was also one of the fastest typists at the lab and a cheerful hard worker who put most of the older secretaries to shame.

She started as an assistant to one of those older women, but before her first month was out Dr. Appleton commandeered her to be his own secretary. The whole lab buzzed with innuendo and off-color jokes. Appleton had never before shown any signs of susceptibility to female charms; everyone at the lab had met his wife at the parties that the Appletons gave at Christmas, and they assumed that Doc and his matronly wife were happily married. Which they were.

It quickly became clear that Appleton took Dorothy under his wing more as a foster father than a potential seducer. He wanted to protect her from the leering men who just happened to be going past her desk each day and stopped to chat or invite her out for a drink after work or ask her if she enjoyed boating on the weekends.

The buzz around the lab subtly shifted. The question got to be: How innocent is Dorothy? She seemed to smile and be pleasant to everyone, yet as far as the rumor mill could determine no one had laid a hand on her. Partly, of course, that was Doc's doing. It was difficult to make time with her when the boss was watching you through the open doorway of his office.

And although she behaved like a very proper young lady, she dressed in skintight miniskirts that drove the men to flights of fantasy. Dorothy had the kind of full-busted, long-legged figure that turns women green and gives men a fever.

She dated a couple of the men from the lab occasionally, but they had nothing to report back to their buddies except a pleasant dinner and maybe a dance or two with a charming, beautiful young lady who smiled her goodnight at the front steps of her apartment building.

"She's a female Nolan Ryan," grumbled one of her disappointed swains. "She keeps throwing shutouts."

"No-hitters," said the guy he was talking to. Wistfully.

Ralph Martinez was still a major in those days, unmarried but a veteran of much more than aerial combat. His first impression of Dorothy was that she was very young, very beautiful, and very lucky that Doc was the kind of fatherly man he was. Major Martinez also thought that it was a good thing that such an attractive Hispanic woman was also a good worker. The Anglos always thought that Latin American women were sluts, he knew. At least Dorothy can show them otherwise. And make them drool in their disappointment.

Dan Santorini had been working at the lab for more than five years at that point, the last two of them with Jace Lowrey. Dan and Susan had married a year earlier, and Sue was pregnant. She spent a lot of her time at her parents' home, comfortably surrounded by her three sisters and her beaming mother, who anticipated the baby even more than Susan did, if that was possible.

Dan's in-laws lived in Xenia, nearly an hour's drive from Wright-Patterson when the traffic was heavy or the weather bad, and even farther from their own home near Vandalia. Dan found himself resenting the extra distance when he had to drive there at night after work. He knew Sue was a little frightened of what was happening inside her; the pregnancy was not without its problems, especially in the first couple of months. It was pretty much of a mystery to Dan, though. Sue did not feel well, that was clear enough to see. It was more than morning sickness. She would phone her mother whenever she felt the slightest twinge, and her mother would drive over and take Sue back home with her. Usually Dan would get a phone call at the lab to tell him to drive to his in-laws after work. As often as not, the call came from his mother-in-law rather than Sue.

It happened on a raw sleety night as he headed out for his car, bent over against the cutting wind, clutching his hat to his head with one gloved hand and fumbling in his pants pocket for the car keys. Humps of graying snow were piled beneath the light standards; Dan could see the cold sleet slanting in their feeble lights. The parking lot was almost empty; Dan had worked more than an hour after their nominal quitting time. Jace, with no transportation except his rusty bicycle, had decided to stay at work until the sleet let up.

"Or until the snow melts, whichever comes first," Jace had said.

Wondering if Jace actually would spend the whole night at the lab, grumbling to himself that he was going to have to drive all the way to his in-laws' and probably end up sleeping on their damned stiff sofa in their stuffy old living room, Dan noticed that somebody in a long belted coat had the hood up on his car and was peering at its engine in the shadowy darkness.

"Need a jump?" he called out as he approached the figure.

She turned, and he saw that it was Dorothy.

"It won't start," she said forlornly.

The first thought to pop into Dan's head was an old joke about Hispanics and the wrecks they drove. He came up beside Dorothy and looked at the engine, as if that would help.

"Try it again," he said. "If it's the battery, I've got jumper cables."

It was not the battery. Dan spent half an hour in the cold wet wind, his ears going numb, the sleet driving into his face. Dorothy's car was dead, and whatever the cause was he could neither find it nor fix it.

"Come on," he said, rubbing his hands together. Despite the gloves, his fingers were starting to tingle. "I'll drive you home."

"Just leave the car here?"

"Nobody's going to steal it on a night like this, and nobody's going to come out to fix it."

She looked doubtful.

"Come on," Dan insisted. "Hell, even if somebody does want to steal it, he'll have to get it started first."

Dorothy broke into a smile. "Yes," she admitted. "That's true, isn't it?"

So she got into Dan's Taurus and gave him directions to her apartment building. The car's heater did not really warm up until he was pulling onto her driveway, yet he could still smell her perfume despite the wet clamminess of their soaked overcoats.

She thanked him, and he watched from the car until she was safely inside the building's glass front door. Then he drove to his in-laws', narrowly missing a head-on collision with some jerk who skidded on the ice because he was driving too damned fast.

Dan did not see Dorothy the next day. Or the one after that. Somehow his work kept him busy out in the hangar or in Jace's rat's nest of an office, far from the quieter and more orderly corridors where the senior staff people and Dr. Appleton's offices were.

She came to see him. Late one morning as he was unpacking the lunch he had brought with him, Dorothy appeared at Dan's office door. She was wearing blue slacks and a gold turtleneck sweater, completely covered from throat to toes. Yet she looked as sexy as a swimsuit model to Dan.

"I wanted to thank you again," she said, smiling brilliantly.

Startled to see her, Dan managed a weak "Uh, it's nothing."

"The car was still there the next day. Nobody stole it."

"What was wrong with it?"

She shrugged, and on her it was a provocation. "The man from the garage said something about a distributor?"

Dan nodded.

"You're eating lunch in? Not at the cafeteria?"

He nodded again.

"Well, thanks again. I really appreciate it. You were my knight in shining armor."

Before he could reply, she left. He sat there thinking that his two-door Taurus, stained and streaked by road mud and highway salt, hardly looked like the steed of a knight in shining armor. Then he realized that his hands were trembling.

The following week, he happened to see her at the cafeteria and sat at the same table with her. Within a few days he had stopped making lunches for himself. No matter how busy he was with Jace, he always took a lunch break. As often as not, Dorothy was there at the cafeteria. She always sat with him.

"Do you want me to make you lunch?" Susan asked him when she finally noticed that he had stopped making his own.

"Uh, no. That's okay. I'll just grab something at the cafeteria." And inwardly he grinned at his double entendre. He wished he could grab Dorothy, even though he knew he would never try.

"I can fix a sandwich for you," Susan insisted. "I'm not completely helpless."

She was getting round, and instead of going to her mother's, her mother had started staying over with them. Like having a live-in nurse, Susan had told Dan. Like having your mother-in-law living with you, Dan had silently retorted.

It was probably not inevitable, but it happened anyway. Susan had gone to the doctor's for another checkup, accompanied by her mother. Late in the afternoon, Sue called and left word that Dan should pick her up at her mother's home. She left the message with Dr. Appleton's secretary.

Dorothy went down to the cold, drafty hangar where Dan and Jace were shoehorning a bulky gray electronics console into the equipment rack already crammed along the catwalk above the hangar floor. Down on the floor, Major Martinez was supervising a crew of mechanics in blue Air Force fatigues, driving them like a mule skinner whipping his team up a steep hill. A big flatbed truck was slowly backing into the hangar, the sawed-off cockpit of an F-22 jet fighter lashed down on its back. It was a brilliant winter day outside, but the wind cut like a saber.

"Maybe Ralph'll freeze his balls off," Jace muttered. "Or better yet, maybe they'll turn Air Force blue. That'd be poetic, huh?"

Dan had had the foresight to wear a sweater under his tweed jacket; still, his hands hurt from the cold. Jace had a thin leather windbreaker over his inevitable T-shirt.

Then he saw Dorothy running into the hangar, arms bundled around her, hair blowing in the wind, long legs covered by nothing more than a chocolate leather miniskirt and sheer stockings. He noticed that her shoes were flat comfortable black sneakers, incongruous against the rest of her outfit.

By the time she had climbed the stairs to the catwalk, her teeth were chattering. She handed Dan his message; she had written it on a pink telephone message slip.

Dan felt his jaw tighten. Sue's off at her mother's again. He did not know why it made him angry. Mother Emerson was as kind and generous as she could be. He had nothing to complain about, really. Except that he wanted his wife home, with him, in the home he made for her, not running off to her mother every couple of days.

Then he saw that Dorothy was shivering.

"Here, take this." Dan pulled off his jacket and slipped it over her trembling shoulders.

"What about you? Won't you freeze up here?"

"I'll be okay," he said.

"But—"

"Go on," he told her. "Go back to your office where the sane people work. I'll pick up the jacket when I'm finished here."

She looked doubtful, but she said, "Thank you," and hurried back toward the warmth of the heated office building with Dan's jacket bundled around her.

Jace watched her go, then turned back to Dan. "Your mouth is open," he said, grinning.

Dan retrieved his jacket just before quitting time. He had intended to go back to the lab and work another hour or so, but as Dorothy smilingly handed him the rumpled old tweed coat he noticed that Appleton had already left; the boss's office was empty.

Suddenly he heard himself ask Dorothy, "Would you like to stop off someplace for a drink?"

Her smile changed subtly. "All right," she said softly. "But under one condition: I'm buying."

Dan blinked with surprise.

"I owe you for the coat," Dorothy explained. "And for the ride home last week."

He grinned—foolishly, he was sure—and agreed. As they walked out to the parking lot together, he realized that if she

bought the drinks she would be under no obligation to him whatever. Smart girl. And she could end their little get-together when
she felt like it.

Dan suggested the Stratosphere, the tavern just outside the
base's gates where the guys hung out. Dorothy suggested a place
nearer to her apartment building. "It's quieter, nicer," she said.
"The Strato's too noisy for me."

He followed her car into the city and parked on the tree-lined
street behind her. It was a quiet residential neighborhood, five-
and six-story redbrick apartment buildings. The Greenwood
Lounge was on the corner, a tasteful small neon sign glowing
above its dark wooden door.

True to Dorothy's word, the lounge was quiet. Almost empty.
People were in their apartments eating dinner at this hour in this
neighborhood. They would come down for a drink and some conversation later. Soft music purred from speakers in the ceiling. The
bartender had a financial news program on his TV by the cash
register. Not like the smoky, raucous Stratosphere at all, Dan
agreed, with its hillbilly music blaring and beer sloshing everywhere.

"I don't know this part of town very well," Dan said as they slid
into a booth.

"It's just two blocks from my apartment building," said Dorothy.

"Do you come here often?" He realized it was an inane question as he spoke the words.

She shrugged. "Now and then."

A middle-aged cocktail waitress in a no-nonsense black dress
took their drink orders: Dan asked for a bourbon and water, Dorothy for a glass of white wine.

"I thought you'd want a margarita."

With a shake of her head, "You can't get a decent margarita this
side of Santa Fe."

"Is that where you were born? In New Mexico?"

She laughed and told him no. In Los Angeles. Their drinks
arrived. Dan asked Dorothy if she had encountered any prejudice
against Hispanics. She talked briefly about it. Dan found himself
talking about his childhood in Youngstown, the kinds of preju-
dices thrown at you when you're weak and asthmatic and the

brightest kid in class. Dorothy told him about the problems of being an attractive young woman.

"You have no idea how many wannabe photographers there are in this world," she said with a scornful little smile.

The waitress returned to their booth. Dan ordered another round. Dorothy did not demur, but as the waitress went back toward the bar she asked, "Doesn't your wife expect you home for dinner?"

"She's staying with her mother," Dan said, surprised at how bitter it sounded in his own ears. "She's used to me working late."

He walked her home after the second drink. She told him that their parking spots were safe until eight o'clock the next morning.

"Let's have dinner," Dan blurted as he recognized the front of her apartment building. He did not want the evening to end so soon.

In the shadowy light of the street lamps shining through the bare branches of the trees, Dorothy seemed to search his eyes for something. Or maybe she was searching herself.

"I can fix something for us," she said, so softly that Dan barely heard it. Then she added, more firmly, "I'm a pretty good cook."

They ended up in bed. They never got to dinner. Once Dorothy led Dan into her apartment, they both seemed to forget everything else except each other. For the first time in his life, Dan threw away all the rules and did what his hormones demanded, all the while amazed in a far corner of his mind that this gorgeous willing warm exciting young woman wanted him as much as he wanted her.

He felt incredibly guilty about it afterward. Stuttering that he had to drive all the way to his in-laws' house all the way out in Xenia, he fumbled himself back into his pants and shirt and shoes and made a hasty retreat toward his car, leaving Dorothy smiling at him from her bed.

By the next morning, he felt more ashamed of himself than guilty. He tried to avoid Dorothy all day but finally had to go past her desk. She smiled at him as if nothing had happened. When he tried to apologize over lunch, hunching over the cafeteria table and whispering his miserable little regrets, Dorothy nodded solemnly.

"I know," she said. "I understand. It was my own fault, really. I wanted it to happen."

"What?" He felt stunned.

Dorothy lowered her eyes but repeated, "I wanted it to happen."

He did not know what to say. He was not certain that he could speak if he tried to.

Tortured, fascinated, wretched, elated, Dan's affair with Dorothy deepened week by week as his wife's pregnancy advanced and she spent more and more of her time amidst her sisters and her mother.

Dan learned what addiction was like. He knew he was doing something terribly wrong, yet he could not find the strength to stop. They explored each other's bodies with the eagerness of teenagers. Dorothy constantly sought for new sensations, new ways of exciting them both. Dan began to wonder how much experience she had already had.

Beside him in bed, she laughed. "In my neighborhood in L.A. they call it breaking the cherry. As soon as I started growing boobs the guys were all around me, sniffing like a pack of dogs. I picked the leader of the pack, and he kept me safe from the rest of them."

Looking up at the shadowy ceiling of her bedroom, Dan asked, "Then why me? Why am I so lucky?"

"Because you're the best man I've found here."

"But I'm married," he said.

"That's part of it. That makes you safe. We can have fun in bed and enjoy each other without worrying about getting tangled up in commitments and all that."

"So I'm protecting you from the other guys?" Dan did not feel much like a protector.

"Kind of," Dorothy answered, turning toward him. "Everybody knows we're a twosome, so the other guys don't bother me so much anymore."

Everybody knows except Sue, thought Dan.

He asked, "Don't you want a commitment? Don't you want to get married someday?"

"Oh, sure, someday," she said vaguely. "But not now. Not yet."

"This can't last forever, can it?" he whispered.

"Us? No, not forever. But let's enjoy it while we can." And she guided his hand down the length of her body to her groin.

Dr. Appleton found out, of course. He called Dan into his office one afternoon, firmly shut the door, and then went to his desk. Dan knew what was coming from the disapproving frown on his high-domed face.

"Dan, I don't want to interfere in your personal life, but I think you're heading for big trouble."

Dan had no reply.

"You know what I'm talking about, don't you?"

"Dorothy."

"What are you going to do about her?"

With a slow shake of his head, Dan said, "I wish I knew."

"All right, then," said Doc. "I'll tell you what you're going to do. You're going to stop this romance right here and now."

"That's what I ought to do," Dan admitted.

"You're going to be a father soon. You have a wife and a child on the way. Those are responsibilities you can't avoid."

"I know."

Appleton's stern visage eased into a fatherly sadness. "Listen, son, we've all been through episodes like this—"

Dan's eyes widened.

"Yes, even me." Appleton blushed slightly. "A *long* time ago. You've got to put an end to it, Dan."

Appleton did not threaten or shout or lose his temper. He talked to Dan for almost an hour, more like an understanding father than an outraged employer. Dan felt grateful. And miserable.

When he left the lab that evening, it was still a balmy springtime outdoors, just after daylight saving time had started, so that it still was something of a surprise to have the sun shining as he headed for his car. He drove to the Greenwood Lounge, and Dorothy was waiting for him there in their usual booth.

His mind was in a turmoil. They ordered their drinks, and before Dan could say anything Dorothy asked, "When is the baby due?"

"Another two, three weeks," said Dan.

"How is Susan feeling?"

"Okay. Tired and cranky, but no real problems."

"Gracias a Dios," Dorothy murmured.

"Huh?"

She rested her long-fingered hand on his, and it sent a tingle all the way up his arm. But her face was somber. She looked just as unhappy as he felt.

"Dan, it's time."

"Time?"

"For us to end this thing. It's getting too heavy. I don't want to break up your marriage, especially with the baby coming."

He grimaced. "Doc talked to you, too, huh?"

"Doc?" She looked genuinely surprised. "He hasn't said a word to me."

Feeling puzzled, Dan asked, "Then why . . . ?"

"If we don't stop now I'm going to really fall in love with you and you'll have to choose between me and Susan and your new baby." Dorothy said it all in a rush, as if afraid that if she hesitated for even an instant the words would stop coming. "I don't want to be in that position and I don't want to ruin all our lives, so we've got to stop seeing each other."

Dan opened his mouth but nothing came out.

"You know I'm right," she said.

"Yeah," he heard himself croak. "I know. But still . . ."

"Do you love me?"

"Yes!"

Dorothy smiled sadly and shook her head. "Wrong answer. You love your wife, Dan. And you will love your baby when it arrives."

"I love you, too."

"Not the same. Not for a lifetime. It was a very good thing for a few months, Dan, but now it must end."

He knew she was right, but still he did not like it. She started dating Major Martinez soon afterward. Dan thought Dorothy was doing that to keep him from trying to get her back. He felt angry, jealous. And incredibly grateful that no one kidded him about his love affair breaking up. No one even mentioned it.

Except Jace.

"She just used you to get Martinez's attention," Jace told him. Dan wanted to hit him.

"Yep," Jace said, as casually as a man reading the time from a clock, "it was Ralphie boy she was really interested in all along.

Friggin' hard-ass was too uptight to go after her, so she used you to make him jealous."

"That's not true," Dan said through gritted teeth.

Jace grinned at him. "Yeah. Sure."

Then Angela was born, and he was like a man coming out of a dream. He was a father now, and he had a loving and lovely wife whom he had betrayed, but he would spend a lifetime making it up to her and never again look at another woman and thank God Sue didn't know anything about Dorothy.

One of the other wives told Susan, of course. At the wedding of Dorothy and Ralph Martinez.

Susan was furious. She took her three-month-old daughter to her parents' home and refused even to speak to Dan on the telephone. Dan knew he deserved every bit of her rage. He wrote her long letters of abject abasement and apology, never once even thinking that he had any excuse to offer, any counteraccusation to make.

It took nearly four months. Dr. Appleton played the peacemaker, even going to Susan's parents' home to ask her to relent and forgive Dan. "I introduced you two," he reminded her. "I feel responsible for you."

Grudgingly, Susan returned home and they slowly began putting their marriage back together. Dan always thought that if it hadn't been for Angela, Sue would have left him for good.

And Dorothy, married now to Ralph Martinez, never spoke to Dan again unless there were other people in the room with them.

CHAPTER 24

For the first time in many years, Susan and Dan had gone to bed angry, spent the night in cold silence, not touching one another. Dr. Appleton phoned at six A.M. with the news that an Air Force plane would pick Dan up at the Kissimmee airport at eight o'clock. Breakfast was tense, broken only by Dan's phoning for a taxi to take him to the airport.

"I'll call you when I land at Wright-Patt," he said tightly as he got up from the kitchen table.

"What about the office?" she asked. "Shouldn't you call Kyle and tell him you won't be in?"

Thinking of the plane waiting for him, Dan said, "Could you call? Please? I've got to run."

She nodded. "It's too early for anybody to be at the office now, isn't it?"

"Maybe Jace," he said, going to the door. "But he won't even notice I'm gone for a day or two."

Like hell, Susan thought. But she said nothing.

"Give Vickie a buzz. Even if she's not there, you can leave the message on her phone machine."

Susan said to herself, I'll phone Kyle. Not Vickie.

She went to the breezeway door and watched Dan climb into the taxi waiting in the driveway. This early in the morning the neighborhood looked like a movie set, clean and new and uncluttered. Neat lawns and shrubs of tropical hibiscus and oleander blossoming pink and red in November. Young trees planted at precise intervals along the curbside. Each stucco-covered house painted a pastel Florida pink or aqua or mint beneath its red tile roof. Not a soul in sight. No one moving about, except for Dan's taxi turning left, heading for the highway. The whole scene as flat as a studio soundstage, uninhabited, antiseptic, sterile as a Moon colony.

Susan sighed. This can't be reality. Reality is the big old houses back in Dayton with their painted clapboards and doodad trim around the eaves. And porches. And real trees, big and lush in the summer, gauntly bare in the winter. Not these palms and bottlebrush pines. Leaves littering the yard in the autumn. Sidewalks! And people who waved to you, people you had known all your life. This isn't home, she thought as she gazed sadly at her Pine Lake Gardens neighborhood. This is a set for some TV advertisement.

Then she noticed a car parked at the curb halfway up the block. A faded old green sedan. Unusual. Isn't there a town ordinance against parking overnight in the street? she asked herself. Maybe I ought to call the police and ask them to look it over.

Dan's cab finally disappeared from her view. I trust him, Susan told herself. I trust him. I shouldn't have gotten mad at him. It's not his fault that something went wrong and Doc needs him. But still she felt anger. Not at Dan; at Dorothy.

She remembered the one and only time she had spoken with Dorothy. It was at the Christmas party Dr. Appleton had given at his house more than a year after Dorothy's marriage to Ralph Martinez. The house was crowded, noisy with holiday cheer and people greeting each other with alcoholic effusiveness, as if they didn't work together every day of the year. Susan saw Dorothy come in with Ralph and kept as much of the crowd between her and Dorothy as possible. Mrs. Appleton, round and white as the Pillsbury Doughboy, bustled from kitchen to living room to enclosed porch, hauling trays of food and drinks. Susan slipped into the kitchen to lend her a hand and get away from the smoke and noise and overheated holiday cheer.

Dorothy stepped through the swinging kitchen door a moment later. Her red sheath clung to her and made Susan feel skinny and plain.

"Oh!" Dorothy seemed surprised, almost startled.

"Merry Christmas," said Susan coldly. It was all she could think of.

"*Feliz Navidad*," Dorothy murmured. She went to the sink. "Do you know where Doc's wife keeps the water glasses?"

Susan gave her a stare, not trusting herself to say anything more.

Turning toward her, Dorothy said in a low, throaty voice, "Look, I'm sorry about what happened. I'm glad you and Dan got together again."

"No thanks to you."

Dorothy accepted the slap without flinching.

"I just hope somebody tries to wreck your marriage someday," Susan spat, "just so you'll know how it feels."

"I wasn't trying to wreck your marriage."

"Like hell!"

"Did you ever think," Dorothy said softly, "that perhaps I *saved* your marriage?"

Susan wanted to pick up the nearest bottle and hit her with it.

"Dan was miserably unhappy. Anything could have happened. I sent him back to you."

"I don't need your leavings!"

"He was yours. All along, he was yours. He never loved me; it was just an adventure for him, a fantasy."

"Bitch!"

"I kept him safe for you. He was ready to explode; he might have done something foolish, something terrible. I'm not the only woman on the base, you know."

Susan glared at Dorothy, speechless. Suddenly she was overwhelmed with such a broiling tangle of emotions that she turned and fled from the kitchen.

And now he's going back to her, Susan thought as she stood in the shaded breezeway in the early Florida morning. She shook her head, trying to clear her thoughts away. That was twelve years ago, she told herself. We're all a lot older. Maybe we're even a bit wiser.

I do trust Dan, she repeated. But I don't trust her.

She went back into her kitchen and started the morning task of getting Angela off to school and Philip his breakfast. Life goes on, no matter what.

At last Angie went running out to the school bus and Phil was safely in his playpen. She could start her business day.

But first she called Kyle Muncrief.

"He *what*?" Muncrief roared into the phone.

Stung by his shout, Sue jerked the receiver away from her ear. Still, she could hear Muncrief shouting, "Took off for Dayton? What on earth is he doing in Dayton?"

"It's an emergency," she said, suddenly uncertain of how much she should tell Muncrief.

"Emergency? What kind of emergency?"

Taking a deep breath, she made up her mind. "Dan said that it could affect the work you're doing at ParaReality. Something's gone wrong with one of the simulations he worked on for the Air Force, and he's worried that something similar could happen with the programs he's developing for you."

That stopped Muncrief. She could hear him breathing, taking in what she had said.

"I don't understand," he said, in a calmer tone. "What went wrong?"

"I'm not sure I can tell you, Kyle. It's Air Force business."

"Well, if you know what it is, why can't you tell me? You're a civilian, too, aren't you?"

That was true enough. Reluctantly, Susan replied, "It seems that somebody's had a stroke while in a VR simulation."

"A stroke?"

"While he was using the simulator."

"That could be just a coincidence, couldn't it?"

"He wasn't the first. There was another one, earlier. In the same simulation. And he died."

She could *feel* his brows beetling as he digested her news. Finally he said, "Look, you get Dan to phone me as soon as he calls you. Understand? I can't have employees traipsing off the job, especially when they're in such a vital position. I want to hear from him this morning! Understand?"

"I'll tell him," Susan said, "as soon as he calls me."

"Do that."

Dan had forgotten how cold Dayton can be in mid-November. A brisk blustery wind smacked him as soon as he ducked through the plane's hatch. A lieutenant in Air Force blue was waiting for him at the bottom of the stairs, young and crew-cut and apparently oblivious to the icy breeze that cut through Dan's sports jacket and light slacks.

The lieutenant bundled Dan into a waiting sedan and they drove to the familiar old concrete building that housed the Wright-Patterson simulations laboratories and offices. Ten thousand memories sprang up in Dan's mind at the sight and smell of the old place.

Dorothy must be in shock, he thought. This must have hit her awfully hard. And he knew that no matter what he had told Susan, he would have to see her. It would be inhuman not to. Sue would understand, he told himself. I've got to tell her how sorry I am. Then a new thought struck him. What if it's my fault? What if the reason Ralph's had the stroke is because I did something wrong with the simulation? What if I've killed him?

Appleton looked as if he had aged ten years in the few months since Dan had last seen him. The Doc was waiting for him by his office door as Dan strode up the corridor he had walked so many times before. Appleton came out past his secretary's desk to take Dan's outstretched hand and shake it solemnly.

"I truly appreciate your coming here like this, Dan," said his old boss. His face was etched with deep lines; his skin looked gray, unhealthy.

"I'm sorry all this has happened," Dan said. "I'll do what I can to help."

Appleton's secretary, an overweight middle-aged woman with bleach-blond hair, said, "Your wife phoned, Mr. Santorini, and asked you to call her as soon as you arrived."

"Oh, yeah. Can I use your phone?" he asked the Doc.

"Certainly." Appleton waved Dan into his office, staying outside with the secretary. "You have to dial nine to get an outside line, remember?"

Dan stood in front of the Doc's desk as he picked up the phone and jabbed at the old-fashioned keyboard. He could not bring himself to go around and sit in Doc's chair.

Susan sounded relieved to hear his voice. Not as frigid as she had been when he left. She told him that Muncrief wanted to hear from him immediately.

"Dan," she said, "I had to tell him what's happened in the simulator there."

"Why'd you tell him that?" Dan flared.

"I had to! He was really pissed off with you. I had to make him see that what you're doing is important to him, too."

"Okay, yeah, you're right." Dan's irritation subsided as quickly as it had risen. "Only—I'm sure as hell the Air Force doesn't want this hitting the news."

"Muncrief isn't going to run to the media to tell them that people are having strokes in VR simulations," Susan said.

"Yeah, I guess. Okay, let me give him a call. I'll phone you tonight. And, listen, can you send my old topcoat up here, Federal Express? It's *cold*."

"Oh, God, I should have thought of that. Don't get yourself sick."

"I won't do it on purpose," he said. "But the topcoat'll help."

"I'll call FedEx right now."

"Better find the coat first. I don't remember where—"

"In the storage box in the back of the garage. We put all our winter coats in there, remember?"

He didn't, but he said, "Great. I'll call you tonight. I think they're going to put me up in the BOQ."

"All right." Then she added, "I love you." But it sounded lifeless, automatic, like a reflex *bless you* when a stranger sneezes.

Turning his back to the office door, Dan lowered his voice to reply, "There's no one in the world for me except you, honey. I hope you know that."

It took several moments for her to reply, "I know it."

"I'll be back home as soon as I can."

"Call me tonight."

"I will."

He hung up the phone, and Appleton took it as a cue to step into his own office.

"My boss wants to hear from me," Dan said. "He's pissed off that I came up here without telling him first."

"I can understand that," Appleton said as he slid into his swivel chair. He gestured to the phone.

"Uh—Sue had to tell him that two men have suffered strokes in the simulation here."

Appleton puffed out his cheeks. "That's classified information."

"I figured it might have been."

"And you told Sue about it?"

Dan grinned sardonically. "Do you think I could have made it here otherwise? Besides, my clearance lapsed when I quit the lab, and you told me anyway."

Obviously unhappy, Appleton said, "You'll have to ask your boss not to mention this to anyone else. For his own good. If our security people find out that you've told him, they'll send an FBI team to check him out."

Still standing, Dan picked up the phone again. He started to tell it to get Muncrief, then realized that the Air Force did not have voice-actuated telephones. It took him a moment to remember ParaReality's number.

"Kyle Muncrief," he told the computer voice that answered. "Dan Santorini calling."

"Dan!" Muncrief's voice exploded in his ear. "What's going on?"

Dan swiftly explained the situation without really telling him more than Susan had, hearing Muncrief's angry huffing every step of the way.

"This could have an effect on the work we're doing," he concluded.

For a long moment Muncrief said nothing, then, "That's nonsense and you know it."

"I don't know anything of the sort, Kyle. It's too important not to check out. Thoroughly."

"And everything here is supposed to stop dead while you play Sherlock Holmes with your old Air Force pals?"

"Do you want people dropping dead at Cyber World when it opens?"

A low, angry grumbling.

Dan said, "I just want to make certain there's nothing inherently dangerous about the VR simulation."

"How long are you going to be there?"

"I don't know. A few days. Maybe a week."

"A *week*?"

"I shouldn't even be telling you so much on an unscrambled phone line," Dan pointed out. "The Air Force regards this whole business as classified information."

"Yeah, sure."

"I mean it. The people here are very serious about it. If they have any doubts about you keeping quiet, they'll send an FBI team to monitor you."

A *long* silence. Finally, "I'll keep quiet, don't worry about that. I won't tell a blessed soul. But you get yourself back here as quick as you can, you hear me?"

"Believe me, Kyle, nobody wants me back home as much as I do."

But as he put the phone down, Dan realized that this office, this laboratory, this part of the world had been his home for much, much longer than ParaReality and Pine Lake Gardens.

CHAPTER 25

They tell us, sir, that we are weak," Patrick Henry was saying, his face red with the emotion boiling through him, "unable to cope with so formidable an adversary. But when shall we be stronger? Will it be the next week, or the next year? Will it be when we are totally disarmed, and when a British guard shall be stationed in every house?"

Angela had never seen a man make such an impassioned speech. The whole audience was sitting on their hard wooden benches, spellbound. Patrick Henry was a little man, not even as tall as her own father. And he wore those funny knee pants with buckles on them, just like all the other men. His long coat was plain brown, and he had no wig covering his brick-red hair.

The room she was in looked more like a church than anything else. The big windows were clear glass, though, and late-afternoon sunlight streamed through them. She was in Virginia and the day was March twenty-third, seventeen seventy-five.

"Our chains are forged, their clanking may be heard on the plains of Boston! The war is inevitable—and let it come! I repeat it, sir, let it come!"

Looking around at the others in the audience, Angela saw stern old men in white powdered wigs and silky embroidered coats. Lots of women, too, up here in the balcony where she was sitting.

And, here and there, Angela recognized some of her classmates. Mrs. O'Connell had explained to all of them that this was a very special VR lesson. Six students would share the same lesson, and they would be able to see each other.

She wanted to wave to Johnny Lundsford or Mary Mackie, her best friend in the class, or even to stuck-up Connie Soscia, but she decided she'd better sit quietly and listen to the speech.

Angela thought that Patrick Henry looked a little like Uncle Kyle. She was accustomed to seeing Uncle Kyle peeking at her in the lessons and games she took in the VR booths. She more than half expected Patrick Henry's face to change in midsentence, to turn into Uncle Kyle's, and for him to wink at her or smile or do something to show that he knew she was there watching him.

But no, Patrick Henry kept right on with his thrilling speech and stayed himself. Maybe his speech was too important for Uncle Kyle to get into. Maybe he wants me to pay attention to what Patrick Henry is saying.

And he was saying, "Is life so dear, or peace so sweet, as to be purchased at the price of chains and slavery? Forbid it, Almighty God! I know not what course others may take; but as for me, give me liberty, or give me death!"

The big room fell absolutely silent. Patrick Henry stood there in the speaker's pulpit, his right arm raised over his head, his face beaded with perspiration. Then, as he slowly let his arm fall to his side, someone shouted, "Hear! Hear!" and all of a sudden the whole audience jumped to its feet and began cheering and clapping and stamping their feet and whistling. Angela had to peek between the two women standing in front of her to see the old man who seemed to be in charge of the meeting banging his gavel on his desktop and angrily hollering, "Order! Order!"

The noise died away and the scene faded. But before Angela could realize that she was in one of the darkened VR booths at the rear of her classroom, she found herself standing beside a wooden house on a warm spring morning.

"It is now April nineteenth, seventeen seventy-five," a disembodied voice whispered in her ear. "This is Lexington, Massachusetts, and these are the local group of Minutemen."

A couple of dozen men were gathering on the village green, across the dirt street from where she was standing. Each of them carried a long gun. They wore plain clothes; several of them had no coat at all, and none of them had fancy buckles or those knee pants that looked so funny. Except the man who rode up on a horse and dismounted in front of them. He looked all dressed up. He even had a sword dangling from his belt.

Angela looked over the houses dotted around the green. She saw two, then three of her classmates. It was like a game: find the hidden faces in the puzzle. Yes, there was David hiding behind those bushes. And Louisa, beside the big gray house.

The Minutemen had lined themselves up in a ragged row, two deep, facing the dirt road that led straight to the common. Angela heard the sounds of marching feet coming from up the road, the thump of a drum beating time.

The Minutemen were fidgeting, some of them looking down at their guns, most of them staring up the road.

Their leader paced calmly in front of them. "Hold your ground," he said firmly. "Don't fire unless fired upon. But if they mean to have a war, let it begin here."

And then Angela saw the British soldiers, all dressed in brilliant red coats with clean white trousers, row after row of them, led by an officer on a beautiful glossy brown horse. They marched like a big machine, all in step, lined up in perfect ranks. There were a lot more of them than the few Minutemen, she saw.

The officer prodded his horse across the green and stopped only a few feet in front of the Minutemen's commander. His soldiers marched mechanically behind him and only stopped when someone with a gravelly voice yelled, "Companyyyy, *halt!*"

For a moment there was silence. Angela could hear a bird chirping in one of the trees. The breeze was cool, the sun warm.

"Disband your rabble, sir," said the officer on horseback. "By order of His Majesty."

"I will not, sir," said the commander of the Minutemen, craning his neck to look up at the British officer. "You have no right to be here. These are free English citizens, yeomen and town men. Go back to Boston."

"Go back to London, lobsterbacks!" came a shout from across the green.

Angela heard a shot, but she was certain that none of the Minutemen had fired. Nor had the redcoats. The officer wheeled his horse about and shouted, "Take aim!"

The first rank of soldiers dropped to their knees and aimed at the Minutemen, while the second rank raised their muskets above their heads. Some of the Minutemen leveled their guns, but most began to back away fearfully.

"Fire!"

The blast of noise was much less than Angela had expected, but maybe that was because she had clapped her hands over her ears. A big cloud of gray smoke covered half the common for a moment, and when the breeze cleared it away the Minutemen were running in all directions, leaving the British soldiers in possession of the green. Angela counted eight Minutemen on the ground, several of them writhing and moaning with pain.

The mounted officer laughed. "On to Concord, then," he said, spurring his horse toward the extension of the road that led to the next town, not even bothering to chase the fleeing Minutemen.

"Things will be different at Concord."

Angela turned to see a young man, a boy really, crouching in the shrubbery slightly behind her.

"Come on," he said, reaching out his hand for her.

Angela let him lead her back behind the house to a small barn. It was shadowy and cool inside, pungent with the smell of horses and hay. The boy—scarcely older than Angela herself—began rooting through a pile of hay next to the horse stalls.

"Who are you?" she asked.

"Names don't matter, not today." His voice was strong, determined. "What matters is this."

And he pulled a long black musket from beneath the hay. "I'm going to Concord," he said.

"You're too young to be a soldier."

"No, I'm not. Not when the lobsterbacks are killing us. We need every gun we can muster at Concord, and that's where I'm going."

"How will you get there?"

"It's only a few miles. I can run faster than those murdering redcoats can march."

Angela felt breathless with the excitement of it all. And with this young man's fierce determination.

He started for the barn door, then suddenly grasped her around the waist with his free arm and kissed her on the lips.

"I'll see you in Concord," he said over his shoulder as he strode out of the barn.

Barely able to breathe, Angela waved to him as the scene faded and grew dark and she found herself sitting in the VR booth at school, tears in her eyes, heart fluttering, dying for the next lesson in American history.

"I don't like it," Jace said as he paced across the office. "It gives me the creeps."

Kyle Muncrief leaned back in his big desk chair, steepling his fingers. "I don't like it either. We need Dan here, not running off to Dayton."

Jace shot Muncrief a glance. "I don't mean that. I mean what you're doing with Dan's kid."

"What *you're* doing."

"For you."

Muncrief conceded the point with a spread of his hands. "It's not hurting anybody. She's even starting to enjoy it."

"Yeah, but why Dan's kid? Why not one of the others?"

"She comes the closest to . . . to what I want," Muncrief said, avoiding Jace's eyes. "I'm not going to hurt her."

Jace kept on pacing, looking unconvinced.

"What's going on back at Dayton, that's what's worrying me," Muncrief said.

"Some asshole of a brass hat had a stroke. Big deal. He was always on the verge of a stroke anyway."

"You know who it is?"

"A guy named Martinez. A real hard-ass. Serves him right. Big friggin' deal."

"Big enough to get Dan to hotfoot it out there, despite all the work he's got to do here."

Jace stopped in the middle of the room and whirled toward Muncrief. "Yeah! What's this special job you've got Dan working on? What's so special he can't tell me about it?"

"You've got enough to do."

"I don't like you sneaking around behind my back, y'know."

His face showing his exasperation, Muncrief said, "I'm not sneaking around. It's a special job that's got nothing to do with your work. It's so absolutely simple that I figured Dan could handle it on weekends and nights."

"But he can't talk to me about it."

"The people I'm doing this job for want it kept very confidential. No leaks. We both know you wouldn't put up with that, so I didn't bother you with it."

Jace stared hard at Muncrief, then pulled up one of the chairs in front of the desk.

"Listen," he said, "this business of recording his daughter's reactions is giving me the creeps. I feel like a friggin' electronic vampire."

"We're almost finished, aren't we?"

"How the hell should I know? How much is enough?"

Muncrief ran a finger across his upper lip, and Jace saw that there were beads of perspiration there.

"I'll go over the disks tonight," he said. "If all the reactions I need are there, we can stop bugging her."

"And if not?"

He shrugged. "A couple more sessions ought to do it. She's not complaining anymore, is she? She's getting a kick out of it, I tell you."

"If Dan ever finds out," Jace said, his voice lowered.

"He won't. How could he?"

"If he ever does . . ."

"If he ever does," Muncrief growled, "it'll be from you. You're the only one who knows about it, besides me."

"What about Vickie?"

"Vickie doesn't know anything important."

"The hell she doesn't."

Waving an impatient hand in the air, Muncrief said, "Let me worry about Vickie."

"Yeah," said Jace. "And I'll worry about Dan."

That evening, while she waited for a phone call from Dan, Susan bathed Philip and laid him in his crib to put on his nightclothes. Angela came into the nursery to watch, her pink terry-cloth robe wrapped around her slim, boyish body.

"Would you get me a diaper for him, honey?" Susan asked her daughter.

Angela brought a diaper to the crib and handed it to her

mother. Lying on his back, pudgy arms and legs churning, Philip suddenly urinated in an arc that spattered his own face. He blinked and batted his little hands at the tiny stream while Susan instinctively ducked out of the way and Angela giggled.

Susan used the diaper to clean up her baby as Angela fetched another from the pile on the table beside the crib.

"Why do they have that thing?" Angela asked her mother.

"You know why," Susan said. "I explained that to you."

"To make babies with."

"That's right."

"Mrs. O'Connell said she's not allowed to tell us anything about sex. She said we're supposed to learn about it from our parents."

Susan sighed. There was no easier way to wreck a PTA than to bring up the subject of sex education.

"Is there something you want to ask about?"

Angela thought a moment. "No, I don't think so."

Susan remembered the inevitable moment, about a year ago, when Angela had finally asked the ultimate question: "I know the man has the seed and he has to put it into the woman," she had said. "But how does he put it into her?"

With some trepidation, Susan explained the process. Angela listened with growing disbelief, then burst into wild laughter. Susan realized that the story must sound awfully improbable on first hearing. She almost wanted to take Angela into the bedroom with Dan and show her a demonstration.

Several months later, Angela started her first menstrual period. For weeks she followed her mother everywhere, asking her everything she could think of about sex and childbearing. Susan tried to answer calmly, clinically, and without offering more information than the child actually asked for. Apparently satisfied with her mother's answers, Angela's interest in sex seemed to have waned.

Until now.

"Marta Randolph says she's slept with four different boys," Angela announced as Susan taped the new diaper on her son.

Susan's guts clenched inside her, but she tried to remain calm. "Do you think she's telling the truth?"

"I guess."

"That's not a very smart thing to do."

"I told her she could get pregnant, or even get AIDS, but she just laughed and said I was a scared bunny."

"You're a very smart young woman, and Marta is either a liar or a tramp. Or maybe both. I'll bet her parents don't know what she's doing."

"She says boys like to put their thing in your mouth."

Ohmygod, Susan groaned inwardly. She busied herself tugging on Philip's pajamas.

"Is that true?" Angela looked as if she were facing a plate full of broccoli.

"Angie, sweet, when you love a man, when you know that this particular man is the one you want to spend your whole life with, the one you want to have babies with, then you can do anything that pleases him. But it's got to please you, too! Remember that. Whatever you do with a man, it's got to please both of you or else it's no good."

Angela considered this for a moment, then asked, "Do you do that with Daddy?"

Susan felt her face flame. "What a man and a woman do when they make love is their business, Angie, and nobody else's."

"Uh-huh. But do you?"

Suddenly Susan understood why her daughter was asking. "Are any of the boys in school trying to get you to have sex with them?"

Angela shook her head. "No, they all go with Marta or Kristy Kelly. They don't like girls with braces on their teeth."

"Oh, that's not true, dear. They think more highly of you than those other girls. They know you're a good girl and those others aren't."

"I guess." Very glumly.

Seeing that Philip was dressed for the night, Susan knelt down beside her daughter and wrapped her arms around her. "You mean the boys don't even look at you? They don't say hello or talk to you on the bus or *anything*?"

"Oh, sure, they talk to me and we play ball in the schoolyard. They like me to help them with their class work. Gary Rusic, he's real nice."

"So you see?" Susan felt immense relief. "You don't have to be a tramp to have boyfriends."

Angela nodded and smiled a bit.

"You can bring some of your friends here after school, you know. I could drive them all home afterward; you don't need to worry about the bus."

"Could I?" Angela's eyes went wide with delighted surprise.

"Certainly."

"Tomorrow?"

"Sure," Susan said, mentally rearranging her own work schedule to free up the late afternoon.

"That's rad!"

"Rad?"

"Totally rad! That means it's real good."

Radical, Susan guessed as she hugged her daughter, happy that something so simple could please her.

But Angela whispered in her ear, "Mommy, what's Deep Throat?"

Kyle Muncrief wandered alone through his big empty house. It had been furnished by the best interior decorator in Orlando, but he still thought of it as empty. No one here but me. All alone.

It was well past midnight, but he knew he could not sleep. Booze didn't help anymore, and he was afraid of getting started with pills. He had spent hours at his office after everyone else had left, playing and replaying the discs Jace had made of Angela. Now he was so wired up over them that he could not sleep.

He was still in the shirt and slacks he had worn at the office. Just before she left for the day, Vickie had told him that the first payment from Washington had arrived. "The cash flow is going to get better and better," she had said, almost triumphantly. Flow. Muncrief snorted. More like a dismal trickle. Just enough to keep the leaky roof over our heads until February.

He looked out at the pool patio. Standing by the sliding glass doors of his living room, he turned on the pool lights. The water glowed ghostlike, and he saw white blurs of insects flitting through the night.

Got to open Cyber World on schedule. We're sunk if we don't. Toshimura's dickering with Sony or one of the other biggies, I can feel it in my bones. Maybe Disney. If we don't open Cyber World on schedule, he'll throw me to the wolves and steal everything we've done. Him and Swenson, both. They won't give me another penny; they're just waiting for me to fall over, like a couple of grinning vultures sitting in a dead tree. Glass might try to stick up for me, but the two of them will pick my bones clean if I give them the chance.

And Dan's off playing soldier in Dayton. God *damn* his eyes! When I need him here. He's supposed to be the reliable one, the steady hand, and he's off on some kind of toot. Says his simulation's giving guys strokes. Absolute nonsense! I need him here and he's running around with his old pals in Ohio.

Muncrief ran a hand over his face. It's too much, he said to himself. It's just too monumentally much. I'm risking everything on this, and they're trying to screw me out of it. They're all against me, every last one of them. Except Crystal. If only I knew where she was. If only she could be here with me.

He licked his lips. Then he made up his mind and strode to the marble table in the foyer, where he had thrown his car keys. I can't have Crystal. Not yet, he said to himself as he headed for the garage. But I can run through those discs again. Dan's daughter. Little Angela. My little angel. I'll turn her into Crystal. Jace will. But I've got to keep control of the company to keep Jace working on this for me. I've got to keep this hardnose Smith happy so I can get the money from Washington. And Dan's not here to do Smith's work.

"Jesus God!" he screamed in the empty house. "They're all pressuring me!"

And he banged through the garage door, jumped into his Jaguar, and headed back to his office. And the discs Jace was making for him.

CHAPTER 26

Dan spent most of the day at the F-22 simulator that stood silent and unmoving in the hangar down by the airfield. Appleton stayed at his elbow as Dan climbed up into the cockpit, checked out all the wiring, and powered up the control consoles. The only thing he found different from his earlier years was that a bank of electrical heaters now sat on the concrete floor, ringed around the simulator, whirring and clanking noisily.

"Guess I ought to see Ralph," he said to Doc toward the end of the afternoon.

Appleton nodded grimly.

Everyone who worked at Wright-Patterson Air Force Base said that the base hospital was the best one in the entire Dayton area. Dan had his doubts, but as he followed Dr. Appleton along a maze of corridors, he realized that the hospital was at least big and well-staffed. Crisply uniformed nurses, serious-looking doctors, orderlies and technicians everywhere; some were scurrying, most strode the hallways with the purposeful assured look of competence. The corridors were sparkling clean, smelling of antiseptic and whatever that particular odor is that all hospitals everywhere have in common.

When he saw Ralph Martinez, Dan realized what that odor was: Pain. And fear.

Dan stood in front of a window that separated the intensive care unit's central monitoring station from the beds laid out in a semi-circle around it. The monitoring station looked like NASA's mission control, bank upon bank of display screens. Three nurses sat before the flickering screens. Only four of the beds were occupied. Martinez's was over at one end, screened off from the others.

He had a clear plastic breathing mask over his face, but even through it Dan could see how horribly distorted his face was, constricted on the left side so badly that his lips were pulled back from his teeth like a growling feral beast. His left eye was squeezed shut, but his right glared red-hot pain and fury. His right arm lay atop the bedsheet, his hand slowly clenching and unclenching like a man enduring torture.

"Can he talk to us?" Dan whispered to the Indian physician standing with him and Appleton.

Chandra Narlikar looked startled by the question. His big liquid eyes flicked from Dan to Appleton and back again.

"He cannot speak at all," Narlikar said. "His vocal abilities are totally gone."

"But he might recover his speech, mightn't he?" Appleton asked, almost pleading.

"Doubtful," said Narlikar, shaking his head sadly. "Extremely doubtful. His condition is deteriorating. He might not even last the night."

"Jesus," breathed Dan.

"If he could only tell us what happened in there," said Appleton. "Adair died without regaining consciousness. If Ralph could tell us what happened to him in the simulation . . ."

Dan put a hand on the older man's shoulder. "Come on, Doc. There's nothing we can do here."

Appleton nodded, his shoulders sagging. "I'll drive you over to the BOQ."

Dan had never been in the bachelor officers' quarters before. Alone in his spartan room, he sat on the bed and phoned Susan.

"You sound exhausted," she said.

"It's been a long day."

"How is Colonel Martinez?"

He let out a breath. "They think he might not last the night."

"Oh, dear."

"I don't know if I'm going to be able to do any good here,"

Dan said, worming off his loafers and letting them drop to the thin carpeting. "I'll see how much I can find out tomorrow."

"Your coat should be at Dr. Appleton's office by ten-thirty tomorrow morning."

"Good. I can use it."

"Anything else I can do?" Susan asked.

He started to say no, then something popped into his consciousness. "Maybe you can look up some background information for me on nerve physiology."

"Nerve physiology?"

While a part of his mind felt almost shocked that he could think of anything except Ralph Martinez, Dan replied, "You know how we were talking with Angie a couple nights ago about learning to play musical instruments?"

"Oh, yes, I remember."

"I need to know about how the nervous system gets trained by constant practice."

A pause. "I'm not sure I'd even know where to begin a search like that, Dan." Susan's voice sounded slightly bewildered.

"Try sports training," he suggested, recalling Jace's idea. "Olympics, professional baseball, stuff like that. It's big business. If there's anything published on the subject, it'll be there."

"I'll try." Then she asked, "Is this on ParaReality or just something of your own?"

Dan remembered the disclosure agreement he had signed his first day on the job. "ParaReality," he said. Glumly.

"Too bad."

"I can't afford your fee." He tried to make it sound amusing, clever. Neither of them laughed.

"Get a decent night's sleep," Susan said.

"Yeah. You too."

"I love you."

"Love you too," he said mechanically.

He hung up the phone, unpacked his garment bag. The other pair of slacks and sports jacket went into the closet. The shirts and socks and underwear into bureau drawers. He placed his shaving kit beside the sink in the white tiled bathroom. And that was it. He had nothing further to do but watch television or try to go to sleep.

At least the TV had a remote-control unit. He sat on the bed again, still in his shirt and slacks, and clicked on CNN.

He glanced at the phone. Putting the TV remote-control unit on the night table beside it, Dan picked up the receiver and dialed information. Then he dialed again.

"You have reached the residence of Colonel and Mrs. Ralph Martinez." It was Ralph's voice, crisp and authoritative. "Please leave your name, number, and time of—"

Dan slammed the phone down. Of course Dorothy would have the answering machine on. She might not even be at their home. She might be staying with relatives or friends or even in the hospital itself. He had no way of knowing. And no car to drive out to her house and see if she was okay.

He undressed and tried to sleep. He kept the TV on, clicking from one idiotic show to another, trying to bore himself to sleep. Still, the vision of Ralph Martinez's madly distorted face haunted him. And with it, his memories of Dorothy.

His dreams were bad. Sometimes it was Jace who gunned him down, sometimes Ralph.

"Jace, you've got to help me," said Susan.

She had invited him to dinner and he had finally shown up just before nine o'clock, as she was getting the kids ready for bed.

"Am I too late for the food?" Jace had asked, standing in the doorway and grinning like a Halloween figure, long lanky skin and bones dressed in threadbare jeans and a T-shirt that read, *Born to Hack*. But the shirt looked clean, and Jace's hair was glistening as if it had just been washed; he had pulled it back into a ponytail with an elastic band.

Susan had thrown on a green and white cotton top that hung loosely on her but went well with her red hair. Matching green slacks. She had dressed for comfort, without a worry of what Jace would think. As far as Susan knew, Jace never noticed what anyone wore, including himself.

Now, with Angela and Philip asleep and his warmed-over dinner reduced to crumbs, Jace leaned back in the dining-room chair and burped contentedly.

"That's a compliment to the cook," he said, by way of excusing himself.

"I'm flattered," said Susan. She did not tell Jace that most of the cooking had been done long before she had brought the meals home from the supermarket. Microwave ovens were the salvation of the working mother.

She got up and started taking the dinner dishes from the table to the pass-through bar that separated the dining room from the kitchen.

"So what kinda help you need?" he asked, not moving from his chair.

"I need an excuse to come over to the lab every few days." Susan watched his eyes as she spoke.

He looked more amused than curious. "What for?"

"To rack up some consulting time," she temporized, not wanting to tell him too much. "Dan got me a consulting contract with the company, did you know that?"

Scratching at his day-old beard, Jace answered, "Yeah, I think he mentioned something about it to me."

"Well, I could use the money."

"What'll you be working on?"

"Nerve physiology," she said, stacking the dishes and glasses on the countertop. "Dan phoned earlier this evening and asked me to look up some background information."

"About nerve physiology?"

Susan said, "Dan thinks there might be something in the area of sports medicine—"

"Bullshit!"

Susan almost dropped the dishes she was holding.

"Dan shouldn't be wandering off into dead ends like that," Jace said, frowning. "There's nothing in sports medicine that'd be useful for us."

"But I thought—"

Jace seemed acutely displeased, almost angry. "Shit, I was just thinking out loud, and he goes off on a tangent. He shouldn't try to get creative, it's not his strong point, y'know."

"No, I don't know," Susan snapped. "Dan has ideas of his own." She went around the counter to the sink.

"He better get his butt back here, y'know," Jace called after her. "Muncrief's about to start hemorrhaging."

"He'll be home in a day or two," Susan said, hoping it was true. She turned on the sink faucet to rinse the dishes before putting them into the dishwasher.

"To stay?" Jace asked over the sound of the running water. "Or is he going back to Wright-Patt afterward?"

I wish I knew, she said to herself. But to Jace she answered, "To stay, I hope."

"He better. We've really ground down to a stop without him. I've been foolin' around with this stuttering stuff, but I don't have the patience for it. And like I said, Muncrief's about to pop his top."

"I'll bet Dan works twenty hours a day," said Susan, "trying to make up for lost time."

"He's gotta do *something* to make Muncrief like him again. Sonofabitch might fire Dan, y'know."

Susan stiffened with alarm. "He couldn't fire Dan! Could he?"

Jace got up from the dining-room chair like a giraffe clambering to its feet. "He'd be an idiot to fire Dan. We need him. *I* need him."

Then why don't you ever tell that to Dan? Susan demanded silently.

"But"—Jace came over to the pass-through and leaned his elbows on the countertop—"people can be assholes, y'know. Muncrief might fire Dan just 'cause he's sore at him."

"You can't let him do that!" Susan said.

Jace made a bony shrug and muttered, "Yeah, I know."

Susan stacked the dishes and glassware and the stainless-steel flatware in the dishwasher, thinking that Jace could protect Dan if he wanted to. And he'll want to, because he needs Dan and he knows it, even if Muncrief doesn't.

"Dishwasher," said Susan firmly. "Full load. Standard."

The machine chugged to life.

Jace leaned over the countertop to stare at the dishwasher. "Hey, I didn't know they had kitchen appliances on voice recognition. That's neat!"

"Would you like an after-dinner drink?" Susan asked, knowing that Jace rarely took anything stronger than Classic Coke.

But he replied, "Yeah, okay, why not? You got any rum?"

"Rum and Coke?"

"Cuba Libre. That's my favorite drink since I was at Cal Tech."

Susan dug into the cabinet where Dan kept the liquor. There was an ancient bottle of rum, two-thirds gone. And Diet Coke in the refrigerator. Jace won't know the difference, she told herself. Then she poured a thimbleful of anisette for herself. Dan had taught her how the Italian liqueur gave a good meal its perfect finish.

"What about that consulting time?" she asked Jace as she handed him his drink, ice cubes tinkling in the tall glass.

He had plopped down in the living room armchair that Dan usually took. "Sure, why not? Only—I'll have to think up some subject for you to work on."

"How about baseball statistics? For the game?" Susan sat on the sofa and took a sip of the anisette. It tasted oily smooth and slightly sweet.

Jace gulped at his Cuba Libre as if it were plain Coca-Cola. "Naw, we already got six people chewing away on that stuff. And it's too easy for you; all the stats are available in a dozen sources."

"There's the nerve-physiology problem," she suggested.

He glared at her. "Forget that crap! It oughtta be something that Muncrief wants us to be doing."

"Stuttering?"

"We need somebody to do the programming, not research the background."

"Then what?"

Jace fell silent. He tilted his head back and studied the ceiling for a few moments. Then he returned his attention to his drink and downed almost half of it in one long swig.

"It'll have to be the nerve physiology, then," Susan said.

His gaze flitted around the room, avoiding Susan's eyes. He took another pull of the rum-and-Coke, then finally said, "I'll think of something for you."

"You're not comfortable with that subject?"

Jace gulped the last of his drink. He smacked his lips and seemed to draw himself together, sit up straighter in the armchair. "You really wanna go digging into that crap? Go right ahead! You won't find anything Dan can use. It's all a blind alley."

"How do you know?"

His look turned sly. "Listen, Sue, I'm the creative genius around here, remember? I bet I can teach you a couple things about nerve physiology you won't be able to find in the friggin' literature."

"Really?"

"I bet." Jace grinned crookedly.

My God, he's drunk! Susan realized. *In less than five minutes.* She had barely sipped her own drink.

"There's a lot you don't know and I do," he said, his grin widening. "A helluva lot. Not even Dan knows what I know, an' he knows me better'n anybody else."

"Would you like some coffee?" Susan asked.

Jace shook his head. "Nope. One's my limit."

"I said coffee."

"It was a joke, Sue."

"Oh."

"I'm all right."

"Are you sure?"

"Sure." He rose to his feet, only slightly unsteady. From her sitting position it seemed to Susan that his neatly combed hair might brush the ceiling.

"I'll brew some fresh coffee," she said. "It won't take a minute."

By the time she came from the kitchen with two steaming mugs of coffee, Jace seemed to have recovered.

"I'm really okay," he told Susan. His smile was back to normal. He was standing by the bookshelf that Dan had built in Dayton, peering at the titles. *"Alice's Adventures in Wonderland,"* he said. "I always wanted to read that."

"You can borrow it," said Susan.

"Naw. No time to read. I saw the video, anyway."

They finished their coffees, and Jace headed for the door.

"You're sure you're all right to drive?" Susan asked.

"My bicycle?" Jace laughed. "Yeah, I'll make it okay, don't worry."

It wasn't until he had pedaled down the lamplit street with a final farewell wave and she had closed the front door that Susan realized she had never before felt the slightest twinge of worry at being essentially alone in the house with Jace. Yet tonight she had felt a flutter of alarm.

Once she finally got to bed, Susan found it difficult to sleep. It was more than Dan's absence. She missed his warm body in the bed beside her, but something was preying on her mind, something just below the surface of consciousness. Something was pecking away at her, trying to get her attention. It would not allow her to sleep.

She lay in the darkness, ears trained to detect the slightest hint of difficulty from her children. At least Angie's talking to me about sex, she told herself as she lay awake. That's a good sign. And once I'm inside the lab, I can look into those school games for myself. There's got to be more to those games than Vickie is admitting. I can't ask Dan to probe into them, but I can do it myself once I'm into their computer system. There's got to be something—

The thought broke through to her consciousness with the force of a wrecking ball demolishing a building.

If a VR simulation can cause a stroke in an Air Force pilot, why can't it hurt a child in a classroom game?

Vickie Kessel was also awake as midnight neared. And working. She had watched the local TV news at eleven o'clock, then gone down to the garage on the ground floor of her condo building and driven out Interstate 4 to the big Marriott Hotel near the Disney World grounds.

The bar was almost empty this late at night. The families that thronged the parks retired early, exhausted. Even the men who had come for conventions or business conferences had gone off to bed, leaving the bar almost empty. But not completely. Luke Peterson sat in a booth in a shadowy corner, a tall drink in front of him, that slaphappy smile of his gone from his jowly face.

He got to his feet and made a little bow as Vickie came up to the booth. She slid in on the opposite side of the table from him.

"Isn't this a little melodramatic?" Vickie asked. "Meeting at midnight." But she kept her voice low.

"I have to talk to you; this is the only time I could arrange it."

"Peeking through keyholes all day long?" Vickie sneered.

He ignored her sarcasm. "I've tried to get to you, more than once. You've been putting me off."

"I'm rather busy."

"Sure, sure." He hesitated a beat, then asked, "What do you want to drink?"

She saw that the bartender had come out from behind the bar and was approaching their booth. Nice-looking boy; athletic build.

"Irish coffee," Vickie said. As the bartender headed back, she said to Peterson, "I don't have anything new to tell you."

"Nothing, huh?"

"Nothing significant. I gave you the complete rundown the last time."

He grimaced, almost as if he were in pain. "Oh, really? Who's this guy Smith from Washington? And why has Lowrey's chief assistant dashed off to Ohio?"

Vickie realized all over again that Peterson, or the people he worked for, had other informants inside ParaReality.

"I don't know anything about Smith," she lied. "He's dealing entirely with Muncrief."

"And you don't know *anything* about him? Or what he's here for?"

"No," said Victoria firmly. "I don't."

The bartender deposited her Irish coffee on the table. It was in a fancy tall cup topped with whipped nondairy creamer, a green cherry, and a plastic straw. Vickie took one look at it and pushed it away.

"Okay, we'll let Smith go for the moment," Peterson said once the kid had returned to the bar. "What about Santorini? What's sent him rushing off to Dayton?"

"The Air Force is having some problems with one of the simulations he worked on before he came to ParaReality. They asked him to come back for a few days and check it out for them."

"And Muncrief let him go?"

Vickie actually laughed. "Dan didn't ask permission. Muncrief nearly had a stroke when he found out."

"And the baseball simulation?"

"Lowrey's still working on it."

"No progress?"

"None that I've heard of."

"You're not exactly a fount of information," Peterson grumbled.

"Look, I don't have to do this," Vickie snapped. "In fact, I don't think I want to play your game anymore."

"What's that supposed to mean?"

"I quit."

"Quit?"

"I'm finished. I don't want to see you again. I'm not going to tell you another thing."

He shook his head like a teacher disappointed over a star pupil's glaring mistake. "It ain't that easy, Victoria. You can't just walk away."

"The hell I can't."

"Listen to me, lady. I'm just a harmless, overweight, middle-aged private snoop. But I'm working for people who can get very angry and very rough."

"What are they going to do, send Minnie Mouse to beat me up?"

He actually looked frightened. "This isn't a joking matter. My client plays hardball. If you don't give me enough material to make him happy, somebody's going to get hurt."

"Are you threatening me?"

"I'm trying to warn you. We made a deal and—"

"What deal?" Vickie snapped. "You still haven't told me who's involved in this."

"We've made a substantial deposit in a Swiss bank account for you."

"You can have it back. I told you I wasn't interested in just money. I want out."

Peterson was almost pleading. "I tell you for your own good, Victoria, my client is going to be very pissed off. Somebody's going to get hurt."

She leaned across the table until their noses were almost touching. "Then tell your goddamned client that I've got protection from the United States government. From the highest levels of the government. Do you know what that means?"

His eyes widened with surprise. "Smith . . ." Peterson's voice trailed off into silence. She could see the wheels turning inside his head.

"That's right, buster. Smith can provide all the protection I need. He can get the FBI on you. *And* your client, whoever the hell he is."

Peterson puffed out his cheeks. "You're a lot more ambitious than I thought. I underestimated you."

Vickie gave him an acid smile.

But he clutched at her wrist. "Let me give you a piece of advice, lady. Don't underestimate the people I'm working for. They're not going to take this lying down."

Vickie pulled free of his grip and slipped out of the booth, leaving her Irish coffee untouched. As she headed out for the parking lot, she told herself, Now you've got to make certain that Smith actually will protect you. It's life or death now.

an remained at Wright-Patterson for more than a week, digging into every line of programming for the flight simulation. He awoke each morning in his narrow little room at the BOQ, went to the simulations lab, and worked through until dinner. At Dr. Appleton's insistence, Dan rented a compact car that the Air Force paid for. At the end of the normal working day, he drove to one of the seedy restaurants near the base, ate a quick meal, then returned to the lab and the intricate unfoldings of the computer program.

Each night he phoned Susan, then went to sleep in his narrow bed at the BOQ. Each morning he awoke weary and drenched with perspiration, his dreams winking out like the picture on a TV tube before he could consciously recall them. But he knew that Jace was in those dreams. Jace and Doc and Martinez and sometimes even Muncrief. And Dorothy. She was there, too, he knew. Never Susan.

His only break from work came when he went to the base hospital to see Ralph Martinez. The colonel had survived his stroke, but he was still on the critical list, still in the intensive-care ward, still half paralyzed and unable to speak. If Martinez recognized Dan, he gave no sign of it. His one good eye burned pain and rage; his right hand constantly clenched and unclenched, the only voluntary movement his body could make.

Dan usually visited the hospital on his way off-base to dinner. He never saw another visitor for the colonel there, until the evening Dorothy came.

She was older, of course, more mature and obviously stricken with grief. But still stunning. Her eyes were rimmed with dark circles. Her face was pale, drawn. But still Dan's knees went watery.

"Hello, Dan," she said, her voice low.

"Hello," he managed.

That was it. Dorothy turned away and hurried down the hospital corridor. Is she running from me? Dan wondered. Or from the sight of her husband? Then he heard a voice in his head ask, Does she blame me for what's happened to Ralph?

It was then that the full enormity of it struck him. For a solid year after Jace had left for Florida, Dan had been the principal engineer on the F-22 simulation: the chief technical guy, the head honcho. It's *my* sim, more than anyone's, he realized. More than Doc's, more even than Jace's. If there's anything wrong with it, it's my fault. Nobody else's. Mine.

That night Dan could not sleep. He phoned Dorothy three times, each time getting Martinez's recorded voice. She did not return his calls.

But the next morning he got other calls:

"I ought to fire you!" Kyle Muncrief bellowed into the telephone at him. "The whole place here is falling apart, and you're off playing games for the blasted Air Force!"

"This Thursday is Thanksgiving," Susan reminded him. "I expect you to be home with your family."

Even Jace called. "It's gettin' real intense around here. Muncrief expects me to put the stuttering program into the baseball game, but I can't get much done without you, pal."

Dan stalled them all off, even Susan. Then Appleton told him firmly, "The lab will be shut down for the holiday weekend, Dan. The entire base will, except for the operational flying units."

"But I haven't gotten anywhere yet," he said.

"Today is Tuesday. Tomorrow I'm putting you on a plane for Orlando. You're going to spend the holiday with your family," Appleton said. "You can come back next Monday if you want to."

They were in Appleton's office, the Doc sitting behind his desk fiddling with his everlasting pipe, Dan standing worriedly at the room's only window and staring blindly at the concrete wall of the adjoining building. This isn't the first time Doc's spoken to me like a stern father, he said to himself.

Dan turned to his former boss. "Okay, then," he said, his breath feeling weak, fluttery, as if he were on the edge of a high precipice or maybe facing the gang of bullies that had bedeviled him when he was a kid.

Forcing his voice to sound calm and unafraid, Dan said, "In that case, I want to fly the simulation tomorrow."

Appleton's mouth dropped open. The pipe fell onto his lap.

"I'll wear the medical sensors. If I get into any trouble, you can terminate the run."

Before Appleton could do more than start to shake his head, Dan went on. "You know it's the only way to break through this puzzle, Doc. Ralph can't tell us what happened, and it'd take months to run through every facet of the computer program. I'm not sure the program would give us the answer, anyway. You need a guinea pig. I volunteer."

"I can't allow it," Appleton said, retrieving the pipe with one hand and brushing tobacco flakes off his lap with the other.

"We don't have any choice. Somebody's got to get in there and see what the hell happens during the simulation."

"Then I'll get one of the jet jocks."

"No! It's *my* simulation. It's my responsibility. I understand what's supposed to be in the program. I'll be able to tell if anything's out of sync."

"You don't know how to fly the plane."

"Yeah, I thought about that. We can program Ralph's moves into the simulation, can't we? I'll just follow along and watch what happens."

"It's too damned dangerous!" Appleton blurted.

Dan had never heard even the mildest swear word from his old boss. He grinned, because he knew he had won his point.

"I'll get the technicians started on their prerun checkouts," he said, heading for Appleton's door. The Doc sat at his desk and did not make a move to stop him.

That evening, Dan dropped by the base hospital again.

"How's he doing?" he asked the nurse sitting at the center of the monitoring screens. She was a middle-aged black woman, hair going gray, munching on chips from a plastic bag.

By now she knew Dan on sight. She did not look happy. "He had a minor incident this afternoon."

"Incident?"

"Another small stroke. Like an aftershock following a big earthquake. It happens."

"Has it done more damage to him?"

"Sure, but it was real minor. Trouble is, his whole system is getting weaker instead of stronger."

"Isn't there anything you can do?"

She answered Dan's question with a reproachful frown. "It's the lungs," she said. "They get pneumonia 'cause they can't keep the lungs from filling up with fluids."

"Is he going to die?"

The nurse huffed out a great sigh. "I didn't tell you, but yes, he's not going to make it."

"How long?"

"Couple days at most. But I never told you, understand?"

Dan walked out of the hospital like a man in a daze. He got into his rented two-door Chevrolet and drove off the base. That Indian doctor said he wouldn't last the night but he did, Dan argued with himself. Now the nurse says he's not going to make it. What do they know? Ralph's a fighter. But somehow the nurse's flat, unemotional prognosis seemed utterly convincing. No bullshit, no tears, Ralph is a goner and nothing any of us can do is going to change that.

It was not until he was parking the car that he realized where he had driven. Dorothy and Ralph lived on a quiet suburban street not far from the base. Dan remembered their house from the occasional barbecues that Colonel Martinez had thrown for the whole simulations-lab staff before he had gotten married. Ralph still threw barbecues afterward, but Susan would never accept the Martinezes' invitations.

As he got out of the car in the chilly darkness of the November night, he wondered how the brain can pick out memories that had lain unused for so many years.

The moon was a thin ghostly white crescent scudding in and out among silver-edged clouds. Dry brittle leaves scratched along the sidewalk. The night felt more like Halloween than approaching

Thanksgiving. Dan half expected to see kids dressed up as ghosts and pirates and Raggedy Anns making their way door to door. He remembered that in Orlando the parents had sponsored a Halloween party for the kids in the school gymnasium. Very organized, very safe. No danger of razor blades in the apples or candies laced with drugs. No problems with vandalism from teenaged "trick-or-treaters." No spontaneous fun.

At the curving walkway leading to the Martinezes' door, Dan hesitated. Should I do this? Should I try to barge into her life? She hasn't returned my calls. She hardly said two words to me at the hospital.

But she looked so—hurt. That was it. Dorothy looked as if she was in pain, vulnerable, alone. And it's my fault. I did this to Ralph. Did it to her. Dan knew he could not stay away from her; she needed someone, she needed him.

Feeling shaky inside, he walked up to the front door, found the doorbell button with its tiny light glowing around it, and leaned on it.

No answer. Dan waited, fidgeting nervously, unsure of what to do. The night breeze sighed; dry leaves grated along the street and the bare limbs of the trees groaned. He pressed the doorbell again. Then he stepped back from the door and looked around. Yes, there was a light on. One light, over at the far end of the house. Must be a bedroom. She must be home. Somebody must be here.

But no one was answering his ring. Maybe she's asleep. Maybe I ought to leave her alone. But he knew he couldn't. He pushed the button again and again.

Through the frosted window alongside the door he saw a light go on and then the shadow of a figure moving. He took his finger off the doorbell just as Dorothy pulled the door partially open. A safety chain dangled between them.

"Dan." Her voice was flat, low, dulled as if she had just awakened from a deep sleep.

"How are you?" he asked. But he could see how she was: eyes hollow, cheeks gaunt, face wan, hair uncombed. She seemed to be half hiding behind the partially open door, a rumpled floor-length robe hastily belted at her waist.

Dorothy did not answer. She simply stared at Dan, as if trying to get her eyes to focus on him. God, is she on drugs? Dan asked himself. She looks punched out.

"Are you okay?" he said aloud. "I mean, do you need anything? Are you alone, is anybody taking care of you?" The words came out in a rush.

Slowly Dorothy shook her head. "I'm all right, Dan. You don't have to worry. Ralph's taking good care of me."

He wasn't certain he had heard right. "Ralph? Ralph's in the hospital."

"I know. It's all right. Don't worry about me."

"Maybe you should see a doctor."

"Don't . . ." Her voice faded out, as if she had lost her train of thought.

"Are you all alone?"

She smiled weakly. "Not alone. I've got Ralph. I'll never be alone."

And Dan realized that on one of her hands she was wearing a data glove.

Dorothy had been making love with her husband.

All through that awful weekend when Ralph had been cut down by the stroke, she had stayed in the hospital with him, watching over him sleeplessly, trying to draw the pain out of him by sheer willpower. Hour after hour she stared into his contorted face, prayed for him, breathed for him, felt her heart beating hard enough to keep the both of them alive.

"Don't die, *querido*," she whispered to her unconscious husband whenever the nurses let her close to his bed. "It doesn't matter how much damage this has done to you, just don't die. I love you. I love you with all my soul."

After thirty-six hours straight, the doctors insisted that either she go home and get some rest or they would put her in a room in the hospital. She chose to go home, but she was back at the hospital the next morning. And that afternoon. Ralph lay there, sometimes conscious, most of the time not. Dorothy did not know which was worse, seeing him lying as if dead, or seeing him awake, knowing what had happened to him, in an agony of helpless rage.

The doctors were very stern with her. They prescribed sleeping pills and instructed the nurses to make certain she went home at the end of the day shift. The nurses were more sympathetic, but they did insist that Dorothy could not stay all night at her husband's side.

"No sense you running yourself down and getting yourself sick," said the head nurse of the intensive-care unit. "You're going to need all your strength over the next few days."

Dorothy nodded and went home and wadded up the prescription and threw it in the kitchen wastebasket. She could not sleep, but she would not take their pills. Instead she tried the VR helmet and gloves that Ralph had smuggled home for her several years earlier.

It had started as a joke. He had to go off for two weeks of flying duty in Nevada to keep up his proficiency. It was an annual requirement. Two weeks of flying in real airplanes, practicing real tactics, dogfighting against pilots who were younger each year.

Dorothy had wondered what he was up to when he spent so much money on a used microcomputer. Big as a two-drawer filing cabinet, it had to be rolled in on a dolly by the kid who drove the delivery truck.

"What's that for?" Dorothy asked her husband when he came home that night. The computer was standing in the middle of their living room.

"It's a surprise." And he went back out to the driveway to tug a big cardboard carton from the hatchback of his Trans Am.

"What's going on?" Dorothy asked again while Ralph tugged and pushed the microcomputer into the bedroom, where he had brought the cardboard box.

"Something to keep you from getting lonesome while I'm away," he said.

"What is it?"

"Me."

After four sleepless nights following Ralph's stroke, Dorothy turned on the computer that still sat in the corner of their bedroom and plugged in the data gloves and helmet. The first time she had done this, the night Ralph had brought the equipment home, she had felt awkward, uncomfortable, nervous.

"This is silly," she had said as he helped her put on the gloves and slid the helmet over her thick dark curls. A fine sensor net of hair-thin wires clung to her torso from shoulders to groin. Otherwise she was naked.

"Maybe. We'll see." He was naked, too. And covered with a sensor net.

"I feel like I'm making a porno movie."

"This'll be better than any porn flick," Ralph said. "If this junk works right you can have two of me, one electronic and one real."

It worked, and she could not tell the difference between them.

Now, alone, she sat on the edge of the bed, naked except for the gloves and the sensor net. She fastened one of the tiny disk sensors on each nipple, arranged the others on her shoulders, arms, belly, thighs, buttocks, groin. She put on the helmet and lay back on the pillows she had piled up. She pulled down the visor.

And Ralph was there smiling down at her, his body glistening, his hands reaching for her. She felt his hands on her body, and she slid her own hands across his chest, down his taut abdomen, and felt his erect penis hard and warm in her hands. He sucked her nipples, left then right, and she could feel the juices starting to flow within her.

From far away a bell rang. It seemed so distant that it might have belonged to another world. She was breathing faster now, her body tingling, Ralph's fingers probing gently into her—but the bell broke into her awareness. It jarred her, even though Ralph was totally undisturbed by it.

"Damn," she snapped, sitting up and raising the visor of her helmet. Ralph disappeared, she was alone in their bedroom. Lifting the helmet off her head, Dorothy wormed off one glove, then simply yanked the wires out of the other one. The bell was ringing steadily now. Something must have happened to Ralph! They must have tried to phone and gotten the answering machine, so they drove all the way out here to tell me—what?

Hastily throwing on a robe, she dashed out of the bedroom for the front door to find Dan Santorini standing there looking worried and upset and just as mixed up as the day she had broken off their affair.

"Dan," she said, surprised, relieved that it wasn't someone from the hospital.

"How are you?" he asked.

Before she could reply, he said, "Are you okay? I mean, do you need anything? Are you alone, is anybody taking care of you?"

Dorothy shook her head. "I'm all right, Dan. You don't have to worry. Ralph's taking good care of me."

He looked confused. "Ralph? Ralph's in the hospital."

"I know. It's all right. Don't worry about me."

"Maybe you should see a doctor."

"Don't . . ." She stopped. How much should she tell him? How much would he understand?

"Are you all alone?"

She tried to smile. "Not alone. I've got Ralph. I'll never be alone."

He seemed puzzled. Poor Dan, she thought, he always shows his heart on his face.

Suddenly his eyes fastened on her right hand. "That's a data glove!"

Clutching the robe tighter around her, Dorothy said, "Yes, that's right."

"I don't get it."

"It's nothing for you to worry about."

"But—"

"I'm really all right, Dan," said Dorothy. "I'm fine."

She did not look fine to Dan. Anything but. Yet it was clear that she was not going to ask him into her house. And she was wearing a data glove.

"Well, okay then," he said reluctantly. "I just wanted to make sure you're okay."

She nodded, more of a dismissal than an agreement.

"And—" He felt himself bite his lower lip. "And I'm sorry about Ralph. I feel like hell about it. I can't help thinking that maybe it's my fault."

It was all that Dorothy could do to keep herself from inviting him in. He looked so forlorn, so guilt-ridden.

"It isn't your fault, Dan," she said. "What happened to Ralph was not your doing."

He nodded unhappily and said good night and went back to his rented Chevy in the driveway. He opened the car's door, then looked back at the house. One by one the lights went off as Dorothy went from the foyer through the living room and down the hallway to her bedroom. The bedroom light dimmed but did not go off altogether.

He got into the car and backed out of the driveway, his mind in a whirling turmoil. She was wearing a data glove! And she said Ralph was with her? Is that what she said?

CHAPTER 28

Quentin Smith was clearly unhappy as he tooled his rented black BMW sedan into ParaReality's parking lot and stepped out into the hot afternoon sunshine. Kyle Muncrief could see the displeasure on his face even through the heavily tinted window of his office. Smith clipped his ParaReality ID badge to the lapel of his suit jacket as he brushed past good-natured Joe Rucker without so much as a smile and strode toward the building's front door. With his gray suit and dark sunglasses he looked like an FBI agent stalking down a student protestor.

Which is probably what he is, Muncrief thought.

He leaned back in his big padded swivel chair and ran a finger around his collar. He knew where Smith was heading.

"The guy who's supposed to be working on my program hasn't been in here in more than a week," Smith began the instant he barged into Muncrief's office, without even taking off his shades.

"You just figured that out?"

"I've been making the rounds of the amusement parks waiting for him to come back and get to work. Where the hell is he?"

"He had to go to Dayton."

"And you let him?"

"He didn't ask me about it; he just went."

Smith strode to Muncrief's desk. "You mean he just took off and went to Dayton and left his work here? Without your permission?"

"Hey, I just pay his blasted salary. I don't own him."

"Well, you damned well better get him back here, and right away!"

"His wife says he's coming back tonight."

"He'd better."

Or else, Muncrief added silently. Or else what? He studied Smith's square, blocky face. Even behind the sunglasses he could see that the man was taut with anger. What can he do? Snatch Santorini out of the Air Force base? Send a squad of FBI goons to grab him? Have Dan arrested on some trumped-up charge? I wouldn't put it past him.

"Look," Muncrief said, spreading his hands in a conciliatory gesture, "you don't want him back here any more than I do. I've got millions tied up in his hands, nearly a hundred million. The whole future of the company—"

"You've got no future at all, Muncrief, unless you deliver my program to me by February first." Smith leaned his fists on the desktop and loomed over Muncrief. "Understand that? No goddamned future at all!"

"Hey, you're scaring the hired help."

Muncrief looked past Smith, who whirled around like a man about to reach for his gun. Jace Lowrey stood in the open doorway of Muncrief's office, leaning against the jamb, a knowing grin on his lantern-jawed face.

"You guys want to have a screaming match, at least close the door." Jace stepped into the office and shut the door with exaggerated tenderness. His T-shirt was black, with a spiral galaxy in white and a *You Are Here* notice pointing to one end of the spiral.

"This is a private matter, Jace," said Muncrief.

"Not anymore." His grin widening, Jace pulled up one of the chairs from the conference table and straddled it backward in the middle of the office, resting his forearms on the chair back, his chin on his arms.

"Get out," Smith growled.

"You want your program by February first, don't you?"

Whipping off his sunglasses, Smith stared hard at Jace. "Where did you hear that?"

"You don't have to be Albert Einstein to know that," Jace replied easily.

Turning back to Muncrief, Smith snapped, "You told me Santorini could be trusted."

"Listen," said Jace. "You got a problem, I can solve it for you."

Muncrief said, "What do you mean?"

With a lazy shrug, Jace replied, "Dan's supposed to be working on your program, right? But he's run off to Wright-Patterson because our old boss has some kind of problem he can't handle for himself. Okay, I'm sitting here with practically nothing to do 'cause Dan's off at Wright-Patt. You're steaming up the place 'cause your program's not getting done. So I'll do your program for you. Simple, huh?"

Smith glowered at him.

"And I'll do it better and faster than poor old Dan could ever do it, y'know. February first'll be no sweat, guaranteed."

"You're supposed to be getting the baseball game into shape," said Muncrief.

Another big shrug. "My end of it's all done. We need somebody to plug the stuttering program into it and get it all debugged. Charlie Chan or one of the other slobs can handle it if Dan's not around. I've got plenty time on my hands."

"If I had wanted you working on this program," Smith said sharply, "I would have asked for you in the first place."

"Sure. So you got good ol' reliable Dan Santorini instead of flaky me. And good ol' reliable Dan's off in the woods someplace. Smart move you made, buddy."

Smith bristled. Muncrief huffed. Jace sat there and grinned at them, obviously enjoying their discomfort.

Then Smith said, "You mean to tell me that you know what this program is all about?"

"I peeked at Dan's work, yeah. It's pretty simple, really. I can show you ways to make it a lot better."

"You can, eh?"

"Sure. And I know why you need it by February first, too." Jace's grin became enormous. "Dan'll never get it done in time, y'know. I'm the only chance you've got."

Smith turned back to face Muncrief, who sank back in his chair and wished that he had never even heard of Quentin Smith. Or Jason Lowrey, for that matter.

"All right," Smith said at last. "You're on. But I'm going to stick to you like flypaper, Lowrey. You're not even going to be able to take a piss without my knowing it."

"Hey, you can come in and hold it for me if that kind of stuff turns you on," Jace said, laughing.

"Wait a minute," Muncrief snapped. "Don't I get to say anything about the way my own blasted company is run?"

Smith looked at him with his cold hard eyes. "I think Lowrey's the man for the job—as long as I can stand watch over him."

Jace said, "Don't get yourself all clanked up, Kyle. I'll do this job for our bright boy here and I'll still work out that special job I've been tinkering with for you."

Muncrief raised his hands as if in surrender. Lord, he thought, if Jace starts talking to Smith about that—

But Jace smiled as if he knew what Muncrief was thinking. "Don't worry, boss. Everything's going to work out just fine."

He got up and headed for the door. With a glance over his bony shoulder, he said to Smith, "Come on, bright boy. I'm going to the men's room, and I know you wanna watch." Then he winked broadly at Muncrief and left the office.

Smith hurried after him.

"You know I don't like this one little bit," said Dr. Appleton.

Dan was sitting on the locker-room bench, stripped to his skivvies, while two technicians—both male—draped the sensor net over his bare skin and began taping the individual sensors to his flesh.

"I don't either," said Dan, trying to hide his nervousness. "But I can't see anything else we can do."

"We can drop the program for good," Appleton said through teeth clenched on his unlit pipe. "Go back to the earlier programs that never harmed anybody."

"And then we'll never know what happened, will we?" Dan countered. "And if we don't find out what happened, we'll never be able to make any advances in VR simulations."

"That's better than killing people."

"It's my sim, Doc," said Dan. "Years and years of my work. I've got to find out what happened. I've got to *know*."

"I still think we should shut it down for good and call it quits."

"It would mean the end of your career, Doc."

Appleton took the pipe out of his mouth. "That might not be such a bad idea. I can go out on an early retirement pension. I can make ends meet on that."

Dan looked into his former boss's pale-blue eyes, magnified by the old-fashioned glasses he wore. He saw fear in Doc's eyes. And defeat. The old man was ready to call it quits, to give up everything he had worked for all these years, rather than face another failure. And Dan knew he couldn't allow that. Not to Doc. Not to the man who had picked him out of the toolroom, literally, and taught him everything he knew. I owe Doc my whole life, Dan told himself. He's been more to me than my real father.

"We're not going to let this beat us," Dan said softly.

"I don't want anybody else hurt. Especially you."

"I won't get hurt," he said. "As soon as the sensors show any trouble, the run will abort automatically. Right?"

Appleton nodded tightly and stuck the pipe back in his mouth. "Dan—" He hesitated, swallowed hard. "You mean a lot to me, you know."

Dan nodded, unable to say a word. He just nodded, feeling embarrassed in front of the technicians. Doc looked flustered, too, almost teary-eyed.

The technicians finished with the sensor net. Now came the flight coveralls, and after that the g suit and all the other paraphernalia. Dan remembered seeing a documentary about bullfighters, ages ago. They had teams of men dressing them in their outfits. What did they call them? "Suit of lights." That was it. And here I am getting myself rigged into a suit of lights, kind of. The sensor net worked on light pulses from minuscule diode lasers carried through a spiderweb of cladded-glass optical fibers ten times finer than a human hair.

All that merely flickered through Dan's mind and disappeared as quickly as a laser pulse. There were other matters at hand.

"Doc?" he asked as he stepped into the flight coveralls and zippered up their front. "Did you know that Dorothy has some kind of VR system at her home?"

Appleton's eyes flashed, more in guilt than surprise, Dan thought.

"I went over there last night. She had a data glove on one hand. I'm certain of it."

"No, you must be mistaken," Appleton said flatly, mechanically. And he jabbed the stem of his pipe in the general direction of the two technicians, who were bringing the g suit and equipment vest to Dan.

"Better get your boots on and make certain they're laced up tight," Appleton said. "We can talk about that later on."

Meaning when the technicians have gone, Dan understood. He nodded and bent over to pull on the flight boots.

Dorothy alone, without Ralph. But with a VR system. Who the hell could rig up a VR system for her? Nobody around here would even know where to start, except Jace. And Jace hated Ralph's guts, especially after their fight.

Dan remembered the fight. It had happened when Ralph had just gotten his silver oak leaves.

"Lieutenant colonel," Jace had grumbled. "Our flyboy's coming up in the world."

Jace and Ralph had never gotten along. It was like expecting a cobra and a mongoose to coexist peacefully. Martinez was all Air Force, hard-driving, demanding the best out of everyone in his laboratory command. He was on his way to the Pentagon, that was common knowledge. He would be a general someday.

"One more promotion and he's out of our hair," Jace said. "Once he makes chicken colonel, they'll move him to Washington. I hope."

Dan had grinned at his partner. "I'll bet Ralph will be more than glad to get out of your hair." He reached over and roughed up Jace's wild tangle.

To keep up his proficiency as a fighter pilot, Martinez took part in a two-week exercise in Nevada each summer. "Bottom gun," Jace called it.

"Better not let him hear you say that," Dan warned.

"Him? I'm not afraid of him."

"Or earthquakes," said Dan.

"Listen," Jace said, "with him gone for two weeks, you've got a chance to shack up with Dorothy again."

Dan felt his jaw drop. "Are you crazy? That was finished years ago. Before she married Ralph."

Jace shrugged. "She dropped you for the flyboy. Now's your chance to get even with him."

Dan took it as a joke. Jace's weird sense of humor.

But later that same day, when they went to the hangar where the simulator stood, Jace took one look at Martinez snapping orders to his scurrying technicians and broke into a malicious grin.

"Hey there, Ralphie boy," he drawled, sauntering up to the colonel, "I hear you're gonna be off in the boondocks for two weeks."

Even with his jacket off and his sleeves rolled up, Ralph Martinez was in proper uniform. His tie was correctly knotted and precisely tucked into his shirt; his collar was buttoned at the throat despite the summer sun beating down on the hangar's metal roof.

He gave Jace a flinty stare. "That's right," he said crisply.

"Defending us from the cactus?" Jace asked. "Gonna pop a few coyotes, come back with a coupla trophies?"

Dan wanted to stop Jace but did not quite know how. The technicians, all Air Force noncoms, edged away like barroom bystanders clearing out before the shooting starts.

"Maybe you don't think this country needs defending," Martinez said, his balled fists on his hips.

"What's to defend?" Jace mumbled, turning away from the colonel.

But Martinez heard him. "You don't think this country *deserves* defending?"

"Like I said, what's to defend?"

Dan stepped between them. "Jace, stop baiting him."

"I'm not baiting him! He's going off to shoot up the countryside. Big deal. If I had a good-looking wife with hot blood, I sure as hell wouldn't leave her to sleep by herself."

Martinez pushed past Dan and grabbed Jace by his loose-hanging T-shirt. "What the hell do you mean by that?"

Jace was half a foot taller than Martinez, but the colonel was clearly the bigger man, stronger, more powerful than the skinny scarecrow he held by one fist.

"She's hot stuff, man. And you're gonna be away for two weeks. You think she's gonna stay in bed all by herself—"

Martinez's punch spun Jace completely around, arms flailing. His knees buckled, and he went down to the concrete floor of the hangar. The technicians rushed toward the colonel as Dan found himself standing squarely in front of Ralph, his hands on the colonel's blue-shirted shoulders, pushing him away from Jace. There was murder in Martinez's blazing eyes.

The technicians pulled at his arms and moved him away. Dan turned and saw Jace sitting on the concrete, knees poking up, one hand rubbing his jaw. Dan knelt beside his partner.

"You all right?"

Jace gave him a slow grin. "I thought he could punch a helluva lot harder than that."

Dan snapped out of his reverie as Dr. Appleton handed him a scuffed Air Force blue plastic helmet decorated with red and gold lightning bolts across its sides.

"All right," he said to the two technicians who had dressed Dan. "Give us a few minutes by ourselves."

They cleared out of the locker room, leaving Dan feeling like a football quarterback about to get a pep talk from his coach.

"You said Dorothy has a VR system in her house?" Appleton asked, his voice low.

Fingering the helmet in his hands, feeling the weight of the flight equipment he was wearing, Dan replied, "She was wearing a data glove, that much I saw for myself."

Appleton nodded and tucked his unlit pipe into his jacket pocket. "Jace jury-rigged a system for Ralph," he said, practically in a whisper.

"Jace?" Dan yelped with surprise. "For Ralph?"

"It was surplus equipment," Appleton said, as if justifying himself. "He was always fooling around with the bits and pieces that we were going to junk anyway, you know that."

"But Jace hated Ralph's guts. Why would he—"

"You remember the fight the two of them had?"

Nodding, Dan answered, "I was just thinking about it. Wasn't much of a fight. Ralph hit Jace, and Jace hit the floor. That was it."

Appleton fished the pipe from his pocket again. "Jace set up the system for Ralph right after that. Said it was his way of apologizing."

"Apologizing? Jace?"

"He didn't want anyone to know about it. You know Jace."

"He sure didn't let *me* in on it."

"According to Jace, Ralph misunderstood what he was saying when the fight broke out. Jace said he was trying to show Ralph how to keep Dorothy from getting lonely while he was away on flight maneuvers."

Dan plopped down on the bench that ran the length of the row of lockers. "So he set up a VR system . . . ?"

Appleton looked flustered. "Apparently he did."

"That's what Dorothy meant," Dan muttered.

"What?"

"She said she was with Ralph." Dan felt as if he had been dropped into the middle of the ocean, drifting without a landmark in sight. "She's using a VR program."

Appleton's face was turning redder and redder.

"But that means," Dan reasoned out loud, "that Jace would have had to get Ralph on tape . . ."

"On tape?" Appleton sat down beside Dan.

"Tape or disc, whatever," Dan said.

"You mean—in the act?"

Dan looked at the Doc. *He's been involved with VR systems this long and he still doesn't understand what you can do with them!*

"Not in the act," he said slowly. "But he'd need a full-body video scan and all Ralph's medical records. God knows what else. He'd have to store all Ralph's parameters in a computer file. Then you can reproduce him whenever you want."

"Jace did all that with surplus equipment?" Doc wondered. "Outdated junk?"

"I'll bet he got Ralph to buy a first-rate microcomputer. The simulation may be pretty crude," Dan mused, "but you can use your imagination."

Doc coughed and clamped the pipe in his teeth.

"Touch is a lot more important than vision when you're making love, anyway."

"By all the saints," Appleton murmured. "A VR system for making love. Who would have thought?"

"Jace would," said Dan. "And he did."

Appleton shook his head as if clearing away evil thoughts. He got to his feet. "Well," he said, his voice firm and clear once more, "let's not keep the crew waiting any longer."

Dan nodded and got up from the bench. The equipment they had loaded on him felt almost ludicrously heavy. What the hell am I doing impersonating a fighter pilot? he asked himself.

CHAPTER 29

You're working with Jace now?" Vickie was startled.

Smith nodded tightly. It was clear that he did not like the situation. "I've got no choice, really."

Vickie had spent most of the morning waiting for Smith to show up so she could talk to him. She had provided him with his own office, one of the nice carpeted ones up in the front of the building, across the hall from her own office so she could keep an eye on him. When lunchtime came and he still had not appeared, she went looking for him. And found him in Jace's lab, all the way at the rear of the building.

It took some talking to get him to leave Jace's side long enough to come to the cafeteria for lunch.

"Does Kyle know about this?" Vickie asked as they pushed through the double doors into the crowded cafeteria. Half the company was there, moving slowly through the food line, sitting at tables, voices echoing off the tiled walls, tableware clattering. The aroma of steamed foods and sizzling deep-fat fryers made Vickie's nostrils twitch.

"Yeah. I don't think he's too happy about it, though," Smith said.

The food line stretched almost to the doors. Smith frowned. "Look, I don't want to leave him alone."

"Jace?"

"Jace."

"He'll be all right."

"Maybe. I just don't trust him by himself."

Vickie felt another jolt of surprise. He knows Jace better than I thought.

"But you've got to eat something," she said.

"I'll get a candy bar from the machine. That'll hold me until dinnertime."

"Can I take you to dinner, then?" she blurted.

He blinked at that. "You take me?"

"We can go dutch if you're worried about your machismo."

Smith laughed, a good-natured boyish laugh. "Okay, okay. You can take me to dinner. I'll let you."

"I have some important things I need to talk to you about," Vickie said, totally serious. "I need your help."

He became instantly serious, too. "I don't know when the big genius packs it in for the day, though."

"Phone me when you're ready to go," Vickie said. "My office phone will forward your call if I'm at home or in my car."

"Okay," he said. Then he stepped out of the line and left the cafeteria. Vickie waited a moment, then went out into the hallway, too. She saw Smith pulling a bag of low-cholesterol trail mix from one of the vending machines along the wall. He headed back toward Jace's lab without seeing her. She nodded to herself and went back to her office. She seldom ate lunch, and even more rarely at the cafeteria. At the moment, she had no appetite whatsoever.

As she headed back toward her office, Vickie thought that it might actually be fun for her to get close to Quentin Smith. Okay, she told herself, so he's young enough to be—well, your kid brother. So what? He's the connection to the power in Washington. Kyle's scared of him, but there's no reason why you should be. Especially if he's stuck here in Orlando over the holiday weekend all by himself.

As she entered her office, Vickie asked herself, How much does Smith know about Kyle's problems? How much does Jace know, for that matter? And how can I use the information?

• • •

Dan pulled the helmet on, keeping the visor up. The oxygen mask covered his lower face like a smothering hand. The helmet felt a bit loose as he fastened the chin strap; he was afraid that if he waggled his head it would slip sideways or maybe fall off altogether. It was a reminder that he was out of his element, an intruder in someone else's realm. But the technicians bustling around him as he sat in the simulator's cockpit did not seem to notice the helmet's poor fit. Or maybe they don't care, Dan thought. Maybe they think this is all a farce, a make-believe run of a make-believe flight.

He pulled on the data gloves, then wiggled his fingers inside them as the two techs checked all the connections between his equipment and the cockpit: gloves and helmet lines, electricity for his g suit and heater, oxygen, radio. They worked silently, as efficient and mechanical as robots, Dan thought. The only thing that would make them react like humans would be if they found something wrong. Then they'd snap back to human emotions and speech.

The female tech gave him a grinning thumbs-up. "All plugged in, sir."

Dan nodded. "Okay. Thanks." He grinned back at her inside the mask. All of a sudden he felt like a kid playing with a big, wonderful new toy. All the years I worked here, he said to himself, and I never tried a flight before.

The technicians clambered down to the hangar floor. Doc Appleton stood by the control consoles, gray and tweedy, unlit pipe in his teeth, looking like a father watching his son take the family car for the first time. The chief technician, sitting at the main console, touched the button on his keyboard that remotely closed the simulator's canopy. Dan heard the electrical motor whine, and the plastic teardrop settled over the cockpit, closing him into a gray featureless world. He felt his pulse racing in his ears.

Dan sat with his gloved hands in his lap while the technicians put the simulator through the engine start-up and the taxi to the runway. Oxygen began to flow through the mask, cold and metallic-tasting. His ears popped. The simulator's sound effects and vibrations seemed thoroughly realistic to Dan. In his earphones he heard the crackling instructions of the traffic controllers. He watched as the flap control lever moved by itself and the throttles pushed forward to full takeoff power. The simulator roared and shook nicely. Dan suppressed an urge to giggle; it would be picked up by his helmet mike and put on tape for everyone to hear.

Instead he pulled the helmet visor down in front of his eyes and saw the runway stretching out ahead of him.

"Flight oh-oh-one," said the flight controller's prerecorded voice, "cleared for takeoff."

"Roger," Dan managed to say.

The controls moved by themselves, slaved to the program tape from Ralph's last flight. The runway slid past and Dan saw the ground fall away below him as the F-22 pointed skyward.

This was a daylight mission. In the stereo display on his visor Dan could see checkered farmland rolling away far below, green hills and fuzzy patches that were supposed to represent groves of trees. Roads were light-brown lines drawn across the cartoon landscape; railroad lines were crosshatched in red. Dan realized how far he and Jace had come in making simulations look truly realistic in their baseball program.

We never needed such realistic graphics for the fighter pilots, he told himself, so we never bothered with it. He felt pleased with the progress they had made at ParaReality. And once I get back and put the stuttering technique into the program, nobody will be able to tell the difference between the sim and reality. No difference at all.

There would be enemy fighters meeting him, Dan knew. He swallowed hard in anticipation. It's only a simulation, he reminded himself. No matter what happens in here, this can't hurt you any more than a bad dream could.

Oh, yeah? jeered an inner voice. Then what happened to Ralph and that other pilot?

"How do you feel?" Doc's voice in his earphones startled Dan, forced him to remember that he was sitting in a hangar on the ground.

"Okay so far," he said, his own voice sounding unnaturally loud.

"The sensor net is working fine. All your parameters are in the green."

Doc's trying to reassure me, Dan realized. "I feel fine, no trouble at all," he said. But the oxygen mask felt tight on his face, suffocating.

"The enemy fighters will be coming up in a few moments."

"Yeah. Okay."

Sure enough, a little girl's voice said in his earphones, "A pair of bandits, Daddy. Five o'clock high."

Dan knew it was a synthesis of Jerry Adair's daughter's voice. Yet it sounded vaguely like Angela's. Nonsense! he snapped at himself. You're identifying with the stimulus, just like the psychologists said a pilot would. And then he wondered, Is that what happened to Angie when she saw me in her game at school?

But he had no time to think about that. The pistol-grip side stick was pulling back, and he felt the plane tilt upward into a steep climb. Dan's arms felt heavy in his lap as the plane nosed upward, as if he were experiencing real g forces that an actual maneuver would put him through. His g suit was hissing away, air pressure squeezing against his midsection and thighs. His chest felt heavy, as if an asthma attack were starting.

This isn't supposed to be happening! Dan knew it was all wrong. A simulator sitting on the cement floor of a hangar *could not* produce the gut-wrenching strains he was feeling. It's impossible. We couldn't figure out how to get that into the program!

Yet he felt as if his arms weighed tons, and his chest was so heavy he could barely breathe. He heard himself wheezing, the noise sounding awful inside the helmet, and he realized that the medical sensors were not programmed to shut down the simulation because of an asthma attack.

Dan felt himself being pushed deeper into his padded seat from the increasing acceleration. His neck, his back, even his legs were feeling the g forces now; the helmet felt like an anvil on his head. And he could not breathe; he tried to fight down the panic that the asthma always kindled, but he could not get his breath.

The helmet visor lit up to show his own fighter as a bright yellow swept-wing symbol in the center of the universe, its nose aimed at the sky, with a pair of red symbols moving in swiftly after him.

The g suit was squeezing his guts. He could not move his arms. His chest was flaming raw now, as if somebody were burning it with red-hot sandpaper from the inside. The oxygen mask was suffocating him, and he could not lift his arms to take it off. He could not breathe, he could not even speak. When he tried to tell the controllers to terminate the program, nothing came out but an agonized wheezing cough.

Everything went black.

It wasn't until he felt the technicians lifting the helmet off his head that he realized what had happened. Doc, or the chief tech, somebody had cut the program. He sat in the simulator's cockpit soaking wet with perspiration, chest heaving, mouth gulping for air like a bloated fish, eyes so teary that it took him several moments to recognize Doc leaning into the cockpit.

"I'm sorry, son. God, I'm sorry. I didn't think." Doc was almost babbling. "I forgot all about your asthma. Are you all right?"

Pointing weakly toward the locker room, Dan gasped, "In . . . halator."

Doc sent the corporal dashing to the lockers. It seemed to take hours of wheezing before he came back with the little plastic bottle and pressed it into Dan's hands.

Dan fumbled with the inhalator, then got it up to his mouth and squeezed twice. A fine mist of epinephrine filled his mouth, acrid, biting, delicious. As best as he could manage, Dan sucked it down into his lungs. It hurt. He waited a couple more moments, then squirted another dose of the aerosol into his mouth. He took a deep shuddering breath and the fire inside his lungs began to fade away.

"Glad . . ." he panted, "I brought . . . it."

"Are you all right?" Doc asked.

Dan nodded. "Yeah. I'll be okay. Give me a minute." His chest still felt raw, but the symptoms were receding quickly. They weren't altogether gone, Dan knew. Not altogether. Never. They would always be there, lurking inside him, waiting to knock him down whenever he tried to do something that he shouldn't. Whenever he tried to reach too far. But for now he was okay.

He climbed out of the cockpit and clambered down to the hangar floor, shaky but on his own.

"The medical subprogram wasn't keyed to asthma, was it?" Dan asked rhetorically.

"I heard you gasping in there," Doc said as they started for the locker room. "It sounded like you were strangling. That's why I terminated the program."

"I don't think an asthma attack would've killed me," said Dan. "But it sure made me useless in there."

"Did you get far enough into the mission to find out anything?"

Dan opened the locker-room door and turned to face Appleton. "I found out what happened to Ralph, I think. And the other pilot. Only, it doesn't make any sense."

An hour later, Dan still felt puzzled.

He and Appleton had gone to the cafeteria. The day before the long Thanksgiving weekend the base was half deserted. The cafeteria, huge and hard-used, usually rang with the clattering of trays and silverware and dishes echoing off the brick walls and stainless-steel counters. Now it was hushed and nearly empty. One cashier perched on a stool glumly; barely a trickle of people came through the line.

Dan was ravenous; he stacked his tray with chili, the biggest sandwich he could find, a large Styrofoam cup of coffee, and a slab of pumpkin pie. Appleton took a salad and a lemonade.

Doc steered them to the farthest corner of the quiet cafeteria, where there was a virtual sea of empty tables between them and the nearest diners.

"What you're telling me, then," said Doc as they sat down, "is that *physiological* inputs have been built into the program?"

"I felt the g forces, Doc," said Dan, nodding. "And it wasn't in my head. I couldn't lift my damned hands out of my lap!"

"But that's impossible."

"Is it?" Dan took a spoonful of the chili and winced. It was bland and tasteless, but steaming hot enough to burn his tongue.

"You know it's impossible," Appleton said.

Wishing he had taken an iced drink instead of the hot coffee, Dan answered, "Doc, there's two kinds of impossibilities here: One, it's impossible to make the VR system put physical stresses into your body; and, two, it's impossible that somebody rigged the simulation to include physical stresses."

Appleton nodded.

"Which impossible are you talking about?" Dan asked.

"Both."

"You're saying it's impossible to make a VR system that gives the user physical stresses?"

"I'm saying it's impossible to make *that* system, the one out in the hangar, do that." Hunching closer over the tray-covered table, Appleton said, "There's no sensory-input devices for the kinds of physical stresses you're talking about, Dan! The system has visual inputs, yes. Audio inputs. But that's it. Not even the data gloves put sensory inputs *into* the user. They're one-way, outgoing. You move your hands and fingers and the system reads the motions as commands to the computer. You know that."

"I know what I felt," Dan insisted.

"It was psychological. It had to be psychological."

"You think psychological stress gave Ralph a stroke? And killed Adair?"

Appleton fell silent.

"Suppose it's not impossible," Dan said, his lunch and his hunger utterly forgotten. "Just suppose, for the sake of discussion, that it could be done."

"All right." Reluctantly.

"Who could have done it?"

"No one could have done it, Dan. You know that. It's just not possible."

"But suppose it *is* possible," Dan insisted, hunching closer to Doc.

Appleton hesitated. "Ralph thought it might have been Yuri Yevshenko."

"The Russian exchange guy?" Dan shook his head. "No. He didn't have the smarts for something like this."

With a beleaguered sigh, Doc said, "Then that leaves nobody but you and Jace."

"It wasn't me."

"Then it has to be Jace."

"But it couldn't have been Jace. He wasn't here for the past year. I was the only one working on the sim after Jace left."

Doc looked lost, bewildered.

"Besides," Dan went on, "why would Jace louse up the sim? He put as many years into it as I did. Even if somehow he could have done it, why would he try to screw things up?"

"Ask him," said Doc.

"But we worked side by side for all those years. Why would he want to ruin his own work? And mine? For chrissakes, Doc, he's my friend! The closest friend I've got. He's your friend, too."

Appleton's pale eyes went cold. "He's not my friend or yours, Dan."

"What do you mean?"

"Jason Lowrey is nobody's friend," Doc said. "I don't think he's capable of friendship."

"No, Doc, you're wrong."

"Face the facts, Dan. Jace would crucify his own mother if he thought it would make an interesting VR simulation."

CHAPTER 30

t was only three o'clock, but as she walked up the corridor toward Muncrief's office Vickie could see that the lab was emptying out. A steady trickle of people passed her, heading toward the back door and the employee parking lot. The day before a holiday, Vickie thought. With all the work we've got to get done in order to open Cyber World on time, they still slink out of here like kids sneaking out of school.

Most of them looked embarrassed as they passed her. Man or woman, they each put on the same shitty little smile and wished her a happy holiday.

"Happy Thanksgiving," Vickie sang back cheerily at each of them. "See you Monday, bright and early."

Maybe I'm being too hard on them, she thought. A lot of them will be back in here Friday and through the weekend. Still, she bristled inwardly that they were leaving before the official quitting time.

Muncrief was at his desk, phone clamped to his ear. There's no Thanksgiving weekend coming up in Tokyo, Vickie knew. Nor in Switzerland. And I'll bet Max Glass is in his office in New York, too.

"Okay, Dan," she heard Muncrief say as she took one of the cushioned chairs in front of his desk. "Thanks for calling."

"Dan?" Vickie asked as Muncrief hung up.

Kyle looked haggard, as if he had not slept in days. His eyes were rimmed with red, dark bags under them. The pressure's really getting to him, Vickie told herself.

"He's coming back tonight," Muncrief said wearily. "The Air Force is flying him into Kissimmee."

"Well, that's something, at least."

Fluttering a hand in the air, Muncrief said, "He sounded apologetic as all hell. Said he'd work through the weekend to make up for the time he's taken off."

Vickie was not as easily assuaged as Muncrief. She knew that Dan would probably have worked through the weekend anyway.

"I see that Jace is working with Smith now," she said.

Muncrief's dejected face settled into a scowl. "Yeah," he said sourly.

"Is that wise?"

"Not a blasted thing I can do about it. He just waltzed in here, told Smith he knows all about it and he can do a better job than Dan can. Smith bought it."

"That's going to be trouble," said Vickie.

"Like we don't have trouble already."

"I know. But Jace—"

Muncrief shook his head like a fighter who had taken too many punches. "Look, the guy wants Jace to do his job, but he doesn't trust Jace as far as he can throw the Washington Monument. So he's going to stick so close to Jace he's going to be like a tapeworm."

Vickie felt her hands gripping the arms of the chair tightly. Forcing herself to relax, she mused, "Well, Jace is certainly the better man for the job, if Smith can keep his nose to the grindstone."

"Maybe, maybe not. At any rate, Smith is going to stay right here for the duration."

"I see," said Vickie.

Muncrief gave her a bleary glare. "Do you? Do you have any idea of what this means? That blasted G-man hanging around here, poking his nose into everything?"

"Kyle—"

"Toshimura trying to slit my goddamned throat, making deals

with who-knows-who behind my back. Reporters sniffing around. We're behind schedule on Cyber World. Money running out. Good God, Vickie, it's all going to come crashing down on my head!"

He looked as if he would burst into tears.

"It's all right, Kyle," she said placatingly. "It's all going to be all right."

"How can it be all right? Everything's coming unglued, for God's sake!"

"Don't get your blood pressure up. Dan's coming back, you said. They'll get the baseball game on track, you'll see. And Jace will keep Smith happy, which means the Washington money will keep coming in."

Muncrief sunk his head into his hands. "That guy scares me, Vickie. If he finds out about me . . . ."

Vickie thought Kyle should be more worried about what would happen if Dan found out about what he was doing. But she said soothingly, "Don't worry about Smith. I'll look after him. He's not interested in your past. I'll take care of him, you'll see."

Dan awoke with a start when the jet's wheels thunked down and the servomotors that actuated the flaps began their high-pitched whine.

The Air Force copilot ducked his head through the cockpit hatch and hollered over the engine noise, "You awake?"

"Yeah," Dan shouted back.

"Seat belt tight? We're on the downwind leg."

Dan nodded and tugged at his seat belt. He had been dreaming. He vaguely recalled being with Dorothy, in bed, the way they had made love years ago. But somebody else was watching them; he could not tell if it was Ralph or Doc or maybe even Jace. Whoever it was, his face was hidden. In his dream Dan wanted to make love to Dorothy, but he couldn't until he found out who it was that was watching them and made him go away.

Jace. Everything boiled down to Jace. He made a masturbation machine for Ralph and Dorothy. That's what it is, Dan told himself. No matter how sophisticated it may be, no matter what kind of visions and sensory inputs Jace was able to build into the system, it's nothing more than an electronic jerk-off. Dan had not been inside a church since Philip's christening, but his childhood catechism classes still triggered a trained reflex of revulsion.

The jet's wheels screeched on the runway once, twice, then the plane settled down. The pilot reversed thrust and slewed the executive twin-jet onto the ramp that led to the modest flat-roofed structure of the Kissimmee Airport terminal.

Topcoat and travel bag in hand, Dan ducked through the hatch and down the shaky metal ladder and saw Susan waiting for him just inside the air-conditioned terminal's glass door. Angela stood beside her and Philip was sitting in his stroller, apparently asleep.

He ran for the door, pushed it open, dropped his bag and coat, and wrapped his arms around his wife.

"I'm glad you're home," Sue said after a long kiss.

"Me too."

Dan saw that Phil was indeed sound asleep as he turned and swooped Angie up in his arms.

"Hello, Angel!"

She grabbed his ears and kissed him wetly on the cheek.

Susan drove the Subaru home, Dan in the right-hand seat and Angela in the back next to Phil's car seat. For a few minutes Dan forgot about the mess at Wright-Patt, the work at ParaReality, about Jace and Doc and everything except the tight little family that surrounded him.

"How's Ralph?" Susan's question brought him back to reality.

"They don't think he'll make it," Dan answered. "But he seems to be holding his own. For now."

"Still paralyzed?"

"His whole left side. He can't talk, either."

"God, he must feel like he's in prison—inside his own body."

Dan felt himself biting his lip. "Yeah. It must be pretty bad."

"Did you see Dorothy?"

A danger signal flashed in Dan's mind. He recalled his dream. "Just for a minute. She's . . . pretty broken up by all this."

"I can guess."

Twisting around inside his shoulder belt, Dan turned to his daughter. "How're you doing, Angel?"

"Fine." Angela smiled widely enough to show both sets of braces.

Dan saw that Philip was awake now and looking at him with a strangely studious expression on his chubby, round-cheeked face.

"Yes, it's your father," he said to Phil, reaching over the seat to tickle his tummy. "I haven't been away so long you've forgotten me, have I?"

Philip laughed and waved all four of his limbs. Angela smiled at her father. Susan kept her eyes on the road as she drove into the deepening twilight.

"Oh, by the way," she said as casually as she could manage, "we're going out to dinner tomorrow."

Dan turned back from the children. "Going out to eat? On Thanksgiving?" He felt almost betrayed.

Susan nodded, eyes fixed straight ahead. "I've got work to do. I won't have time to cook; I haven't even had time to shop. So I made a reservation at the Empress Lilly in Disney Village."

"The Empress Lilly?"

"It's a very nice restaurant on a Mississippi River paddle-wheel boat," said Susan.

"With the kids?"

"Yes."

Watching his wife's profile, Dan saw that Susan's chin was up in her no-nonsense posture. The decision had been made, and there was no use arguing about it. He realized that in all the time they had been living here in Florida, he had not yet taken the family to Disney World. He made a weak grin.

"Okay, honey," he said. "I was planning to spend most of the day at the lab, anyway."

"Me too," said Susan.

It was almost nine when Smith finally called Vickie. She was half undressed and half asleep on her bed watching a rerun of *Dynasty* when the phone rang.

"That guy Lowrey has no concept of time," Smith complained.

"We have to be patient with genius," said Vickie with a small smirk, glad that her phone was not a video instrument.

"I appreciate your invitation for dinner," he said. "But it's probably too late for you, huh?"

Vickie realized she had not eaten a thing since breakfast. "Well, it is rather late . . .ʺ

"I'm starving," he said.

He sounded hungry, she thought, for more than food. "All right. But there won't be many places open at this time of night."

"How about the Moroccan Pavilion at EPCOT? They keep their restaurant open until midnight."

Without further thought, Vickie said, "Fine. I'll meet you there in three-quarters of an hour."

As she swiftly dressed and put on her makeup, Vickie smiled at his choice of restaurant: there would be belly dancers at the Moroccan Pavilion, she knew. She decided to wear a white belted tank dress with a gold-trimmed white jacket over it. Simple and modest, with a knee-length skirt.

When she saw Smith waiting for her at the restaurant's bar, he was in the same light-gray suit he had worn all day. She had never seen him in anything else. Did he bring only one suit or did he have several, all the same?

Once they were seated at their table and picking at an appetizer of stuffed grape leaves, Vickie said, over the reedy Middle Eastern music, "Quentin seems such a formal name."

"It's a family tradition. Actually, I'm Quentin Wayne Smith the Third."

"That's a mouthful. What do your friends call you?"

"Mr. Smith."

That brought Vickie up short. Then she saw he was grinning at her.

"Chuck," he said. "My friends call me Chuck."

"Not Smitty?"

"No." He shook his head. "Never Smitty. I hate that."

He was rather handsome when he smiled, Vickie thought. Good-looking in a boyish, athletic way. But he didn't come across as boyish. This was a man, an adult who looked out at the world through those startling blue eyes and measured everything very rationally. He was ambitious, that Vickie could see easily. Already working in the White House. It seemed perfectly clear to her that he had plans to move higher.

But apparently his mind was on things closer to hand.

"I guess I'll be in the lab all day tomorrow with your resident genius," he grumbled. "Is there a portable TV I can bring into his lab? I don't want to miss the Thanksgiving games."

"I don't think there are any portables in the building," Vickie replied, reaching for a piece of the round, flat pita bread.

"Rats."

"But there's a tabletop TV in Muncrief's conference room. You could watch the games in there. Or unplug it and carry it down to Jace's lab if you want to stay there with him."

His face brightened. "Okay. That'll work."

"Just remember to bring it back again after you're through with it."

"Sure. Okay."

They made innocuous conversation through dinner. Vickie wanted to tell him about her problem with Peterson and whoever he was working for, but she hesitated, waiting for the right moment, the right mood. Then the belly dancer came out and she saw that Smith pulled a pair of eyeglasses from his jacket pocket and wiped them carefully before putting them on. The dancer was young and lithe and buxom. Smith never took his eyes off her.

She made a mental note of that.

After dinner, they went out to the artificial lake and watched the nightly fireworks display. As the crowd gasped and applauded the colorful bursts, Smith asked, "You said you needed my help?"

"I think I do," she said, keeping her voice low.

"What's the problem?"

"Security," she replied, hoping that it was a word that would catch his interest.

It did. In the shadowy light she could not make out the expression on his face, but his whole body seemed to tense.

"We have competitors—"

"We?"

"ParaReality. There are plenty of big corporations who are very curious about what we're doing."

She saw his teeth flash into a grin. Smith gestured toward the lake, the fanciful buildings, the crowd, the fireworks. "Our genial host, for one, I imagine."

"Disney, yes. MGM. Plenty of others. From overseas, too."

"Foreign competition," he murmured.

"They've hired a private investigator. At least one, that I know of. He contacted me—"

"How?"

"Phoned me at home one night. Said he wanted to meet with me and make me rich. Not in so many words, but his meaning was pretty clear."

"What did you do?"

Victoria took a deep breath. She was walking a tightrope here and she knew it. "I went along with him. To find out as much as I could. Find out how much he already knew, who he was working for. You know."

"That can be pretty tricky."

"So I discovered. He seems to know quite a lot about ParaReality. He must have informants inside the company. And he knows you're from the government."

"Damn!"

"I don't think he knows what you're doing here," she added hastily.

"Who's he working for?"

"I haven't been able to find out. I—" Vickie realized that her voice was shaking slightly and it was no act. "He scares me, Chuck. He's starting to threaten me. I told him I wouldn't talk to him anymore and he said things could get very rough for me."

For several moments Smith said nothing. Vickie looked up into his face, lit by the flickering glow of the fireworks. He looked grim.

"I'll take care of it," he said at last. "Give me his name and everything else you know about him. I'll have some people check him out."

Vickie gushed thanks all over him while a part of her mind marveled at the fact that she actually felt almost as relieved and grateful as she was telling him.

Then she said, "Look—there's no reason to tell Kyle about this."

"He doesn't know?"

"I haven't told him. He has enough to worry about."

Smith's expression seemed to go stony. It was hard to tell in the stroboscopic light of the fireworks, but he seemed to be eyeing her suspiciously now.

"Besides," she added quickly, "Kyle's very sensitive about having you around. He doesn't like having to deal with the government. He wants to keep ParaReality entirely under his control."

"But it isn't, is it?"

Ignoring his jab, Vickie went on, "He's almost paranoid about the company. If he found out that you're going to involve more government people—"

"For his own company's protection."

"Even so," Vickie said. "Just leave him out of this, okay? You and I can handle it without getting Kyle involved."

He nodded, but Vickie thought it was reluctantly. He can see through me, she told herself. He knows I haven't told him the whole truth.

The fireworks ended and everyone headed for their cars. Smith started to stroll around the perimeter of the lake.

"Give them a little time to clear out the parking lot," he suggested. "Be easier to find your car then."

"Good thinking," said Vickie.

"You'll be okay to drive home alone?"

"I think so. But I feel a lot better about everything now that you're going to do something about Peterson. Thanks again."

"Nothing to it. I ought to thank you for taking pity on a lonely man and having dinner with me," Smith said as the meager crowd moved past them.

"My motherly instinct," she said.

He smiled in the darkness. "Do I come across like a lost little boy to you?"

"Not really. But I was surprised that you didn't fly back to Washington for the holiday. Don't you have family there? Friends?"

"I've got to stick close to Jace," he said tightly. "He may be a genius, but I can't trust him to do what I want without blathering about it to everybody he sees unless I'm right there with him. And now I've got this Peterson thing to worry about. I'm not going anywhere until this job is finished."

"But you let him go home alone?"

Again that tight smile. "He's being watched; don't worry. If he sneezes, I'll know it."

"Oh." Vickie was surprised for a moment, then relieved that

Smith already had helpers on hand. She returned to her original line of questioning. "Do you have family and friends in Washington?"

"In Washington what I have mostly are associates, teammates, a few helpers, a lot of hinderers." He hesitated a beat, then added, "Plenty of competitors."

"Esther never told me exactly what you do in the White House. . . ."

"Esther Cahan. Nice woman. Very bright."

"What do you do there?"

He stopped and leaned on the railing that circled the lake, asking, "What are you after, Vickie?"

"Me?" The question caught her by surprise, and she had to make time to think. "What do you mean?"

"You're an extremely attractive woman and the boss's right hand. I'll admit that I'm young and handsome and incredibly attractive. And unattached. But why did you invite yourself to dinner with me? You could've told me about Peterson in your office. What are you after?"

Vickie decided that he was too sharp to play games with. "Your job in the White House," she said. "Whatever it is."

He gaped at her, then threw his head back and laughed. "My job? And then what do I do? Retire to Disney Village?"

"No," Vickie replied. "You move up."

For a long moment he made no reply. Finally, "I don't think you have any idea of what a shark pool Washington really is."

"I have some idea," she said. "I've been there."

"And you want to help me get ahead, is that it? Because of your motherly instinct?"

She ignored his sarcasm. "If I help you, then you can help me. Isn't that the way the game is played?"

"This isn't a game, kid. It's deadly real."

"So am I," Vickie snapped. "I don't intend to be Kyle Muncrief's nursemaid forever."

"Are you sleeping with him?"

"With Kyle?" She almost laughed aloud. She almost said that Kyle was not interested in any woman older than twelve. But she caught herself. "Never sleep with the boss. It's foolish."

"Amen." He said it with a fervor that made her wonder. Then

he added, "My hotel's about a fifteen-minute walk from here."

"Let's get my car from the parking lot."

"Good thinking. You can park all night at the hotel."

And Vickie said to herself, This will seal the bargain. He knows I'm not telling him everything, but he's willing to go along with it as long as I'm willing to go along with him. Smiling inwardly, she thought that it might be the best deal she had made in a long time.

CHAPTER 31

I t felt really strange toting Susan and both kids to the lab. The front parking lot was empty, Dan saw. Still, he drove slowly around to the back. Nothing there either, except Joe Rucker's beat-up T-Bird with its handicapped license plate. And Jace's bike. Yes, it was there. Dan felt his teeth clamp together. I've got to face him down and find out what the hell he's done. I've got to. Can't let him off the hook this time. Can't let him push me around, either. I've got to get the truth out of him. Lives depend on it, and there's nobody else to get it done except me. I've got to do it. Got to.

Dan parked his bird-spattered Honda under one of the live oaks.

He had told Susan nothing about what had happened at Wright-Patt. Nothing about his near-certainty that somehow, in some weird way, Jace was at the bottom of the problem there.

"Brung the whole family, did ye!" Joe Rucker's cheerful voice called across the parking lot as Dan tugged Philip's car seat from the back of the Honda.

"Hello, Joe. Happy Thanksgiving."

Rucker limped across the lot, touched the bill of his cap as he smiled at Susan. "Mornin', Mizz Santorini."

"I thought I was the only one working today," Dan said as he headed for the rear door, lugging the car seat and a slim briefcase.

Rucker took the bag of toys that Susan was holding and, with the bag dangling from his hand, pointed toward the bicycle leaning against the loading-dock wall. "Nope. Ol' Jace is here, workin' his head off. And me, o' course. Place needs guardin' even on Thanksgiving."

Angela stared at Rucker. She had never seen a one-armed man before.

"I'll have to make out visitor's badges for y'all," Rucker said as he limped toward the rear entrance. "Can't go into th' building 'less you've got a badge. 'Cept fer the front lobby, o' course."

"There ought to be a consultant's badge for Mrs. Santorini," Dan said as they reached the door.

"I'll check in the security office," said Rucker.

Dan led the little procession down to the Pit, the computer center, where Rucker left them and shambled up the corridor. He was back moments later with a red consultant's badge and green temporary badges for Angela and the baby. Susan peeled the back off Angie's badge and let her stick it onto her blouse. She put Philip's badge in her purse.

"I reckon that's all right," Rucker said, "seein' how he's too little to wear it regular-like." Satisfied that the company's security regulations had been followed, he left them in the Pit and headed back to his post at the rear door.

"He looks familiar," Susan said. "Wasn't he one of the guards at Wright-Patterson?"

"Couldn't have been," Dan said.

"I'm sure I saw him there a couple of years ago."

"They wouldn't hire a cripple for guard duty," Dan said. "They use the Air Police."

"I saw him somewhere," Susan insisted. "I know I did."

Dan shrugged it off as he set Susan up at one of the desks in the computer center. It was a square room big enough for a dozen people to work in simultaneously. Along the back wall stood the big IBM and DEC mainframes, tall and blocky as refrigerators. The Cray supercomputer was against the side wall. No windows. The whole ceiling was covered with glareless light panels. The tile flooring was slightly spongy, easy on the feet.

Angela immediately went to the copying machine. "This is bigger than the one in your old lab, Daddy," she said.

Dan grunted agreement as he unfolded Philip's playpen and put the baby into it while Sue unpacked a hamper full of Phil's toys and dumped them in with him. Both Susan and Angela were in jeans; their Thanksgiving dresses were hanging in the back seat of the car.

Dan pecked his wife on the cheek and marched toward Jace's cluttered lab like a soldier heading for the battle front.

"Back from the wars, huh?" Jace barely looked up from the desktop computer he was hunched over, bony knees poking up almost to the keyboard's level. The other machines were silent, their screens blank.

Dan took off his suit jacket, hung it on the peg behind the lab's door, then plunked his briefcase down on the table beside Jace.

"Briefcase?" Jace looked surprised. "You going executive, kiddo?"

"Got a fresh shirt and a tie in it," Dan explained tightly. "Taking the family out to dinner around four o'clock."

Jace laughed. "The joys of married life, huh?"

"Ralph's still alive, if that's of any interest to you," Dan said.

"Too bad. He could've been a hero if he had sense enough to die."

"Jesus! Even if he lives, he's going to be crippled for the rest of his life! He can't even talk, for God's sake."

"Tough."

Before Dan could answer, he saw what was on Jace's display screen: a videotape of last year's economic summit meeting in Copenhagen. "Hey! That's the Washington program. That's my work!"

"Not anymore, pal." Jace hooked a gangly arm over the back of his chair. "I talked Smith and Muncrief into letting me do it. You concentrate on the stuttering program."

"But I was supposed to be—"

"You ran off to play with the flyboys. Smith needs his job by February first, remember? So now I'm doing it. It's fun, really. I'm putting in a few wrinkles you would've never thought of."

Dan pulled up one of the wheeled secretary's chairs and sat down next to Jace.

"Watch this," said Jace. He flicked his fingers across the keyboard and three of the men sitting around the broad conference table disappeared, replaced by women. Dan recognized each one of them.

"They're movie stars."

"Uh-huh." With a jack-o'-lantern grin, Jace tapped the keyboard again and each of the women was suddenly nude. The men continued their earnest discussions, oblivious to Jace's manipulations.

Dan shook his head, more in disappointment than awe. "You sure know how to waste your time," he said.

"Like hell," Jace snapped. He pecked a single key and the scene returned to its original form. "The whole point of this program, Danno, is to manipulate the data."

"Smith wants to be able to *handle* the data efficiently, not manipulate it," Dan said.

Jace gave him a sorrowful look. "Dan, you're so square, you've got edges on you. When Smith says 'handle,' what he really means is 'manipulate.' "

"There's a difference."

"Damn right. Control a guy's information input and you control the decisions he makes."

"Everybody knows that."

"Sure." Jace hunched closer to Dan, brimming with excitement. "But with VR we can make the guy *experience* the results of his decisions, right? We can show the President of the friggin' United States what would happen if he told the economic summit to go take a flying leap into the nearest toilet bowl. We can show him how the leaders of the other nations would react."

Shaking his head strongly, Dan said, "We could only show the President how his aides *think* the other leaders would react."

"Oh, yeah? With a VR system we could make the aides' guesses so real the President would swallow 'em hook, line, and sinker."

Dan felt a surge of something close to anger. "That's why it's important to do this job right, with no messing around. If what we do is going to go to the President, then we've got to make certain he's getting the absolute straight stuff. Not somebody's biased version."

"Aw, come off it, pal," Jace countered. "There ain't no such thing as a totally unbiased version of anything. You know that! Everybody manipulates the data, one way or the other."

Dan sank back in the little chair. It rolled slightly backward, wheels squeaking against the concrete floor.

"But then you're not just manipulating the data. You'd be manipulating the President."

"Now you've got it." Jace patted Dan's knee the way a teacher would when a slow pupil finally arrived at the right answer.

"But that's not legal!"

"It's not against the law," said Jace.

"It's not right!"

Jace made a pitying smile. "I looked it all up. I did a computer search. There's nothing in the Constitution or anywhere else that says the President's aides have got to give him straight, unbiased information. Hell, I even spent all last night looking up old TV documentaries about Presidents: Lyndon Johnson during the Vietnam years, Nixon and Watergate, all that stuff. Most Presidents *want* their aides to massage the raw data for them. They want to be told what they want to hear, man! Ever since good ol' George Washington."

"That still doesn't make it right," Dan insisted.

Shrugging, Jace answered, "So what? Nobody's talking nuclear war anymore."

"Look," Dan said, "one of the input tapes I was working with dealt with the rain forests in South America—"

"Yeah, yeah," said Jace impatiently. "The environmentalists want us to muscle those countries and make them stop chopping down the trees."

"But suppose the lumber interests, the people who make money out of chopping down the trees, get control of the VR system. They could play scenarios for the President that downgrade the environmental impact and support the economic benefits of stripping the forests bare!"

"Right."

"And the President would *believe* it!"

"Damned right."

"But that's wrong!" Dan nearly shouted.

"Who the fuck cares? I'm going to be manipulating the friggin' President! Me! I'm gonna make him jump through hoops, pal. Just wait and see."

"But, Jace, with that kind of power comes a responsibility. This isn't a game anymore."

"Sure it is. Don't take everything so seriously."

"But VR's *powerful,* Jace," said Dan. "You know that!"

Jace grinned knowingly. "You mean like that gunfight sim that you won't get into anymore?"

Dan sat there blinking at his friend for several moments. "You really want to manipulate the President."

"Why not?"

"But why should you? What do you want—"

"For the hell of it," Jace said, almost gleefully. "Just to see how it feels. And besides, Smitty can get me all kinds of good stuff for whatever else I wanna do. I'll be able to get my hands on anything the government's got. Think of it, Danno! Whole computer networks! Think of what I could do with that!"

"You can't be serious."

"The hell I'm not."

"But . . . the President of the United States."

Jace tapped him on the knee again. "Listen, kiddo, why do you think Smith's in such a friggin' sweat to have this system on-line by the first of February?"

Before Dan could respond, Jace gave the answer, "Because the President gives his State of the Union speech in February. Right? Right."

Susan knew that she could have ensconced herself and the children in Dan's office instead of the computer center. For that matter, she could have done the work she claimed she was doing from her little kitchen alcove at home. But she had told Dan that she had to have access to ParaReality's computer center, and her husband—too preoccupied with his own problems to pay that much attention to her—had delivered her unquestioningly to the company's nerve hub.

Ostensibly, Susan was hunting down every possible reference to nerve physiology that she could find in the literature on sports medicine and cross-referencing them by author, subject, and the places where the authors did their work. And she actually was doing that task, using one of the computer center's modem-equipped machines to tirelessly track down the literature, based on a long string of keywords that she had found in a search she'd done the week before.

But in addition to the task she was getting paid to do, the task that her husband had asked her to do, Susan was at the computer center for a reason of her own. The literature search was going on, the computer doggedly tracking down every reference that could be supplied by the National Research and Education Network, plus half a dozen more specialized medical information services. Susan hardly glanced at that machine as page after page of journal entries flickered across its screen almost faster than the human eye could register.

Her real concentration was on performing a delicate bit of electronic burglary, or trying to. It was not easy, because she did not want to leave any trace of her intrusion into the files of ParaReality's personnel chief, Victoria Kessel.

Phil suddenly wailed and Susan snapped her attention from the display screen in front of her to her baby. Angie, happily making color copies of her own drawings, turned from the copying machine toward her brother. The baby had thrown each and every one of his cuddly toys out of the playpen and now wanted somebody to give them back to him. Susan smiled at the incongruity of the scene: a yowling baby sitting in a blanket-lined playpen in front of a row of desktop computers.

Angela dashed from the copying machine to Philip's playpen. "I'll pick them up," she said to her mother.

"Thanks, Angel," said Susan.

Scooping up an armful of the soft animal shapes, Angela said firmly to her brother, "Well, if you throw them all away, silly, then you won't have anything left to play with."

She's playing mother, Susan thought. I guess that's what I sound like. Not too bad, I suppose.

Angela took her thumb-sized Amanda doll from the toy box she had brought and handed it to her brother. Susan watched, fascinated, as her daughter said to the baby:

"Now this is a very special friend. You take good care of her, understand?"

Philip grasped the little doll and immediately stuck it in his mouth. Angie shook her head in disappointment, then turned to her mother.

"It's all right, Mommy. He can't hurt Amanda."

Marveling at her daughter's forbearance, Susan turned her attention back to her work. All the school's VR games were controlled by Vickie from her office. Which meant that there was a program in the ParaReality system somewhere that operated the school games. Vickie could send a certain game to a certain VR booth at the school with a few strokes on the keyboard in her office. Susan was searching for that program, and for the complete list of games.

She was certain that there were different variations of the games, certain as only a mother can be. Faced with a choice between her pubescent daughter's distressed tales and the repeated assurances of her husband's employer, Susan knew with absolute conviction that her daughter was telling the truth and the others were lying.

She did not know why. At this stage she had not really given it that much thought. She was driven to prove that her daughter was not overreacting, not imagining things, not hypersensitive to the suggestions of an ordinary VR game that had not affected any of the other children in the school. Angie's a normal, healthy child, Susan assured herself. If there's something wrong here, it's not her. It's the games that Vickie programs into the school's equipment.

She needed to do this snooping into ParaReality's files from the company's own computer center because she did not want Vickie to discover that she had been rummaging through the files. Susan had taken the precaution of altering the mainframe's internal clock, so that if Vickie or anyone else saw that their files had been accessed, the computer would tell them it had been done in the middle of the afternoon two days earlier, a normal working day when dozens of different employees had access to the computer center.

Got to remember to reset the clock before we leave, Susan reminded herself for the fortieth time.

She glanced at Phil. The baby seemed happy enough, sitting in the midst of his toys. He had a stuffed tiger by one rear leg and was pounding it merrily on the back of a frayed-looking teddy bear. It doesn't take much to keep a baby happy, Susan thought. Or a twelve-year-old, for that matter. Angie had spread her papers and colorful felt-tip pens on the floor and was busily drawing pictures.

The list of school games she had found showed no variants. Yet

Susan was certain there must be some. She accessed Vickie's personal files and found that most of them were locked from her view. She needed special code words to open these files.

Susan stared at the list like a burglar studying a growling Doberman. It's such a long list, she said to herself. How can Vickie possibly remember all the code words for each individual file? She must have a separate file of code names. But what would she call it?

Susan was no hacker. She tried straightforward possibilities such as "file codes" and "list names." Nothing. The screen remained stubbornly blank, except for a message line across its bottom: ERROR. FILE NOT FOUND.

She got up from her chair and walked across the room toward the big bulky mainframes. Glancing at the children, she saw that Angie was now folding the papers she had been drawing on, turning them into lopsided origami figures of birds and animals, and dropping them into Philip's playpen. The baby delightedly batted at them with his dimpled fists.

Susan leaned over the keyboard of the big IBM and booted it up. It hummed to life, lights winking across its front panel. Still standing at the keyboard, Susan looked over the menu of options on its display screen. This is like using a nuclear weapon to kill a mosquito, she thought as she plugged Vickie's entire set of files into the mainframe.

FILES LOADED, the screen reported.

Susan returned to the machine's basic menu and scanned the list for two items. She found neither one of them.

"Okay," she muttered to herself, "we can fix that."

Pulling up a typist's chair, Susan used the IBM to search for Vickie's word-processing program. She found it: WordPerfect 9.0. Good. She accessed the program. The screen showed a string of symbols across the top, information on how to use the program. She touched the List Files key.

The screen filled with a brief list of words and symbols. Fourteen file names. One of them, Susan knew, was the file that contained Vickie's code names. She ran down the list, seeking the word that would unlock Vickie's secret code words. But each time she tried to gain entry into one of the files, the screen asked: ACCESS CODE? and would go no further.

Susan clenched her teeth as she stared at the screen. One of these files contains all the code names, she told herself, but I can't get the damned codes unless I know the code name of that particular file. Catch-22.

What would a real hacker do? she asked herself. She had read news stories about ten-year-olds who had broken into computer files of national banks, investment houses, even the Pentagon, using nothing more than their home computers, a telephone link, and their ingenuity.

GET DICTIONARY, she typed. Then she pressed Enter.

The screen split into two parts: one retained the file list, the right-hand side showed a string of words beginning with "A, a (a) *n;* (pl) A's a's As, as: 1. the first letter of the Roman and English alphabet . . ."

WORD SEARCH, Susan commanded. CORRELATE A/B. Enter.

The right side of the screen disappeared in a blur too fast to follow. In a few minutes, Susan knew, the computer would display every word used in Vickie's file names. Maybe the list would include the words that were hidden from normal access. Would Vickie be so security conscious that she would hide access to her code words even from the dictionary search subprogram?

Susan hoped not.

The day had started strangely for Vickie Kessel. She had awakened with a jolt, startled that she was not in her own bed. Blinking the sleep away, she remembered: Quentin Wayne Smith III. Chuck. It had been some years since she had made love with a man so young, so insistent, so—powerful. That was the word. Chuck Smith exuded power: exciting, passionate, animal power.

She turned and saw that she was alone in the king-size bed. Vickie sat up. "Chuck?" she called, modestly tucking the bedsheet over her bosom.

No reply. She heard no sounds from the bathroom. The door to his sitting room was shut. Then Vickie glanced at the digital clock on the night table: 9:46. My God, she thought, I haven't slept this late in ages. She smiled, realizing that she probably hadn't fallen asleep until two or three in the morning. It was a busy night, she said to herself.

She padded naked to the bathroom, thinking, He's probably gone to the office to keep an eye on Jace. And to watch his football games. I'll call him there. After all, we have to make plans for Thanksgiving dinner tonight. And then afterward.

CHAPTER 32

As Chuck Smith used his temporary security card on the electronic lock at ParaReality, he thought about getting Vickie into bed again. Shouldn't be too hard, he thought to himself. It's obvious she's hot for me, unless those screaming orgasms were all faked. And even if they were, who cares? Might not be such a crummy Thanksgiving after all, he thought smugly.

Halfway down the corridor to Jace's lab, he saw Joe Rucker puffing his way toward him, an electronic clipboard in his one hand.

"Oh, it's you, Mr. Smith," said Rucker. "I saw yer car go past out t' the back."

"I parked up front," Smith said to the guard.

Rucker consulted the display screen of his clipboard. "Yep, you're okay. You're allowed to park in front."

Smith started to smile at the hillbilly's earnestness.

Then Rucker added, "But ye got to wear yer badge, Mr. Smith. I got to be able to see it on ye."

Smith's smile turned to a grumble, but he fished the red temporary badge out of his jacket pocket and clipped it to his lapel.

"Thank ye, sir. An' happy Thanksgiving to ye!"

Go fuck yourself, Smith answered silently.

•   •   •

Jace stuck his head through Dan's office doorway. "Hey, you using a mainframe?"

"No."

"Somebody's using one of them."

"There's nobody else here except us—and Sue, she's down in the Pit with the kids. But she wouldn't need a mainframe to do a literature search."

Jace shrugged loosely and gangled into the office. "Doesn't matter, I don't need it right now."

"How do you know it's in use, then?"

"I know everything, pal. Haven't you figured that out yet?" Jace plopped down on the leather sofa. "I am all-seeing, all-knowing."

"All bullshit," Dan said.

"Like hell."

Dan blurted, "You set up a VR system for Ralph to use at home, didn't you?"

Jace's narrow eyes shifted away from him. "Aw, that was years ago."

"After that fight you two had."

"Some fight. I was trying to help the sonofabitch and he pops me in the mouth."

"The system was for Dorothy?"

"Yeah. To help her while away her lonely nights while her true love was away slaying dragons."

Dan was accustomed to Jace's sarcasm where Ralph was concerned. But now, with Ralph dying, it angered him. He asked, "How the hell did you do it?"

"Do what?"

"Make a sex machine."

"It was really for you, y'know."

"For me?"

"Yeah. I figured if Dorothy could play with herself while Ralph was away, she wouldn't come on to you. I saved your marriage, buddy."

Dan stared at him. Jace never does anything for anybody except himself, he knew. And yet—why would he help Ralph? He hated Ralph.

"You really did it for me?" The question came out high-pitched, almost like a little boy talking to an elder.

Jace nodded solemnly. "Sure did."

For several moments Dan could say nothing, think of nothing except Jace's concern for him. He did it for me? At last he shook his head, as if trying to clear his mind and get back to the subject he had started with.

"But how did you do it? How does the sex machine work?"

"Why? You want one?"

Suddenly impatient, Dan said, "I want to know how it works. I don't understand how you did it."

Jace scratched at his stubbly jaw. "Come on, Dan. You know better than that."

"Dorothy's using it right now, for chrissakes."

"Good."

"How the hell did you do it?"

"It's better than watching porno movies, I betcha."

Dan stared at his partner, his friend, the man he had built his career around. His life around.

"Don't give me that hound-dog look," Jace said. "What the hell. You know that a VR system—*any* VR system—makes imaginary experiences seem real. It's a wonder nobody's made a sex machine before."

"Maybe they have," said Dan.

The slightest little grin wormed across Jace's lips. It made him look sly, almost smug. "No, they haven't," he said. "Nobody knows how to, except me."

"You took measurements of Ralph's body, his nervous system, and then used them as input into the system you gave him."

"Just his brain, buddy boy. All I had to do was map the electrical activity in his brain. The rest was what they call cape work."

"Cape work?"

"Fancy dancing, just to keep Ralph or anybody else from figuring out what I was really doing."

"The electrical activity in his brain."

Jace's grin broadened, but his eyes looked somehow sad, weary. "The one thing I remember from the freshman English course they made me take: 'The mind is its own place, and in itself can make a heaven of hell or a hell of heaven.' "

"What's that supposed to mean?"

Jace pulled himself up from the sofa. "Figure it out, pal. Figure it out for yourself."

Susan stared disconsolately at the display screen. She had tried every one of the keywords that her dictionary search had turned up; all but four of them were useless. And for those four, the screen stubbornly demanded ACCESS CODE. She was no better off than when she had started.

She shut down the IBM and returned to the desktop mini that was still faithfully searching all the medical journals in the NREN.

The door opened, and Dan walked into the computer center, looking strained, uptight.

Angela bounced happily toward her father. "Can I play a game now? Is it time now?"

Dan looked down at his daughter as if he did not recognize her. But then he broke into a tight smile and tousled her blond hair.

"We did promise you could play a game, didn't we? Only one, though."

Angela clutched her daddy as he made his way past the unoccupied row of desktops and minicomputers to where Susan was sitting.

"How's it going?" he asked.

Pointing to the display screen that was still flashing medical references, Susan replied, "There's a mountain of data about sports medicine and nerve physiology. You won't be able to sort it out in a month."

His face went grim. "That's okay. Long as we've got the data, I can put a couple of researchers on the job of sorting it all out."

"What's the matter?"

"Jace."

"What's he done now?"

"He's taken over the special job I was supposed to be doing. You know, the one for Washington."

"Good!" said Susan. "Now you can come home nights at a decent hour."

But she saw from the way he was gnawing his lip that there was more.

"Can you check into Jace's requests for computer searches?"

Dan asked. "I mean, can you find out what he's been looking for over the past couple of days?"

"Does he log in to the search services like everybody else?"

"I guess so."

"Then I can trace his requests, yes."

"Okay. How about his searches from six, seven years ago, back at Wright-Patt?"

"My God, Dan, I don't think anybody keeps records that far back."

"No, I guess not," Dan muttered. He went back to gnawing on his lip.

"What are you looking for?"

"I want to see what *he's* been looking for."

"I can try."

"It's time for my game now, isn't it?" Angela asked, unable to contain herself quietly.

Susan turned to her daughter. "Not until we have some lunch," she said. "You and Daddy go out to the car and bring in the picnic basket while I see to Philip."

They picnicked on the floor of the computer center, sitting on the rough old blanket that they had used on outdoor picnics, chewing on sandwiches that Susan had made and drinking iced tea.

"I helped with the sandwiches," Angela informed her father.

"They're good, honey." But Susan could see that Dan's thoughts were a thousand miles away. He sat cross-legged on the blanket, wound up into knots of anxiety.

"Why do you need to see what Jace was doing back at Wright-Patterson?" she asked.

Glancing at his daughter, who was trying hard to finish her sandwich without getting any of it on her blouse or jeans, Dan said, "Jace made a VR game for Dorothy."

"For Dorothy? How do you know that?"

"For her to use at home. When Ralph's away. Hell, maybe they used it together, too."

"How do you know?" Susan repeated.

He avoided her eyes. "Doc told me. And I talked with Jace about it this morning."

"A VR game? For the bedroom?"

Dan nodded solemnly.

"That's kinky."

"I'm finished!" Angela announced, brushing crumbs off her jeans.

Dan climbed slowly to his feet and put on a smile. "Okay, honey, I'll take you to the lab. Just one game, now, right?"

Susan watched them walking away from her, Angela's hand in her father's. Neither one of them so much as glanced back at her. Philip, sitting up in his car chair, waved both hands at them, but they did not see him.

"Which game do you want to play?" she heard Dan ask their daughter.

"Cinderella," said Angela. "Or maybe Alice in Wonderland! No, not that one. Green Mansions! Mary Mackie told me about that one, it's all about this deep, deep forest and there are birds that talk to you and you wear a dress made of spiderwebs and . . ."

They reached the door, went through, and let it swing shut behind them. Leaving Susan sitting there on the floor with the baby, wondering what a VR sex simulation would be like.

Then she thought, If Dan's going to set up Angie in a VR game, at least I can watch which programs are put into use. Maybe I can get a clue to Vickie's damned code words that way.

She scrambled to her feet, startling little Philip so badly that he broke into a bawling cry.

The forest-green Jaguar convertible purred to a stop in the roofed parking slot marked K. MUNCRIEF. PRES.

Muncrief got out and squinted into the bright sky as he patted his windblown hair into place. He did not expect to meet anyone at the office on this Thanksgiving Day, so he had dressed casually. Still, he knew he looked stylish. Like the picture of Dorian Gray, he thought. Good-looking outside, but inside a real mess.

There was only one other car in the front lot, he saw: Smith's rented BMW. He must be in there keeping an eye on Jace. Good. Let the two of 'em get in each other's hair. As he strode through the lobby toward his office, Muncrief laughed to himself at that image: Jace with his long tangled mane and Smith's military-type buzz cut.

He waved to Joe Rucker as the guard came lurching and grinning toward him like an eager Saint Bernard puppy.

"How do, Mr. Muncrief, sir! Happy Thanksgiving to ye!"

"Same to you, Joe," Muncrief called as he strode through the lobby.

For the past week, Muncrief had been feeling more and more helpless. Out of control of what was happening around him. Vulnerable. He sat heavily in his high-backed swivel chair and flicked on his desktop computer. Nobody in the office, nobody calling on the phones. All the sane people in the country are out enjoying the holiday. Good time to get some work done without interruptions. A chance to study the cash flow and the work schedules and see just where in hell we stand. Quiet enough to think and make plans. Got to get Cyber World running by April first. Got to get Smith off my case and back to Washington.

Out of ingrained routine and a touch of curiosity he checked the security log to see who else was working this Thanksgiving afternoon. The screen showed a list of names and their personnel numbers.

Jace, of course. He just about lives in his lab, Muncrief grumbled to himself. I ought to charge him rent, the way he uses the showers and all. And Smith. Joe Rucker; dumb hick has no place else to go, I guess. Why on earth did I ever let Jace talk me into hiring a one-armed, one-legged security guard?

He saw that Dan Santorini was in the lab—well, at least he's trying to make up a little for the time he's wasted off in Ohio. Muncrief's brows rose slightly when the screen showed three other names under Dan's. He's brought his whole family in here with him! The daughter, too. Angie.

He leaned back in the chair, as if afraid to touch the computer keyboard.

I wonder—would he let her play one of the games? Good way to baby-sit her.

Muncrief felt the familiar hollow sensation in the pit of his stomach. As if he were going to be sick. Like a teenager trying to work up the courage to touch his date's breast.

With a trembling finger, he pecked at the keyboard. Yes! She's in there playing Green Mansions. Then he checked the other machines in use: Jace in his own lab; Dan in his office; somebody in the computer center. He remembered that Susan Santorini had taken on some computer searches for her husband and Jace. Must be her, Muncrief thought. There's nobody else in the building except Rucker.

And little Angie is in the game booth.

Don't do it, he warned himself. Her parents are here in the building with her. Her mother's using one of the minis in the computer center, for God's sake. If her father finds out . . .

He sat there for almost a quarter of an hour, struggling against his common sense. He won.

CHAPTER 33

It was the most beautiful world she had ever been in.

Angela walked almost on tiptoe along the soft mossy trail that wound through the lovely green forest, her arms held out in anticipation, her gauzy dress of spiderwebs soft and cool against her skin. The trees were tremendous, soaring up and up and up until their branches mingled with one another in a leafy canopy that let in just enough sunlight to make everything warm and bright down here on the ground.

Birds called back and forth. Jeweled insects chirruped. The breeze was soft, caressing.

A jaguar stepped onto the trail in front of her, its tawny coat adorned with handsome black designs. It stretched its front legs and bowed its head.

"Hello, Angela," said the jaguar.

Not surprised in the slightest at the talking jungle cat, Angela returned, "Hello. What's your name?"

"What name would you like to give me?"

She thought a moment. "Are you a boy cat or a girl cat?"

"That's up to you, my dear."

"You look like a boy cat to me," said Angela. "I'll name you Georgie."

"Georgie the Jaguar," said the cat.

"Can I pet you?"

"*May* I pet you?" Georgie corrected. "And yes, of course. I like to be petted by pretty young ladies."

Angela came up beside the jaguar and stroked his back, feeling the warm silkiness of his fur. The jaguar purred for her and rubbed against her legs, gently, though, so she wouldn't be knocked over. She felt the strength in the cat's smoothly rippling muscles.

"Where are you heading?" Georgie asked.

"I'm exploring. This forest is really very beautiful, isn't it?"

"You mean you haven't seen your house yet?"

"My house? No! Where is it?"

"Right down this trail and across the stream. It's a tree house, you know, built up high where the birds make their nests."

Angela clapped her hands with joy. "Let's go see it!"

"Of course. Just follow me."

The jaguar padded off along the trail and Angela followed him. Birds of every color flitted through the trees, singing so beautifully that Angie almost wanted to cry. Beetles glittered like precious stones as she hurried along the path, and she saw squirrels and deer and even an auburn-coated fox by the time she reached the bank of the swift-flowing stream.

"How deep is the water?" Angela asked.

"Not very," said Georgie. "Look, there's a set of stones arranged for us to cross on. You know, I don't like to get wet very much."

"I'm learning to swim."

"You mustn't swim in this stream," Georgie said. "There are crocodiles and alligators and piranhas and all sorts of evil things in the water."

"Really?"

"Every world has its dangers, Angela dear, and in this world the dangers are in the streams and rivers. As long as you are on dry land, you are perfectly safe."

"How strange," said Angela.

The stones were broad and flattopped, although they looked wet and slippery. Georgie padded across easily.

Angela was just starting to put her bare foot on the first stone when she saw an alligator on the opposite bank, sunning itself next to a huge fallen log. It was staring at her, smiling broadly with a mouth full of crooked sharp teeth.

"Come on," Georgie called from the far bank. "Nothing can hurt you—unless you fall into the water."

Angela stepped onto the first stone. It felt cold, slimy. The alligator's smile widened.

"You can do it, Angela," said Georgie. "Come on."

She hopped from one stone to the next. They were close enough together so that she could skip across them easily.

"That's the way!" Georgie encouraged her.

Halfway across, though, Angela glanced down into the dark, swiftly swirling water. It looked cold and menacing. There were strange shapes flickering in the darkness down there, gathering around the stones as if waiting for her to lose her balance and fall in. She saw evil little eyes glinting at her, and hard sharp teeth.

Angela's foot slipped on the wet slithery rock and she teetered, arms windmilling.

"Look out!" cried Georgie.

Then she righted herself, swallowed hard, and raced across the remaining few stones to land safely on the far bank beside the jaguar.

The alligator smiled toothily at her from beside its log. "You were lucky not to fall in the water, young lady," it said.

Angela did not know what to answer, so she said nothing. But a chill shivered up her spine at the thought of the cold dark water and the evil things in it. She saw that the alligator's eyes were cold and cruel and watching her hungrily.

"She's not going to be your dinner," Georgie said to the gator. "She's going to see her very own home up in the trees where ugly old things like you can't bother her."

Kyle Muncrief had closed his office door and locked it. He had pulled down the blinds on his windows so that the office was cool and shadowy despite the afternoon sunshine. He had pulled open the bottom drawer of his desk, where Jace had installed the VR equipment.

Not even Vickie knows about this. Muncrief grinned to himself as he fondled the rough-textured data gloves, their wires trailing to the gray electronics box built into the drawer. She thinks she knows everything about me, but she doesn't know about this. If she did—

He broke off that train of thought abruptly. The only person in the world who knew about this equipment was Jace Lowrey. Jace had built it for Muncrief, Jace had programmed the system and was continuing to refine it. He bitches about it and worries out loud about what'll happen if Santorini finds out about it, but actually Jace gets off on it. Not the way I do, of course, but he practically creams his pants over this.

Muncrief smiled inwardly. Of course, not even Jace knows everything I can do. That's the secret of success, Muncrief reminded himself. Never let the right hand know what the left hand is doing. Jace knows some of it. Vickie knows some of it. Neither one of them knows it all, and as long as they don't compare notes they won't find out. How much does Smith know? That's the real problem. That's what I need Vickie to find out for me.

He turned his swivel chair around and bent down to slide open the cabinet behind his desk. The helmet was there, bright and glistening and smooth to the touch. Warm, almost as if it were alive. Muncrief ran his hands across its warm smooth curving surface. He raised the helmet in both hands, then lowered it onto his head like Napoleon crowning himself. He pulled the data gloves on, flexed his fingers inside them, admired the craftsmanship of their design, their manufacture. Then he bent down again and powered up the electronics.

Finally he leaned back in his comfortable high-backed leather chair and slid the visor down over his face. He knew he should try to relax, but every nerve in his body was tingling with anticipation.

There were delicious-looking fruits hanging from the trees along the trail, but when Angela picked a russet-golden one and tried to eat it, it turned out to have no taste at all. It was like biting into air.

"You don't need to eat anything here," said Georgie, padding along beside her. "This is a land to look at and listen to, not to taste."

Tossing the tasteless fruit into the bushes, Angela asked, "Would the alligator have tasted anything if he had eaten me?"

"I suppose so," the jaguar replied. "I imagine you would taste absolutely delicious."

They walked on through the delightful forest for what seemed like hours.

"When do we get to my tree house?" Angela asked.

"It's just around the bend in the trail."

Angela broke into a happy run, and when she rounded the bend in the trail, sure enough, there was a house high up in the trees, with windows and a slanting roof of palm fronds and even a porch in front of its door. Long looping vines hung from the trees, and flowers blossomed everywhere, red and gold and brightest blue and purple and sunshine yellow.

"It's beautiful!" said Angela.

The house seemed to be made of living branches and vines, green and leafy, graceful yet strong. And it looked quite large to Angela, more like a palace than an ordinary house.

"How do I get up to it?" she asked, craning her neck as she stood near the base of the huge old tree.

"Use the elevator," said Georgie.

And Angela saw that amid the vines hanging from the tree's upper branches there was a wooden platform with a railing all around it. She heard the powerful trumpeting of an elephant, and sure enough a big gray elephant stepped out of the jungle foliage as daintily as a ballerina, spread its huge ears, and lifted its trunk in greeting.

Laughing, Angela skipped onto the elevator platform and gripped its railing. The elephant grasped a particular liana in its trunk and started backing away. The platform rose swiftly into the air, and in no time at all Angela was stepping onto the front porch of her very own tree house.

"What about you?" she called down to Georgie. "Won't you come up?"

"I'm not allowed to," the jaguar called back. "Don't worry, I'll be down here waiting for you. You won't be lonely up there, I promise you."

"Hello, Angela darling."

She whirled and saw a handsome young prince standing in the

doorway, smiling at her. He was tall and slim and wore a soft white shirt and skintight pants with a wide leather belt, highly polished leather boots, and a long velvet cape so deeply violet that it seemed to glow. He looked a little like the young patriot she had met in Lexington. Yet when he smiled he almost looked like her father did when he wasn't too busy to pay attention to her, gentle and strong and loving. His eyes were like Daddy's too, she thought: deep warm brown.

Angela felt her heart beating fast.

"I've been waiting for you for a long time," the prince said. But his voice was not a young man's voice, she realized. It was a voice she had heard before: Uncle Kyle's.

"Are you Uncle Kyle?" she asked, her own voice trembling.

"Is that who you want me to be?"

"No!"

"I'm whoever you want, Angela darling. I'm your dream prince. The only reason I'm here is to make you happy."

Angela realized she felt a little afraid of all this. "Could—could you change your voice?" she asked.

The prince looked very sad. "Is that what you truly want, Angela?"

"Yes. Please."

For a long moment the prince simply stood there before her, smiling sadly. Then at last he spoke again. "All right. This is your world, Angela, and whatever you ask for in it you shall have." His voice was young now, rich and soft and matching his appearance perfectly.

"Oh, thank you," said Angela, feeling truly grateful. Yet she still had the feeling that somewhere in this delicate green world she was being watched by eyes as coldly glittering as the alligator's, by someone whose teeth were waiting to sink into her flesh.

Muncrief yanked the helmet off his head and mopped his face with a handful of tissues.

You came on too strong, you damned idiot! he raged at himself. You scared her again.

He tugged off the data gloves, turned off the electronics box, stored everything back where it belonged, shut the cabinet and drawer, locked them both, and then collapsed into a tearful mess, arms on his desktop, head in his arms, sobbing softly to himself.

She doesn't love me. She's afraid of me. All I've done for her, and she doesn't care about me at all. The little bitch.

But she will, he vowed to himself. She *will* love me. I'll *make* her love me.

CHAPTER 34

usan was sitting in the computer center with Philip on her lap. The desktop machine at her side was still searching for the sports-medicine reports that Dan had asked for. The search had slowed down considerably. She had gone through NREN and had the computer double-check the Library of Congress files. Now the program was seeking out smaller data banks, oddball medical journals, and popular magazine articles. Even newspaper items.

There's enough material here to keep Dan reading for a year, Susan thought as she tickled her baby's tummy. Philip giggled and hiccuped happily. He'll have to set up a program to scan the whole file by keywords, once he figures out which keywords he's really interested in.

Dan stuck his head through the open doorway.

"Working hard, I see."

She gave him a mock frown. "The computer's working. I'm keeping an eye on it. And doing some mothering at the same time."

He made a tight grin. "Angie's in the VR booth up the hall. Give me a call when she's finished the game she's playing."

"How will I know—"

Dan pointed to one of the minis, a few desks up the line from where Susan was sitting. "That's the machine running the program. When it beeps and its lights go out, the program's over."

She nodded.

"Pretty easy, having the computer do all the work for you," he teased.

"I'm thinking."

"About what?"

"About how to track down all the files Jace has accessed. How far back do you want me to go?"

"To the year one."

"A.D. or B.C.?"

With a shrug, "Take your pick. I don't want to make it too hard on you."

"The hell you don't."

Dan's grin turned sheepish. "Okay, okay. I've got to get back to my own work. Give me a call when Angie's program is over."

"In your office?"

"Or down at Jace's lab."

He left, and Susan could hear his footsteps echoing down the hallway. But as she sat in the curved little typist's chair holding her baby in her arms, Susan wondered how she could possibly track down Jace's requests for data from all the information services in the country.

Then one of the minis beeped. The noise made her look up. No, it wasn't the machine Angie was using for her VR game; that one was still humming softly to itself. But the one next to it had beeped to life.

Curious, Susan carried Philip on one hip as she walked to the blinking, chugging computer.

She bent over the keyboard of Angie's machine and tapped out a query in yellow letters against the display screen's pale-blue background: PGM RNG?

GRN MAN 1.0, answered the display screen. The Green Mansions game, version 1.0.

Okay. Susan shifted Phil's weight slightly and turned to the next machine.

PGM RNG?

ACCESS RESTRICTED. ENTER ACCESS CODE.

She felt her teeth clenching. Susan walked back to the playpen and deposited Philip in it. He started to squawk, but she handed him a squeeze toy that honked like a duck. That seemed to satisfy him for the moment.

Rushing back to Angie's machine, she sat in its chair and typed:
LIST ALL PGMS RNG

GRN MAN 1.0

"So you won't talk, eh?" Susan muttered. Computers are like very obedient children, she knew. They will do exactly what you tell them to. But not a jot more than you tell them.

LIST ALL GRN MAN PGMS

The list was very short:

GRN MAN 1.0

GRN MAN 1.5

There's another version of the game Angela is playing! Susan felt neither triumph nor vindication; only the sudden shock of realization that all her fears were true.

She typed, CD\GRN MAN 1.5

ACCESS RESTRICTED. ENTER ACCESS CODE

She typed, GRN MAN 1.5 IN USE? Y/N

Y

Susan felt a constriction in her chest. The other version of Green Mansions was in use. Angie was playing with 1.0, but somebody else was using 1.5.

Breathing heavily, she typed, LIST ALL NEPTUNES KINGDOM PGMS

NOT FOUND

Damn! The program's listed under some abbreviation, she realized. It took her four tries before she hit it:

LIST ALL NPT KGM PGMS

NPT KGM 1.0

NPT KGM 1.5

There *is* another version of the game! Despite what Vickie said, there is another version of the Neptune's Kingdom game, god damn it! There must be alternate versions of all the games. And somebody's using the second version of Green Mansions right now, while Angie's playing the regular version. That's how Angie keeps seeing people she knows in the games; somebody's injecting himself into her games!

She scooped up Philip again and went racing down the hallway toward the VR booth. Peering through the darkened glass of its door, she saw Angela sitting back in the chair, visor over her face.

Susan could just make out her daughter's lips below the edge of the visor, smiling faintly. Her hands twitched now and then inside the data gloves.

Susan turned and made her way toward Victoria Kessel's office like an Old West sheriff heading toward a shoot-out at high noon. *The lying bitch told me there were no other versions of the school games.*

But Vickie's office was empty, its door wide open, its computer cold and quiet.

Then who? Susan asked herself. *Who else is here besides Dan and Jace?*

She went out to the lobby and saw Muncrief's green convertible in the parking lot. And a black BMW sedan.

Kyle? Could it be Kyle?

Philip was squirming in her arms. He wanted to get down on the floor and be free of his mother.

"Not yet, baby," she whispered, heading up the corridor, looking for Muncrief's office.

There it was. The nameplate on the door said KYLE MUNCRIEF, nothing more. It was closed. Susan tried the doorknob. Locked. She tapped at the door. No reply. She knocked harder. Still no answer.

He's in there, she knew. *He's in there injecting himself into my daughter's game!*

Wait, she said to herself. *Wait. Calm down. Don't go off half-cocked. Who else is in the building?* Closing her eyes briefly, she recalled that when Dan drove into the parking lot out back earlier in the morning the only other car had belonged to the guard, Joe Rucker. And Jace's bicycle had been there.

Again Susan hurried down the hallway, Philip starting to squall unhappily. She checked Angela once more. Still looking relaxed, no apparent trouble. Then she went back toward Jace's lab in the rear of the building. On a hunch she went to the loading dock and checked the back lot: still nothing but Dan's dark-blue Honda and the guard's battered Thunderbird.

There was a stranger in the lab with Jace when she popped in. Jace looked surprised to see her.

"Hi!" Susan said, her voice too loud with tension. "I thought Dan might be back here."

Jace was sitting at a desktop, looking slightly annoyed at her interruption. The other man, square-jawed and clean-cut as a movie version of an FBI agent, was watching football on television.

"He's in his office," Jace said, not bothering to introduce the man with him. Nor did the man do more than flick a glance at Susan before returning his attention to the TV screen. She assumed he was the man from Washington that Dan had spoken of.

"Oh. Sure. I should have looked there first."

Philip was putting up a real struggle as she hurried back up the hallway, yowling loudly enough to echo off the bare painted walls.

Dan was almost around his desk when she burst into his office. "What's wrong?" he asked. "I could hear Phil halfway across the building."

Susan bent down and let the baby crawl across the office's thin carpeting. His yowling stopped immediately once he had the freedom to explore.

"Kyle's messing into Angie's game," Susan blurted.

"What?"

Breathlessly, she said, "He's got alternate versions of the school games. Green Mansions and Neptune's Kingdom, at least. I didn't have time to check them all out. Kyle's in his office with his door locked. Didn't answer when I knocked. *He's putting himself in Angie's game, Dan!*"

"Angie's still in there?"

"She's all right. I looked in on her. Twice."

"Then what—"

"It's Kyle," Susan insisted. "He's been interfering in the games Angie plays. Right from the start!"

Dan sagged back on the edge of his desk. "But that's not possible."

"The hell it's not!" Susan snapped. "There are alternate versions of the games, Dan. I found them in the files."

"That doesn't mean he's injecting himself into the games Angie plays, for God's sake!"

"He's running the alternate version now!" Susan fairly screamed. "While Angie's in the booth!"

"Why would anybody . . ." Dan's voice trailed off. He looked at his wife. Her blue eyes were fiery, but she wasn't hysterical. Never had been, no matter how mad she got. Always had a level head, even when things were at their worst.

"Let's get Angie out of that game," he said, heading for the door.

Susan scooped up the baby and headed after him, saying, "Let's break in on Kyle first and catch him red-handed."

They raced to Muncrief's office, Dan holding Philip in one arm as he followed Susan's frenzied dash up the hallway. Muncrief's door was still closed and locked. With his free hand Dan knocked on the door. No response. He glanced at Susan, then pounded on it harder. Almost immediately Muncrief opened it, looking half startled, half angry. Maybe there was guilt in his expression, too; Dan could not tell.

"What are you trying to do," Muncrief demanded, "break my blasted door down?"

Dan eyed the frowning man, wondering, How do you accuse the boss of messing with your daughter electronically? While holding a squirming ten-month-old baby in your arms? Muncrief looked flustered, all right, but there was no helmet, no data gloves, nothing of a VR system in sight. Muncrief's shirt was rumpled a little and his hair slightly out of place, but otherwise he seemed perfectly normal.

"Someone's interfering with Angela's VR game," Susan snapped from behind Dan's shoulder.

"What?"

"There are alternate versions of the school games," Susan insisted, pushing past Dan, past Muncrief himself, and into his office.

"What on earth do you mean?"

"Alternate versions of the games the children play at school," Susan said impatiently, her eyes scanning the office like a detective looking for evidence. "Versions that allow *somebody* to get into the game with the child and interact with her."

Muncrief followed her, his face white as if in shock. Dan followed him in and let Philip down on the thickly carpeted floor. Phil immediately crawled toward the window, where the blinds had been drawn against the afternoon sun.

"That's ridiculous, Susan," Muncrief was saying. He turned to Dan. "Tell her how absolutely idiotic that is, Dan."

"She saw the alternate versions listed in the files," Dan said.

Muncrief's face regained some of its color. He swung his gaze from Dan to Susan.

"Okay," he said, gesturing toward his desk, "show me."

Susan marched to the desk, plopped herself into the oversized swivel chair, and booted up Muncrief's desktop. In less than a minute she had the screen displaying:

GRN MAN 1.0
GRN MAN 1.5
NPT KGM 1.0
NPT KGM 1.5

"There must be others, too, but I don't know their names," Susan said.

Muncrief had come around the desk to look at the screen. He made a sour face. "Did it ever occur to you that we have a backup program for each of the school games? In case one goes down, or two kids want to play the same game?"

Dan said, "Is that what they are? Backups?"

"What on earth else?"

Susan glared across the desk at her husband. "Then why was the backup in use just a few minutes ago?"

"How the hell would I know?" Muncrief snapped, his face reddening with the beginnings of anger. "I've been in this blasted office all afternoon, trying to get some work done in peace and quiet, when you two come pounding down my damned door!"

"Angie's still in the game," Dan said to his wife. "Maybe we ought to get her out."

Susan was clearly seething. "Somebody was using the alternate version of the game, and nobody else is here. The building's empty except for us."

"And Smith and Jace," Dan added.

"It wasn't Smith or Jace," Susan said, getting up from Muncrief's chair. "I checked them."

"Look, Susie," said Muncrief patiently, "I know you're very concerned about your daughter. She had a bad experience with one of the games early on, and you're still worried about her. That's what mothers are all about, I guess."

"Don't patronize me!"

Dan was horrified that Susan would speak to his boss that way.

But Muncrief raised his hands, as if in self-defense, and answered placatingly, "Okay! Okay! I'm sorry. I can understand how worried you are. But nobody's hurting your daughter. Don't let that one bad experience override everything else in your mind. Don't be an overprotective mother."

Susan's nostrils flared like a bull about to charge.

"He's right, Sue," said Dan, trying to head off the explosion. "Come on, let's get Angie out of the game and go to dinner. It's getting late."

Susan said not a word more. Dan went over and picked up Phil, who was happily batting the cords of the window blinds.

"I'll check the alternate versions," he said to Susan. "Then we'll know for sure."

"Have a nice dinner," Muncrief called to them as they left his office. Dan thought his voice sounded weak, shaky.

Angela was in love with the young prince. He was so handsome and kind, so considerate. They rode the forest trails together, he on a magnificent golden steed, she on a pretty little chestnut pony who had a white blaze on his forehead.

They stopped by a swift stream and let the horses drink. Angela gazed worriedly into the rushing dark water.

"The jaguar told me there are evil things in the water," she said to her prince.

"Not if you don't want them to be," he said, his voice as melodious as a cello to her. "This is your land, Angela, and nothing bad can happen unless you want it to."

"Really?"

He smiled, and her heart fluttered. "Really. This is truly your very own land, Angela dear. I'm only a visitor here, but I'm very glad that you're allowing me to stay with you, even if it's only for a little while."

"I wouldn't want you to go away," she said. "Not ever."

He reached out and took her hand in his. "Thank you, dearest one. I'd like to stay here in this beautiful land with you forever."

"Me too!"

The prince brought Angela's hand to his lips and kissed her fingers. Her knees went watery.

"ANGELA? ANGELA!" The sound was like a bell tolling, far off in the distance.

"ANGELA, IT'S TIME TO COME BACK NOW. TIME TO END THE GAME."

"But I don't want to come back," she whispered, gazing into the prince's dark romantic eyes.

"COME BACK, ANGEL BABY." Her father's voice, coming closer, growing stronger. "COME BACK TO US, SWEET-HEART."

"I want to stay here with you," she told her prince. "Forever."

He smiled sadly. "I'll be here, my dearest one. I'll wait for you. No matter how long it takes for you to come to me, I'll wait for you."

Dan was standing in the narrow little control room where the VR simulations were monitored, Susan behind him with Philip in her arms.

"Come on, sweetheart," Dan was saying softly into the microphone he held before his lips. "Time to go now."

Susan still looked furious, but whether she was sore at Muncrief or Dan himself he could not tell. Probably both. His wife had still not spoken a word as they had gone to the VR control booth and Dan began talking Angela out of her game.

"You don't just turn the game off," he explained to the air. "You bring the player back into the real world first, let the player terminate the game himself. Or herself."

Susan's eyes were riveted on the door of the booth where her daughter was. Dan was watching the screen of the computer that monitored Angela's game.

"Okay," he said, exhaling slowly. "She's out of it. I'm terminating the program now."

Susan rushed out of the control room and yanked open the door of the booth. Angela stepped out, rubbing her eyes as if she had just awakened from a dream.

"Why did you call me out?" Angela asked. "It was so nice in there. . . ."

Susan took her by the shoulders and studied her face. Angela was half smiling, half rueful.

"Are you all right, honey?"

She nodded. "Of course I'm all right. Why wouldn't I be?"

"Come on," said Dan. "Let's get changed and go to dinner."

"Can't I go back and finish the game?"

Susan shot a worried glance at Dan, who said to their daughter, "Not now, Angel. Some other time."

"It was so wonderful," Angela said.

"You can tell me about it while we change into our dresses," said Susan. Turning to Dan, she asked, "Are you really going to check out the alternate versions of the games?"

"Not now," he answered. "You need the access codes, and Vickie's the one who keeps them. I'll call her tomorrow and get them."

Susan glared at him but said nothing.

As Dan drove his family to Disney Village, Susan sitting beside him still blazing-eyed with anger, he cleared his throat and said firmly, "You shouldn't have barged into the boss's office and accused him of something like that without any real evidence."

"He did it," Susan snapped.

"You *think* he did it. You don't know for certain."

"He did it, and Vickie helped him."

Dan shook his head.

"And you're taking his side."

"No, I'm not," he said firmly. "I'm just saying that there's no evidence to show that anybody did anything. Not yet."

From the back seat Angela asked, "Who are you talking about? Uncle Kyle?"

Susan whirled on her daughter. "He's not your uncle!"

"But you said—I mean, I thought—"

"He's not your uncle," Susan repeated, louder. "I don't want to hear you ever call him that again. Not ever!"

Glancing at his daughter in the rearview mirror, Dan saw that Angela was on the verge of tears.

Dinner was a roaring fiasco. Susan was still raging mad. Angela seemed confused and upset. The restaurant was crowded, noisy. They had to wait in line more than half an hour despite their reservations. Half the items on the menu were gone by the time Dan and his family were seated. The waiters and waitresses, mostly young and inexperienced, were harried and overworked, clearly tired and longing to get home to their own dinners.

And just as dessert was being served, Philip upchucked his dinner all over their table.

The end of a perfect day, thought Dan miserably as his own dinner burned its way up into his throat.

CHAPTER 35

Vickie had almost driven over to the office to see Chuck Smith in person, but she decided that would be foolish. It would make her seem too eager, too much like a moonstruck girl. So she phoned him instead. ParaReality's computerized telephone system located him in Jace's lab. Vickie told him she had already made a reservation at the posh Gran Cru restaurant for seven o'clock.

"They don't open until six, and besides, they're too expensive for families having their holiday dinner out," she said. "We can have a nice quiet supper without children yapping all around us."

"You don't like children?" Smith's voice had a chuckle in it.

"They're fine," Vickie replied. "In their proper place. In cages, like chimpanzees."

Smith laughed and agreed to meet her at seven. Vickie hung up, pleased with herself. She had been crisply efficient. No goo or gush. What had happened last night was not going to dissolve her brain. What might happen tonight was strictly a form of entertainment, without any emotional attachment. None at all.

Still, that evening as they sipped wine from crystal goblets she could not help wishing that she were twenty years younger. Well, maybe not twenty. Ten would be just about right.

Chuck was smiling handsomely at her, perfect white teeth and wonderful blue eyes catching the candlelight.

"I spoke to a couple of people back in Washington," he said lightly. "They're going to take a look at your man Peterson."

"He's not my man," Vickie replied.

"Well, whatever he is, I don't think you'll have to worry about him anymore. They'll scare him off."

"Do you really think so?"

"They can be pretty scary when they want to be."

Vickie said, "Just like that? You just talk to some people and Peterson gets scared away?"

His smile seemed to shift slightly. "Do you have any idea of what I do in the White House?"

"Not yet," murmured Vickie. She had leafed through the papers that Smith had left in the desk of his hotel room. Nothing much there. A yellow legal-size tablet with a couple of handwritten lists that meant nothing to her. A few bills forwarded from his address in Washington. No personal mail. She was pretty certain that he had a notebook computer, but he must have carried it with him.

"I work for a guy you never heard of," Smith said. "He's in charge of coordinating information inputs from the various departments: you know, state, defense, agriculture, labor—all that."

"Cabinet-level departments."

"Right."

"Don't they meet with the President face-to-face?"

"Of course. But I'm talking about the detailed info. The big cheeses all talk at cabinet meetings and in private sessions with the President, sure, but they can't go into much detail. Heck, they don't *know* the details. They don't even want to know, in most cases. All they want to do is convince the President to do what they want, which is usually what their staffers have convinced them to want."

"The President must get bombarded with all kinds of pressures from them."

"Every day," Smith said fervently. "Now, I came up with this idea of using virtual reality to help give the President's staff a better grasp of the information that's pouring into the West Wing."

"Not the President himself?"

Smith shrugged. "Probably not, at first. His immediate staff, the people he trusts to give him usable information."

"I see," said Vickie.

"Do you? If this works, I'll take over my boss's function. He's already on slippery ground; a lot of people would like to see him resign. I can save his ass with this and he'll be grateful to me forever."

"And your boss will become a figurehead."

He looked impressed. "You catch on pretty quick."

"You'll be the one who's actually in charge of coordinating all the President's information inputs."

"Not all of them." Smith put up both hands, as if to slow her down. Then he grinned. "Just the most important ones."

"The VR inputs."

"If virtual reality is as powerful as I think it is, I can become the most important guy in the White House. *Everybody* will come to me to get their story across to The Man."

"And where do I fit in?" Vickie asked.

"You can be my link with the science guys, like Jace. You can be the right hand of the most important person in the White House."

"That would be nice," she said, thinking, It can't be that simple. There must be more to it than that. You don't just walk into the White House with a VR system and take over the place.

But Smith was smiling pleasantly and asking, "Any other little problems I can help you with?"

Vickie arched an eyebrow at him. Why not see how powerful he really is? "You can scare off a private detective," she said, "but how good are you at scaring off the Japs?"

"What do you mean?"

She hesitated long enough to let him know that she was debating inwardly over how much to tell him. Then she said, "The Japanese are trying to take over ParaReality."

"Oh?"

"I don't want this spread around, obviously. But one of Kyle's backers is Hideki Toshimura. Maybe you've heard of him?"

Smith's mind began racing. She needs my help. And I can be a hero in Washington by stopping a Jap takeover of a vital American technology. I love it! The President himself will talk to me about this one; he's always yakking about preventing American technology from being taken overseas. And Vickie will have to depend on me for this as much as I have to depend on her for the VR stuff in the first place. That's what makes politics work: two people who owe favors to each other.

He smiled and leaned back in his chair, twirling his wineglass in one hand. "Tell me all about it, Vic," he said.

As Dan drove the family home from the restaurant, Susan worried about Philip's getting sick.

"It might be an allergic reaction," she said. "Maybe we should call a doctor and get him checked out."

Dan glanced at his wife. Philip seemed happy enough in his car seat.

"He probably tossed his dinner out of excitement," he said to Susan. "Or maybe he's coming down with a cold. There's nothing wrong with the boy."

Looking doubtful, Susan said, "I'll take his temperature when we get home."

Angela looked worried, Dan thought. "You okay, Angel?"

He saw her bob her head up and down in the rearview mirror. "Feeling all right?"

"Yes, Daddy."

"Can you make a smile?"

She grinned.

"Bigger?"

Angela hooked her fingers in the corners of her mouth, pulled her lips wide, and stuck out her tongue. Even the baby laughed.

When they finally got home, the phone's message light was blinking. Dan picked it up and heard Dr. Appleton's recorded voice:

"Dan, it looks like Ralph's taken a turn for the worse. He's failing. The doctors don't expect him to last the weekend. Thought you'd want to know."

Susan was taking the kids to their bedrooms, but she saw the expression on her husband's face. "What is it?"

"Ralph. He's dying."

A strange expression flickered over Susan's face: sorrow, a hint of fear, maybe anger.

Despite her, Dan said to the phone, "Dr. William Appleton."

Susan turned her back to him, shooed Angela down the hall, and carried Philip toward his room. The phone's computer tried Appleton's office line, then was shunted to his home number.

Doc sounded somber as he repeated the news about Ralph Martinez.

"He's our only link to what really happened in that simulation," Dan said.

"He's dying," Doc repeated.

"If only there was some way we could get inside his mind and find out just what happened to him."

"He can't even speak, Dan."

"Yeah, I know." Dan was surprised at how cold-blooded he was being. "Does he understand what's going on around him? When people talk to him, does he know what they're saying?"

"I think so. But I don't really know. He can hardly move, hardly blink his one good eye."

"Can he type?" The question popped out of Dan's mind before he even realized he had thought of it.

"Type?"

"He can move one hand, can't he? He knew how to type. Maybe we can ask him some questions and have him type the answers on a keyboard."

"Dan, he's dying!" Doc's voice sounded agonized. "He's only got a day or so left."

The whole idea came into focus in Dan's mind. But Doc won't be able to do it, he told himself. Doc's too damned emotionally involved. I'll have to do it myself.

"Doc, can you get a plane here to pick me up tomorrow morning?"

"I suppose so."

"Okay. We've only got this one last chance to get any information out of Ralph. We've got to act fast."

"But—"

"Doc," he said sternly, "Ralph's going to die no matter what we do, right? We've got to take this last shot while he's still alive."

Doc reluctantly agreed. "I'll have to talk Narlikar into letting us do it. He's not going to like it."

"Neither do I. But it's got to be done."

Dan hung up, then saw that Susan was watching him.

"You're going back to Dayton tomorrow?"

"As soon as Doc can get a plane here for me."

"And what about checking those alternate games back at the office?"

Dan consciously kept himself from gnawing his lip. "That'll have to wait."

"If you wait, he'll have time to change the alternates, erase them altogether," Susan said.

"Maybe."

"Ralph Martinez is more important than your daughter?"

"Ralph's dying."

"And Angie? Kyle's fucking her mind, Dan!"

Dan stared at his wife for a long, silent moment; saw the anger there and, behind it, the fear.

"Listen," he said. "Whatever Muncrief's doing, he couldn't do it by himself. Somebody had to set up those alternate programs for him—*if* he's really doing what you think he is."

"If?" Susan's whole body went rigid with fury.

"It's not Kyle!" Dan snapped. "Not by himself, at any rate. He'd need somebody to rig the games for him. The same guy who's screwed around with the flight simulation so much that it's killing people."

He saw understanding dawn in her eyes. "Jace?"

"Who else could it be?"

"Jace is . . . killing people? Hurting my Angie?"

"That's what I'm going to Wright-Patt to find out," said Dan. "I want proof, and I think I can get it out of Ralph Martinez. If he doesn't die first."

Kyle Muncrief spent the rest of Thanksgiving Day in his office, too shaken to leave. They almost caught me, he kept repeating to himself. He saw the fury in Susan Santorini's eyes, but what frightened him more than that was the deadly flat calm of Dan's voice. He wasn't emotional, he wasn't raving or threatening or even worried. He was like a robot, a machine. He's going to check it all out, and when he's convinced that he knows what's going on he's going to come in here and beat my brains out.

I've got to erase the alternate games. No, that won't work. I told them that the alternates are just backups. If I erase them, they'll know I was lying. Got to change the alternates so that they really are nothing but backups. But how? When? Get Jace to do it. Now. Tonight. Before Dan gets back here tomorrow morning.

Muncrief pushed himself up from behind his desk and bustled through the building toward Jace's laboratory, hardly noticing that it was fully dark outside.

Sure enough, Jace was still there, tinkering with one of the VR helmets. He had it clamped in a vise on the workbench, its inner lining removed and hair-thin optical fibers trailing from it like a jumbled network of nerves.

"I've got to talk to you," Muncrief blurted.

"Not now," said Jace, without looking up.

"Now!"

Jace ignored him.

"What the hell are you doing?" Muncrief asked, striding up to peer over Jace's shoulder.

"Brain surgery." Jace had the pencil-size probe of a voltmeter in one hand, a pistol-like laser welding gun in the other.

"Listen, I need—"

"Hang in there," Jace said. "Gimme a minute or two."

Muncrief fumed impatiently, strode the length of the laboratory. It looked like a disorganized electronics junkyard to him. Reaching the end of the long narrow room, he turned back. Jace was still bent over the workbench. Smith was nowhere in sight.

"Where's Smith?" Muncrief demanded.

"I dunno. Went out to dinner, I guess."

Muncrief remembered Smith saying he was going to stick as close to Jace as a tapeworm. Some tapeworm. But it's a good thing he's not here, Muncrief told himself. Now I don't have to pry Jace loose from him.

He saw the flash of the laser and heard Jace mutter, "Damn!"

"Hey, you're supposed to wear protective goggles when you use that thing," Muncrief called, hurrying back toward Jace.

"I got contacts."

"Contacts! Who on earth ever heard of protective contacts?"

"Don't get close unless you've got goggles, man," Jace warned.

God, Muncrief said to himself. If anybody sees him working like this, my insurance rates'll triple.

"O-kay," Jace said slowly, straightening up to his full height. He put the tools down and stretched his arms over his head. "Whew."

"What the hell was that all about?" Muncrief demanded.

"Rewiring a helmet. For Smitty's program. Got to remember to ask him the President's head size."

"Since when do you do menial work like rewiring? I don't pay you to waste your time—"

Jace cut him off with a sly grin. "You don't want anybody else doing this work, boss. I can get my hands dirty when I have to. I know what I'm doing."

Muncrief huffed. "I thought you were the theoretical genius and guys like Dan did the manual labor."

"I can do whatever needs to be done. Dan and the others help out, sure, but I don't really need them—except to save time," he added before Muncrief could get a word in.

"I'll have this program for Smitty by February," Jace went on, "and Dan can put all his time into the stuttering job so the baseball game'll be ready for April first. Everything's coming up roses, huh?"

"For God's sake, will you stop patting yourself on your blasted back and listen to me?" Muncrief shouted. His voice echoed off the lab's bare cinder-block walls.

Jace gave him a crooked grin, then planted both elbows against the workbench and leaned back. "Okay," he said casually. "I'm listening."

Muncrief stared at him. Jace seemed completely relaxed, happily at work, as if everything was going along as smooth as chocolate pudding, a messy scarecrow in blue jeans and a T-shirt that announced, *King Kong Died for Our Sins.*

"You gotta learn to relax, buddy," Jace was saying, with an easy smile. "You look like you're gonna pop your cork, all red in the face like that."

"You've got to erase the special games," Muncrief said. "Not erase them, really. Change them so they're nothing more than duplicates of the regular games."

Jace's beady eyes became suspicious. "Susan's getting wise, huh?"

"How do you know?"

"She popped in here today looking for blood. Tried to make like it was nothing special, but I can tell when somebody's pissed off."

"She found out that there are special versions of the games. I told her they were just backups."

"Okay. No sweat. Just get rid of the program disks. I'll make copies of the regular games on some blank disks."

Muncrief blinked at him. "Then I can keep the special games?"

"Sure, why not? No sense throwing them away."

Muncrief felt a rush of relief. But then, "They're not working," he mumbled, so low that Jace hardly heard him.

"What's not working?"

"Every time the kid sees me in a game, she gets scared."

Jace made an *I told you so* face. "You're coming on to her too strong, I guess."

"No, I'm not! Not anymore. She just doesn't want me in her games. She told me to get out, for God's sake!"

Jace pulled up one of the stools by the workbench and lowered himself onto it like a construction crane lowering a load of girders.

"She doesn't have to know it's you," he said. "You can play the handsome prince for her, or whatever the hero of any particular game might be. You don't have to show yourself."

"But that's the whole point of it!" Muncrief insisted. "I want her to know it's me! I want her to like me. Me! Not some imaginary prince. Me myself!"

Shaking his head, Jace said, "That's tough. Maybe if you hadn't scared her so much that first time out, she wouldn't be so cranked up about you."

Muncrief was breathing heavily. It made him angry to think that Angela didn't like him. It made him even angrier to see the cool amusement in Jace's narrow eyes.

"You can't force her to like you," Jace said.

Muncrief growled, "Why not?"

CHAPTER 36

Dorothy was there.

It was the day after Thanksgiving, the busiest shopping day of the year. Santa Claus had paraded into countless towns and cities all across the United States. Stores were thronged. The airwaves were filled with advertisements for holiday sales and jokes about turkey leftovers.

And in the intensive-care ward of the Wright-Patterson Air Force Base hospital, Lieutenant Colonel Ralph Martinez was dying.

Dorothy was sitting by her husband's bed, already dressed in a black sheath. Dan could see that her eyes were red and filled with tears when he was ushered into the cubicle by a very reluctant Dr. Chandra Narlikar. Appleton was right behind Dan, who clutched a notebook computer in one hand, scarcely bigger than a schoolboy's tablet.

Martinez had wasted noticeably since Dan had seen him last, less than a week earlier. His face was still horribly contorted, but the burning fury in his one open eye was gone, faded into pale hopelessness by the pain that was conquering his body. Tubes ran from one nostril and both arms into the machines that hummed and buzzed behind his bed. Small display screens played out his life story: heartbeat, blood pressure, breathing rate, electrical activity in the brain.

Dan stopped at the foot of the bed. "Hello, Dorothy," he whispered.

She got up from the white straight-back hospital chair but did not move toward him. "Hello, Dan."

"I'm sorry as hell."

"It's not your fault," she said, her voice trembling on the verge of tears.

"Even if it's not, I'm still sorry that it had to happen."

She nodded, not trusting herself to say more.

Dr. Appleton pushed past Dan in the suddenly crowded cubicle. "Dorothy," he said, his face grave, "we want to try to get a statement from Ralph. If we can."

Her dark wide eyes went from Appleton's face to Dan's and then to the even darker liquid eyes of Dr. Narlikar.

"I am not in favor of it," Narlikar said. "Not at all. He should be allowed to rest."

"He's dying," Appleton said, his voice so low that Dan barely heard the words.

"Still . . ." Narlikar made an uncertain gesture with one hand.

"We need to find out what he experienced in the simulation," said Appleton. "If we can."

"It could push him beyond his limits," Narlikar warned.

Dan watched Dorothy's face. *She knows he's as good as dead already. She knows that even if he doesn't die he'll be a helpless cripple. But he could not open his mouth to say a word to her. How the hell can I ask her to let us do this to her husband? It might be the final straw that kills him. I've already done this to him. If he dies, it'll be my fault.*

Appleton's voice seemed to gain strength. "It's our only chance to find out what really happened to him."

Dan stared at his former boss, then turned his gaze to Dorothy. She seemed awash in conflicting emotions.

"I know Ralph," Appleton said, steady and insistent. "He always pushed himself to the limit. He wants to tell us what he knows, and we've got the means to allow him to do it."

Narlikar shifted uneasily.

"You've got to let us do this, Dorothy," Doc went on, pitiless, unswerving. "You owe it to Ralph to let us help him tell us what we need to know."

Leave her alone! Dan wanted to scream. But he said nothing, his body paralyzed as Doc ground down Dorothy's resistance. Doc's made his choice, Dan realized. He's not giving up. He's going to push on this to the bitter end. Dan wanted to reach out to Dorothy, to tell her not to listen to Doc, to do what her heart told her was best. But he could not. Doc was fighting to save his own life, Dan knew, and he could not go against the man who had been so much of a father to him.

"It's your decision, Dorothy," Doc said, his voice low but edged with steel.

She nodded so slightly that Dan was not sure until she whispered, "I understand. Go ahead."

"Do you want to leave, take a break?" Appleton asked.

"No. I want to be with him."

With trembling hands, Dan popped open the little computer and moved to the right side of the bed. Narlikar sighed like a man who wished he were someplace else. Appleton stayed beside Dorothy.

Bending over Ralph's madly contorted face, Dan said softly, "Ralph, can you hear me? It's Dan Santorini."

Martinez mumbled something unintelligible. Dan winced at his odor. Beneath the hospital antiseptics and the crisp smell of freshly bleached sheets was the cloying stench of death.

"I've got a computer here," Dan said, putting the notebook machine on the bed. "You know how to use a keyboard, don't you?"

Martinez might have tried to nod. His right eye seemed to focus on Dan's face.

"We need to know what happened in the simulator, Ralph. You're the only one who can tell us what happened to you."

Another mumble. This one ended in a gargling cough.

"He should be resting!" Narlikar hissed.

Ignoring the physician, Dan took Ralph's right hand and placed the fingers on the keyboard. The colonel's hand felt cold, lifeless.

"You're on the keyboard, Ralph. Can you feel the keys? Type a 'yes' for me if you can."

For agonizing moments the hand did not move. Then, slowly, as if with enormous effort, his index finger moved across the keys:

UES

Dan glanced up at Appleton and Dorothy across the bed.

"Close enough," he said. Looking down at Martinez again, he said, "Good, Ralph. Good."

The finger typed, LOV U DOR

She fell to her knees and put her face next to her husband's. "I love you too, *querido*. I love you!"

He could not turn his head, but his eye swung toward her. Slowly his fingers moved across the keyboard.

PLS DON CRY

One of the machines behind the bed changed the tone of its monitoring hum. Dan looked up and saw that Ralph's heart rate had quickened. Is that good or bad? he wondered. Narlikar did not seem to notice it.

"Ralph," he said swiftly, "can you tell us what happened to you in the simulation? Anything at all. What happened?"

MY FAILT

"What does he mean?" Appleton whispered, staring at the letters glowing on the little screen.

"Was it a normal mission?" Dan asked. "Did the simulation go the way we programmed it?"

Y N

"Yes or no?"

BOTH

"I don't understand," Dan said. "How could that be?"

JAVE

"Say again." Dan unconsciously lapsed into the clipped jargon of the fliers.

JACE

"Jace was a thousand miles away, Ralph."

No response. The monitoring machines were all running at a higher pitch. Narlikar was looking at them worriedly. "We must stop," he said.

But Dan went on. "Ralph, tell us what happened to you. We've got to know what happened."

JACE

"Jace couldn't have had anything to do with it."

JACE DID THIS TI ME

"It must stop!" Narlikar insisted. "It must stop now!"

The monitors were all screeching thin high-pitched wails of danger. Dan saw the jagged peaks and valleys of the display screens

smoothing, flattening into pencil-thin straight lines. Narlikar
punched the red emergency button on the bedside console.

"Get out!" he screeched. "Clear this area!"

Dan took the computer with him and followed Doc Appleton,
who was holding Dorothy by the shoulders and helping her
through the doorway as a team of grim-faced medics barged past
them pushing a cart full of emergency equipment.

They stood outside the cubicle, surrounded by the intensive-
care ward's semicircle of desks and monitoring screens. The two
nurses on duty gave them unhappy glances but said nothing. For
fifteen minutes they waited in morbid silence while the emergency
team surrounded Ralph's bed, shouting, flailing at his dying body.
Dan felt as if he were underwater trying to hold his breath for fear
of drowning. Another pair of green-suited medics raced into
Ralph's cubicle. Another ten minutes went by.

Then Narlikar came out, ash gray, exhausted.

"There was nothing we could do," said the physician. His face
hardened as he turned to Dan. "Your interrogation was too much
for him."

Dorothy half-collapsed in Appleton's arms, sobbing. Dan stood
there. Narlikar, the two deskbound nurses, even Doc Appleton all
stared at him accusingly. But in his hand he held the open computer, and its screen still read JACE DID THIS TI ME.

CHAPTER 37

Somebody's following me," said Luke Peterson.

He was driving his Cutlass through the Friday-afternoon traffic on Interstate 4 with one hand, his other holding the cellular phone clamped to his ear.

"Following you? Are you certain?" The cold voice of the Inquisitor sounded more incredulous than alarmed.

"I know when I'm being followed," Peterson said, glancing into his rearview mirror. "It's a bronze Dodge Intrepid, and it's been tailing me since this morning. Everywhere I go, it's right behind me."

"They're not very good if they let you spot them."

"I think they want me to know they're watching me."

The Inquisitor fell silent for a moment. "We've been checking out this man Smith. He's not FBI."

"These aren't FBI men," Peterson said. "I know the local feds."

"They could have brought agents in from Washington."

Unconsciously Peterson shook his head. "They don't behave like FBI. Not the same MO."

"Can you see their license number?"

"No, they're behind me," Peterson answered with some irritation. "But it's a rental, I can tell you that much."

A long silence while he weaved one-handed through the four lanes of heavy traffic. He cut in front of a station wagon full of kids; the woman driving it blared her horn angrily at him.

"Well," Peterson demanded, "what do you want me to do?"

"Do nothing," came the response. "Stay away from Santorini for the time being—"

"That's easy. He's gone back to Dayton."

"And his family?"

"They're still here."

"You've tapped their phone?"

The Intrepid slid in behind him. Faintly he heard the station wagon's horn blasting again.

"Nothing so crude as tapping," Peterson answered. "I just pick up their phone conversations remotely with the ELINT gear. But I've got to be within a block of their house to do it."

"Let it go for now. I can get someone else to monitor their phone."

"And what do I do?"

"Nothing. Not until I find out exactly who this man Smith is and who is following you."

"I don't like this. He must have some pretty strong friends back in Washington," Peterson said.

"We have friends in the capital also," said the Inquisitor. "Powerful friends."

"So I'll just spend the weekend taking life easy and hoping these guys behind me aren't licensed to kill, is that it?"

"Don't be melodramatic."

"You're not the one being followed. And don't think diplomatic immunity is going to help you if they put the screws to me. I'm no hero."

"I can take care of the situation, don't worry."

"I'm already worried."

"You just take the weekend off and spend the time thinking of a way to deliver Santorini."

"From Dayton?"

"No, he will be back. We checked into the situation there. He will most likely return this evening."

They've got contacts inside the Air Force, Peterson thought. Impressive. Maybe he really can take care of the men following me. If he feels it's in his own best interest. The main thing is to keep him from throwing me to the wolves.

"Once Santorini has settled down once again, you must find a way to get him to me."

"Not while I'm being tailed."

"Of course not. I will take care of that part of it."

Peterson had always known that the kind of games he played could occasionally get rough. But as he glanced in his rearview again at the big bronze Intrepid planted on his tail, he worried that this time he would be the one on the receiving end. Plenty of cubes in that engine; they'll be able to outrun me even if she's not souped up. And all I've got to give them is the Inquisitor's name and phone number. One lousy contact. His name's probably a phony, and he'll leave the country the instant he realizes I've been grabbed.

He clicked the phone back into its holder and reached into his jacket pocket for a handkerchief to wipe the perspiration from his brow and bald pate. What other cards do I have? he asked himself. If they grab me, what can I offer them?

Not a damned thing. He found himself hoping that the Inquisitor would not be able to peel the tail off him and would call the whole operation off. Not even the amount of money they were paying him was worth this kind of risk. A guy could wind up dead in a game like this. A nice convenient car wreck or maybe a heart attack or a fatal stabbing by muggers. Peterson felt scared. Best thing to do is call the whole thing off.

But he knew the Inquisitor wouldn't do that. He wanted Damon Santorini, and he always got what he wanted.

Dan's on his way home, Susan said to herself as she hung up the phone. At least that's something, she thought. His voice had sounded so down on the phone, so utterly exhausted, that she hadn't had the heart to ask him any details about what had happened. Ralph Martinez was dead and her husband was coming back to her. That was all that really mattered. For the moment.

As she went back to her desk in the kitchen alcove, Susan glanced out the bay window at Angela, running across the lawn of stiff Bermuda grass with a handful of neighborhood kids. That's the way children should play, she told herself. Out in the open air and sunshine, running and laughing. Not locked up in some VR booth with electronic LSD pumping into their brains.

Still, she worried about fire ants and sunburn and a thousand other dangers that the world could throw at a twelve-year-old girl.

Phil was sitting on the kitchen floor, happily banging on a pair of lids from Susan's pots. Surrounded by a month's income worth of toys, he still preferred the shiny noisy lids. Boys, thought Susan. Before long he'll be outside, too, playing baseball and skinning his knees and getting into fistfights with his friends. The baby was showing increasing signs of rambunctiousness. A month ago he had been content to spend half the afternoon in his playpen. Now he wants to get out and explore. They don't stay babies for long.

But as she sat in the little secretary's chair in front of her computer, Susan's seething anger rose up again. Dan had driven his own car to the airport to meet the Air Force jet that Dr. Appleton had sent. He would drive himself home when the plane returned him to Kissimmee. Out and back on the same day. At least he did not have to stay in Dayton overnight again.

Susan had been glad to see him go. The smoldering rage she felt about Muncrief and Vickie lying to them, tampering with the school games, assaulting Angela's mind and then blandly insisting that nothing of the sort had taken place, that hot wrath of hers blistered Dan, too. It wasn't his fault, she knew that, but still it infuriated her that he could not accept what seemed so obvious to her.

"They're trying to rape your daughter!" she had raged at him the night before.

"Sue, for chrissake, stop exaggerating!"

"Rape her mind."

"Maybe so," Dan had answered. "When I come back, we'll get to the bottom of this. I'll find out what's going on and then we'll know who's doing what to whom. But until we have some real proof you can't go barging around making wild accusations."

They had argued half the night, Susan getting angrier and more frantic while Dan struggled to stay calm and under control. His asthma started, the way it always did when he was faced with a crisis, and he'd spent the remaining hours until dawn sitting up in bed, wheezing, struggling to breathe. Which just made Susan angrier at Kyle and Vickie and Dan and herself.

Her first instinct, after Dan had left the house that morning, haggard and tight-lipped, was to go down to the lab and face Vickie in her own den. But the offices were closed for the Thanksgiving weekend, and when she tried to phone Vickie's apartment all she got was a stupid answering machine. So Susan spent her Friday morning setting up the keyword list Dan would need to search the files she had pulled on Jace's information requests, fuming inwardly. Ever since lunch, though, she had been trying to ferret out more information about the VR games in the ParaReality programs.

To no avail. Yes, there were backups to each of the fourteen school games on file. But she could not access them from her home computer.

Still, Susan worked at it doggedly, trying to crack the security codes that guarded the games and their backups. She glanced at the window every now and then, though, and saw that Angela was still playing with the neighbors' kids. Philip was happily clanging away a few feet from her. She looked up at the kitchen clock and saw that Dan's plane would be leaving Wright-Patterson in less than an hour. If it took off on time.

"I'll take Dorothy home," said Dr. Appleton.

Dan had just hung up after calling Sue from one of the pay phones lining the wall of the hospital corridor. Appleton looked grim, but he no longer had the defeated, hangdog look he had worn a few days earlier.

"Maybe I should," Dan said.

"No," Doc answered firmly. "You go home to your wife. I'll take care of Dorothy. It's my responsibility."

Dan heard the unspoken words: I may have helped you to kill her husband, but I'm not going to let you destroy your marriage.

"Does she have any relatives in the area?" Dan asked.

"I don't think so. She told me some friends are coming over to stay with her tonight."

Stepping along the corridor beside his former boss, Dan saw Dorothy standing in the little waiting area outside the intensive-care ward. All in black, already mourning, her eyes staring into infinity. This wasn't the vibrant, exciting woman he had made love with all those years ago. This was a widow, a woman struggling to keep herself from breaking in two, a woman whose husband had been killed. By me? Dan accused himself silently. But Ralph said that Jace did it.

I ought to say something to her, Dan told himself. But what? I'm sorry Ralph died? I'm sorry I pushed him to the limit? He looked across the distance between them into her dark, dark eyes, rimmed with red now, circled with grief and sleeplessness. Dorothy looked through him, as if he weren't there, staring at images that only she could see.

"Doc." Dan pulled at Appleton's tweed jacket sleeve. "We've got to talk."

The older man nodded, but said, "I've got to get her home."

"Ralph said that Jace did this to him."

"And the plane's waiting for you."

"Let it wait!" Dan snapped, gripping Appleton's thin arm. "What the hell did Ralph mean by that?"

Startled, Appleton turned to face Dan. "I don't know, Dan. I don't know if it means anything or not."

"He said Jace killed him!"

"He might have been delirious. Or maybe that's not what he meant. He never liked Jace."

Dan stared at the older man. I owe this man my career, my whole life, Dan thought. And I'm bullying him as though he's a murder suspect. Yet he tugged Appleton across the corridor, away from the waiting area and Dorothy.

"Why would he say Jace did it to him?" Dan insisted. "Did he mean that Jace programmed something into the simulation? Something that we don't know about?"

"You've gone over the program," Appleton replied. "Did you find anything?"

"Two men have died, Doc. That's not a coincidence. And I'm working for a company that's going to use VR sims in an amusement park. For the general public. If somebody can be killed in a VR simulation—"

"Murdered," Appleton corrected. "When you deliberately kill a human being, it's called murder."

Dan gaped at him.

Appleton nodded solemnly. "There's something in that simulation that kills people," he said, his voice low but unshakably certain. "And Jace put it in there."

"But he hasn't been here for more than a year," Dan pointed out. "You said it yourself. I'm the only one who worked on the sim for the past year."

"Jace did it."

Miserable, Dan pleaded, "You're sure? It couldn't be—"

"No one else would know how, or even want to," Appleton said. "You'll have to find out what he did."

"But why—"

"It's up to you, Dan. I'm keeping that simulation shut down unless or until you can tell me how to make it safe again."

It's up to me, Dan said to himself. There's nobody else. He stood there rooted to the spot, realizing that Doc was right, feeling the weight of all the responsibility pressing on his shoulders. Doc turned away and started walking toward Dorothy. Dan shook himself like a man waking from a dream, squared his shoulders, and strode across the waiting room to catch up with Doc and Dorothy.

"Wait," he said. "We're not finished yet."

"I've got to get Dorothy home," Doc murmured.

"Dorothy—" Dan's voice caught in his throat when he looked at her, close enough to touch.

She said sadly, "We had a good life together, Ralph and I."

"If there's anything I can do," Dan said, "anything you need . . ." He could not help staring at her, remembering.

"No. I'll be all right. Ralph has provided for me very well."

"But where will you go? What will you do?"

"It's all finished, Dan. What we had was finished a dozen years ago. We can't relive the past. You know that."

"Too much has happened," he agreed reluctantly.

"Good-bye, Dan," said Dorothy in a throaty whisper.

"Not yet," he said, so sharply that her eyes widened with surprise. "I've got something to say—"

"Dan, I don't blame you for what happened to Ralph. Honestly I don't."

He could see the effort it took for her to speak the words. The pain. The grief.

"I may have helped to kill him," Dan said, his voice low.

Appleton started to protest.

"But I promise you this, Dorothy," Dan said urgently, silencing Doc. "Whoever did kill Ralph—I'll find him. I'll find out who did it and see to it that he's brought to justice. If I have to do it all by myself," he said, glancing at Doc, "I'll get the job done."

For a long moment Dorothy said nothing. Then, at last, "I know you will, Dan. I knew it all along."

Doc seemed to straighten up slightly. "What do you want me to do, Dan? What help will you need?"

"I don't know, not yet. But the answer's not here; it's back in Orlando."

"Jace," said Doc.

"Jace," Dan agreed.

Jace was grinning as he watched Chuck Smith pull the helmet over his sandy crew cut. Smith's air of crisp authority had melted away like a pat of butter left out in the sun. He looked doubtful now as he stood alone in the bare VR chamber, uncertain, almost afraid.

Leaning toward the microphone, Jace asked softly, "Can you hear me okay?"

Through the one-way window he could see Smith twitch with surprise at the voice in the helmet earphones. He nodded.

"You can talk, y'know," Jace said. "There's mikes built into the cheek flaps."

"I hear you."

"Good. Put on the gloves and connect the wires. They're color-coded. Don't get them mixed up."

"Right."

Jace settled his bony frame in one of the squeaking little typist's chairs and surveyed the control board like the captain of a star ship. He laughed inwardly. That's just what I'm gonna do, take our uptight Mr. Smith for a long ride.

The gloves felt strange to Smith: stiff, like leather that had been left out in the rain. And kind of nubby inside, as if they were inside out. The light in this bare, low-ceilinged chamber wasn't all that good. He had to squint to match the colors of the hair-thin optical fibers to the plugs on the gloves. The helmet had already been wired up when he had put it on.

He looked at the window and saw only a reflection of himself in the helmet. He had taken off his suit jacket and tie, rolled up his shirtsleeves. All at Jace's suggestion.

"You wanna be as comfortable as possible in there," Jace had told him.

Okay, so I'm as comfortable as I'm going to get, he thought, surprised that his throat felt so dry.

"I'm ready," he said in a gritty croak.

"No, you're not."

"Yes, I am," he insisted.

"The visor."

"Oh."

His hands trembled slightly as he reached up and lowered the visor over his eyes. The world went totally dark, like a planetarium before they turn the stars on. Smith stood in the middle of the chamber, arms spread out as if to balance himself, thinking, Jace must've turned out all the lights in here, otherwise I'd be able to see some stray light from under the visor's rim. Or maybe—

"Here we go." Jace's voice sounded amused.

Smith saw a swirl of colors, heard the unmistakable background hum of a mediocre sound system in his earphones. He started to feel slightly dizzy; his stomach knotted.

And he was high up above the Earth, out in space looking down at the vivid green expanse of the Amazonian jungle. His stomach dropped out of him; his breath caught in his throat. He was floating in space, weightless, like a tiny one-man satellite, arms and legs spread-eagled like a sky diver. Broad ugly brown scars slashed through the rain forest where logging companies had cleared away the trees. There was no wind, no sound. Within moments his nausea faded away. He felt fine.

"You're in charge now," Jace's voice whispered to him. "It's your ball game."

Smith licked his lips. "Bolivia," he said. "False-color infrared imagery."

Like a ghost he drifted across the continent, saw the Andes as a set of gray bony wrinkles topped with lean clutching fingers of white snow. The forest below him was still green, but now he could see yellow and blue patches: cultivated farmland in the clearings.

And red dots here and there: coca plantings. Even beneath the sheltering trees the satellite sensors picked up the coca farms. Good. As he moved closer to the Andes he saw more and more areas of red, broad swaths of red in the rugged mountainous valleys.

"Initiate ECS delivery," he said, barely mouthing the words. "Fast-frame forward."

The red areas shriveled. Many of them winked out altogether. Smith smiled. Stealthy jet bombers, invisible to radar and flying so high no one could see or hear them, were delivering cargos of bioengineered bacteria over the coca-growing areas. The genetically altered bugs can wipe out most of the coca crop, just like the science guys had promised. The cocaine industry would go broke within six months.

"All right," he called, his voice firmer. "Let's move to the processing-plant scenario."

Darkness again for several heartbeats. Then he was on solid ground, standing behind a massive tree looking out through thick foliage at a low, long cinder-block building painted ugly olive green. Big trees swayed in the hot breeze and the building's roof was covered with camouflaging sod and greenery. Insects buzzed around him in the humid jungle air, but Smith felt no discomfort at all; he was not even perspiring.

Several trucks were parked at the far end of the building. Men lounged in the shade of a low overhang on benches along its side, while others came and went through the big open front doors, toting wooden crates.

Smith nodded and whispered, "Now."

A multiengined jet plane swept low over the little clearing, disgorging soldiers with jet packs on their backs and assault rifles in their hands. The men lounging along the building leaped to their feet and dashed toward their trucks. The soldiers landed in clouds of jet gases and kicked-up dust, firing at the fleeing truck drivers. Others threw grenades into the open doorway of the building. Smith heard no explosions but saw thick white smoke billowing out. Then he realized the soldiers were all wearing gas masks.

It was over in a few minutes. The soldiers dragged out the men and women who had been gassed inside the building and then took off their masks. Several of them looked familiar to Smith; the tall one he recognized as the star of several martial-arts films. Medics bent over the bodies of the truck drivers, a chaplain among them to give the last rites for the dead.

"Incredible," Smith muttered. "Absolutely incredible! Now let's go to the hacienda. And this time I want to go in with them."

Again the moment of utter darkness. Then he was standing behind flowering shrubbery on the edge of a parking lot. Beyond the luxury European cars rose a beautiful stucco-walled house with a red tiled roof. Intricately wrought iron gratings on all the windows and delicate iron railings on the house's many balconies. The sky above was crystal blue, and in the distance Smith could see the purple masses of the Andes and snowcaps that seemed to hover in midair.

Armed men were patrolling the grounds, submachine guns casually slung over the shoulders of their rumpled jackets. Their faces were brown, weathered, accustomed by generations of heredity to the cruelty and violence of serving their *patron*.

Instinctively Smith ducked down behind the shrubbery. He felt the bulk of a leather holster beneath his left armpit. He pulled out a Colt automatic and hefted it. The gun felt solid and heavy in his hand.

Again a jet plane roared out of nowhere, disgorging soldiers. But this time the guards scattered around the grounds and immediately began firing at the troops as they swooped to the ground. Smith saw men hit in midair, jerking convulsively as the bullets slammed into them. One soldier's jet pack exploded in a shower of flame, flinging bloody pieces of his body everywhere.

Smith gripped his pistol so hard his fingers began to ache. Men all around him were shooting, killing and being killed. Soldiers landed on the hacienda's sloping rooftop and tossed gas grenades through the windows up there. But he stood frozen at the edge of the parking lot, screened by the shrubbery, unable to move.

The real battle was taking shape on the parking lot, right in front of Smith's stunned eyes. Several of the drug lord's men had taken refuge behind the heavy bulletproof cars parked there and were firing back at the slowly advancing soldiers. And he stood frozen, terrified, his heart thundering in his ears, his mouth dry and burning.

The noise and the confusion were shattering. Guns firing, grenades exploding, men screaming and yelling, smoke billowing.

Smith saw that three of the men were slinking into one of the Mercedes sedans, starting the engine, ready to use the bulletproof car as a tank against the soldiers.

Their backs were to him. Each of them had a submachine gun and extra clips of ammunition poking out of their pockets. If nobody stopped them they were going to kill a lot of the soldiers, maybe break the back of the attack. And nobody had noticed them except Smith himself. It was up to him. There's nobody else, he knew. It's up to me.

Gritting his teeth, forcing himself to move, Smith pushed through the bushes and yanked open the back door of the Mercedes. He stuck his gun into the back of the nearest man and pulled the trigger. Nothing happened. The man turned toward him awkwardly, crouched between the front seat and the rear, his lean hard face wild-eyed with rage and terror, an ugly short-snouted Uzi in his hands.

Desperately Smith cocked the gun with his left hand and fired point-blank. The man's head exploded in a shower of blood and bone and brain. Smith shot again, and the driver splattered forward over the steering wheel. The third man jumped out of the open front door, flat onto his belly on the blacktopped parking lot. Smith whirled and emptied the gun into him.

And it was over. He leaned against the car, smoking gun in his shaking hand, and watched the soldiers pushing their prisoners out of the house. Dead bodies littered the parking lot and the grounds. Many of them were American soldiers. Smith's knees barely held him up. He felt sick and his trousers were wet. He had pissed himself.

The scene faded away into darkness.

"Program's terminated," he heard Jace say in his earphones. "You can lift the visor. And, uh—I guess you'll wanna clean yourself up, huh?"

For a moment Smith felt embarrassed, ashamed. But then a new feeling swept over him. I killed those guys. I saved the attack. So I was scared for a minute; who wouldn't be?

Lifting the helmet off his head, he smiled at his image in the one-way window, stained pants and all. He felt strong. He felt powerful. He felt great.

CHAPTER 38

Dan sat staring out the tiny window of the Air Force executive jet, seeing neither the landscape far below nor the snowy mountainous clouds that floated in the air all around the plane. His mind was spinning thoughts over and over and over, faces and memories and snatches of words tumbling past one another endlessly. Dorothy. There's no place in her life for me now. She won't let me near her. I could feel the attraction, it's still there. And she could, too, I know she could. But Ralph's standing between us now, more real than he was when he was alive.

He pictured himself with Dorothy again. I'm sorry I killed your husband, but let's run away together; I'll leave my wife and children and we can pretend none of this ever really happened. Yeah. In your dreams, pal. Maybe in a simulation. But this isn't a game. There is the real world, and you're in it for life.

And Doc. His career, his whole life is on the line. I owe him so much. I can't let him down. I've got to get to the bottom of this so he can reopen the sim and keep developing new ones.

Unbidden, the memory of how he met Doc came surging up into his awareness. The memory of why he left Youngstown, why he had to leave.

In gym class, in his senior year of high school. A skinny, pale, asthmatic teenager sitting on the bench that ran along the far side of the gym while the other guys played basketball. The teacher had gone off to his office, leaving the guys to spend the period any way they wanted. None of the jocks wanted a hopelessly inept nerd on their side, so Dan sat, hating the smell of sweat and sneakers, while the other guys ran and shouted and did their best to imitate basketball players.

He never saw the ball bounce past him. Dan was deep in thought, wondering about what kind of a job he could get after graduation, worrying about facing a lifetime of jobs and wages and eventually maybe getting married and supporting a family. On what? What can I do? What do I like to do?

The slap across his face didn't really hurt. It shocked Dan, though.

"I said get the ball for us, asshole!"

Totally surprised, Dan looked up to see one of the muscular jocks looming over him, fists on hips, gym shorts and baggy T-shirt soggy with sweat.

He grabbed Dan by the hair and yanked him to his feet. "When I tell you to get the ball, shitface, *you go get the fuckin' ball!*" he shouted. And he shoved Dan in the direction that their basketball had rolled, out by the parallel bars and weight-lifting equipment.

The other guys were grinning, standing there watching with stupid monkey grins on their sweaty faces. Dan turned wordlessly and walked toward the corner where the ball rested among the barbells and weights. He ducked under the parallel bars and around the worn leather horse, the anger inside making his heart pound so loudly he could hear it in his ears.

He picked up the ball and flung it two-handed back to the players. His tormentor took it, and they all broke back onto the basketball court. Dan picked up one of the hand weights and walked back toward the players. No one paid him any attention at all.

The bully shot for the basket, missed, and turned to run down to the other end of the court. He looked surprised to see Dan stepping methodically toward him. He didn't realize Dan had the weight in his hand until Dan swung it up and rammed it under his chin, knocking the kid off his feet. Suddenly blind with rage, Dan planted his knees on the fallen kid's chest and raised the weight over his head.

He would have smashed the guy's skull in if the other kids hadn't grabbed him and pulled him off.

As it was, the youngster's jaw was fractured, his tongue bitten almost in two, and eight teeth were either knocked out completely or so shattered that they had to be surgically removed. Dan was suspended from school for two weeks, saved from worse punishment only because of his unblemished previous record. The other guys all admitted that the bully had slapped Dan and pulled his hair, but the viciousness of Dan's retaliation shocked everyone in the school.

The parents sued, of course. Dan's father lost his automobile and nearly their house. Dan worked for a solid year after graduation just to pay his father back. His father screamed and bellowed at him. His mother cried. His younger brother and sister looked at him as if he were a stranger. Eventually, the screaming and the crying stopped. But not the strange looks. The family turned to cold silence. He had brought shame upon them. And worse, lawyers. He was a potential killer, a savage in their midst. "How could I have raised such a child?" his father railed.

After that episode, it was inevitable that Dan would leave Youngstown. He got a job at a local gas station and worked there long enough to buy his father a used car to replace the one he had to sell. Then he answered an advertisement for a job at Wright-Patterson Air Force Base in Dayton.

It was Dr. Appleton who plucked Dan out of his dead-end job in electronics repair. Doc Appleton who had gotten the Air Force to pay for special schooling. Doc who had teamed Dan with Jace, made Dan part of the top VR team in the country. Doc had introduced Susan to him. Doc had been more of a father than his own disappointed old man.

When he had been riding the bus from Youngstown to Dayton, alone and knowing that he was not really welcome in his family's home anymore, Dan realized that the one time he had given vent to his anger it had shattered his life completely. He had to start all over again. He vowed he would never lose his self-control again. It cost too much.

"I've never lost my temper without it costing me more than it was worth," Dan muttered to himself as the Air Force plane threaded its way through the clouds.

You've got to stay in control, he told himself. Don't let your emotions run away with you; that won't solve anything. But the burning, rasping ache in his chest told him that he was not in control of himself. Not entirely. It was impossible.

He took out his inhalator and squeezed a squirt of epinephrine down his throat. Look at it rationally, he told himself. Like an archaeologist looking into a newly excavated pit filled with the shards and fragments of an ancient civilization. It all fits together somehow; all those chips and bits can be pieced together into a coherent whole that will tell you what you need to know. But how to do it? Where to start?

And unlike a coolheaded scientist who can attack the puzzle before him with a certain level of detachment, Dan felt deep within him this terrible surging anger. Anger at Jace for turning their simulation into a death trap. Anger at Muncrief for hiring him to be Jace's lackey. Anger even at Doc for saddling him with this responsibility and at Dorothy for walking away from him. Anger at whoever it was who was messing around with his daughter's head. Even anger at Susan's fiery insistence: "They're trying to rape your daughter!"

She's right, Dan admitted to himself. Muncrief or Jace or somebody's going after Angela. And Vickie's covering up for whoever it is. An overwhelming tide of rage swept over him, but he fought it down, battled with every atom of self-control in him. Don't go off half-cocked. Don't let your emotions ruin everything. Find out who it is first. Find out *why*.

And even as he fought to control himself, Dan felt a smoldering implacable inescapable anger at himself for letting them do these things to him, to his child, to his family, to his work, to his life.

The bastards, he cursed silently as the Air Force jet cruised toward Florida. The sneaking murdering child-molesting bastards. I'll get them. I'll get each and every one of them.

And do what? challenged another voice in his head. Who do you think you are, Wyatt Earp? Going to march in there and have a shoot-out with Muncrief? With Jace? You already tried that once, and you haven't had a decent night's sleep ever since. Get real! Get a grip on yourself. You're not going to accomplish a damned thing if you let your temper get the better of you.

So Dan struggled with himself all during the flight home. By the time the jet landed and he set foot on the airport's concrete apron, he was trembling inside with pent-up fury. Blindly he walked through the tiny terminal and out onto the parking lot. Automatically he unlocked the Honda, cranked down all four windows, started the car, and turned the fan up to maximum.

He might have driven past a presidential motorcade, for all he noticed on his way home. But by the time he got out of the car and saw Susan standing at the breezeway door smiling at him, Philip in her arms and Angie by her side, he had made up his mind about what he had to do.

Susan's welcoming kiss was warm. "I'm sorry about Ralph," she said as Dan took the baby from her. He hoped that she meant she was sorry about their argument, as well.

"Yeah," he said. "Me too." Then, looking down at his daughter, "How're you, Angel?"

"Okay."

Dan held Phil in the crook of his arm and tousled Angie's hair. "Miss me?"

She smiled up at him, all braces and coltish awkwardness and happy eyes. "Sure."

Pushing his inner furies deeper below the surface, Dan followed his wife into the kitchen. "I won't be going back to Dayton," he said. "What I need to find out about is right here. Has been, all along."

"Jace?" she asked.

He nodded grimly.

"I've got about a hundred pounds of journal articles and books and whatnot that Jace's looked up since he came to ParaReality. No luck with Wright-Patt, though. They won't let me into their files."

Dan said, "I'll call Doc. He'll get you cleared." Putting the baby down on the kitchen floor, he said to Angela, "Keep an eye on your brother for a minute, will you, honey?"

"You're calling Doc now?"

"Why not?"

"It's almost seven o'clock."

Dan picked up the wall phone. "He'll either be home or in his office."

"It's Friday."

"We're going to work the weekend on this, Sue."

"*We* are?"

"You and me, right."

"But will Dr. Appleton?"

Pecking Appleton's number from memory, Dan replied, "All he's got to do is give me the access code for the library files. You and I will take it from there."

Susan saw the look of absolute certainty on her husband's face. She turned and scooped up the baby, saying to Angela, "Help me get Phil ready for bed, dear, and then we can have dinner with Daddy."

Two hours later, Dan had kissed his daughter good night after tucking her into her bed. He turned out the light in her bedroom and walked back to the kitchen where Susan was putting the last of the dishes into the washer.

"Angie seems okay," he said.

"She's glad you're home. It makes her feel safer."

He felt a slight touch of surprise.

"Makes me feel safer, too," Susan added.

"This business scares you?"

"Yes! Didn't you know? I tried to tell you—"

"Hey, hey," he said gently, sliding his arms around her. "Don't be scared. Whatever happens, I'm here now and we're going to handle this thing together."

Susan looked into his eyes. "I don't know how you can stay so cool about all this."

He almost wanted to laugh. "Cool? Me? If you tried to take my temperature, the thermometer would pop."

"You hide it awfully well."

"Come on," he said, changing the subject. "Show me what you've dug up on Jace."

Susan pointed to a four-inch stack of paper sitting next to her computer printer. "I printed out about one piece in ten so you could sample the material. If you need more, I can print out the rest."

Dan grunted. "Looks like a weekend's work."

"You're not going to the lab tomorrow?"

"Not until I've waded through this stuff," he said, stepping into the alcove and hefting the pile of paper.

"Don't you want to call Jace?"

"Not yet," he said, feeling the anger surging again. "Not until

I've gone through this material. I don't want to accuse him of anything unless I can back it up."

"Okay," said Susan, following him. "I'll start accessing the Wright-Patt files."

"Now?"

"Right now. You read while I work."

He grinned at her, but there was no mirth in it. "This isn't work, huh?"

"You know what I mean." Susan sat at her little chair and booted up her computer.

"I never knew it could be like this," Chuck Smith was saying. "It was fan-fucking-tastic!"

Sitting beside him in his rented BMW, Vickie tried to keep as straight a face as she could, allowing only the slightest of smiles to curl her lips. Smith took no notice, he was so wrapped up in describing his VR session.

"I mean, I've been in simulations before, but I've never gone through anything like this. I was there! I was really there. I thought one of those greasers was going to kill me. For real! I popped him, though. *Bam,* right through the head."

He was speeding toward a new restaurant that Vickie had read about in the local newspaper, weaving through the evening traffic as if he had a siren and blinker on the car.

One session in the VR system and he's bubbling over, Vickie said to herself. That tough no-nonsense facade of his has crumbled away; he's like a little boy who's just seen Santa Claus for the first time.

"Jace has pulled it off, all right," Smith was saying, gesturing with one hand as he roared through the highway traffic. "In just a couple of days, too."

At least his eyes are on the road, Vickie thought gratefully.

"I mean, he's really done it. The guy's a flake and all that, but he really can produce when he wants to. I could take this system to the White House tomorrow if I had to. But Jace says he's got some refinements he wants to add to it. Improvements. We'll make the February first deadline with no sweat, and it'll be *incredible!*"

"You have to be careful about Jace's refinements," Vickie

warned. "Sometimes he starts down a side alley and doesn't come out for months on end."

Smith waved his hand again. "Doesn't matter. I can bring the program we've got right now to the White House, if I have to. It'll do—for starters."

Vickie leaned her head back against the headrest and watched the evening traffic zooming by. Smith was leaning on the gas pedal, passing everything in sight, impatiently blinking his high beams at cars in the left lane doing a mere seventy-five.

"They do have unmarked patrol cars along this highway," she warned softly.

He laughed. "Am I going too fast for you?"

"You wouldn't want to get a ticket. They're quite steep around here."

"So what? I'll put it on my expense account."

"Then I'll have to pay for it out of my taxes," she countered.

"Hey, I'm going to make you a powerful woman, remember? When I go back to Washington, you're going back with me."

"I am?" Vickie sat up straight, shocked.

"You sure are, sweetie. You're going to be my pipeline to Jace and those other technical guys while we set up the VR system in the West Wing."

"Nice of you to ask me so politely."

"Come on, Vic. It's what you want, isn't it?" He laughed again, louder. "I think we'll set it up right in Quigley's office. Move him out into a broom closet or something."

"Who's Quigley?"

"The fat fart who thinks he's my boss."

He slid the BMW between two big tractor-trailer rigs. Vickie saw the speedometer's digital readout pass eighty.

"I would appreciate it if you'd slow down, Chuck," she said.

"Really?" He leaned harder on the accelerator.

"Please!"

"Say pretty please."

"Damn you!"

"Pretty please or else." They were doing eighty-six now. The other cars on the road were blurring past in the gathering darkness. A big semi loomed ahead, rushing up on them.

"Pretty please!" Vickie squealed.

He roared past the semi on its right, then slowed back to seventy-five and turned to her, grinning so widely that she could see all his teeth even in the shadowed dusk.

"That was nasty," Vickie said.

"Don't be sore."

"I don't like you like this. It's as if you're drunk."

"Drunk with power, maybe."

Vickie grimaced.

"You've got to try it, Vic. It's better than coke. Better than designer drugs!"

"No, thank you," she said tightly. "I haven't done any drugs since high school, and if this is the way a VR session affects you—"

"Do you realize what a tiger we've got by the tail here?" Smith ignored her displeasure. "It's even greater than I had expected it to be, and I had expected something pretty damned powerful. It's incredible, Vickie, it really is. You're not just watching it happen; you're *there*. You're taking part in the scene! I've never experienced anything like it."

"You said that before."

"But it's wild, Vic. It's so goddamned powerful! Whoever controls the VR system will be able to control the President! The whole fucking government!"

"And that's what you want, is it?"

"Sure as hell is! You and me, kid. We're going to be the two most powerful people in Washington. In the world!"

"If you don't kill us in a car wreck first."

He grinned again. "I'll get you safely back to your own bed, don't worry."

She saw that he had slowed down almost to the speed limit.

"You've never tried it, have you?"

"No," said Vickie.

"You ought to. There's nothing like it."

Never, she said to herself. I've seen how it's taken hold of Kyle. I watch Jace getting deeper into it day by day. And now you've turned into a VR junkie after just one hit. You'll never get *me* into a VR booth. Never in a million years.

After dinner and a bottle of champagne that Smith insisted on, he drove Vickie back to her apartment just as feverishly as he had driven her to the restaurant. And once in bed . . .

"Hey, you're hurting me!"

"Then move the way I want you to."

"You don't—"

"Come on, bitch. Take it. Take it!"

"You're brutal."

"Damned right. On your knees, cunt. That's the way I want you, and you're going to do what you're told like a good little bitch, aren't you?"

Vickie did as she was told.

CHAPTER 39

Kyle Muncrief was on the road that night, too. Ever since he had fled from Toronto, all those years ago, he had known that a man needs a hideaway, a safe house that no one else knows about. Absolutely no one. When he lived in New York, he had rented a loft in SoHo in addition to his apartment in the Gramercy Park area. No one knew about the loft except the pathetic young girls he brought there from time to time.

Now he had found the perfect place, a suite of rooms in one of the second-rate chain hotels that lined International Drive. Thousands of tourists came and went every day; no one would notice a single middle-aged man who just slipped in now and then. He took an annual lease with the hotel chain's corporate headquarters and paid by postal money order so that there would be no way to trace the transaction.

He drove past the hotel's main entrance and down the side street to the entry ramp at the rear, slowing to a crawl over the speed bumps because he did not want to jar the box filled with a pair of VR helmets and two sets of gloves resting on the back seat of the Jaguar. There were also two complete body-sensor nets in the box. That goddamned idiot Joe Rucker had insisted on helping him tote the box out to his car, him with his one arm and artificial leg and endless good cheer.

He had literally bumped into Rucker that morning in the receiving room just off ParaReality's loading dock, where the equipment package was waiting for him. It had arrived several days earlier, but Muncrief had waited until Friday, when the office was closed and the receiving-department people were out of the way, before he picked it up.

"What the hell are you doing here, Joe?" Muncrief had demanded of the security guard. Rucker was obviously not on duty. He was wearing threadbare old slacks and a baggy short-sleeved faded blue shirt with one sleeve hanging loose.

"I'm helpin' Jace," Rucker had replied with a broad smile.

Muncrief gave him a sour look. "Helping Jace do what?"

"We're playin' soldiers in the VR. Mr. Smith's in th' game, too."

Smith was the last man Muncrief wanted to run into. "Well, then, go back to the lab. I can handle this by myself."

But Rucker had insisted in his cheerful bumbling way that he had to help. Fuming, but not wanting to cause a row that might bring Jace or Smith, Muncrief allowed the guard to struggle one-armed with the box while he trotted down the ramp and opened the Jag's door and pulled down the front seat. Muncrief's heart spasmed in his chest as Rucker limped toward the car, nearly dropping the delicate equipment onto the hardtop.

Once the box was safely on the rear seat, Muncrief thanked Rucker and went around to the driver's side of the Jaguar.

"And Joe," he said, mopping perspiration from his brow, "for God's sake don't mention to Jace and Smith that I was here this morning."

"No?"

"Not a word, understand? I don't want them knowing every move I make."

"Whatcher doin' is a secret?"

"It's my business, not theirs," Muncrief growled.

Rucker bobbed his head up and down. "Yes, sir, Mr. Muncrief. I reckon I can keep a secret good's anybody, if that's what you want."

"That's what I want."

All day long, Muncrief wondered if he had handled Rucker in

the best way possible. Even after darkness fell and he drove out to his newly acquired hotel suite, he still mulled it over. As he parked his Jaguar next to the door of his ground-floor suite, he thought that maybe telling Rucker to keep his mouth shut hadn't been so smart, after all. Goddamned hillbilly thinks he's in on something now. If I had just let it go he probably would've forgotten all about it by the time he got to Jace's lab.

No way to change it now, though. He hauled the box out of the back seat, put it down to lock the car, took it up to the door of his suite, and had to put it down again to fish out the door key and open it up.

There in the middle of the suite's sitting room sat a brand-new minicomputer, about waist tall, gray and square and almost shiny-looking, like a small refrigerator. Muncrief put his box down on the coffee table and went to the wall to turn the air-conditioning up full blast. The stupid maids always turned it down to minimum. Then he locked the door and put on the safety chain and pulled all the window blinds shut. "A hundred thousand dollars' worth of computer in here and they leave the goddamned curtains open," he muttered.

Finally he pulled a slim plastic folder from the inside pocket of his sweaty, rumpled jacket. In it were the disks on which Angela Santorini's reactions had been recorded. Muncrief grinned to himself, alone in the shadows. He plopped himself down wearily in one of the sagging upholstered armchairs and took stock. The computer stood in the middle of the room, an incongruous oblong of clean smooth metal and plastic standing on a worn gray carpet amid seedy chipped furniture.

For several minutes he merely sat there, waiting for the tension in him to ease off. All those people pounding on me. It's good to get away. Got to have some time for myself. Got to have a place where they can't find me.

My little love nest, Muncrief thought to himself, not without some bitterness. The plastic folder with the disks in it was on his lap. He opened it and took out the glimmering compact discs. My electronic love nest. And nobody knows about it, not even Vickie.

It was well past midnight before Muncrief got everything working to his satisfaction. He sat in the darkened room, the minicomputer humming, his VR helmet and data gloves on.

He swam beside Angela Santorini on their way to Neptune's

Kingdom. He led her through the forest woven out of Beethoven's Pastorale. He explored the Green Mansions world with her. He was her guide, her companion, her prince.

He could see clearly that she was Angie, the little girl he often drove to school. But now and then, if he half closed his eyes and did not look directly at her, she was Crystal, his sister, his love. He had found her at last; she had been waiting for him all along, inside Angela. In some part of his mind, he realized that he did not even remember clearly what Crystal looked like. She might even be dead, out there in the real world where people hurt each other.

But none of that mattered. Crystal was here with him, and he loved her and would protect her from any harm that might threaten her.

He desperately wanted Crystal to love him, too, but whenever he came too close to her she changed back into Angela again and became frightened.

"Love me!" he begged her. But she ignored his pleas, as if she could not hear a word he said.

The sun was starting to brighten the drawn curtains. The last disc had spun out its electronic images. Kyle Muncrief sat in the armchair soaked with sweat, his hair flopped down over his eyes, his breathing ragged, a frown of bitter disappointment on his flushed face.

"It's not enough," he muttered in the darkness. "There's just not enough fucking material in there."

All these weeks. All the risks he had taken. And still what he wanted was not in the machine.

He ran a weary hand across his eyes, pushed his hair back in place. There's only one way to get what I need, he told himself. I've got to make her love me. And then I'll have her forever.

In the clear bright sunlight of early morning, Vickie Kessel studied her image in her bathroom mirror. Chuck had been a brutally different man the night before. One session in a VR simulation had brought out all the frenzied power dreams he had kept under control before. He had pawed her in bed, used his physical strength to put her where he wanted her, make her do what he wanted her to. He had insisted on oral sex in the most degrading manner possible. And she had done it, because she feared he would hit her if she didn't.

He was out of control last night, Vickie said to her image in the mirror. He was ugly. She saw that there was a bruise on her shoulder the size of his thumbprint. Another bigger one on her thigh.

That's the last time I crawl into bed with *him,* Vickie told herself. He's not going to play his domination games on me.

The phone rang. Naked, she went to her bedroom to answer it. The security guard in the lobby:

"Delivery for you, Ms. Kessel. Flowers."

"You can let him come up," she said.

Swiftly she pulled a robe around herself, then went back to the bathroom mirror to brush her hair. The doorbell chimed. She kept the chain on the door, accepted the box of flowers, handed the delivery man a dollar.

Roses. A dozen red roses. Expensive but not very original, she thought. The note said, "I got carried away last night. Please have dinner with me this evening and let me apologize. Chuck."

Dinner, Vickie said to herself. And that's all. She went to the phone and left a message on the answering machine in his hotel room. She did not try to track him down at the lab. I'm not going to chase after him, even on the telephone; let him play with Jace and check his machine to see if I called him.

She put the roses in a vase and then went back to getting dressed for her Saturday morning's shopping. She dressed slowly, thinking, planning, reviewing her options. Every opportunity carried risks. Every danger she faced held the chance of reward.

Chuck will protect me from Peterson, but that means that I've got to depend on Chuck and forget about making a deal with whoever Peterson represents. Chuck says he wants to bring me to Washington. Good. But from now on we'll be business partners, not lovers. I'm not going to make a whore of myself for him or anybody else.

Then she thought of Kyle. Maybe I'm not a whore, Vickie thought, but Kyle's got me pimping for him, just about. ParaReality stands to make millions out of virtual reality when and if Cyber World opens. But Kyle's a man set for self-destruction. She realized that now. He's doing something with Dan's daughter, invading her VR sessions at the school, and sooner or later that will explode in his face.

If Kyle nukes himself, what does that do to the company? I could run it, as long as Jace and Dan and the rest of the technical staff stay on board. Would the investors back me? Swenson's a chauvinist pig, and Toshimura couldn't even imagine a woman in charge of anything. Glass is seduceable, but he's not strong enough to swing the other two.

Besides, if Kyle blows up it'll take Jace with him. Jace has been helping him, and once Dan finds out about *that* there'll be earthquakes and tidal waves.

So Smith is the best option. Go to Washington, get onto the power train. You've got to keep Chuck in line, though. Last night was a revelation. He's a macho creep under all that Beltway gloss. If I go to Washington with him, I'll have to fight every inch of the way for my own self-respect.

Unless—there's still Peterson and whoever he's working for: Disney or Paramount Communications or one of the other corporate biggies. What if I offered to work for them? Vickie asked herself. What if I brought them ParaReality on a platter and showed them how they could use virtual reality in their own parks? I'd have to get past Peterson and talk to whoever he's working for.

She hesitated. Chuck said his people will scare Peterson off. But will the corporation behind him scare that easily? If they contact me again, maybe I could get them to give me the kind of deal I'm looking for. That would be stabbing Kyle in the back. But if he destroys himself with this child-porn thing, why shouldn't I try to land on my feet? It could even work out to my benefit.

Finished dressing, Vickie gave herself one last critical look in the mirror. Not bad for an old lady, she told herself. You'd look all right in Washington. Or in the corporate offices of Disney or MGM.

As she headed for the door, she thought, It all depends on Kyle. If he actually gets Cyber World running on schedule, we're golden. But if he cracks up before then, I've got to be able to get clear of the wreckage.

Quentin W. Smith III was trembling with eagerness. He had been angry, at first, because the phone call had come while he was in the VR simulation. He had been forced to terminate the session, to leave his gorgeous manipulation of the cabinet meeting, to come to the goddamned stupid phone.

But this call was important. This was the one that counted.

"So it really works?" Perry was asking.

"It works," Smith said, surprised at the tightness in his throat. "It works better than I thought it would. You've got to come down here and experience it for yourself."

"Do you think that's wise?"

"Why the hell not? Who's going to know? Take a couple days off and tell them you're going to Disney World, for chrissakes."

Perry's tone was cautious. "Look, we're not playing games here. If word about this leaks out, we could all end up in Leavenworth. Or worse."

"Jesus!" Smith snapped. "What kind of a pansy are you?"

"Hey, I don't like—"

"Never mind. Okay, I'm sorry. But you've got to get down here and try this for yourself. Then you'll see that it's *exactly* what we hoped it would be. Even better! In six months, we'll have the whole cabinet eating out of our hand! In a year, the whole Congress!"

"It's that good?"

"Come and see for yourself."

"Maybe I should."

"You should."

"But what's this business about Army intelligence? Why have you put them into the picture?"

"They're not in the picture. They don't know a damned thing about us."

"The hell they don't!" Perry's voice sounded tense, almost frightened.

"I needed some help to protect the security of our operation here," Smith explained. "They don't know what the operation is all about. I'm not that stupid."

"You had to get a pair of Army intelligence goons down there to follow some private investigator?"

"It was necessary. For security."

"It was necessary to bring Army intelligence into this? When McMasters finds out about this, your name is going to be horse manure!"

That's not what Perry's worked up about, Smith knew. He's terrified that *his* name will be shit if things go wrong.

"Don't worry about it," Smith said.

"Don't worry? Have you gone nuts, Chuck? Do you realize—"

"Just haul your ass down here and take a look at what we've accomplished," Smith insisted, adding silently, And stop acting like an old lady.

"This video thing of yours better be god-awful impressive," he warned. "McMasters won't be happy if it's just another fancy-dancey television gimmick. Neither will Ingram."

Smith grinned into the phone. "Don't worry. This is all we hoped it would be, and more. We'll be running the whole damned government inside of a year, you'll see."

Perry huffed. "Okay, I'll come down. I've got to see this for myself."

"Good. Do that."

"But I'm calling off those Army men you requisitioned. I don't see why you need the goddamned U.S. Army to deal with one lousy private eye. I don't like having them involved."

Smith thought briefly of Vickie. What the hell, I just did it to make her dependent on me. "Okay," he said into the phone. "I think maybe they've already done the job I wanted them to do."

CHAPTER 40

t was Sunday morning when Luke Peterson realized he was no longer being followed. The big bronze Intrepid had gone away, and he could not spot any replacement. He drove from his home in the trailer park south of the airport and spent the whole morning doodling around, looking for a tail. Nothing. Not at church, not at the shopping mall, not along the highway. Nobody was following him.

Which gave Luke Peterson reason to think hard. Maybe his contact actually did have friends in Washington high enough on the pecking order to get his tail removed. Or maybe he just alerted whoever was tailing him so that they've gotten a whole lot smarter. Maybe they're watching me from the air, he thought. They could even do it from a satellite if they wanted to.

Peterson felt more worried without the obvious Intrepid behind him than when it had been there.

Sunday night. Dan sat wearily on the living-room sofa, reading page after page of a report on brain physiology from a research group at Johns Hopkins University. It made little sense to him; the jargon was completely unfamiliar. But Jace had accessed this research paper from the Wright-Patterson library search system more than five years earlier.

The rest of the sofa was piled with papers. More report printouts lay scattered across the living-room floor. The words were blurring in Dan's vision; he found himself struggling through the same paragraph for the third time. Or maybe it was the fourth.

Susan had spent the weekend alternating between her computer and the children. Her printer had chugged out a steady stream of reports on subjects as wildly divergent as computer-chip manufacturing methods and sensory pathways in the human nervous system, optical data processors, and the medical phenomenon called phantom limbs.

He had hardly seen Sue all weekend, except when she brought in more papers for him to read or handed him a tray of sandwiches and coffee. She kept the kids away from him entirely; they might have gone to Alaska, for all he saw or heard of them.

Finally he let the paper drop from his fingers. Its unattached pages fluttered to the floor. Leaning his head back on the sofa, Dan rubbed his aching eyes.

"Do you have a minute to kiss the kids good night?" Susan whispered.

He looked up, focused blearily on her at the doorway to the hall that led to the bedrooms.

"Yeah. Sure."

Philip was already blissfully asleep in his crib. Dan smiled down at his son and realized that the boy would soon be too big for the crib; he would have to convert it to a child's bed, if he could remember where he had put the instructions that had come with it.

Angela was tucked into her bed in her pink and white room, lit only by a Mickey Mouse lamp on the night table beside her.

"You want Amanda with you?" Dan asked her.

"Oh, Daddy, I'm too big for that," she said, with no small disdain. "I haven't slept with Amanda in a *long* time."

He looked at his daughter. She was growing up, true enough. Soon she'll want to sleep with boys. But then he remembered that somebody was tampering with her VR games, invading her electronic fantasies. I've got to put a stop to that before they hurt her.

Bending down, Dan kissed Angela on the forehead. "Sleep well, Angel. Have happy dreams."

"You too, Daddy."

He clicked off the lamp and left her bedroom, closing the door softly as if she were already asleep.

Susan was waiting for him in the hallway.

"Until we get this thing settled," Dan said to her, "I don't think we ought to let Angie play any more VR games at school."

"I've thought that for weeks," Susan replied.

"You'll tell her teacher?"

"First thing tomorrow."

"Good." He started for the living room.

"How's your reading going?"

He took a look at the paper blizzard and shook his head. "Jace seems to be interested in everything from computer architecture to phantom limbs."

Susan started to pick up the papers from the floor. "I only picked a small percentage of the papers he accessed over the years."

Dan knelt down to help her. "I guess if you tried to get all the papers he's looked at, it would've filled the house."

"And then some." She stacked a pile on the coffee table. "I tried to give you as wide a sampling as possible. You know, picking as many different subjects as there were on the list."

"Yeah."

"I have the number of papers he accessed on each descriptor keyword, so you can tell which subjects interested him most."

"What's the top subject?"

"Biofeedback."

"Biofeedback?"

" 'A method of controlling mental reactions and physical functions that are normally involuntary by the use of electronic monitoring devices,' " Susan recited. "I looked up the definition in the dictionary."

Squatting on the living-room floor, surrounded by the scattered papers, Dan said, "Isn't that what people used to do back in the sixties—change their pulse rate and stuff like that by listening to a tone in their earphones?"

"I think so," said Susan.

"But I didn't see any papers about biofeedback in the stuff I read."

"It's all in the oldest material. Seven, eight years ago. I didn't bother printing out material that old, but when the computer added up all the papers by subject, biofeedback was number one. Jace did a *lot* of reading on the subject back then."

"The library has records going back that far?"

She nodded. "I don't think the Air Force ever throws anything away."

Dan went back to picking the papers off the floor. The coffee table was starting to look like a library cart, but at least he could see the carpet again.

"Is the subject of phantom limbs what I think it is?" Susan asked.

He looked up at her. "An amputee still gets feelings from the limb that's been cut off. He feels as if the arm or leg is still there. It hurts him or itches or something."

"And he thinks he can move it? Like, reach out and grasp something with the amputated arm?"

"Yeah, I think so."

"Jace accessed a lot of papers about phantom limbs. Duke University, MIT, the University of Milan, London School of Medicine, a lot from McGill and a couple of other Canadian schools."

Dan picked the last of the papers off the carpet and brought it to the coffee table. He sat on the cleared sofa; Susan sat down beside him.

"Apparently Jace got Joe Rucker his job," he said.

"Joe Rucker?"

"The security guard at the lab."

"The guy with one arm?"

"And one leg. He's got an artificial leg."

"You know," Susan said, "I thought I had seen him in Dayton."

"Yeah, you told me that. But he couldn't have been a security guard at the base."

"It wasn't on the base. I think it was at one of Doc's parties."

"Joe's never been to Dayton. I'm pretty sure of that."

"Then maybe it was somebody else who only had one arm."

"At a party at Doc's?"

Susan nodded.

"Was Jace at the party?"

"I'm not sure. I think maybe he was."

Dan felt his brows knitting into a frown. "I guess I could call Doc and ask him if he remembers. I sure as hell don't."

"You only remember numbers," Susan said.

"And dates. I've never missed a birthday or an anniversary, have I?"

"Because they're numbers," she teased.

"Still . . ."

Susan grew serious again. "There's another thing, now that I think of it. A lot of those papers were cross-referenced under pain control."

"Pain control?"

"Pain control. The subject seems to be linked to the work on phantom limbs."

Thinking out loud, Dan muttered, "Biofeedback, phantom limbs, pain control . . . Jace has been studying all three."

"For years."

He glanced at his wristwatch. "Geez, it's not even nine o'clock yet. Feels like half past midnight."

"You've had an exhausting weekend."

He pushed himself up from the sofa. "Doc should still be up."

"You're going to phone him now? On Sunday night?"

Heading for the wall phone in the kitchen, Dan replied over his shoulder, "I'll be seeing Jace first thing tomorrow morning—or at least as soon as he drags himself into the lab. I want to have all my ducks in a row before I face him."

Susan watched him through the pass-through, wondering if Dan really had the strength to face Jace down. She had always felt that Jace depended on Dan, but her husband felt the other way: that he was nothing but a glorified technician; that if it weren't for Jace, he would be a total nonentity. Now he's going to have to stand up to Jace, she told herself. I hope he can do it.

Dan heard the phone ring once, twice. In the middle of the third ring, it was picked up. Doc's flat thin voice said, "Appleton residence."

"Hello, Doc. It's me, Dan."

Immediately, Appleton's voice took on a more urgent tone. "Is something wrong with the access codes I gave you?"

"No, no. They worked fine. Sue dug up a ton of material."

"And?"

"I need to ask you a question."

"About Jace?"

"I think so. You remember a party you threw, oh, it must be more than five years ago, more like seven or eight, maybe—"

"Dan, I give parties every year at Christmas and the Fourth of July."

"There was an amputee at this one. A man with only one arm."

"Why in the world are you asking about that?"

"Jace has pulled a lot of papers on phantom limbs over the years. Right now, here at ParaReality, he's buddy-buddy with a North Carolina redneck who's lost an arm and a leg."

"Jace?"

"That's what I said."

A long silence on the phone. Then, "The only amputee I ever knew well enough to invite to a party here at the house was Hoot Johnson."

"Who was he?"

"He's still alive," Appleton said, a tang of irritation in his voice. "Retired major from the medical service. Lost his arm on a combat mission in Vietnam. He worked at the base hospital for a few years before he retired from the Air Force."

"Do you know where he is now?" Dan asked.

"Haven't the foggiest notion."

"Can you track him down?"

He sensed Appleton shrugging. "I can try. If you really think it's important."

"I don't know, Doc. But I think we've got to track down every possible lead, don't you?"

"Dan, you sound like a detective investigating a murder."

Without hesitation Dan replied, "Two murders, Doc. Two of them."

Jace cranked his black recliner up to its sitting position. He could not relax, could not sleep. This business with Muncrief is getting to be a real crock of shit, he told himself. But I don't know how to get myself out of it.

The friggin' sonofabitch isn't satisfied with what I've done for him. He wants more: more realism, more physical sensation. Maybe I oughtta just put enough amps into the feedback loop to fry his brain altogether. Serve him right, the friggin' pervert.

He swung his long legs off the chair and bent over to tug off his boots. It was always a struggle, but somehow the physical exertion helped to make his mind work better.

This time, though, all he could think of was Muncrief's sorrowful, almost tearful pleading for a more realistic simulation. The only way to make it more realistic, Jace knew, was to get more emotional reactions out of Dan's kid.

If Dan ever finds out! Jace finally yanked one boot off his foot and tossed it halfway across his cluttered room. If Dan ever finds out, he'll go gonzo on me. All that Italian crap in him will explode. He'll turn into a nutcase.

Straining at the other boot, Jace wondered if there was some way to satisfy Muncrief while leaving Dan's daughter alone. Maybe I can cross-link the program I did for Ralph and Dottie; use the physical sensations I recorded there and plug 'em into Muncrief's program. If Kyle wants to feel like he's fucking the kid, let him fuck Dorothy. Only, she'll look like a twelve-year-old to him. That could work.

The boot pulled free at last, and Jace nearly toppled off the edge of the chair.

Naw, he realized. It won't work. Muncrief would be getting the reactions from a grown woman who likes to fuck. That's not what he wants. That's not what makes him sweat. He wants an innocent little kid. He wants to be the big daddy screwing his own daughter.

Jace got up and paced the room in his stocking feet, oblivious to the computer chips and other debris littering the bare plywood floorboards.

How much does Dan know? Or suspect? Susie's been complaining to Vickie, I know. But what do they know for sure?

Hell, I'm not hurting their kid. Scared her the first time, I guess, but that was Kyle, not me. Dumb bastard's too damned eager, doesn't listen to what I tell him. I won't hurt the girl. But Dan wouldn't see it that way. It's his daughter, and he'll want blood.

Jace stopped his pacing and stared at the scuffed VR helmet

sitting next to one of his computers. His long, lantern-jawed face eased into a slow smile.

Okay, pal. If he's gonna come after me, I guess I better get ready. I can handle Dan. Always could and always will. But I've gotta deal with him on *my* terms.

The poor bastard won't have a chance.

CHAPTER 41

At breakfast Monday morning, Susan sat between her two children, munching on a slice of thin toast, while Dan sat opposite her in his crisply starched short-sleeved white shirt, hardly touching his plate of sunny-side-up eggs.

"Angel," said Dan, "there's something I want to tell you. Something important."

Angela looked up from her cereal.

"Your mother and I want you to stop using the VR games for a while—"

Her eyes widened. She began to whine, "Da-aa-dy!"

Susan reached out and grasped her slim arm. "Only for a while, baby."

"But why? I *like* the games."

Susan looked across the table at her husband. Dan's stomach was already clenching inside him.

As calmly as he could, he said, "There are a few things I need to check out about those games, Angel. As soon as I've done that, you'll be able to play them again."

"You can still use the VR for your lessons. It's only the games that we want you to stay out of."

"What's *wrong* with the games? I *like* them!"

Dan had spent half the night rehearsing this, yet he still felt totally unprepared to face his twelve-year-old daughter.

"Well," he said, hoping he had the right argument to convince her, "it's sort of like eating chocolate. You like chocolate, don't you?"

"Sure."

"And what happens when you eat too much of it?"

"You get zits."

Dan blinked with confusion. He had expected her to say she would get a bellyache.

"And fat," Susan chimed in.

"Sometimes," Dan went on, trying to cover up his surprise, "we have to stop doing things we really like to do because they're not all that good for us."

"The VR games aren't hurting me."

"Maybe not," he admitted. "But I want to check them out and make sure."

Angela's fair-skinned face clouded into a childish frown. "If there was anything wrong with them, Mrs. O'Connell wouldn't let us play them."

"I've already talked with her on the phone this morning," said Susan.

"And you told her I can't play the games?" Angela looked shocked.

"It's for your own good, sweetie," Dan said.

"All the other kids can play the games!" she shouted. "They'll all laugh at me!"

"No, they won't—"

"They will! They will! You don't want me to play because I'm happy in the games! The prince loves me and he wants me to stay with him, and you just want to make me miserable!"

"Prince?" Susan looked startled.

"If I can't play the games, I won't go to school!"

"All right," Susan said. "You can stay home today."

"No," Dan snapped. "School's important. You go to school today and every day. You just don't play the VR games until I tell you it's okay. Is that clear, young lady?"

There were tears in Angela's eyes, but she nodded silently.

"Now go wash your face and get ready for the school bus," Dan said sternly.

Slowly she got up from the table, lower lip trembling.

"I'll help you," Susan said. She got up, too.

Dan sat there, morning sunlight streaming through the alcove windows, his eggs congealing into an unappetizing mess. Philip banged his spoon on the high-chair tray, grinning widely, his face smeared with his breakfast.

Dan made a smile for his son, hoping that boys were easier to raise than daughters.

Susan came back and untied Philip's bib. She started to clean the baby's face with the back side of it.

"The bus come already? I didn't hear—"

"She's sitting in her room for a few minutes. She's really upset, Dan."

"We've got to do this."

"I know, but she can't understand why."

"Maybe we should tell her."

"*No.*" The sharpness of her voice made the baby jump. Philip looked up at his mother, reached for her. Susan automatically patted his cheek as she said to Dan, "That would just frighten her."

He realized he was gnawing his lip. "Maybe a little scare would help her to see how serious this is."

"She knows we're serious."

"What was that about a prince that loves her?"

"Something in the games. I don't know. She's that age, you know. She's looking for romance."

Dan's nostrils flared. "That's how girls get pregnant."

"Oh, for God's sake! We're talking about virtual-reality games here, not real boys."

"We're talking about Kyle or Jace or somebody trying to get into her mind, Sue. And maybe more than that."

Susan stared at him for a moment. Then, "You're right," she whispered.

"She seems attached to the games, doesn't she?"

"She's just afraid of being ridiculed by the other kids. You know how children tease."

But Dan shook his head. "I wonder if it's more than that. She seems really hooked on the games. Like an addict."

"You're exaggerating," Susan said. But there was no conviction in her tone, and inwardly she worried that Dan was right.

"You spoke to her teacher already?"

"That was a white lie," Susan answered as she lifted Philip from his high chair. "Eleanor wouldn't be at the school this early. I'll phone her as soon as the school bus picks Angie up."

"Better tell her to keep an eye on Angie, see if she seems emotionally bothered by all this."

Susan nodded grimly while Phil examined her ear with his sticky fingers.

The reception lobby was empty this early on a Monday morning, Chuck Smith saw as he headed for Vickie's office. He glanced at his wristwatch: not even seven-thirty yet. Plenty of time to meet Perry's plane at the airport. Time to mend fences with Vickie, he thought.

She was already working at her keyboard, looking stylish and capable in a gold silk pants suit. She sensed Chuck at the office door, looked up and smiled coolly at him. She had been very cool the past two nights. They had dined together at quiet romantic restaurants, but that had been it. Vickie had said good night to him and driven home by herself. Smith realized he had gone too far with her on Friday night. He blamed it on the power rush from his first VR experience.

"It won't happen again," he had promised, over candlelight and wine.

Vickie had nodded, smiling knowingly. Now he wondered if she would ever go to bed with him again. Well, he rationalized, maybe it's better that we don't. If we're going to be working together, maybe we shouldn't let sex snarl things up between us. Besides, there are plenty of other twats available. Younger ones, too.

So he smiled back at Vickie as he stepped across her Oriental carpet and sat himself on the little love seat.

"You're in early," she said.

"Yeah. I don't think anybody else is in the building this early except you and me—and the security guard at the front door."

"How are things in Washington?"

For an instant he felt a pang of alarm. How much does she know? he wondered. How much should I tell her?

Then he relaxed and gave her a satisfied grin. "Everything's fine. An . . . associate of mine is coming in this morning at ten-thirty."

"If the plane's on time."

"This one will be. It's a private jet, special VIP service."

"Courtesy of the American taxpayer," Vickie murmured.

Smith let it pass. "By the way," he said, "I don't think that man Peterson will be bugging you anymore. We've scared him off."

Vickie looked genuinely relieved, but all she said was "Good." Then she added, "Thank you."

He got up from the love seat.

"Don't go," Vickie said.

Smith let himself settle back in the little sofa.

"Chuck, I've got to know what this is all about. This job that Jace is doing for you."

"I told you—"

"The *real* reason, Chuck," Vickie said. "I've been thinking hard about this. There's more to it than creating an information system for the White House."

He gave her a long, silent look. She was utterly serious. She's bright, Smith told himself. And ambitious.

"If I'm going to be a part of your game," Vickie said, "I want to know the whole story. Otherwise . . ." She let the thought hang in the air between them.

"Otherwise what?" he asked, trying to keep the anxiety out of his voice.

"I can pull Jace off the job. I can tell Kyle we should stop the project. I could even let the news media know who you are. Then you'd have to tell *them* why you're here."

"That wouldn't be smart, Vic."

She made a smile for him. "You know I don't want to do any of those things, Chuck. But I have to know the whole story. What are you really up to?"

Again Smith hesitated, thinking, How far can I trust her? She's ambitious, sure enough, but can she be loyal? Would she be willing to go all the way with us?

"Chuck?" she prompted.

You've got to make decisions in this business, he told himself. There's nobody else here to fall back on. It's my call.

"Okay," he said, letting out a breath he had not been aware of holding in. "Okay."

Vickie sat up straighter in her chair, expectantly.

"How do you like the way your government works, Vickie?"

"What?"

"How do you like the way your elected representatives keep on screwing up everything? The economy's in a mess, foreigners are buying up the whole damned country, the cities are falling apart, drugs are destroying our children, our so-called allies thumb their noses at us, the Congress is in a perpetual gridlock, and the President's more worried about his popularity ratings than getting anything done."

"So what else is new?" Vickie quipped.

"Virtual reality. That's what's new."

"I don't understand."

"Yes, you do," Smith said. "You just haven't taken it to its logical conclusion."

"What do you mean?"

"Control the information input and you control the decision, right?"

Vickie nodded.

Deadly earnest, Smith said, "Control the information input to the President and you control the President. Every powerful chief of staff knew that: Eisenhower's chief, Sherman Adams; Nixon's Ehrlichman; Bush's Sununu—they all made certain that the only access to the President was through them."

"But they all got fired, eventually, didn't they?"

"That's the beauty of it. I'll be strictly behind the scenes. The media won't even know I exist. They won't know a thing about the VR system. I'll just be an assistant to the guy who has to take the heat."

"The power behind the throne."

"Right on! And it doesn't matter if The Man gets reelected or not. I'll be just one of the administrative staff guys who stays there no matter who's in office. Part of the faceless bureaucracy. With you and a couple of other people I know, we can run the works!"

"A few other people?"

"I mean," he went on, ignoring her question, "this country needs good, solid, reliable government. But what've we got? One party gets in and tries to do its thing; the other party works its ass off to block everything until they get their own guy into the White House. That's got to stop!"

"And you're going to put an end to that?" Vickie murmured.

"Hell yes! We're going to give this country *good* government, get the job done, put this nation back on the road to greatness."

"With virtual reality."

He nodded grimly. "First the White House. Once the cabinet secretaries find out how the President gets so sharp, they'll all want access to a similar VR system. Then the clucks in the Congress will want it, too. We'll get them all, and they'll all see the world the way we want them to see it."

"You'll be running the entire government," Vickie said, surprised that the thought appealed to her.

"It's this drug business, Vic," he said earnestly. "It's destroying our children; it's destroying the fabric of our society, for Lord's sake! We've got to stop them."

"Them?"

"The dealers. The pushers. Organized crime. The whole damnable drug cartel. I mean, we've got the armed forces. It's time to use them! Get the President to declare a national emergency. Suspend all these damned civil-rights laws temporarily. It's been done before. Lincoln did it, and look what a saint he's thought to be!"

"I don't understand," Vickie said.

"The President can activate the National Guard. With them and the regular Army we can go into the cities, rout out the pushers and dealers and all those other crooks and pimps. Clean 'em all out! And their goddamned crooked lawyers, too! Put 'em all behind barbed wire."

Vickie felt almost breathless. "Chuck, that's—that's not possible. Is it?"

"Control the information input, remember? We start with the White House. Put in a VR system in time to shape the President's State of the Union message. Get him to see things the way we want him to see them."

"Through VR."

"Right on. VR for the White House staff. VR for the Oval Office. Pretty soon the cabinet officers are going to want their own VR systems. So we start to control them. Then the Congress. A small group of us is going to take over the decision-making process in Washington. And that group includes you, Vickie. You're part of this."

"I am?"

"You are now. The guy who's coming down here, Hal Perry, he's with the Security Adviser's staff. He's a key man in our group. There's only a handful of us, but we're positioned in the most influential spots in the White House."

"You really intend to run the White House?"

"The whole government, Vickie. The whole goddamned mother-loving shebang. And you're part of it. You're going to be the most powerful woman in the country, Vickie. The most powerful woman in the world!"

Nodding, Vickie saw a vision of herself in the White House. But the vision disappeared almost instantly.

"Jace," she said.

"What about him?" asked Smith.

"How are we going to control him? You can't trust him to keep his mouth shut."

Smith smiled tightly at her. "That's going to be your problem. You're our liaison with the technical types."

"Thanks a lot!"

His smile widened into a toothy grin. "Don't worry. Jace'll be okay as long as we give him toys to play with. I told him he can have anything he wants in the way of hardware, and he seems happy as a pig in shit."

"For now," Vickie said. "But I wonder how long he'll stay happy. And under control."

"As long as we need him." Then Smith's grin vanished. "Once he's finished this first job, of course, we could get rid of him if we have to."

Vickie nodded again, slowly, but said, "It would be better to keep him. He's tremendously creative."

"Sure," said Smith easily. "As long as he's useful. And under control."

"I feel like a kamikaze pilot," Dan muttered as he stood at the breezeway door, keys in hand.

"You can do it, Tiger," Susan encouraged him.

"Yeah." He kissed her lightly and then went out through the door toward his Honda, a slightly built man in a short-sleeved shirt and beltless gray slacks, navy-blue sports jacket slung over one arm, heading for a showdown with his best friend and his boss.

Susan's heart went out to him. She knew he would rather be a million miles away from this, yet he was finally marching out there to face Jace and Muncrief. But Dan did not look like a soldier heading into battle or a flier going off to attack the enemy. To Susan he looked more like a grimly determined man heading toward a suicide mission.

CHAPTER 42

All the way to the office Dan kept muttering to himself, "Stand up to him. Don't let him evade the issue. Come right out with it, and don't let up until he's told you everything."

Yet he remembered the shoot-out simulation. Jace gunned me down. He killed me. He could do it again. I've got to keep him out of the VR chamber and pin him down to reality. The real world. I've got to keep him in the real world and make him tell me what he's done.

That was going to be tough enough, he knew. But he also dreaded the fact that before the day was out he would have to face Muncrief, too. If Muncrief's actually messing with Angie's games, I'll have to deal with him as well as Jace. And there goes the job, the career, everything. It doesn't matter if I'm right or wrong about him, Kyle will throw me out on my ear as soon as I accuse him of fooling around with Angela's games.

Maybe I should ask Vickie for help, he thought. Or maybe she's a part of this mess, covering up for Kyle. Sue doesn't trust her, and so far Sue's instincts have been one hundred percent on the mark.

He was driving slowly over the speed bumps as he headed for the back parking lot before he realized he had reached the ParaReality building.

No, he told himself as he parked the Honda beneath one of the swaying willows. Jace gimmicked the F-22 sim and he's rigged Angie's school games. If I'm right, he's killed two men and he's helping Muncrief mess with my daughter's mind. I talk to Jace face-to-face, and if Muncrief's involved the way Sue thinks he is, then I brace him, too. Not Vickie. No in-betweens. They're messing with my daughter, and I'm going to find out who and why.

He was trembling inside by the time he reached his office. Without bothering to do more than hang his sports coat on the peg on the back of the door, he started down the corridor toward Jace's lab.

He saw that the light over the door to the VR lab was blinking red. Somebody in there already? Dan cracked the metal door slightly. Three technicians sat in the cramped control booth, hunched over the glowing, humming monitor screens. Surprised, Dan slid into the booth and let the heavy door spring shut behind him. Sure enough, Jace was in the VR chamber, decked in helmet and gloves, shuffling around like a gawky scarecrow, windmilling his arms in dreamy slow motion.

Leaning between two of the techs, Dan flicked the intercom switch. "Jace, it's me. I need to talk to you."

"Not now."

"Now," Dan said firmly.

"No! I'm busy."

"Jace, if I have to shut down this sim—"

The scarecrow figure looked straight at him, as if he could see through the opaque visor on his helmet and the one-way window. "Listen up, Danno. Our buddy Smith's bringing some hotshot from Washington in here this morning to see what I've done for them. I don't have time to talk to you now. This afternoon. After lunch."

All three of the technicians were staring up at Dan. Fuming, frustrated, desperately wanting to have it out with Jace yet knowing that he should let him get on with his work, unwilling to make a scene in front of the technicians, Dan clenched his fists in helpless fury and stamped back to his own office.

You can't let him off the hook, he told himself. You've got to pin him to the wall.

He felt a tendril of irritation in his chest; not pain, exactly, but a raw burning sensation, the warning of worse to come. Dan sat at his desk and tried to will the asthma away. As always, the more he fought against it the tenser he became and the more difficult it became to breathe. A biofeedback loop, he realized. A negative one.

Turning to his keyboard, he angrily punched up the latest results of the AI system's debugging work on the stuttering program. I should have been doing this myself, he grumbled inwardly. This is my responsibility, and I've turned it over to a set of algorithms.

Well, okay, so the Chan kid is riding herd on it, Dan said to himself as he peered at the lines of programming. But still . . .

He did not realize that three hours had gone by. He was deeply into the debugging routine, his chest feeling better, his cares about Jace and Muncrief buried for the moment, when he heard Smith's loud, self-assured voice coming down the corridor.

"Wait'll you see it," Smith was saying. "It's like nothing you've ever been into before."

Dan looked up from his display screen and saw Smith pass his open doorway, walking beside a slight, sallow-faced young man in an expensive-looking gray silk suit. Must be the big shot from Washington, Dan told himself. Can't be any older than Smith himself. It puzzled Dan. He had always thought that the government was run by older men. Even the women in Congress and the White House were gray, mature. Yet Smith was a puppy in comparison, and this so-called big shot was just as young. Are these the staff people who make the decisions that really count?

Vickie was trailing behind them while Smith continued to extol virtual reality almost at the top of his lungs. The guy with him must be deaf, Dan thought. Or Smith is wired really high. Curious, he got up from his desk and went into the corridor, leaving his work on the computer screen.

"Is that our visitor from Washington?" Dan asked Vickie.

She seemed startled. "You're not involved in this anymore, Dan."

"I started this work," he said.

"It's Jace's project now."

Smith and his visitor had reached the door to the Wonderland chamber. Smith had his back to Dan; the visitor was turned so Dan saw him full-face. It was a sour face, young but as pinched and bitter as a man on a diet of lemons. The guy was already balding; his high forehead gleamed in the overhead lights. His thin mouth turned down at the corners.

"Listen, Chuck," he said, breaking into Smith's nonstop sales pitch. "I just hope you're not wasting the taxpayers' money on some cockamamie super-high-tech bullshit. This stuff never works right, and I'm not going to let you or anybody else sell us a bill of goods. Understand me?"

Spreading his hands like an innocent facing martyrdom, Smith replied, "Hey, I'm not selling you a bill of goods. All I want you to do is try this for just a few minutes. See what we've got here. That's all I ask."

"You made me come all the way down here just to play some video game for a few minutes?" The man's voice was like an audible toothache.

"Try it," Smith urged. "Just try it."

The other man huffed and hawed with unconcealed poor grace.

"Dan, this does not involve you," Vickie said firmly.

He looked into her eyes, noticing for the first time that they were a strange opalescent gray, almond shaped, almost Oriental. For an instant he wanted to confront her with his suspicions about Muncrief and Angela, but something in him made him back away from that.

"Yeah," he said flatly. "I've got work to do."

And he went back to his office, where his computer still displayed the debugging program.

Hal Perry was shaking with fear, soaked with sweat. All through the battle at the hacienda, he had done nothing more than cringe behind the bushes edging the parking lot, shaking with terror as the soldiers and drug gang's men fought it out with submachine guns and hand grenades. He had hunkered down on his hands and knees, buried his face in the dirt, while the bullets whined and explosions rocked the air.

But now the battle was over. The drug lord's men were dead or captured, the hacienda burning furiously; flames shot through the roof higher than the trees towering around the compound. The soldiers were leading their prisoners to waiting helicopters; the medics were tending the wounded. Other soldiers were drag-

ging their own dead toward the team who waited by one of the
choppers with the body bags.

We won, Perry told himself. It worked. The attack was a success.
We won. Still, he shook with fear. He had never even watched a
gun being fired before.

He tried to regain control of himself, wondering if the soldiers
were real and able to see him, wondering if Chuck Smith and
those other guys in the control booth could tell how frightened he
was. It's natural, he told himself. Totally natural. They threw me
into the middle of a fucking firefight! Naturally I'm shook up a
little. It's so damned realistic, I thought I was going to get my ass
shot off. He took deep breaths, trying to calm himself, trying to
regain control of his trembling knees.

Gradually the scene dimmed, faded. He sighed with relief. It's
all over. They'll take me out of it now.

But instead the soft grayish light flickered, shifted, and then a
different scene slowly built up before Perry's eyes. He was standing before a joint session of the Congress, giving his State of the
Union speech.

"The drug lords of Latin America long ago declared war on the
United States." His voice was suddenly powerful, commanding.
"For decades they have been killing our people and destroying our
property. Well, we have declared war against them and their kind.
Real war, not rhetoric."

The entire cabinet was sitting there watching him with rapt attention. The joint chiefs of staff, the whole Congress. The gallery
was packed. Television cameras focused on him.

He went on, "Now, thanks to the courage and sacrifice of the
finest fighting men and women in the world, we are at last winning
that war!"

The applause was thunderous. Perry stood behind the podium
and let it wash over him, wave after wave. At last it quieted and he
could continue.

"But this war has many different fronts. There are battles to be
fought in our own cities, even in our own schools. I have declared
a National Emergency to deal with the drug problem. I have activated the National Guard. I ask the Congress to agree to a temporary suspension of the habeas corpus and certain other provisions
of civil-rights laws, so that we can fight this war and win it!"

The entire chamber rose to its feet and cheered wildly. Hal Perry stood there basking in their applause, forgetting the nausea and terror that had clutched at him only a few moments earlier. He made a mental note to see how the scenario worked out if they used cruise missiles against the drug-processing plants instead of troops. Cut down on the casualties that way. Tactical nukes. Clean bombs, low radiation.

He smilingly accepted the Congress's plaudits. It was a huge letdown when the scene faded out and he found himself in the bare VR chamber once again.

Dan worked through the usual lunch hour, all track of time lost as he slowly convinced himself that the stuttering program was being debugged properly. Grudgingly he admitted that the artificial-intelligence system was doing a reasonably good job. Better than reasonably good, actually, although he still wanted to go through every line of the program for himself before he would really trust it. I'll have to tell Gary that he's doing fine.

The voices in the corridor shook him out of his work once again. This time, though, it was the needle-sharp voice of the visitor from Washington that Dan heard.

"It's fantastic! It's incredible!"

Dan looked up as they passed his door. The sour-faced guy was sour-faced no more. He was glowing. He was gesticulating exuberantly. He had not yet bothered to comb his thinning hair, mussed by the helmet he had worn. Even at this distance, Dan could see that his eyes were alight.

"Didn't I tell you that you've never seen anything like it?" Smith said, smiling broadly.

"When you're right, Chuck, you're goddamn right. We've got to get this set up in the West Wing right away."

They headed on up the corridor, Vickie still keeping a few paces behind, wearing a feline smile of satisfaction.

Now's the time to grab Jace, Dan said to himself as he slid out from behind his desk and practically sprinted toward the VR lab.

He saw that the light over the lab door was still blinking red. Jace must be still in there. Good. The control booth was empty, although the monitor screens were still lit up and running. Jace was in the VR chamber again, in helmet and gloves, just standing there with one finger slowly tracing along his lips, just visible beneath the helmet's visor.

Dan leaned on the intercom switch. "Jace, it's me again. Time for us to talk."

A wait. Then, "Come on in, the water's fine."

"No. You come out."

"No way, Jose. You wanna talk to me, you come into my world."

"No!"

"What's the matter, scared I'm gonna shoot you again?" Jace laughed softly. "Don't be afraid, Danno. This isn't the gunfight sim."

Dan swept his eyes across the monitor screens. He could not tell what simulation Jace was into; the screens showed alphanumeric symbols and data graphs, not visual imagery.

"I'm going to turn everything off," he said. "I have to talk to you right now."

"You can't turn it off, pal. How d'you think I can run this sim all by myself, without any of those asshole technicians in the booth?"

His voice sounded slurred. Dan looked through the one-way window and saw that Jace was tapping one gloved finger on an electronic black box hooked to his belt.

"I'm running the whole show by myself, Danno. All by myself, in my own little world. Come on in. You wanna talk to me, you gotta join me in my world."

"Dammit, Jace, stop this shit and come out here!"

"I can't hear you."

Dan fumed and stared at the scarecrow figure. Jace wore a black T-shirt with one word emblazoned on it: *Baaad*.

"If you're saying anything, Dan old pal, I can't hear it. I turned off my earphones. The only way you can talk to me is by coming into my world."

"Sonofabitch," Dan muttered. But he grabbed a helmet and a pair of gloves from the shelves lining the end of the cramped booth and pulled them on like a soldier grabbing his helmet and rifle: reluctant, afraid, yet almost anxious to get it over with.

Then he yanked open the door to the VR chamber and stepped in. Jace stood waiting in the center of the bare room, skinny arms folded across his narrow chest, visor pulled down over his eyes. All Dan could see of his face was a lopsided smirking grin.

"Didn't know I built a remote-control unit, did you?" Dan heard as soon as he connected up his helmet. "I can run the whole kit and caboodle while I'm in it. Don't need technicians or anybody. Just me myself."

"All right, I'm here. Now let's talk."

"Pull your visor down, Danno. You're not here with me until you're here with me."

With an angry snort, Dan pulled down the visor of his helmet. For a moment he felt blindfolded, vulnerable. But then vague lights began to stir in the distance and . . .

He gasped involuntarily. He was floating in deepest blackest space, beyond the stars, out in the cold emptiness where there was nothing at all except the faint distant spindle shapes of galaxies, so far away that they looked like flickering candle flames. Everywhere Dan looked, galaxies and more galaxies, the smallest of them containing billions of stars.

"We're going backwards in time," Jace said out of the nothingness. Then his voice took on the deep hollow tones of grandiloquence. "You're going to see . . . How It All Began."

"Jace, I want to talk to you about—"

"Shut the fuck up, willya, Danno? We can talk after. Lemme get this done first."

The galaxies were drawing noticeably closer, rushing together in eerie silence. Dan knew what he was seeing: the Origin of the Universe exhibit, one of the first that ParaReality had created, before Muncrief had hired Dan. Jace bragged that he had put it together over a weekend. It was a simple cosmology tour of the universe, from its beginning to its end, all in twelve minutes. He was witnessing the end, the Big Crunch, when all the galaxies coalesce into a single point of incredible energy density that explodes and starts the universe all over again.

"Jace, why are you—"

"Silence, mortal!"

Dan breathed out an impatient sigh. There was only a couple of minutes to go, and at least Jace hadn't turned on the sound track of ethereal music and schmaltzy commentary about the mystery and beauty of it all.

All the galaxies were streaming together now like drops of water sliding down a funnel. Dan could see them elongating, stretching out into thin lines of blue Cerenkov radiation as they streaked down to the single point of blazing brilliance at the center.

Then it all stopped. There was nothing in all of creation except that one incredibly bright point of light. Everything else was total darkness: not a star, not a cloud, not a molecule to be seen.

"Jace—"

"In the beginning," Jace's voice intoned, slightly raspy despite his attempt to be sonorous, "I created the heavens and the earth."

Oh my God, Dan thought.

"And the earth was without form, and void; and darkness was upon the face of the deep. And my spirit moved upon the face of the waters."

He's gone off the deep end, Dan said to himself.

"And I said, LET THERE BE LIGHT!"

The tiny point of light in the center of nothingness exploded soundlessly. Blazing light flooded the universe, almost blinding Dan, sending him staggering backward with its ferocious brilliance.

"And there was light," Jace said. "And I saw the light, that it was good."

"Dammit, Jace, you're not God!" Dan shouted.

"I have the power of life and death in my hands, Danno. Isn't that God?"

Streams of light were rushing outward, pulsating, making Dan's eyes tear with their intensity.

Jace said, "I'm going to tell the President of the United States what to do, what to think. Isn't that godly power?"

"Jace, for Christ's sake, we have to talk."

"And the Congress, too. They'll all come to worship me, Danno. I'll have them all eating out of my hand."

"Now, Jace," Dan demanded. "You talk to me *now*."

"I didn't mean to kill him, man." Jace's voice dropped several notches, took on an almost apologetic tone. "You gotta believe me, pal. I didn't think it would kill him."

"Ralph?" Dan guessed.

"You know how he was always pushing me to make the simulation tougher, more realistic. It was his own friggin' fault, really."

The light was dimming slightly. Modulating. Evolving into vast clouds of shimmering colors.

"What did you do to Ralph?" Dan asked.

"When I set him up with the sex sim. It was easy, Dan. Poor bastard never knew it. I got his brain-wave patterns six ways from Tuesday. Alpha rhythms, beta—all of 'em. Dumb sucker even let me make CAT scans of his brain, over at the base hospital. He thought it was for his stupid sex sim; he was *eager* to do it!"

"But what did that have to do with the flight simulation?"

Jace laughed, a low sly chuckle. "I mapped out his sensory receptors, man. In his brain. I figured out how to stimulate sections of his brain directly, with electrical inputs from circuitry in the helmet."

"That's impossible!"

"Not for me, Danny boy. That helmet Ralph wore was like a live bomb. I rigged it to pump enough current into his sensory receptors to sizzle 'em good. Rev up his heart rate, boost his blood pressure, the whole nine yards, pal. Fear is a *physical* thing, Danno. It makes your body react, and your body's reactions make you even more scared. Basic biofeedback loop."

"And it worked on the other flier, Adair?"

"Sure as hell did. Took me years to track down those biofeedback loops. Did you know there are musical notes that can make you afraid? Did you know that the noise from a rocket engine can make you cry? Took me years to figure it all out. Every night, for years and years. I even worked with amputees and made them feel like their arms or legs were back in place."

"But you didn't like Ralph. Why did you—" And even as he started to ask the question, Dan realized what the answer was.

"Didn't like him?" Jace replied softly. "I *hated* the sonofabitch. He always thought he was better than me. Always pulling that crap on me: he puts his ass on the line and all I do is tinker around with toys."

"You murdered him."

"Damned right! I snuffed him and what of it. Was his own damned fault. He hadda fly the simulator himself, big brass-balled hero. I knew he'd do that. I *knew* it! And that's when I had him. I didn't even have to be there. The program was waiting, buried in the computer. Not even you could find it, could you, Danno? It was right there under your big wop nose and you never even smelled it!"

"Jesus Christ," Dan muttered.

"It's so friggin' simple, once you know how," Jace said. "All those nights I worked in the lab, back in the old days. You thought I was just amusing myself, didn't you? Jerkin' off. But I was learning how to get that brass-balled sonofabitch. Learning how to put feedback into the simulations that zap right into the brain's autonomous control systems."

"You deliberately raised Ralph's blood pressure to the point where he had a stroke."

"And the other guy, too. I didn't mean to snuff him, but by the time I got the system finished Ralph had got himself redlined and taken off flight duty."

"Jace, you're a murderer!"

"Not me. I didn't murder anybody. I didn't force those guys to fly the simulator. I even left the joint and moved to Florida, remember? I was a thousand miles away."

"You killed them!"

"I executed them. It was all Ralph's fault, and he paid for it."

"I can't believe this. Jace, what the hell are we going to do?"

"Not a friggin' thing, pal. There's nothing you can do."

"I've got to warn Doc, tell him what you've done."

"The hell you will!"

"Jace, you need help."

He laughed. "Me? I don't need anything or anybody, buddy boy. I have the power of life and death in my hands. And I'll have protection from Washington. Smitty promised me that. Protection from the White House itself."

"And Angie?" Dan snapped. "What are you doing to my daughter?"

"Nobody's hurting the kid."

"What are you doing to her?"

"It's almost finished."

"Goddammit, Jace, what are you doing to my daughter?"

A long silence. Dan was about to rip off his helmet and go after Jace physically. The universe was speckled with blazing blue points of light: quasars and the beginnings of galaxies flickering faintly in the eternal dark.

Jace said, "I told you, nobody's hurting her. She's perfectly all right."

Dan had to take a deep breath before he could say, "You just told me you've killed two men, and now you're saying I shouldn't worry about my daughter? When I don't even know what the hell you're doing to her?"

"I'm just mapping her emotional reactions," Jace replied, almost carelessly. "Like having her sit to have her picture drawn. Just takes a little longer, that's all."

"Why? For what purpose? Who for?" Dan croaked. He felt stifled inside the helmet, choking.

"Don't try to take the helmet off, Dan," Jace said softly. "I've got to make you understand who's in charge around here."

All around Dan galaxies glowed warmly in space, majestically sailing outward in an expanding universe, generating swarms of bright blue stars as they revolved smoothly in the void. But his chest was constricting, his breath gasping. Christ, not an asthma attack. Not now!

The helmet was smothering him. He had to get it off. But he could not move his arms.

"I can make amputees have their arms back," Jace said. "I can also make your arms useless."

Dan sank to his knees. His chest was aflame. He could not catch his breath.

"The helmet you're wearing now," Jace said, his voice flat and deadly calm, "it's rigged just like Ralphie boy's. I don't have your brain patterns mapped out, but I can do a job on you, Danno, just like I did on Adair."

The universe swam around Dan. He could not get air into his lungs. He was suffocating, his lungs rasping as if a red-hot sanding machine were blasting away inside him. A thousand-ton weight pressed on his chest as he tried to crawl, gasping, all his strength seeping away while he desperately, painfully tried to draw a single breath.

"All these years we've worked together," Jace said. "You

thought they were just simulations, didn't you? You thought they were just electronic games. I don't play games, Danno. I play God."

Dan collapsed on the floor of the VR chamber, visions of star-filled galaxies swimming in his blurring sight.

CHAPTER 43

A ngela sat unhappily at her desk, staring at the book in her hands. Six of the students were in the VR booths. The rest of the kids were waiting their turns at the games that Mrs. O'Connell let them play at the end of the day.

But not me, Angela knew. She won't let me play a game because my parents told her not to. I hate them! I hate them both and I hate Mrs. O'Connell, too!

But she knew she did not hate her parents or her teacher. She did not understand why they were keeping her away from the games, though. Or maybe she did know! She suddenly realized that her parents wanted to keep her away from the handsome young prince who somehow worked his way into almost every game she played. I shouldn't have told Mommy about him. She doesn't want me to be with him. She's jealous.

Why? she asked herself. It's only a game. He can't do anything to me. And even if he did, he wouldn't want to hurt me in the first place. And I love him!

That's why Mommy doesn't want me to be with him. She thinks I'm too young to be in love. But I'm not. I'm not.

"How's the book?"

Angela was startled by Mrs. O'Connell's question. She saw that her teacher was standing beside her, bending over slightly with a kind little smile on her face.

"Okay, I guess," said Angela.

"How much of it have you read, Angie?"

"Not much," Angela said, glancing around the classroom. All the other kids were busy with their own work or huddled together in one of the workshop corners, talking to one another about their study projects. Thank goodness nobody was paying any notice to her, stuck with this dumb book.

"You know," Mrs. O'Connell said, "books are like virtual-reality games. You only have to use your imagination a little, and a book can take you anywhere you want to go."

But Angela shook her head. "It's not the same."

"I know. You have to do some of the work—inside your head."

"In a VR game everything's right there," said Angela. "You see it and hear it and everything."

"Try reading the book, dear. You'll see the scenes and hear the people talking, and you don't need anything except your own mind to do it."

Angela knew that her teacher was wrong. How could a bunch of words on paper compare with being in a VR game? But she dutifully stared at the open page, desperately hoping Mrs. O'Connell would go away before any of the kids noticed. Angela felt like a retard, unable to do what the others could, getting special attention from Mrs. O'Connell because she was different from all the rest.

Several kids laughed, and Angela's face flamed. But then she saw that they were laughing at a paper airplane that sailed across the room, right over the teacher's head, and landed smack on her desk.

Mrs. O'Connell turned away from Angela and headed for the boys in the far corner of the room who were supposed to be working on a map of the original thirteen American colonies.

Angela held the book up and tried hard to get interested in it. *Heidi,* by someone with the weird name of Johanna Heusser Spyri. Yuck!

The minutes crawled by. Every time Angela peeked up at the clock above the chalkboard at the front of the room, the hands seemed to be exactly where they had been the last time. If the second hand had not been sweeping along—slowly—she would have thought the clock was stopped.

But by the time the bell rang to signal the end of the day, she was getting engrossed in the story of the Swiss girl. It wasn't like a VR game, for sure, but she could see Heidi in her mind and the rugged snow-covered Alps and the green meadows with spring flowers beneath the clear blue sky and the sheep with their bells tinkling in the crisp mountain air.

The school bell jarred her out of the story. Angela looked up, surprised that the clock actually showed three-thirty. While all the other kids trooped to the door and lined up, Angela went to Mrs. O'Connell's desk to return the book.

"Would you like to take it home with you?" the teacher asked.

"Could I?"

"If you promise to take good care of it and bring it back tomorrow."

Angela nodded eagerly. "I will."

Mrs. O'Connell smiled. "All right, then. I'm glad you're enjoying it. I read *Heidi* when I was about your age. I loved it."

Angela got into the line, the book tucked under her arm.

"Is she making you read that whole book?" Gary Rusic asked her.

"Uh-huh," Angela replied. "It's really good."

"Not as good as the VRs," said Kristy Kelly. She had thick red hair and perfect teeth.

"Yes it is," Angela countered.

"Quiet now." Mrs. O'Connell opened the classroom door and led her students down the wide hallway to the double front doors of the school building.

"Why won't she let you into the VRs?" Marta Randolph whispered. "Afraid you're going to *faint* again?"

"She likes reading books," Kristy said with a laugh. "Angela's real old-fashioned."

"I am not!"

"Quietly, please," called Mrs. O'Connell from the front of the line.

I am not old-fashioned, Angela repeated to herself. But my parents are.

She heard Marta snickering, "Her father *builds* the VRs and she can't even go in them."

Angela fought to keep the tears back.

"Well," said Kristy, "maybe when they take the braces off her teeth they'll let her back into the VRs."

Several of the girls laughed, and Angela felt her insides burning.

They went out in a fairly orderly line, joining the other lines of students trooping to the yellow minivans that served as school buses. Angela went along glumly, the book under her arm now a badge of shame.

Then she heard a car horn toot.

"Hey, Angela! You want a ride home?"

It was Uncle Kyle. Mr. Muncrief, Angela remembered. Her mother did not want her to call him Uncle Kyle anymore. He was sitting in his totally awesome green Jaguar with the top down, smiling and waving at her.

Mrs. O'Connell looked at Angela.

"May I go home with Mr. Muncrief?" she asked.

Eleanor O'Connell walked slowly down the line toward Angela. She recognized Muncrief, of course; she knew him as the founder and president of ParaReality, the man who had made the Pine Lake School the unique educational establishment that it was. Still . . .

"Do your parents allow you to ride with him?" she asked.

"Oh, sure! He drives me to school all the time."

"Wait here while I phone your mother," Mrs. O'Connell said.

"But he drives me to school," Angela repeated.

"Yes, I understand that, but I still must call your mother. Those are the rules, Angela. Wait right here; I'll be back in a few moments."

Angela watched Mrs. O'Connell walk back to the school's front door while all the other kids were climbing into the school buses. She looked over at Uncle Kyle in his convertible. He waved to her.

She decided not to wait for Mrs. O'Connell.

Angela wanted to run, but instead she paced slowly toward Uncle Kyle and his convertible, enjoying the envious stares of Marta and Kristy and all the rest of the nasty bitches filing into the school buses. She knew her mother did not want her to call him Uncle

Kyle, but she didn't care, he was rescuing her from ridicule and she loved him for it.

The first hazy thought that drifted through Dan's mind as he struggled back to consciousness was that hardly anybody ever died of asthma. You just wished you could die, gasping and wheezing, your lungs on fire while you fought to get air through your constricted bronchial passages. It was like drowning, only dry and painful.

A black nurse was standing over him. He saw that he was in a little cubicle with lime-green walls. Hospital emergency room, he guessed.

He pulled in a breath of air, gently, cautiously. His chest ached, but the asthma seemed to be gone.

His butt was sore, too, and he realized he was in a drafty white hospital gown.

"How long have I been here?" he asked.

The nurse eyed him suspiciously. "You're supposed to ask, 'Where am I?' "

"I can see where I am." Dan started to push himself up on his elbows.

The nurse pushed him back down flat. "You just rest for a while more. Doctor will be in shortly."

"How long—"

"Nearly two hours. Worst asthma attack I ever saw. We had to put a quart of adrenaline into you, just about." She smiled to show she was exaggerating.

"With square needles, huh?" Dan understood why his backside hurt.

"You just rest now and you'll be all right by suppertime."

The nurse left, and Dan lifted his arm to see his wristwatch. Almost four-thirty. He remembered being in the VR chamber and Jace acting crazy. Jace *caused* this asthma attack? He realized he was chewing on his lower lip and opened his mouth as if yawning. If Jace didn't outright cause the attack, he sure made it worse than it would have been.

What he had thought to be walls were actually curtains. He was lying on a gurney or a makeshift bunk of some sort, partitioned off from the other cubicles by thin pale-green curtains. He could hear someone moaning softly: woman or man, he could not tell. Swell background music, Dan thought. Where the hell's that doctor? I've got to get out of—

The curtain was pushed aside, and Jace Lowrey stepped in. Dan blinked at him. Are we still in the simulation? he wondered.

"How are you?" Jace whispered.

"Not dead yet."

Jace fidgeted a little, raised his hands and let them fall to his sides again. "Hey, I didn't mean to make it so bad. I was just— well, kinda showin' off, I guess. I'm sorry."

"Some show."

"I got carried away."

"You're going to get carried right into jail, you know."

Jace shook his head.

"You tried to kill me," Dan accused.

"No, I didn't. Honest, I didn't mean to make it so bad. I got carried away."

Dan said nothing. In the back of his mind he still wondered if this was a simulation or the real world. Must be the real world, he told himself. Jace would never be apologetic in one of his own creations.

"I just wanted to show you. You know. I wanted you to see what I can do."

"Okay, you didn't try to kill me. You just tried to scare me into keeping my mouth shut."

"About what?" He looked genuinely puzzled.

"Aw hell, Jace. You admitted that you killed Ralph and that other pilot."

Jace looked over his shoulder, as if afraid they would be overheard. "I didn't mean to kill him," he whispered. "I didn't mean for them to die. It was just supposed to—y'know, to show him."

"Just to show who?"

"Ralph. Who else?"

"Show him what?"

"Show him what I can do. Make him admit that I'm as good as he is. Better, even. Thing is, once I start workin' on a sim, I can't just go halfway. I gotta push it as far as I can, see what I can do."

"See if you can give somebody an asthma attack?" Dan growled.

Jace's eyes narrowed into a truculent stare. "I said I was sorry, didn't I?"

"See if you can kill people?"

The frown deepened for a moment. Then Jace grinned slyly, making his long, lean face look almost wolfish.

"Try to prove it," he said, leaning over Dan's bed. "I'll deny I ever said a word."

"Two men have died."

"So what? I was a thousand miles away."

"I'll dig out the subprogram you put into the sim. The biofeedback loop."

"Loops. Plural. And they're all erased. By phone, pal. I set it all up so I could destroy the evidence whenever I needed to. That's what modems are for."

"You can't just pick up the phone and get access . . ." But Dan's voice trailed off before he finished the sentence.

Jace grinned at him. "Hell, Danno, teenage hackers can break into secured systems. Don't you think I set up everything in the computer before I left Wright-Patt?"

"You did it all deliberately. Cold-blooded, premeditated murder."

"Sure I did. I can see you telling that to the cops. They wouldn't believe a word of it, not in a million years. Not without proof."

"So it'll be my word against yours."

"Doesn't have to be anything," Jace said. He backed away from the bed, scratched at his stubbly jaw. "You don't have to say a word. Not to anybody."

"The hell I don't."

Spreading his long arms, "Hey, it's over and done with. Ralph's dead. You're not gonna bring him back."

"You killed him."

"He killed himself, the big heroic motherfucker."

"He was killed by your simulation."

"It was your sim as much as mine," Jace said. "You had it to yourself for a whole year, just about."

"And you stuck your death trap into it. You turned my work into a murder machine."

Jace raised his face to the ceiling and sighed as if to ask the gods why he was being persecuted.

"Look," he said to Dan, "if I left a pistol in Ralph's office with one bullet in it and he went in and blew his friggin' brains out with it, is that murder? Is it my fault?"

"It sure as hell is, and you know it."

"Well," with a shrug, "you're gonna have a damned tough time provin' it, y'know."

"If you don't kill me first."

Jace gave him a sour look. "Aw, for crap's sake, Danno, don't make it all so friggin' dramatic. I'm not going to kill you. Go ahead and tell Appleton or the cops or the friggin' FBI, if you want to. Nobody's gonna believe you."

"Doc will."

"Big friggin' deal. The sim's safe now. Anybody can use it, no trouble. It's all fixed."

Propping himself up on one elbow, Dan asked, "Don't you feel any guilt at all?"

Jace turned away slightly, avoiding his eyes. "I really didn't mean for them to die," he mumbled. "I just wanted to kick Ralph's ass a little."

Dan stared at his partner. This was a different Jace from the would-be god in the VR chamber. He's got a split personality, Dan thought. But then he corrected himself: No, it's the same personality. Only, in the VR sims he makes his own rules. All the limits of the real world are off and he can go as far as he wants to. As far as his imagination or his hatred can take him.

"You really hated Ralph that much?" Dan asked. "Enough to kill him?"

"Hey, listen. I'm gonna be workin' in the White House. Smith is gonzo about what I've been doing for him. I'm gonna be the friggin' hero!"

"You think Smith's going to protect you?" Dan asked.

"You bet!"

"And you're going to be developing VR systems for the White House?"

"And Congress, too."

"Jesus Christ."

"Hey, you can come along, pal. We don't need Muncrief and all this chickenshit game stuff. We're goin' to the big leagues, Danno!"

"What about my daughter?"

Jace froze for an instant, then put his grin back on. "What about her? She's okay."

"Just what have you been doing to her? The real story, Jace. No more bullshit."

"I already told you. I'm recordin' her emotional reactions for a sim that Muncrief wants."

Dan pushed himself up to a sitting position. He noticed his clothes heaped on a white chair in the corner of the cubicle.

"What's Muncrief want a simulation of Angela for?"

Looking more and more uncomfortable, Jace answered, "It's not Angela in particular. He wants a kid. A young girl."

"A twelve-year-old girl?"

Jace nodded.

"For what?"

"A simulation."

Knowing the answer but hoping he was wrong, Dan asked, "What *kind* of a sim?"

Jace's face screwed up into a frown that was half guilt, half exasperation. "Shit, man, what do you think?"

"For sex," Dan said.

"What else?" Jace snapped.

Dan just stared at him, his mind spinning. The sonofabitch wants to fuck my daughter. Sue was right. He wants to fuck my daughter.

"It was part of our deal," Jace explained. "Kyle hired me and swore he'd give me anything I needed, long as I developed this sim for him. Why do you think he blew all that money on the school?"

Dan's gut went hollow as he realized the truth of it.

"And when I told him I needed you," Jace added, "it didn't hurt that you had a twelve-year-old kid."

"You bastard," Dan said, his voice a stiletto-thin whisper. "I thought you were my friend, and all along you were doing this."

He planted his bare feet on the floor and stood up, fists clenched, pulse thundering, fury blazing through him.

"You goddamned sonofabitch bastard." Dan advanced toward Jace.

Jace backed away. "Hey, now wait, Dan. Don't get yourself all worked up."

"We're not in a VR chamber now," Dan said. "This is the real world, Jace, and I'm going to break every bone in your face."

Jace spun around and tried to duck through the curtain, but he bumped into a chunky balding middle-aged man wearing a white hospital jacket with a stethoscope jammed into one of its pockets.

"What are you doing in here?" the doctor demanded of Jace. Despite his question, he was smiling amiably.

"Leaving," said Jace over his shoulder as he disappeared past the curtain.

Dan stood rooted, shaking inside, jaws clenched so tight they hurt.

"Maybe they gave you too much adrenaline," the doctor said, smiling at Dan. "You look like you're ready to kill somebody."

"Maybe I am," Dan said.

The doctor glanced thoughtfully at the curtain where Jace had just left, then turned back to Dan, the smile still spread across his face. "Well, I guess you're ready to go home, huh?"

"Damned right," said Dan. He grabbed for his clothes as the doctor turned and left the cubicle.

Dan was buttoning his shirt when the black nurse came in again, holding a portable phone in one hand.

"It's your wife," she said.

Dan took the phone from her. "Hello, Sue. I'm okay, it was just—"

"Dan!" Sue's voice sounded frantic. "Angie hasn't come home from school! Muncrief picked her up and she hasn't been seen since!"

CHAPTER 44

here are you?" Dan shouted into the phone.

"In the Subaru," answered Susan, "heading for the police station. I can't stay on the phone, Dan. If Angie calls the home phone, it's programmed to forward the call here. Are you okay?"

"It was just an asthma attack," he half-lied, watching the black nurse watching him. "I'm at the hospital. I'll drive over to the police station as soon as I can get out of here."

"See you there." And the connection clicked off.

"You can't get out of here without one of the doctors signing a release form," said the nurse warily.

"Then you'd better get a doctor in here fast," Dan said, sitting on the edge of the bed to tug on his shoes. "My daughter's missing, and I'm heading for the police station."

The nurse wheeled around and ducked through the curtains. Dan did not wait for her to come back. He pushed through the curtains and made his way through the waiting room with its sorrowful handful of old people in pain and mothers with injured children. He heard the nurse yelling behind him but kept on going through the door out into the warm late-afternoon sunshine of the parking lot.

And realized that his car was still at ParaReality. They must have brought me here in an ambulance or somebody else's car.

Dan stood at the top of the hospital entrance's stairs, his mind racing. If I go back to phone the lab, the nurse'll grab me and make me sit around until all her forms have been signed off. Dan looked wildly around the parking lot. He did not recognize any of the cars. Not even Jace's bicycle was in sight.

A faded green four-door sedan slowed to a stop at the bottom of the stairs.

"Need a lift?"

It was the doctor who had told him he could get dressed. The white coat was gone, replaced by a wrinkled lightweight suit jacket. He was still smiling amiably.

"I need to get to the police station right away," Dan said.

The man's eyebrows hiked up a notch, but his smile stayed in place and he said, "Okay, hop in."

Dan sprinted around the front of the car and slid into the right-hand seat. Luke Peterson put the old Cutlass in gear and pulled smoothly away just as the nurse barged through the hospital's front doors waving a fistful of papers in her hand.

The Pine Lake police station was nothing more than a wing of the community-center building, quiet and cool and modern. Sergeant Wallace, chief of the three-man police squad, was a solidly built man with graying hair clipped short, a leathery tanned face etched with deeply weathered seams, and sad hound-dog eyes. He was leaning back in his chair, fingers steepled over his slightly bulging middle. His desk was like a barrier protecting him from the distraught woman sitting in his office.

"We've notified the county sheriff and the state police," he was saying to Susan. "Both my boys are out in their cars scoutin' around for her."

"What about the FBI?" asked Susan.

The hound-sad eyes focused on her. "Yew want to treat this as a kidnapping?"

"I want my daughter back!" Susan snapped.

Sergeant Wallace nodded understandingly. "We been to Mr. Muncrief's house. Nobody there. Place is locked up tight and his car's not in th' garage."

Susan was holding Philip on her lap. She had thought about asking one of the neighbors to mind him, but that would have taken too much time. The baby seemed to understand that something serious was going on; he was sitting quietly, without squirming or squalling, watching the police sergeant in his blue shirt and shiny badge.

"Would the FBI be helpful?" Susan asked. She felt tense with strain, ready to crack apart.

"They could be," said Wallace. "But they get kinda huffy if we call them in and it turns out to be jest a kid runnin' away from home for a few hours."

"It's been more than four hours," Susan said. "He took her from the school."

"I know. Mebbe he just took her to a movie or over to Disney World."

"No. Angie would have called—"

Sergeant Wallace smiled slightly. "I got the Disney security people lookin' for the two of 'em. And checkin' out their parkin' lots for his Jaguar." He pronounced the car's name with three syllables. "Not much more we can do now, 'cept wait."

Susan wanted to scream.

The sergeant smiled patiently. "Maybe y'all ought to go home. Be there by the phone. She'll prob'ly phone yew when she gets tired of runnin' away."

"She didn't run away," Susan flared. "Kyle Muncrief abducted her."

"Yes'm, I know. Yew told me."

Susan had tried to explain that Muncrief had been invading Angela's VR games at school, but the sergeant seemed to understand little of it and believe less.

"I honestly think home's the best place for yew," he said, getting up slowly from his chair and coming around the desk.

Susan got to her feet, the baby in her arms. Wallace planted one heavy hand on her shoulder, guiding her firmly toward the door.

"Now, I know yew got all kinds of horror stories runnin' through yer mind," he said gently. "In ninety-nine cases out of a hunnerd like this, nothing bad really happens. We'll get yer little girl back and she'll be fine, you'll see."

Susan said nothing. She allowed the sergeant to walk her outside to her station wagon in the parking lot. He even helped her buckle Phil into his car seat.

"Yew okay to drive?" Sergeant Wallace asked. "I can get somebody to take y'all home."

It was full night now, and in the fluorescent light of the parking lot's lamps the sergeant's skin looked sickly.

"I'm okay," Susan said tightly. "If my husband gets here, or if he calls—"

"I'll tell him you're on yer way home."

"Yes. Fine."

Susan got in behind the wheel and started the engine. Sergeant Wallace watched her as she drove carefully off the parking lot. But once she got the Subaru onto the street leading home, Susan said through gritted teeth, "What's he *doing* to my baby?"

Angela was exploring the castle. It was just like a castle out of a fairy tale, with tall spires and a high wall and a moat outside. Inside it was wonderful, each room she wandered through more beautiful than the last. Curtains of shimmering gold, servants in colorful uniforms who bowed to her as she passed, beautiful tapestries on the walls. It was her very own castle, she knew, and everyone here loved her.

She had been a little afraid, at first, when Mr. Muncrief had told her that he wasn't taking her straight home.

"There's something I want to show you," he said as he drove his convertible through the bright sunny afternoon. "Something special."

At first Angela thought he was taking her to Disney World. But he pulled off the highway at International Drive, passed the Wet 'n Wild amusement center, and drove onto the parking lot of the Travelers Inn Motel.

"Why're we going here?" Angela asked.

"This is where the special thing is," he said, beaming at her as he drove slowly through the crowded parking lot, off toward the rear of the sprawling hotel complex.

Angela remembered hearing some of the kids in class sniggering about motels. Or was it *hotels*? Either way, she had not understood what all the giggling was about, but it didn't sound good to her.

"I should be home, Mr. Muncrief," she said. "My mother will be worried."

"I'll phone her and tell her you're with me. It'll be okay." He parked the car in the nearly empty area next to the big Dumpsters. "And what's this 'Mr. Muncrief,' Angela? I thought you called me Uncle Kyle."

Angela felt a little frightened. She knew her mother did not want her to call him Uncle Kyle, but she didn't want to upset him. More than anything else, she wanted to be home.

"I think you should take me home," she said, not getting out of the car.

Muncrief held the door open for her. "We'll phone your mother. Everything'll be fine. I've got a great surprise for you; you'll love it."

Reluctantly, Angela got out of the Jaguar and followed Muncrief up to the door of the ground-floor suite. He unlocked the door and ushered her inside the darkened room with a sweep of his arm and a little bow.

"After you, Princess," he said.

Once she saw the VR helmets and gloves and the gray box of the computer that was almost as tall as she, Angela felt both better and worse.

"My parents told me I'm not allowed to play any VR games at school," she said.

"Oh?" Muncrief looked slightly surprised as he shut the door and turned on the lights. "Well, we're not at school now, are we?"

"No," Angela had to agree.

"And I've got a really special program for you, Angie. That good-looking prince is waiting for you. He's in love with you, you know."

"My prince?" She felt her heart leap.

"Right in here," said Muncrief, tapping a fingernail on the computer box. "All you've got to do is put on the helmet and gloves."

Her worries about her mother were swept away. Angela pulled on the data gloves and then slid the helmet over her hair, tangled from the ride in the convertible. In less than a minute she was in the castle, completely lost in its wonders.

"But where's the prince?" she asked as she moved through room after room.

"He's waiting for you," replied Mr. Muncrief's voice. "You'll find him, don't worry."

She climbed a marble staircase that spiraled up one of the castle's many towers. Each time she passed a window she saw more of the enchanted landscape out beyond the castle's walls, a green flowering land where fruit trees were always in bloom and unicorns frolicked in the meadows.

At the top of the winding stairway was a huge airy room with magnificent views of the entire world through its sweeping open windows and the most beautiful furnishings Angela had ever seen.

And, standing in the middle of the room, in front of the big canopied bed, stood the prince, her prince, young and strong and handsome and smiling at her.

"Hello, my love," he said. "You don't know how long I've waited for this moment."

Angela realized that her prince spoke with Mr. Muncrief's voice.

"Why're you going up on the highway?" Dan asked.

Luke Peterson's perpetual smile dimmed just a little as he slid the Cutlass into the stream of traffic. "There's somebody wants to meet you, Mr. Santorini. I'm taking you to him." He revved past seventy and swung into the left lane, passing a big semi rig chuffing sooty black smoke.

"What the hell do you mean? What's going on?"

Peterson glanced in his rearview mirror, then nudged the accelerator even more. "I'm not a doctor, Santorini. I'm a delivery service."

"My kid's been kidnapped, for chrissake!" Dan yelled over the roar of the rushing wind. "I've got to get to the police station!"

"I'm afraid not."

Peterson weaved in and out of the highway traffic, constantly looking around for any cars that might be following him. The Inquisitor had been as good as his word. The tail was gone. He had been planning to nab Santorini in the ParaReality parking lot, knowing that the guy usually worked so late that the lot would be dark and empty by the time he came out. Lucky thing he parked himself back behind the building before quitting time, though. He saw two ParaReality employees lugging Santorini's half-unconscious form out to a car; he followed them to the local hospital. It had been fairly easy to insinuate himself into the hospital's busy, disorganized emergency room. Santorini had suffered a crippling asthma attack, but a healthy shot of adrenaline had fixed him up.

As he drove through the darkening night, Peterson wondered if he should tell the Inquisitor about the asthma. Might be a way to make Santorini more cooperative. Probably the Inquisitor already knows about it. I'll tell him anyway, win some points with him.

"Goddammit, stop this car and let me out!" Santorini was yelling.

"Calm down," Peterson said softly. "You don't want to have another attack, do you?"

Santorini grabbed for the door handle.

"It's locked, and I've got the only working controls on my side. Anyway, you don't want to jump out of a car doing nearly eighty, do you? They'll pick up what's left of you with a shovel."

CHAPTER 45

Susan gripped the wheel with both hands, staring straight ahead as she drove through the deepening shadows of evening. There were only a few other cars on the streets; the going-home rush was over.

She saw the turnoff that led to Pine Lake Gardens and drove past it without a second thought. If Angie or Dan or anybody else phones home, I'll get the call here in the car. I don't need to be home.

She headed for Kyle Muncrief's house.

The police had already checked there, she knew. But Susan wanted to see for herself, wanted to be *doing* something. If I just go home and sit by the phone I'll go crazy, she thought.

Maybe I should go to the hospital, she thought. Or at least phone and see if Dan's still there. But she could not bring herself to touch the telephone. She glanced down at it, on the console between the front seats. Ring, damn you! Ring and let it be Angie telling me she's all right.

The phone remained silent.

Susan turned onto the entry road for Muncrief's housing development. The Subaru's headlights picked out the sign, Fairway Estates, and the little stucco security post with the barrier gate blocking the road.

She pulled to a stop. The blue-uniformed security guard looked up from the television show she was watching, slid the glass door open, and stuck her head out.

Susan fumbled in her purse and pulled out her red ParaReality security card.

"Susan Santorini to see Mr. Muncrief," she said to the guard.

The guard nodded and ducked back inside to check her computer screen. Then she came back outside.

"Mr. Muncrief isn't in," she said.

Susan had expected that. "I know. I work for him. He wanted me to drop off some computer programs that he's got to have tonight. Big meeting tomorrow, and he's got to look over this stuff before it starts."

The guard looked puzzled more than suspicious. Susan waggled her ID card. "See?" she said, holding it out to her. "If he doesn't get these disks tonight I'm going to be in a peck of trouble."

"But he's not home."

"He told me to drop them into his mail slot."

"I can take them and hold them here," the guard said. "I'll leave a message on his phone."

Susan said, "He told me he wants them in his mailbox by the time he gets home. If they're not there, I could lose my job."

The guard looked at Susan, then at Philip sleeping in the right-hand seat. Then she smiled. "Well, you don't look much like burglars. Okay, go on through."

"Thanks!"

The guard went back into her cubicle and her TV show. The barrier arm swung up, and Susan drove slowly down the dark tree-lined curving street.

I'm glad I'm not black, she thought. That's all they really worry about: blacks or anybody else who looks poor.

The big houses all looked pretty much alike, especially at night with nothing but the far-spaced street lamps lighting the curved roadway. But Susan recognized Muncrief's house from a staff party he had given weeks earlier. Besides, all the other houses were lit within; Muncrief's was totally dark.

Susan swung the station wagon onto the driveway. The headlights swept past a mailbox at the curb, dark gray with the house number painted in white on it and below that the name, Muncrief.

The house was not totally dark, after all. There was a single dim light glowing faintly in the front foyer through the frosted panes lining either side of the double front doors. Susan braked to a stop in front of the garage doors. She looked down at Philip; the baby was sleeping peacefully. Good. She got out of the car quietly and went to the front door. She tried the doorknob. Locked. The garage was closed, but by crawling up on the warm hood of her Subaru she could peek through the window at the top of the garage door.

Totally dark inside. She could see nothing.

She walked around to the back. The screen door by the pool was also locked. There's no other way in, she saw.

Susan started back for the car. I ought to go home. I ought to try to find where Dan is; he must be frantic with worry about us by now. And get Phil into his bed.

The baby seemed to be sleeping soundly enough in his car seat, though. Susan opened the passenger-side door and unhooked Phil's car seat from the safety belt. She knew what she had to do. She took the baby out of the car and placed him, still in his plastic seat, gently on the grass of Muncrief's front lawn, well removed from the driveway. Philip snoozed undisturbed as Susan gazed down at her son in the faint light of the tree-shaded street lamps. She thought he looked like an angel.

Susan hoped that the noise of the car's engine wouldn't wake the baby. But even if it did, it couldn't be helped. She started up the engine. Glancing at the car seat over on the grass, she saw that Phil was still sleeping peacefully. This is crazy, she thought. But she put the Subaru in reverse anyway and backed down almost to the street without turning on the headlights.

Susan braked the car to a stop, then revved the engine. This is really crazy, she told herself again as she pulled on her seat belt and tightened it hard against her chest. Crazy or not, she thought, here goes. She slammed the car forward straight into the garage door. The crash sounded enormous. The air bag exploded in her face, but still she could hear each individual part of the crash: breaking wood, metal shrieking against metal, tinkling glass.

The air bag engulfed her as she jolted against the seat belt, both her feet jammed against the brake pedal. For a moment she thought the air bag would suffocate her, but then it started to sag and deflate. Susan sat there, jaw hanging open, the front end of her wagon rammed into Muncrief's dark garage, the garage door bashed to pieces.

She turned off the engine. Susan pushed her door open, it banged against something that toppled to the concrete floor with a dull thud. She made her way out of the dark garage, ducking under a dangling chunk of the door.

"Now we're in," she said to Philip as she picked up his car seat. The baby stirred but did not wake up. "Good boy," Susan said. She carried her baby into the battered garage.

She did not hear any alarms going off, but she thought that maybe the neighbors had heard the crash and would come out to see what had happened. Or phone the security guard at the gate. Maybe they would call the police. Whatever. She knew she only had a few minutes.

The garage connected directly with Muncrief's kitchen. The ceiling-panel lights went on automatically as soon as she entered the room. Susan could see the pool and patio outside, where the party had been.

She went straight toward the bedrooms, lugging the car seat. Each room lit itself as soon as their body heat tripped the sensors in the doorways. Nothing. There were two bedrooms, both of them empty. The beds were neatly made, undisturbed. She put Philip's car seat down and yanked open the closet doors, then started checking out all the closets in the other rooms and the attic crawl space, anywhere that he might have hidden Angie.

Every moment she expected the police to come screaming up to the house. But outside it was as quiet as before. I guess he didn't set his security alarm, Susan told herself. And none of the neighbors is curious enough about the crash to come and look, or phone the security guard. Maybe they didn't even hear the crash; the houses are pretty well separated.

Still, she felt harried. There was a dim overhead light in the attic crawl space. The area was totally bare, not even a cardboard box up there.

She came down and swung the ladder back into the ceiling. Then she noticed a smaller room, down the hall from the bedrooms. A mini-office, with Muncrief's home computer in it. She sat herself at the desk and booted up the machine. No time to even start going through his files. But Susan found Muncrief's communications program and set up his modem to answer her when she phoned. I'll be able to check out all his files from home. There might be something in them, and it'll be better than sitting around doing nothing but waiting.

She heard Phil squawk. Not crying, just a complaining noise that said he was awake and unhappy. Turning off the display screen of Muncrief's computer, she went back to the bedroom. The baby was squirming unhappily. Probably wet, Susan thought. The baby's things were in the wagon.

Forcing herself to stay calm, Susan changed Phil's diaper in the darkness of the shattered garage, then tucked him back into his car seat and buckled it securely to the passenger chair beside her. The air bags hung limply from the steering column. If she weren't so wired she would have giggled; the air bags looked like giant used condoms.

Grimly she backed the Subaru down Muncrief's driveway. No time to look at the damage to the front end, but she could see a nasty gouge in the teal blue of the hood. My beautiful new wagon; what have I done to you? The car seemed to drive all right. No shimmies or rattles. One headlight was out, though.

Susan drove with exaggerated care toward the development's exit, trying to remember if there was a barrier gate on that side of the security shack or not.

There was, but it swung up automatically, she saw to her immense relief. If the guard saw the bashed-in hood with only one headlight working, she would want to hold them there while she checked out what she had done. But she was bent over her television show and only glanced at the Subaru as Susan drove past.

I wonder if she took the license-plate number when we came in? Susan asked herself. Then she remembered. What's the difference? What does it matter? Muncrief has taken Angie! And where is Dan? Where in the hell is my husband?

Dan's chest was tightening as if someone were knotting rawhide thongs across his lungs. The oddly smiling man kept the speedometer near eighty as he roared along the left lane of the highway, passing everything in sight. Dan felt trapped, panicked. This is a nightmare, he told himself. A crazy wild nightmare.

And then he realized what was going on.

"This is a simulation," he said aloud. "Jace, you sonofabitch, terminate the program."

The balding little man shot him a quizzical look from behind the driver's wheel.

"Goddammit, Jace, this is a helluva thing to do," Dan shouted. "Come on, terminate the program and let me out of this."

"Who are you talking to?" the driver asked, his pasty smile replaced by an anxious frown.

"You're not real," Dan told him. "None of this is real. Come on, Jace, end this program."

"I don't know what you're talking about, friend, but this is real, believe me."

Dan stared at him. How the hell can I tell the difference? He lifted his hands to his face; he could not feel a helmet or gloves. But then I wouldn't, not if Jace has programmed this with as much detail as the baseball sim.

"It won't do you any good to act crazy, you know," said the balding man.

Is this reality or a simulation? Am I still in the VR chamber? Was the hospital real? Sue's phone call—

"Somebody's kidnapped my daughter," he said. "Somebody's really kidnapped her!"

"Wasn't us."

"Who the hell are you? What do you want? I don't have any money—"

Peterson shook his head the barest fraction of an inch. "Money's not a factor. They just want to talk to you, ask you about your work."

"Who?"

No answer. Just that pasted-on grin as he stared straight ahead, both hands on the steering wheel.

"Let me find my daughter first. After I get her back—"

"No way," said Peterson. "My friends want to talk to you now. My job is to deliver you to them."

The highway was blurring past, big semi rigs with their glaring lights, a pickup truck packed with beer-drinking kids. Not a cop in sight when you need one. It's a simulation, Dan told himself. It's got to be. Who would kidnap Angie? Why?

Turning in his seat, Dan saw that the back of the car was filled with cameras and electronic gear. "Okay, Jace," he yelled, "if you want to play games, we'll play games."

He leaned back and picked up one of the cameras.

"That's an expensive piece you've got there," Peterson said, glancing out of the corner of his eye.

"Yeah." Dan forced himself to take a deep, painful breath. His lungs were burning. If this is a sim, then I can't get hurt. If it's not, if this is reality, then I've got to stop this clown and find Angie.

Dan smashed the camera against the windshield with every ounce of his strength. The glass starred but did not break, and the camera slipped out of his hands.

"Are you crazy?" Peterson screeched.

Dan twisted in his seat and grabbed for a bigger black electronic box. He bashed that against the windshield. Peterson pawed at him with one hand, ineffectually. The car swerved wildly across the highway. Holding the black box in both his hands, Dan smashed it again and again at the windshield. It finally shattered into a blizzard of tiny frosted pieces as Peterson skidded off the highway and up onto the shoulder of the median strip, plowing heavily into the grassy uneven ground.

Dan's seat belt cut into him as Peterson braked the car to a bumping, lurching stop. He turned toward Dan with wide, frightened eyes as he fumbled with one hand for the gun he kept beneath his seat.

Dan bashed him in his bald head with the electronics box once, twice. His eyes rolled up into his head and he collapsed onto the steering wheel, his scalp bleeding. The horn blared.

Tossing the black box through the shattered remains of the windshield, Dan yanked Peterson's unconscious body off the wheel. The horn stopped and the black box slid along the Cutlass's hood and off onto the grass of the median. Peterson's head was bloody, his eyes half closed. But he was moaning. He was alive. Dan unbuckled both seat belts, leaned across him, opened the driver's door, and pushed him out. Then he clambered over the console, slid in behind the wheel, and drove off, leaving him sprawled on the grass.

Christ, this isn't a sim, he said to himself. It's real. It must be real.

He did not head for the police station. Not even for home. He drove as fast as he dared, squinting into the night wind, straight to the ParaReality building. Jace will be there, he knew. Either there or at his bungalow. Muncrief has kidnapped Angie, and if anybody knows where Muncrief is, it'll be Jace.

He'll tell me, Dan said to himself. I'll get it out of him if I have to kill him.

CHAPTER 46

A t first Angela had been afraid, especially when her prince spoke to her in Uncle Kyle's adult voice. But before she could ask, his voice became brighter, younger, and he began to show Angela the lovely kingdom that would be theirs.

Through leafy woods and across sparkling streams they traveled, sometimes on magnificent horses decked in colorful trappings and jingling leather harnesses, sometimes walking across sunny warm meadows rich with the fragrance of new flowers.

"Nothing dies here," said the prince as they drifted lazily in a golden sailboat across a crystal-blue lake, lying on silken pillows and watching the soft white clouds gliding across the gilded sky. "It's always springtime, always as warm and beautiful as you are, my Angel."

"Always?" Angela asked dreamily, watching a pair of swallows flit overhead.

"Always," said her prince. "Unless you want it otherwise. If you would prefer winter and snow and palaces of ice—"

"No, no!" Angela laughed. "I like the springtime much better."

Kyle Muncrief watched Angela carefully as she reclined on the pillows in the stern of the little sailboat. He had dressed her in a gown of pink and white, covered her with jewels, and curled her blond hair. He had even removed her braces and made her teeth white and straight and perfectly even.

This is how Crystal would look, he told himself. This is what Crystal deserves, to be a princess, to be happy and loving and without a care. Beyond pain, beyond fear and hunger and everything that the world can do to us. This is what we deserve, Crystal. This is what I bring to you.

Angela saw a shadow pass over the prince's youthful face. His smile faded. He looked solemn, almost somber.

"What is it?" she asked gently. "What's wrong?"

"Nothing is wrong," he said. "Now that you're here with me, my love, the whole world is fine and right."

"But you look sad."

"I was thinking of all the years I spent searching for you. That's all." He brightened, smiled. "Now those dark years are over. You're here and we'll be together forever."

"Forever," Angela agreed. In the back of her mind she wondered what her mother was thinking, what her father might be doing. How long have I been here? But it didn't matter. Time had no meaning in this enchanted world. She wished she truly could stay in it forever.

And yet— "I'm getting hungry," she said. "Aren't you?"

"Of course," said the prince. "I should have thought of that."

He got up from the cushions and moved forward in the boat, ducking low beneath the boom. Angela could not quite make out what he was doing, but when he turned around and started back toward her, he was carrying a magnificent ebony tray inlaid with ivory, with a feast set out upon it.

He placed the tray at her feet. "Pheasant, pomegranates, sweetmeats from Arabia, the finest wine of France."

Angela gaped. "I've never eaten pheasant. Is it good?"

"Try it and see."

"And the only time I've had wine was at special dinners, like birthdays, and then my Daddy would only let me have a little sip of it."

The prince smiled at her. "You can drink all you want here. It's delicious and it won't harm you in any way."

Angela smiled back as she accepted a goblet from his hand.

Muncrief watched her sip the wine and then taste the dishes he had laid out for her. If Lowrey told me the truth, he thought, the system will stimulate the appetite centers in her brain and she'll feel as if she's really eaten a meal.

Angela thought that the food was quite bland. Almost tasteless. And the wine didn't fizz in her nose the way grandpop's champagne did at Christmas dinner. She nibbled at this and that, taking precisely what she wanted and no more, without a parent at her elbow to tell her to finish her plate.

"Do you like it?"

"Oh yes," she said. It was not exactly a lie. She did like it, all of it, even if it was rather tasteless. And it seemed to fill her up. Her hunger was gone.

The sun was setting behind the hills on the far shore of the lake. The boat turned around all by itself, as if guided by magic, and pointed its prow back toward the castle. Angela saw its proud towers jutting high against the reddening sky.

"It will be night soon," said the prince.

"I'll have to go home," Angela said.

"Not yet. Time doesn't matter here, you know. It's not the same as in that other world."

"No, I suppose it isn't."

"This is a much better world, isn't it?"

"Much," she agreed.

The tray had disappeared, with all the dishes and goblets and everything. Nobody has to clean up after dinner, Angela said to herself. This is a much better world!

"Crystal," said the prince.

"Crystal?"

"Do you mind if I call you Crystal?" he asked. In the deepening shadows of twilight, his face seemed to change slightly.

"My name's Angela."

"Yes, but Crystal is a pretty name, too, don't you think?"

"I like my own name."

He made a smile. "Very well, Angela dearest."

A breeze blew across the water, rippling the placid lake, making the sail strain, chilling her.

"Angela," asked the prince, "do you truly love me?"

"Yes," she said without an instant's hesitation.

"Would you like to stay here in this world with me forever?"

"Yes." Angela knew that she would have to go back home to her parents and her brother *sometime*. But not now. Not yet. This game was too wonderful to leave so soon.

The prince saw that she was cold and put his arm around her shoulders. "Do you know how long forever is?" he asked.

She nestled close to his warmth. "Forever is forever."

"We'll grow old, you know."

"You said nothing ever dies in this kingdom."

"Yes, that's true. But we will grow old."

"That's all right."

"Would you love me if I were old, Angela? If I were old and ugly and fat?"

She laughed. "But you're not. You're young and thin and handsome."

Muncrief decided not to press the issue any further. He did not want to alarm her. Not yet. Not before night had fallen and it was time for bed.

It took a concentrated effort of will for him to slide the visor of his helmet up. He looked through the doorway into the motel bedroom. Yes, the sensor net was draped across the bed, waiting for him to put it on her.

It was tough to drive with the windshield gone. Dan pulled off the highway as soon as he could. His eyes felt raw with grit, and he imagined he looked like one of those old-time open-cockpit fliers, face caked with dirt and windburn.

Once he got his bearings, Dan realized that he was closer to Jace's house than the lab. He decided to try the bungalow first. As he stopped at a red light a car full of kids pulled up beside him.

"Hey, whyn't you trade that junker in?" called one of the boys, grinning at him.

Dan grimaced, hoping that the police did not find him before he found Jace. He glanced down at the telephone between the seats. Pulling over to a dark, tree-lined curb, he dialed home.

"Yes?" Susan's voice was quivering.

"It's me, honey."

"Dan! Where've you been? I've—"

"No time to talk now," he said. "I'm okay and I'm going after Jace. He should know where Muncrief is."

"Oh."

"Have you heard anything?"

"No."

"I'll get Jace to tell me where Kyle is. And if he's got Angie, I'll get her back."

"He's got her." There was not a shred of doubt in Susan's voice.

"Then I'll get him," Dan said.

"Dan, I—"

He interrupted. "What do you say when I use words like testosterone or coitus?"

"What? What are you talking about?"

"I've got to hear it from you, Sue. I've got to know this is reality and I'm not stuck in one of Jace's simulations."

"This is no time—"

"Sue, I don't know if you're real or not! I don't know if I'm really here or if I'm still in the VR chamber at the lab."

She hesitated, then replied, "Well, I usually say something like . . . uh, I love it when you talk scientific."

Dan felt his breath gush out of him. "Yeah. Right." Jace wouldn't know that. No one would know that. This *is* reality, Dan told himself, not a sim.

"Thanks, honey. Now I'm going to find Muncrief." He hung up before Susan could reply. I've got to find Jace first, he thought. He'll know where Muncrief is. Then I'll get them both.

It took a bit of hunt-and-seek before Dan found the street where Jace's bungalow was located. He nosed the Cutlass slowly down the unpaved driveway behind the houses on the street itself, then stopped in front of the place. It was hard to tell if Jace was home or not. Dan turned off the car lights and studied Jace's bungalow for a few moments. With all the windows painted black and the front door shut, the place would look abandoned even if he had a party going on inside.

He turned off the ignition and got out of the car, gravel crunching underfoot as he went to the door. It was locked. He rapped on it once, twice, and then suddenly banged on it with both his fists as if he wanted to tear it apart.

Great! he raged at himself. Take it out on a door. Break your stupid hands on a goddamned door when what you really want to do is break Muncrief's neck.

He stood puffing, glaring at the unyielding door. No, he told himself. What you really want to do is find Angie. Find her and get her home safe. *Then* I'll break his fucking neck.

If Jace was home he wasn't answering Dan's pounding. Or maybe he can't hear it. Maybe he's got himself caught up in one of his own sims. Or he's sleeping. Drugged, drunk, whatever.

But he knew Jace hardly ever drank and never used even recreational drugs. Doesn't need them; he gets high on his own simulations.

Then Dan realized that Jace's bike was nowhere in sight. He walked around the bungalow, nearly stumbling over some junk piled up in the backyard where the distant street lamps were shadowed by the trees. No bike.

He must be at the lab.

Sure enough, Jace's scrofulous bicycle was leaning against the wall next to the rear door as Dan parked alongside the dimly lit loading platform.

But Jace was not in his lab in the rear of the building nor in the Wonderland VR chamber. Puzzled, Dan hurried along the corridor to Jace's office, barely noticing as he passed the computer center that two of the mainframes were busily humming and blinking. Jace's office was empty, except for the usual snowdrifts of papers.

Dan went to his own office, glancing at his wristwatch, figuring he'd phone home again and see if anything had developed.

Jace was stretched out on the black leather couch, snoring softly. He had put on a clean T-shirt, sky blue with white script lettering: *Who Dares Wins.*

Dan rapped his knuckles against the sole of one of Jace's worn boots. "Hey! Wake up!"

Jace's eyes popped open. "I wasn't asleep."

"The hell you weren't." Dan went to his desk. He wanted something to lean on, something solid to keep him from grabbing Jace by the throat and throttling him. I need him now, he told himself. I have to get him to help me.

"I wasn't," Jace insisted, swinging his legs to the floor and sitting up straight.

"You were snoring."

"That doesn't mean I was asleep."

He's already moving me off the subject, Dan realized. "Never mind that," he said, sitting in his desk chair. "I want your help."

Jace gave him a suspicious look. "Why should I help you?"

"Because I'm asking you to."

"You were ready to hand me over to the cops a couple hours ago."

"The sonofabitch has kidnapped my daughter, Jace!"

"Huh? Whattaya mean?"

"Muncrief took Angie from school. They've been missing since three-thirty."

Jace looked away from Dan and muttered, "He can't hurt her."

"How do you know that? How do you *know*?"

"Look, you think I'd give him a program that could hurt anybody? I'm not that dumb."

"What makes you think he's using a VR program, Jace? He's got Angie in his hands, for chrissake!"

But Jace just shook his head. "I know the bastard better'n you do. He's not hurting your kid."

"Jace . . ." Dan felt his hands clenching into fists.

"Didn't you see the mainframes perkin' away in the computer center? Who d'you think is usin' them at this time of night?"

"Muncrief?"

"It ain't the Wizard of Oz."

"Where is he?"

A shrug. "I don't know."

"But you said—"

"He doesn't tell me *everything*, pal. I don't know where the hell he is, but wherever it is he's got a processor and a phone link. Probably a DEC mini and an optical-fiber line."

"Christ, he could be anywhere."

"Guess so."

"Help me find him, Jace."

"Why should I?"

Dan's first impulse was to yell, *Because you've helped him set up this simulation that's based on my daughter, you stupid sonofabitch, and that makes you an accessory to kidnapping!*

But he swallowed his anger, took a deep rasping breath, and

said, "Because my Angie's in trouble, Jace. Even if he's just fucking around with her mind, he's going to hurt her. Mentally. Emotionally. Can't you see that?"

Jace said nothing. He looked away from Dan, like a kid
who's been caught sneaking a peek at his father's girlie magazines.

Forcing himself to stay calm, Dan thought, There's a way to get
to him. There is a way.

"Okay, so you don't know where Muncrief is."

Jace combined a nod and a shrug.

"You haven't any idea of where he could be."

He hesitated, then said, "Nope."

"I guess it was too much to expect," Dan said.

"What was?"

"That you'd be able to track him down."

Jace's close-set eyes focused on Dan.

"I just thought you'd have the smarts to locate the bastard.
Through the computer, maybe. Thought you'd have been bright
enough to figure out how to find him."

"You didn't ask me how to find him," Jace said slowly, as
though he knew he was stepping into a minefield. "You just asked
me where he is."

"And you don't know."

"That's right. I don't know."

"And you don't know how to find him."

"I didn't say that."

"But you don't. Come on, Jace, admit it. You don't know how
to find Muncrief. He's outsmarted you, just like he's outsmarted
me."

Grudgingly, "I wouldn't put it that way."

Dan reached back with one hand and tried to massage the stiffness in his neck. "He's beaten us both. You're no better off than I
am, are you?"

"I could find him," Jace snapped.

"Sure you could." Dan strained to make it sound as skeptical as
he could.

"You don't think I could?"

Dan shrugged elaborately. "Hey, you're the boy genius, right?
Only, I don't see any genius at work here."

Jace shot to his feet. "You just don't know much about anything, do you?" And he turned toward the door.

"Where're you going?" Dan called, scrambling from behind his
desk.

"Computer center, dickhead. Wherever he is, his *mind* is connected to the friggin' computer."

CHAPTER 47

B

AD COMMAND

The words blinked on the computer screen. Susan rubbed her eyes, hoping they would go away, but when she looked again, they still blinked at her, white letters against black background.

Then she looked at the command she had typed.

SHOW AKK BOLLS/MP

God, my hands are shaking so bad, I can't even type straight.

With deliberate care she retyped SHOW ALL BILLS/MO.

She had already gone through Muncrief's data bank of telephone numbers, accessing his computer through her modem. Nothing in there that gave her a clue as to where the man might have taken Angie; the phone numbers were almost entirely home phones for ParaReality employees. The man seemed to have no friends outside the company, no social life of his own.

Now she was examining his personal bills: rent, telephone, utilities, food, credit cards, car payment—it all looked maddeningly ordinary, except for a rather high bill from the local liquor store.

Of course, Susan reasoned inwardly, everything else must be in the company's files. He uses company money to pay for most of his expenses, I bet. It's a wonder he's paying for the Jaguar out of his own pocket.

She thought she heard Phil cry out. Looking up from the computer screen, fingers poised over the keyboard, Susan held her breath and listened. She heard nothing but the hum of the machine. Still . . .

She got up and padded barefoot to Philip's room. The baby was sleeping soundly, none the worse for his evening's travels. Maybe he enjoyed the excitement, Susan thought. Then she went back to her alcove office. She saw the kitchen phone on its wall rack. It had not rung since Dan had called. Angela's still out there with Muncrief, wherever the hell he's taken her. Maybe I should phone the police and ask them just when they're going to start considering this a kidnapping.

But instead she sat in front of the computer again. There has got to be *something* in here that will tell me where he's taken Angie. There's *got* to be! Otherwise we have no way of knowing. He could be anywhere. He could be doing anything—

Susan clenched her fists and forced herself to take a deep breath. Don't start that! Don't draw pictures in your mind. That's not going to help. Dig into his records, find out where he spends his money. Find him. Find him. Find him and you'll find Angie.

But will I find her before he rapes and murders her?

"I'm getting really sleepy," Angela said.

The prince smiled gently. "Your bed is waiting for you, up at the top of the tower. It's the loveliest room in the castle."

"Doesn't anyone else live here?" she asked. "I mean, are we all alone?"

He gestured vaguely. "Oh, there are servants, of course. They appear when you want them."

"I haven't seen any since we came back from the lake."

His smile turned just a trace sad. "Aren't you happy being alone with me? I thought it would be more romantic, just the two of us."

"Oh yes, I'm happy," Angela said quickly. Then she added, "I was just wondering."

"Come on, I'll take you to your bedchamber. Would you like to have ladies waiting upon you?" He held out his hand.

Angela slipped her arm in his and they started toward the grand staircase that spiraled up to the tower room.

But she hesitated at the first step.

"I really should go home."

The prince looked surprised. "But Angela, my dear, this is your home."

"No, I mean my real home. With my mother and father and my little brother."

He blinked in confusion. "Don't you want to stay with me?"

"I can come back to you."

"No, I'm afraid they wouldn't let you return here."

"But I can't stay—"

"They'll keep us apart, Angela. They'll take you away from me."

"You said you'd wait for me," she replied. "You said you'd wait forever, if you had to."

"I don't want to wait! I want you with me, now and forever."

"But I'll come back, I promise I will."

"Don't you love me?" he asked, heartbroken.

Her own heart almost broke to see him so sad. "Of course I love you. I'll always love you."

"Then don't leave me. Please. Not now. Not when we mean so much to each other."

"But my parents will be worried about me. I can't stay here all the time. I have to go home. But I'll come back to you."

"Angela! Angel baby, is that you?"

She whirled around and saw her father coming through the high arched doorway at the other end of the room.

"Daddy!" She ran to him.

"Angie," he said, taking her into his arms. "I've been looking for you."

"Daddy, I want you to meet—"

But when she turned back, the prince was gone.

"Where did he go?" Angela asked, bewildered.

Her father smiled at her. "He's upstairs waiting for you, Angie. He loves you a lot."

"I love him, too, Daddy."

"I know you do, Angie. That's why you must go to him. So you can love each other."

She stared at her father, almost overcome with happiness that he understood and did not object. And yet she felt afraid at the same time.

"I thought you'd want me to come home," she said.

"This is your home now, Angela. You and your prince will live here happily ever after."

"But you . . . and Mommy . . ."

"We'll come and visit you," her father said. "Your mother and I will come, you'll see. And your little brother, too."

"Will you? Will you really?"

"Of course we will. But you're a grown-up woman now, Angie. And you love the prince very much, don't you?"

"Yes," she said, trembling. A grown-up woman, she thought. The thought frightened her a little.

"Now you're going to love your prince the way a grown-up woman loves a grown-up man. The way your mother and I love each other. That's what being a grown-up is all about, Angie."

"Can't I come home with you?" she blurted.

Her father's eyes flashed, and for just a moment, just a flicker of an instant, she thought she saw someone else's eyes in her father's face.

"Daddy, I—I'm afraid!"

He made a mechanical smile at her. "There's nothing to be afraid of. The prince loves you. He won't hurt you."

"Where's Mommy?"

"She's busy."

"Can't I see her?"

"Not now."

Her father grasped her by the shoulders and kissed her on the forehead. "The prince is waiting for you, Angie. Don't make him unhappy."

He turned her around so that she faced the staircase. The prince was standing halfway up the first flight, in a splendid uniform of deep blue and gold, reaching both hands out to her.

Angela turned toward her father. But he was gone. She was alone in the castle with the prince.

Kyle Muncrief blinked sweat from his eyes. Jace had been as good as his word. The simulation of Dan Santorini was just about perfect, except that Kyle couldn't remember the baby boy's name. Didn't matter. He had gotten through it. Too bad he couldn't run both the prince and the father at the same time, but the girl isn't smart enough to figure that out. I've got her now. I've got her.

Angela felt her throat go dry. She was alone in the castle with the prince. She *did* love him. And she knew that he loved her.

She started up the stairs toward him. She did not know whether the shaking of her legs was from love or fear. It did not matter, though. There was nothing else for her to do but to go to her prince.

He led her to the bedchamber. It was a magnificent room, richly tapestried, with a wide bed piled high with pillows beneath a silken canopy. And on the bed was a strange glittering web of jewels, like a necklace except that it was big enough to cover her whole body.

"This is for you, my love," said her prince, gesturing to the sensor network. "The finest jewels from Persia and India. All for your lovely skin."

"They're beautiful," Angela said, marveling at the gemstones.

"They must be worn next to your skin," said the prince. "Just as I am wearing mine."

And when she turned back to him, she saw that his beautiful uniform was gone and he was standing there with nothing on his handsome muscular body except a network of sensors that glittered like jewels.

Susan stared wearily at the computer screen. She had gone through the past six months of Muncrief's bills and found nothing useful. Why should there be? she asked herself. It was just wishful thinking. Wherever he's gone, he hasn't left any paper trail for me to follow.

Leaning back in her typist's chair, she rubbed at her eyes. The house was perfectly still, not a sound except for the hum of the computer. Not even a car going past outside. Susan got to her feet, surprised at how her back ached. Then she looked at the kitchen clock: she had been at the computer for nearly three hours straight.

And not a word from the police! Glancing at the wall phone, she thought again about calling Sergeant Wallace. But he would call if he had learned anything, she told herself. And the memory of Muncrief's smashed-in garage door held her back, too. Sooner or later, somebody's going to find it and question the security guard and come here looking for *me*.

Automatically, her mind numb and frantic at the same time, Susan took out a mug and spooned in some instant coffee. She half-filled the mug with boiling water from the special tap at the sink; the coffee frothed and steamed as she padded back to Philip's room to look in on the baby.

She tried to push away the images of what Muncrief might be doing to Angie. Instead she pictured what she would do to him. She wanted a knife, a big butcher's knife, she wanted to slash his face into bloody ribbons, cut off his balls so he would never bother another little girl, stab him in his fat gut and twist the blade until he screamed.

Shaking her head, Susan murmured, "I'll be happy if we can just get Angie back safe and unharmed. That's all I ask. Please, just bring her back to us okay." And she wondered whom she was praying to; she had not been in church since last Easter, with her mother and the whole family back in Dayton.

The computer screen still spelled out the list of Muncrief's monthly bills: rent, telephone, utilities, food, credit cards, car payment. He made out checks for those bills every month. Too bad his computer file doesn't have the itemized bills from the phone company and the credit cards. Might be something in there. Something.

She sat at the curve-backed typist's chair again and put the steaming coffee mug down beside the computer. Could I get the phone company's records? It's worth a try. If I can access their computer.

Susan got up again and went to the two-drawer file cabinet in their bedroom closet where Dan kept all the household bills. Thank God he's such a neatness freak, she thought as she pawed through the precisely lettered manila folders. She found their latest phone bill, with the number she was looking for:

Problem with your billing? Call our customer-service hot line, 666-5915.

Clutching the bill in her hand, Susan searched for their credit-card bills. Each of them had a customer-service line, also. Now, if Muncrief has the same credit cards as we do, I can access their records. Maybe.

She had to pass Angela's room on her way back to the kitchen, and the sight of the empty bed clutched at her heart. I'm trying to find you, baby. I'm trying my hardest.

As Susan expected, United Telephone's customer-service hot line was fully automated.

"If you wish to check your most recent billing," said their computer's synthesized voice, "press one. If you wish to—"

Susan pressed one. The voice started droning a new menu of options. ". . . If you have a computer modem and wish to have your bill displayed on your home computer screen, press four."

She pressed four, then followed the phone's instructions until she linked up through the modem and could read the further instructions off her display screen.

NAME? blinked at her.

KYLE MUNCRIEF, she typed.

TELEPHONE NUMBER?

Susan had expected that one and had it jotted down on the pad at her elbow. She typed it on her keyboard.

SOCIAL SECURITY NUMBER?

Damn! That was their security check. She wouldn't get anything out of the phone company's files unless she could give them Muncrief's Social Security number. Thinking furiously, Susan split the display screen and searched through the Muncrief files she had put into her own machine's memory. Somewhere, *somewhere,* Muncrief had listed important numbers and dates and— Yes! There it was!

She returned to the phone company's flickering question and typed in 646-28-6017.

Muncrief's latest phone bill filled her screen. Susan copied it to memory, then asked for the previous month's bill. And the one before that. Then she cut the modem connection and accessed the Directory Assistance computer. Within minutes she had a complete list of everyone Muncrief had telephoned from his home for the past three months.

But it wasn't much, she saw. He hardly used his home phone, except to call the ParaReality office.

Susan slumped with weariness. But the thought of Angela out there somewhere in the night straightened her spine. She took a healthy slug of the cooling coffee and cleared the computer screen. There's still his credit-card bills. Maybe something'll show up there.

•   •   •

The computer center felt chilly, colder than the rest of the building. Dan shivered involuntarily and wished he had brought his jacket with him.

Jace went straight to the control console of the Cray that was running and folded his lanky frame into the little wheeled chair in front of its keyboard. He pecked at it for half a minute, then got up again.

"Come on," he said, grim-faced. Whether his expression was anger or something else, Dan could not tell.

Wordlessly Dan followed the tall lean scarecrow down the corridor to the Wonderland VR chamber. The control booth was thick with ominous shadows, lit only by the dim safety lamps atop the consoles. Jace pulled a scuffed helmet and a pair of gloves from the storage shelves and pushed them into Dan's hands.

"Go on in," he said, pointing at the one-way window. "I'll set you up."

Dan remembered being in the chamber only a few hours earlier, the crippling asthma attack he had suffered at Jace's hands. And he remembered the shoot-out, the bullets smashing into his chest.

"I'm not goin' in," Jace said, reading his thoughts. "I'll stay out here and run the board."

Still Dan hesitated. In the dim lights he barely recognized the man standing before him. Jace looked utterly serious, strangely purposeful, like a man about to enter battle.

"You wanna get to him before he does anything to your kid?" Jace urged. "This is the way to do it. Step into his simulation. Enter his fantasy."

Dan swallowed hard. "Right. Okay."

He put on the helmet and opened the door to the simulation chamber, both gloves in his free hand. As he wormed his fingers into the fuzzy gloves and hooked up the optical-fiber connecting lines, Dan began to feel like a trapped animal. The big, empty, low-ceilinged chamber was like an elaborate cage. On the other side of the one-way glass stood Jace, grim and grave as death. *Is he really going to inject me into Muncrief's fantasy, or is this just Jace's way of getting me out of his hair for a while?*

Dan felt the first scratches of rawness in his lungs. *Not now!* he snarled at himself. *Not an asthma attack now!*

"You ready?" Jace's voice in his earphones.

Dan pulled down his visor. "Ready."

"Here we go."

The darkness flickered, then vanished. Dan was standing in some kind of elaborate bedroom, like a cross between a fairy-tale castle and a Las Vegas casino hotel. The walls looked like stone where they weren't covered with colorful tapestries. The floor was thickly carpeted. There was a huge canopied bed over against one wall, with candles burning softly on the night tables on either side of it.

A young man was standing beside the bed, gazing out the window at the starry night, stark naked except for a strange web of glimmering jewels draped across his bare shoulders and extending down to his thighs. Like a sensor network, Dan recognized.

But no Angela.

"Where is she?" Dan snapped, coming around the bed toward him.

He whirled around, startled. "How did you—"

It was Muncrief's voice in this phony VR Prince Charming's naked body. Dan saw that he was erect, anticipating.

"Where's Angela?" Dan bellowed. "What've you done to her?"

"Daddy?" Angela appeared at the arched stone doorway. "You're back!"

Angela was naked, too, except for a sensor network. Dan stared at her budding breasts, the thin patch of hair at her crotch, absolute fury boiling up within him.

Angela ran into her father, and he wrapped his arms around her protectively.

"Angie, baby, he didn't hurt you, did he?"

"No," she said, almost sobbing. "He loves me, Daddy, just like you said. But I was afraid."

"I said?"

"A couple minutes ago, downstairs. Don't you remember?"

Dan looked over at the young prince. His face seemed to be wavering, melting like candle wax.

"That wasn't me, Angel. That was a fake."

He could feel her body go stiff with alarm. Angela looked up at him, wide-eyed. "But—but how do I know it's you now?"

He smiled down at her and patted her golden hair. "Because I'm taking you out of here and back home where you'll be safe and sound and sleep in your own bed with Mom and Phil and me right there under the same roof with you."

"You can't take her away," said the prince, in Muncrief's gruff voice.

"The hell I can't," Dan said to him. "And once she's safe, I'm going to find you and kick the shit out of you, Kyle."

"I'm your prince, Angela," he said, his voice breaking. "I love you. You said you loved me, too!"

"I do love you," said Angela. But she did not leave her father's arms.

"Then stay with me."

"I'll come back," she said.

"No! He won't let you come back. He won't let you ever see me again!"

She turned back to Dan. "Daddy?"

"Angela, baby, this is all an illusion. A VR game. There is no prince. It's really Kyle Muncrief running a VR game. Like the games at school, remember?"

"Uncle Kyle?"

"Yes," said Dan.

"Is it really you, Uncle Kyle?"

The prince wavered and shimmered like an image seen under water.

"Tell her the truth, you sonofabitch," Dan demanded.

The handsome young mask melted into Muncrief's unhappy face. The slim youthful body aged before their eyes, belly sagging, muscles slumping, erection gone. He crumpled to his knees, face in his hands, blubbering.

Jace could not see what Dan was experiencing, but he heard the voices over the tinny loudspeaker built into the command console.

Muncrief's such an asshole, he grumbled to himself. And now he's gone down in flames. Probably wind up in a funny farm for perverts.

The phone rang, startling him. Who the hell would be calling at this time of the night? Who'd have this friggin' number?

He let it ring two, three, four times. When it became clear that whoever was calling was not going to hang up, Jace snatched the instrument from its cradle.

"What?" he snapped.

"Dan?"

"No."

"Jace, is that you?"

"Sue?"

"Yes. Where's Dan?"

She sounded excited. Jace looked through the one-way window and saw Dan standing in a weird, half-stooped posture, his arms wrapped around empty air.

"He's not here," he half-lied.

"Jace, can you get him? Do you know where he is?"

"I think so."

He could hear Susan's breath gasping through the phone. "I've found him! Tell Dan I've found him! He's at the Travelers Inn Motel on International Drive. I'll bet anything on it! I traced him through an invoice the delivery company faxed to him. He had a DEC minicomputer delivered there!"

"Muncrief? That's where he's at?"

"Yes! Tell Dan. I'm phoning the police right now."

"But wait—" Too late. She had already hung up.

Jace put the phone down and stared through the window at Dan. *Shit, if she gets the cops in there, Dan's gonna find out that I copied him, too. He'll find out that I knew what Muncrief wanted all along. Muncrief'll blab everything to them, and Dan'll want to kill me.*

He shook his head. *Shit on all of them,* he said to himself. And he began to manipulate the controls of the VR equipment.

CHAPTER 48

Dan held Angela in his arms, his anger seething like molten lava within him. His daughter seemed unharmed physically, but what about mentally, psychologically? What's this done to her?

He had not seen his daughter naked in more than a year; she had become very shy.

But Kyle's seen her naked. Kyle was going to fuck her; maybe just in a VR sim, but it would've seemed real enough to him. And to Angie.

Muncrief was still rocking back and forth on his knees, weeping.

"I love you, Crystal. I've always loved you. I didn't want to run away, but I had to. I *had* to. You can understand that, can't you? Can't you?"

Angela clung to her father, whispered to him, "I think he's talking to me, Daddy."

"No, honey, it's somebody named Crystal."

"The prince wanted to call me Crystal. I wouldn't let him."

Dan wondered who Crystal might be.

"Daddy?"

"I'm right here," Dan said. He could feel his daughter pressing against him, see her as clearly as if she were really in the same place with him and not separated by miles of distance, naked except for the sensor net that was disguised in this simulation to look like jewels linked by fine golden chains.

Dan unbuttoned his shirt, tugged it off, and wrapped it around his daughter.

"The prince was Mr. Muncrief all along, wasn't he?"

"Yes, Angel."

"He said he loved me."

Now comes the tricky part, Dan thought. "He's not well, Angel. He's sick in his mind. When he said he loved you, it wasn't the way that I love you or your mother loves you."

"He loves this Crystal person, doesn't he?"

"I guess so. He keeps saying he does."

"And he wanted me to be Crystal."

Cripes, she's got a better grip on this than I do, Dan told himself. "Maybe he did," he said to his daughter. "Maybe he did."

"He didn't want to hurt me," Angela said. "He tried to make me want to love him. That's why he disguised himself as the young prince."

Dan nodded, stroking her hair, his eyes on Muncrief's blubbering form. The bastard could still be dangerous, Dan thought. He's bigger than I am, and if he goes from self-pity into anger we could have an ugly situation here. He started to call to Jace to have him take Angela out of the simulation, but then he realized she would be alone in a room somewhere with Muncrief.

"Where did Mr. Muncrief take you when he picked you up at school?" Dan asked his daughter.

Angela screwed up her face, trying to remember. "Oh, sure— the Travelers Inn Motel."

A shock wave shivered through Dan's guts. A motel. The sonofabitch wanted more than a simulation, after all.

Gently, so he wouldn't frighten her, he asked, "Which Travelers Inn, Angel?"

"The one near Wet 'n Wild."

"Jace!" Dan called. "Did you hear that? They're in the Travelers Inn on International Drive."

"Got it," Jace's voice replied. "Help is on the way."

Angela looked back at Muncrief. "He really is sick, isn't he, Daddy?"

"I'm afraid he is. He didn't—hurt you, did he? Touch you?"

"No." She sighed painfully. "I thought the prince really loved me. I kinda knew he wasn't real, but that made it even better, in a way."

"Did you love the prince?" Dan asked.

"I guess."

He held her tighter. "Angel darling, there are going to be lots of boys who'll love you even more than your make-believe prince, believe me. I'll have to buy a baseball bat to keep them away from you."

She almost giggled. "Don't keep them *all* away, Daddy."

"Not all of them. But not until you're a little older."

Muncrief had grown silent. He was still hunched down on his hairy calves, leaning against the brocade-covered bed, face buried in his hands. But he had stopped weeping. Now he looked up at Angela and Dan, face red, eyes swollen, hair disheveled.

"I can't get out," he muttered. "I want to get out, but I can't."

"Help is on the way, Kyle," said Dan, thinking, It's just as well that you can't get out of the sim, you pederastic sonofabitch. I don't want you in the same room with my daughter. I don't want you in the same county as my daughter.

"I didn't do anything," Muncrief whined. "It was all a game. Just a game."

Dan's anger broke through. "Yeah, a game. With my daughter. Well, you're not going to play any more games, Kyle. They're going to put you away, lock you behind padded walls where you won't be able to threaten little girls anymore! And if they don't, I'll kill you, you sneaking bastard. I'll kill you with my own two hands!"

"Daddy!"

Muncrief leaned heavily on the corner of the bed and pulled himself to his feet.

"So kill me!" he shouted. Spreading his arms wide, standing there naked and vulnerable, he screamed, "Here's your chance! Kill me! You think I want to live like this! *Go ahead and kill me!*"

His eyes wild, Muncrief staggered toward Dan and Angela. Dan moved his daughter behind him and took a step forward to face him.

Muncrief stopped in midstride, his eyes flaring as if they were going to pop out of his head. His back arched so violently that his arms flung themselves almost out of their sockets. He spasmed, mouth open to scream but nothing coming out except a gargling, strangling groan.

Muncrief fell backward onto the bed and slid to the floor with a limp thud. Angela screamed as Dan stood watching the man die.

By the time Susan drove up onto the Travelers Inn's entryway, Philip was back asleep. The baby had squalled as hard as he could when Susan had lifted him from his crib and bundled him into the car seat. But she shushed and cooed at him as she strapped him into the front seat of her Subaru. Then she had forced herself to walk around the front of the station wagon; the molded bumper was crumpled on the left side and the headlight was shattered. The hood's finish was terribly scratched up. But it had been worth it. She had found Angie.

Philip settled down once they were moving, and the street lamps flicking by soon lulled the baby back to sleep. In the darkness of the hotel's parking lot she saw the flashing lights of several police-car gumballs and headed for them, down the side of the hotel's sprawling complex and out to the back lot.

She parked, dashed out of the wagon around to the passenger side, unlatched the safety belt, and eased Philip's car seat out. Leaning it against her hip, she ran toward the gathering crowd, pushed her way through the curious onlookers until a tan-uniformed sheriff's deputy held up a beefy hand.

"Where d'you think you're goin', little momma?"

"That's my daughter in there!" Susan shouted, frantic. "I'm the one who phoned you!"

The deputy put a hand on her shoulder and led her toward the door of the hotel suite.

"Is she all right? Is she all right?"

Sergeant Wallace stepped out of the door, blue uniform in contrast to the deputies' tans. He smiled at Susan.

"Mrs. Santorini, yer little girl's safe and sound. A mite confused, though. She's sayin' her daddy came and rescued her."

"She's all right!" Susan almost collapsed into Wallace's arms.

"Here, take the baby for a minute," the sergeant said to the deputy. "Come on inside and sit down, Mrs. Santorini. Yer daughter's right inside there."

With a deputy's jacket draped over her, Angela came running to her mother the instant she stepped inside the room. Susan hugged her and kissed her and hugged her some more.

"You're all right, baby. You're all right."

Angela was laughing and crying at the same time, apologizing for not coming home from school and kissing her mother back.

Breathless, Susan let the police sergeant guide her to a chair. As she sat down, she looked through the open doorway into the suite's bedroom. Kyle Muncrief lay on the carpet, stark naked, eyes staring sightlessly at the ceiling.

Sergeant Wallace looked slightly flustered. "Yer daughter was all undressed 'cept for that rig over there." He pointed to a sensor net thrown carelessly over one of the chairs. "Her clothes are in the other room, on the bed."

Half a dozen state troopers and one woman in street clothes were in the bedroom. One of the troopers was photographing Muncrief's body. The woman was sitting on the bed, tapping on the keys of a notebook computer.

"Daddy came and rescued me," Angela was saying, "just like in the videos."

"He's dead?" Susan asked Sergeant Wallace.

"Yep. Looks like a stroke, the medical examiner says. It's Kyle Muncrief, 'cording to his wallet."

"Yes," Susan said, "that's Kyle Muncrief."

"Daddy saved me," Angela repeated.

Susan turned her attention to her daughter. "Mr. Muncrief didn't hurt you, did he? He didn't try—" Suddenly she was embarrassed to ask such questions in front of strangers.

"No," Angela said. "He didn't touch me at all. He was going to, but Daddy came and stopped him."

"Daddy found you?"

"Yes!"

The sergeant looked as if he thought Angela's experience had bent her mind. Susan tried to explain what virtual reality was all about, pointing to the minicomputer in the sitting room and the helmet and gloves lying discarded on the floor.

Wallace grunted. "That explains the helmet he was wearin' when we found him. Looked like a biker's helmet, 'cept it was hooked up to the computer in here."

Susan made herself look back at Muncrief's body. He was still wearing data gloves and a sensor net.

"Can I take her home now?" Susan asked.

The sergeant cocked his head to one side, staring down at Angela. "Yew want the medical examiner to look her over? She's right in the next room."

"I'd rather get her home," said Susan. "I'll take her to our own doctor tomorrow morning."

Wallace nodded as if he agreed with her. "Okay. We'll need a statement from yew. And yew, too, young lady. The state police can send somebody over to yer house t'morrow, I reckon."

"In the afternoon," Susan said, getting up from the chair.

"Surely." The sergeant's face flushed slightly. "Uh, yew want to get her dressed, I s'pose."

He went into the bedroom and came out with Angela's clothes in his arms. Then he closed the bedroom door and went out the front door, ushering the sheriff's deputy who was still holding Phil in the car seat. Susan helped Angela to dress, both their hands shaking.

Angela wrapped an arm around her mother's waist and Susan clutched her daughter's shoulder as they left the hotel room. The sheriff's deputy was still standing by the door outside, holding Philip in his car seat.

"He's still sleeping," the deputy whispered hoarsely.

"Thank you." Susan reached for the car seat.

"I'll take him to the car for you," said the deputy. "Got one of my own comin' in a coupla weeks. Be good practice for me."

It wasn't until they were halfway home that Susan remembered what she had done to Muncrief's garage door. I should have told Sergeant Wallace, she said to herself. Then she thought, No. It's better that I didn't. Let me get the kids home and settled in bed.

"Daddy killed Mr. Muncrief," Angela whispered in the darkness of the car.

"What?"

Her voice trembling slightly, Angela said, "Daddy said he was going to kill him, and Mr. Muncrief just fell down and died."

"Your father didn't kill Mr. Muncrief, Angie. He had a stroke and died, just like Grandpop Santorini, remember?"

"Daddy was awful mad at him."

"I know. I don't blame him for that, do you?"

"No. He came and rescued me."

"Yes he did, didn't he? But he didn't kill Mr. Muncrief. Your father is too sweet a man to kill anybody."

Angie had screamed when Muncrief collapsed. Dan had whirled about and scooped her back into the safety of his arms.

"It's all right, Angel. It's all right. Nobody's going to hurt you. I've got you, and nobody's going to touch you until the police come and bring you home."

Angela peeped around her father's protective form. Muncrief had disappeared.

"He—he's not there anymore," she said, her voice wavering.

Dan turned back and saw that Muncrief had indeed disappeared. The bed, the tower-top room, all the trappings of the castle simulation were still there and solid as rock. But Muncrief was gone.

He knelt on one knee to be on eye level with his daughter. There was a lot of explaining to do.

"Now, listen to me, Angel. You remember the motel room where Mr. Muncrief took you?"

She nodded, on the verge of tears.

"Well, in a few minutes you're going to find yourself in that room again. Just like you come back to the VR booth when you play the games at school, you'll be back in the room where you started. Do you understand?"

Angela nodded.

"There'll be policemen in there with you, honey. They've been searching for you, because your mother and I didn't know where Mr. Muncrief had taken you. You're not afraid of policemen, are you?"

"No." Weakly.

"They'll be in the room with you because we asked them to find you."

"But you found me . . ."

"That's right, I did. But I've found you in this game, right? We're still in the game, in the castle. See?"

She glanced around, then turned her gaze back on her father's eyes.

"The policemen will be in the real world. Your mother's waiting for you in the real world, honey. So's little Phil. He misses his big sister."

She almost smiled. "He's asleep by now."

He conceded the point with a nod. "I'm in that real world, too, honey. But not in that hotel room. I'm at my lab, but I'll come right home so we can all be together again."

"I'm sorry I stayed away after school."

"That's all right, Angel. It's all okay now."

She threw her arms around her father's neck and kissed him on the cheek. Dan clasped his daughter for a moment longer.

Then, "One more thing, Angel. When you go back into that room, with the police and all, Mr. Muncrief is going to be there."

He felt her stiffen in his arms.

"He'll be dead, sweetheart. I'm pretty sure of that. Or at least he'll be unconscious. The police will be there to protect you, in any case."

"Will Mommy be there?"

"I don't know. Probably not. But either she'll come to where you are or the police will bring you home and she'll be there."

Angela nodded solemnly. Dan knew this was a lot for a kid to absorb in just a few minutes, especially after what she had just been through.

"Daddy?" she whispered into his ear.

"What is it, honey?"

"Did you *kill* Mr. Muncrief?"

The question stunned him. And before he could even try to frame an answer, Angela disappeared from his arms. Suddenly Dan was alone, kneeling in the fantasy-castle bedroom, his arms empty as if Angela had never been there. She never was, he realized, getting to his feet. She never really was.

His shirt lay on the carpeted floor. Dan picked it up and realized that Angie would be naked except for the sensor net when she came out of the game. The anger flared in him again. She'll be stark goddamned naked in front of a bunch of policemen.

Dan waited impatiently for the illusion to disappear as he pulled on his shirt and stuffed it into the waistband of his slacks. He knew he was in the VR chamber at ParaReality. Time to go home and hold his daughter for real. Dan felt tired, drained; it would be good to go to bed and sleep with Susan beside him.

The tower bedchamber remained.

"Come on, Jace," he called. "Wrap it up." And he started to remove his helmet.

"Not just yet, Danno." Jace's voice in his earphones was low, strained.

"Come on—"

"I mean it, Dan! You try to take that helmet off and I'll zap you just like I zapped Muncrief."

CHAPTER 49

What the hell do you mean?" Dan said. But he took his hands off the helmet.

"I don't know what to do about you, Dan. You're such a friggin' straight arrow. You're gonna make trouble for me, aren't you?"

Feeling only slightly ridiculous to be talking to a disembodied voice in a castle-tower bedchamber that did not really exist, Dan replied, "You just murdered a man, Jace. That makes three you've killed."

"Ralph and the other flyboy were accidents. I didn't mean for them to die, not really. I just wanted to teach Ralph a lesson. I *told* you that," Jace said, his voice growing irritable.

"And Muncrief?"

"He wanted to die. He said so himself, you heard him. I just put him out of his misery."

"That's called homicide, Jace. Murder."

"And you're gonna turn me in?"

As calmly as he could, Dan said, "I'm going to see to it that you get help. No matter what you've done, Jace, you're still my friend, my partner. I won't let you down. I'll help you all I can."

"By puttin' me in some funny farm? No, thanks."

Dan's chest felt raw, tight. "So what are you going to do, kill me, too?"

"Naw, I don't wanna do that."

"Then what?"

"I don't know what to do! Lemme think a minute."

"The first thing to do," Dan said slowly, "is button up this sim so we can talk this over face-to-face."

A long silence. Dan waited for a reply, but none came. He tried to calm his breathing, tried to soothe the rasping in his lungs. *Maybe I could snatch the helmet off my head and then I'd be out of this. Maybe he's not paying attention to me, not fully. I could get it off before he knows I've made a move.*

But Dan found that he could not move his arms. It was as if the gloves on his hands weighed ten tons each. He could no longer raise his hands from his sides.

Jace laughed. "You're as transparent as glass, Danno. And don't you think that if I could make that hillbilly Rucker think he's got two good arms I can fix *you* so you can't move your arms at all?"

"Jesus Christ, Jace, what're you going to do, keep me in here forever?"

That hushed, tense voice, almost a whisper, answered, "No, that wouldn't work."

"Then what?"

"Look outside."

Dan looked at the wide window. It had no glass. In this fantasyland there were no insect pests, no cold winds or rain. He saw that it was full daylight out there, bright sunshine bathed the wooded hills and gently rolling meadows.

"Go to the window and look down," Jace's voice instructed.

Dan did as he was told. A knight in black armor sat on a powerful black charger at the base of the castle wall. He held a lance in one mailed fist upright like a flagpole. At the lance's pointed end fluttered a sky-blue pennant with white lettering emblazoned: *Who Dares Wins.*

"What's that all about?" Dan asked the empty room.

"Who dares wins. That's what it's all about, Danny boy. That's what it's always been all about. Who dares wins."

"I don't get it."

"It's simple, pal. I'm not leaving you alone in the simulation. I'm coming in with you. I'm the black knight. You're going to fight me. Who dares wins."

Unconsciously rubbing at the pain in his chest, Dan replied, "I've got to fight you?"

"Until you admit that I'm right and you're wrong. Until you swear to me that you won't make any trouble out there."

"Jace, you can't do—"

"I can do anything I friggin' want to! You're in *my* world now, Danno, and you're gonna play by my rules."

"You're just as crazy as Muncrief!"

"Yeah? By the time I'm through with you, pal, you'll be on your knees worshiping me."

"Turn off the goddamned simulation," Dan shouted.

Jace laughed. "There's only one way out of my world, Danno. You've got to beat me."

Dan remembered the asthma attack that had crippled him only hours earlier. And the gunfight where Jace had killed him. The crazy sonofabitch wants to keep me in here until he's got me completely cowed. He wants to dominate me so completely that I'll do whatever he wants.

"Come on, Dan. Go down and get into your armor. Prepare to meet your maker. Pronto, Tonto."

Anger flared through Dan like crackles of electrical sparks along his nerves. His chest was raw, tightening painfully. But he told himself, It's only a matter of time until somebody gets to the lab and shuts down this sim. Maybe Gary Chan or one of the technicians will see what's going on and turn off the power. Maybe the police will come in. What time is it? How long until the office opens in the morning?

"Nobody's gonna bother us, Danno," Jace said. "Anybody tries to shut down this sim, it'll zap your brain automatically."

"Not yours?"

Jace laughed. "Hey, d'you think I'm stupid enough to rig my own suicide?"

"Jace, this isn't the way—"

"Better get your armor on, Tonto. I wouldn't want to zap you in cold blood."

"I'm not going to fight you, Jace."

"You wanna die like Muncrief did?" Jace's voice flared with anger. "I'm givin' you a chance."

"With the deck loaded in your favor."

"Hey, I'll be fair and square! All you've gotta do is beat me. If you can."

Dan looked out the window again. The black knight held his lance aloft. The pennant fluttered in the breeze. And when Dan turned away he saw that the bedroom had changed into some sort of armory, with shields hanging on the walls and lances stacked in rows and two silent, stolid men standing waiting for him, sections of armor in their hands. The armor was dazzling white.

"You're the good guy," Jace's voice said, with an audible sneer.

It took only minutes for the two armorers to suit Dan from head to toe in the steel plate. The armor weighed nothing. They buckled a huge sword to his side and then slid an armored helmet over his head. None of them had any weight. Dan found that he could move his hands and arms once more, but shod in the armor, he could no longer feel his VR helmet.

"You can't get out of the game, Dan. Just like the laws of thermodynamics: you can't win, you can't even break even, and you can't get out of the game. Only, *I* make the laws here."

"This is ridiculous," Dan grumbled as his two armorers led him to his horse, caparisoned in white with crisscrossed red arrows, waiting patiently for him in the castle courtyard.

Dan squinted through the helmet's visor slits. It was hard to see anything except straight ahead. His armorers helped him up into the saddle and placed his armored feet into the stirrups. Then they handed up a big curved shield, white with the red arrow symbol.

"I don't know how to drive a horse," Dan complained.

"Like I do?" said Jace. "Don't worry about it, the horse knows the rules."

Dan's powerful steed trotted across the bare earth of the courtyard and through the big castle gate, hooves booming on the wooden drawbridge across the moat. Then they were out on the grass. The black knight sat on his mount a hundred yards away. Dan's two armorers had disappeared, or at least he could no longer see them in the restricted view through his visor.

"Hey, don't I get a lance?"

"Oops! Almost forgot."

Another squat, sour-faced man in grimy jerkin and trousers appeared at the horse's side and handed a six-foot-long wooden lance to Dan. It felt surprisingly light. Dan saw that its tip bore a needle-sharp steel point.

His horse trotted a few more paces out onto the green meadow. The black knight remained where he was, but lowered his lance and pointed it straight at Dan.

Dan's horse suddenly bolted into a flat-out charge, jouncing and banging across the grass so hard Dan almost fell out of his saddle. The black knight charged straight at him, smooth as a well-oiled machine. No telling how many times Jace has practiced this damned game, Dan thought. He tried to get the shield in front of him, between his body and the sharp point of that lance that was flying toward him with terrifying speed. He tried to aim his own wavering lance at the black knight's body.

The impact lifted him out of the saddle and flung him through the air. Dan felt nothing at first. The world tumbled dizzyingly in the slit view through his visor: black armor rushing past, then bright blue sky, fleecy clouds spinning past, and finally green grass and solid ground. He hit the ground with a crash, and it felt as if every bone in his body had been broken. His shield hung from his left arm, bent almost double from the impact of the lance that had struck it squarely in its center. Dan's own lance had been torn from his grasp.

Painfully, slowly, he pulled himself to his knees. The black knight was dozens of yards away, reining in his charger and turning the horse around. Dan fumbled for his sword, still on his knees, too weak to stand up.

The black knight swung a vicious spiked ball of iron at the end of a short chain and spurred his charger straight at Dan again. Dan held his sword in his right hand and tried to use his left to push himself to his feet. The black horse thundered down on him, and he raised his shield feebly to protect himself from the spiked iron mace. The black knight caught his shield with it and ripped it from Dan's arm. Dan screamed with the pain of his arm being torn out of its shoulder socket.

The black knight wheeled his horse around and swung the mace again. The iron ball caught Dan on the side of his helmet, knocking him flat again, ears ringing, head spinning dizzily. He saw the great black body of the horse stamping over him, those terrifying hooves pounding the grass next to him. *He's going to trample me!* Without thinking, Dan tightened his grip on his sword and rammed it upward into the horse's unprotected belly.

Everything went black.

"Goddammit, Danno, that's not fair! You killed my friggin' horse."

Dan lay panting in the darkness. He could feel the hard surface of the VR chamber floor beneath him. The fantasy world of armored knights was gone. He tried to bring his hands up to his face, but again his arms were just too heavy to move.

"You're not gettin' out yet, man," Jace said. "We haven't settled a friggin' thing yet." His voice in Dan's helmet earphones sounded surly, annoyed.

Dan lay flat on his back in utter darkness, struggling to breathe, the pain of his simulated wounds submerged by the real pain of asthma. *I've got to get out of this,* Dan thought, wheezing, straining for each breath. *He's going to kill me, one way or the other. He's gone crazy.*

"Let it go, Jace," he said, gasping. "This isn't going to solve anything."

"The hell it won't. I want your promise to keep quiet about the Air Force sim and Muncrief. You're a man of your word, Danno. I trust you. Just give me your word and I'll let you out."

Dan stayed silent.

"Okay, then," Jace taunted. "It's you against me. One on one. *Mano a mano.* You want to turn me over to the cops, you've got to beat me first."

Dan pushed himself up into a sitting position. Inside the VR helmet his breathing sounded like a ragged calliope. He remembered when the kids in school would laugh at him, make fun of his gasping struggles for breath. Even at home, his sister would giggle and his brother jeer.

"You're not gettin' out of this by pretending to be sick, Danny boy," Jace demanded, his voice hardening. "I didn't give you any asthma attack; you've done it to yourself."

Dan remembered his father hollering at him, exasperated, frightened, angry, "It's your own damned fault! If you'd go out into the air once in a while instead of sticking your nose in books all the time, maybe you'd breathe better!" And the doctors, even when he was a grown man, "Asthma has a large psychological component, Mr. Santorini. In your case, it's almost entirely psychological. Have you seen a psychologist about your condition?" And even Susan, "You've got to learn how to relax, Dan. You never get asthma when we're making love, do you?"

They all blame me. Like I want this. Like I enjoy gasping like a motherfucking fish out of water.

"Come on, Danno," said Jace. "You've had enough time to rest. On your feet. We're going to the O.K. Corral, pardner."

Dan felt icy fear clutch at his heart. He remembered Jace gunning him down, the shock and pain of the bullets, the bottomless pit of death. Slowly he struggled to his feet as if in response to Jace's command.

But his mind was racing. "Wait a minute," he said. "Don't I get a chance to pick the game we use?"

"What's the matter? Scared of the gunfight scenario?"

He could sense Jace's amusement. But Dan felt something else flowing through him: burning anger, rage at himself, at everyone he had ever known, everyone who had poked fun at him or muscled him around. Soaring fury at Muncrief and Jace, who had tried to take his daughter, tried to destroy his family. And now Jace is trying to destroy me. He thinks he owns me. Thinks he can beat me and kill me, thinks he's God inside his machine.

"You're the one who's scared, Jace. Scared to let me pick the game we use."

"I'm the boss in this universe. I do whatever I friggin' feel like."

"Some boss. You're scared of the real world, aren't you? You're just an overgrown kid hiding from his mommy and daddy, aren't you?"

"You're gonna regret you said that."

"What are you going to do, kill me?" Dan countered.

"I could."

Dan's mind was searching frantically. Any edge I can find, anything that'll shake him out of a scenario that he's obviously played a thousand times. "Then do it in the Moonwalk sim," he blurted.

"Charlie Chan's game?"

"Show me how good you are on the Moon, Jace."

He heard Jace's low chuckle. "You think the low gravity's gonna give you some kind of edge, don't you?"

"Maybe," he said, hoping desperately for exactly that.

"Okay," Jace said, amusement in his voice. "We can have a shoot-out on the Moon, I guess. With laser pistols instead of six-guns. You'll be just as dead at the end of it; what's the difference?"

"So do it," Dan snapped. "Set up the Moonwalk game."

"Hold on a minute."

Dan thought that now was the time to take off his VR helmet and get out of this, but his hands would not leave his sides.

"You don't think I'm that dumb, do you, Dan?"

He's still got me locked in here. Christ, are we going to stay in this fantasy of his forever? No, Dan realized. Just until he kills me. Jace is going to keep playing these stupid games until he kills me. Like a cat playing with a mouse. He'll keep it going, no matter how many simulations it takes. He'll stay locked inside his own fantasy universe until the games actually do kill me. Or maybe he'll get tired of it and kill me outright, the way he killed Muncrief.

The best I can do, the best I can hope for, is to kill him first. Or take him down with me.

Susan was drowsing on the living-room sofa when the front doorbell chimed. She awoke with a start and glanced at the clock on the wall between the two front windows: 1:21. Dan's not home yet!

She got to the door as the chime sounded again. It was Sergeant Wallace, looking like a worried grandfather.

"What's wrong?" she blurted. "Where's my husband?"

The sergeant shifted his feet slightly, broad-brimmed hat in both hands. "He's at the ParaReality building, just like yew said, missus."

"Is he all right?"

"I think so. Kinda hard to say, really. We got that one-armed security guard of theirs out of bed to open up the building for us. Mr. Santorini and that other fella, Lowrey—they seem to be locked inside one of the laboratory chambers or whatever that room is. None of my people knows how to get them out. The two of 'em seem to be cut off from seeing us or hearing us."

Susan clung to the door for support. She felt totally drained. She needed Dan here, home. "They're in a simulation together?"

"If that's what you call it."

Why? Susan asked herself. Why would Dan still be in the simulation? And with Jace.

"I got a policewoman in the car," Sergeant Wallace said. "State trooper. She can sit with yer kids if yew want to come to the building with me and see if yew can figure out how to get them out of there."

Feeling dazed with fatigue, Susan managed to mumble, "Yes . . . all right. Let me—"

"Yew take all th' time yew need, Mrs. Santorini. From the looks of things, those two guys aren't going anywhere."

The state policewoman looked terribly young to be carrying a pistol, but she smiled reassuringly at Susan. "I have two little brothers at home; I was baby-sitting before I learned to read."

Susan worried that Angie would be frightened if she woke up and found this stranger with her instead of her mother.

"Don't worry about nothin'," said the policewoman. "I can change diapers blindfolded, and if your little girl wakes up I'll tell her you've gone out to fetch her daddy."

"All right," said Susan at last. "Thanks."

Sergeant Wallace showed her to the front seat of his cruiser. As they started off for the ParaReality building, he muttered, "Damnedest thing I ever saw: your husband and this other guy inside this spooky room with some kinda helmets on, like bikers, you know, with visors down over their eyes. They were jumpin' around like a coupla freaks in there."

"It's all right," Susan said, staring into the night darkness whizzing past her window. "It's a kind of game. An electronic game."

Joe Rucker let them in the front door and they hurried down the corridor to the VR lab, Rucker limping along behind them.

Wallace yanked open the door to the control booth. Seeing the array of dials and screens, Susan realized that she did not know any more than the police sergeant about how to operate the equipment.

"We'll have to call one of the technicians," she said. "Dan told me he had worked with somebody named Chan."

"Gary Chan," said Rucker, leaning against the open doorway. "I can look him up in th' phone directory and call him."

Wallace looked at Susan, who nodded. "Do that," the sergeant said to Rucker.

As the security guard lumbered eagerly away, Susan stepped to the bank of consoles and peered through the one-way window into the darkened simulation chamber. Her heart clutched in her chest.

She saw Dan lying facedown on the floor, as if he were dead.

CHAPTER 50

D an waited in total darkness in the VR chamber. He tested his strength again but he still could not move his arms.

"If I wanted to murder you, Danno, I could've done it about six million times," said Jace's disembodied voice. "But I always give the other guy a fair chance."

"Like Ralph?" Dan snapped.

"That asshole could've stayed out of the sim. He wanted to be the big-shit hero. He killed himself."

Dan did not reply. The anger that had boiled within him had damped down now, but it simmered hot through his blood. Dan nursed his anger, fed on it. Adrenaline, he knew. That's what they inject you with in the hospital to stop an asthma attack. That's what happened to me when I had to fight Jace. My own glands pumped adrenaline into my bloodstream. I stopped the asthma myself.

Despite himself, the anger was ebbing away. Dan's lungs felt okay, but he wondered how long that would last. Got to think clear and fast, he told himself. This is life and death, this game Jace is playing. The only way out of this is over his body. I hope I don't have to kill him. But if that's the only way out, that's what I'll have to do. Just stay calm, think clearly. You've got to stay at least one jump ahead of him. The Moonwalk gives you an edge. Maybe. Maybe.

I just hope he really is setting up the Moonwalk, Dan thought. I can handle that. I'm sure of it. And maybe he doesn't know that Chan worked out the low-gravity stuff. Maybe that's the edge I need.

It was like being bound and blindfolded. Dan could not move his arms or see anything but blank darkness. He stood there waiting like a prisoner facing a firing squad. Nothing to be afraid of, he told himself. He's just using his remote-control box to set up the programming. Maybe he's taking his time just to make me sweat. He's enjoying this cat-and-mouse stuff. All those years, and he never really saw me as anything but a fucking mouse for him to use.

Well, we'll see about that soon enough.

"Okay, Danno, we're off to the Moon."

The darkness lightened, but not much. Dan saw that he now wore a bulky space suit of gleaming white. He was standing on the utterly barren landscape of a lunar plain. The uneven ground was bare, crusted over like a poor blacktop job, pockmarked with little craters as if somebody had been poking fingers into the surface. Rocks and pebbles everywhere, some considerable boulders a hundred yards or so away. Tired old smooth-worn mountains slumped over by the horizon. A gibbous blue and white Earth hung in the black sky, fat and glowing.

Is this the version with Chan's gravity subprogram? Dan took a few tentative steps. Yes! His booted feet seemed to float off the ground; each stride was like a broad jump.

"Hey, I'm over here," Jace called. "This-a-way."

Dan turned and saw a dim figure standing amid a jumble of house-size boulders, half the distance to the horizon. Jace was encased in a shiny black space suit with a bubble helmet that glinted slightly in the wan earthlight. It was night on the Moon, but in the airless lunar landscape the glow from the daylit side of Earth made an eerie twilight.

"A black space suit?" Dan said.

"That's 'cause I'm the baaadest badass this side of Copernicus."

Dan realized that although Jace was standing amid the boulders, he himself was out in the open with nothing bigger to protect him than a scattering of fist-size rocks strewn along the ground.

"Your space suit is nice and white," Jace said. "I can see you fine."

Dan saw that Jace wore a metallic holster fastened to his left hip. Reaching down with his gloved right hand, Dan felt the butt of a pistol.

"So what do we do?" Dan asked. "Count to three and draw?"

"Sure. But let's do it like a countdown, NASA style." Without waiting for a reply Jace swiftly counted, "Three, two, one, *draw!*"

Dan was still tugging at the pistol clipped to the flank of his space suit when a pencil-thin beam of ruby red lanced through the darkness and exploded at his feet. Startled, Dan jumped sideways, a long lunar jump, like floating in a dream. He had time to realize that the beam of laser light was an artifact Chan had put into the game; on the airless Moon, any light beam would be invisible. Landing on the thick soles of his boots, Dan staggered and struggled to stay upright.

"That's right, buddy! Dance!" Jace laughed wildly and fired again at Dan's feet.

Dan dodged backward. Jace's having fun, is he? Dan held his arm out straight and fired his laser pistol. A beam of electric-blue light shot out and hit the boulder nearest Jace. His black-suited figure ducked behind the boulder.

"Come on, chicken!" Dan yelled, forgetting that they were speaking to each other over their suit radios. "Don't hide. Come on out and fight!"

"No more Mr. Nice Guy," Jace's voice replied, flat and hard.

Dan had no cover. He knew that if he tried to run in this low gravity, he would end up floating like a balloon from one stride to another, an easy target. Got to get him out from behind those rocks. Got to get him before he gets me. Carefully he got down on his hands and knees and began crawling slowly, hoping that Chan hadn't made the simulation so realistic that he could tear his space suit and kill himself by blowing all the air out of the suit.

A glint of light off Jace's helmet warned him. Jace popped out from the other side of the boulder, fired, and ducked back again. The beam went wide.

"Is that the best you can do, chickenshit?" Dan called as he inched carefully toward the boulders.

"I'm just giving you a chance to say your prayers, pardner," Jace retorted.

"The hell you are." Dan fired at the spot where he had last seen Jace. Then he squirted a blast at the other side of the boulder. The rock exploded where the blue beam touched it, puffing out silent bursts of gas and rock chips in the airless vacuum.

Hoping that would keep Jace behind the boulder, Dan crabbed sideways, scuffing his boots and one gloved hand across the lunar soil, scraping up clouds of dust that blossomed and fell back to the ground with the slowness of a dream.

Got to get to those boulders so I can have some protection, Dan thought. But the closer I get to them, the closer I get to him.

He didn't see Jace this time until the red laser beam seared the left shoulder of his suit. There was no impact, but from inside the suit Dan heard the hiss of escaping air. How long before the suit decompresses? He had no idea.

"How's that, wiseass?" Jace taunted. "Got you, didn't I?"

He had ducked behind the boulder without looking to see how much damage he had done.

Dan stretched himself onto the ground facedown. He lay sprawled on the cold lunar dust; the only sounds he could hear were his suit air hissing away and his own terrified breathing.

"Dan?" Jace called.

He said nothing. Let him think I'm dead. Or passed out, at least.

"Dan?" That was Sue's voice! "Dan, it's me! Susan! Are you all right? We're going to get you out of there!"

"No!" Jace yelled. "Anybody touches the controls and Dan gets fried! Understand? Don't touch a friggin' thing or you'll kill him!"

Stretched out on the ground, his chin plastered against the transparent plastic of his helmet, Dan looked up and saw Jace pop up from behind one of the boulders, waving his arms, screaming:

"Stay out of it! This is between him and me. Don't touch any of the controls. None of 'em, you understand?"

Jace was bobbing sideways as he yelled, floating in the low lunar gravity like a scarecrow being blown by puffs of wind.

Sighting carefully, Dan squeezed the trigger of his laser pistol. The blue beam struck Jace's suit squarely on the chest. Dan moved the beam upward to Jace's helmet. It exploded in a silent shower of air and blood and brains.

And Dan was lying facedown on the floor of the simulation chamber in his pants and sweat-soaked shirt, his data-gloved hands empty, the helmet on his head the one he had put on to get into the VR simulation. Dan felt weak, drained, but he found that he could move his hands. He pushed himself to a sitting position and slid the visor of his helmet up, squinting to focus his eyes in the dim lighting of the VR chamber.

Jace was across the room, slumped against the wall in a sitting position, chin on his chest, VR helmet twisted slightly awry.

"You cheated," Jace accused, like a sullen little boy. "Susie distracted me."

"Give it up, Jace," Dan said.

"Like hell."

"Susan must have brought the police with her. It's all over now."

For several moments, Jace said nothing. He just sat there limp as a scarecrow, staring at Dan, his narrow eyes red with something close to hatred.

"I'm gonna kill you, pal," Jace said at last. "This is the end of the game."

Dan saw that Jace held the remote-control unit in his left hand. He tried to scramble to his feet and take off his VR helmet at the same time, but suddenly his legs would not work and his arms were once again too heavy to move. He flopped to the floor with a painful thump.

"Dan! Are you all right?" Susan called.

"Don't touch any of the controls," Jace warned again, scrambling to his feet. "They're slaved to my remote unit. If you try to change 'em, it'll kill Dan."

"Dan?"

"I'm all right, Sue," he said, still lying on the floor helpless as a boated fish. "Do what Jace says; leave everything alone."

Dan watched, paralyzed, as Jace slowly walked over to him. Jace dropped to his knees beside Dan and carefully, almost tenderly, adjusted Dan's helmet.

"We coulda done really big stuff, Danno. I would've let you be my number-one man, my friend. But it's not gonna work out like that, is it?"

"Jace, you need help—"

He snorted angrily. "I don't need *anything*! Or anybody. I've got the power of life and death in my hands, pal. Just like God."

He slid the visor of Dan's helmet down over his eyes.

"Time to get this over with," Jace said.

Dan lay there, immobilized, waiting for the inevitable. He knew what Jace was setting up. The gunfight. He's going to kill me again. Only, this time it's going to be for real.

Susan and Sergeant Wallace watched the two men capering in the simulations chamber. To Susan it looked like two little boys playing a game of imaginary cops and robbers. Bang, bang, I got you! No, you missed!

But that was her husband in there, and Jace had gone insane. Could he really kill Dan? Is there any way I can stop this game and get Dan out of there? Jace said if we touched the controls we would kill Dan. Is he bluffing or did he really kill Ralph and Kyle?

The outside door of the control booth squealed open and a young Chinese-American stepped in. He had obviously been rousted from his bed; eyes still puffy, stiff black hair uncombed, wrinkled white shirt tucked unevenly into his dark slacks. He looked terribly worried, almost afraid.

"I'm Gary Chan," he said in a whisper. "You must be Dan's wife. What's going on?"

"Can yew turn off this machinery?" Sergeant Wallace asked curtly.

"I don't see why not." Chan slid into one of the chairs and looked over the control board.

"Jace said if we touched the controls it would kill Dan," Susan blurted.

"That's Jace and Dan in there?"

"Yes!"

Chan pulled his hands back from the board as if it were a hot stove. "Who's been running the controls?"

"Nobody," said Sergeant Wallace.

"I think Jace has some sort of remote control in there with him," Susan said.

Chan blew out a breath and tugged at his ear. "And Jace said if we tried to shut down the sim it would kill Dan?"

"That's what he said."

He kept scratching at the ear. "Let me think about this. Jace must have rigged the controls in some way, but it'll take a while for me to figure out what he's done."

"Can you undo it?" Susan asked.

"I don't know. First I've got to see what he's done."

Sergeant Wallace said, "Well, get to it, son. From what we've overheard on this intercom, this man Jace intends to murder Mr. Santorini."

"For God's sake, Jace," Dan was saying, "Susan's in the control booth watching us. The police must be here by now. You can't get out of this. Give it up."

Jace giggled. "Let 'em watch. I'd like to see them try to prove I murdered anybody."

Dan was still sheathed in darkness, unable to move. Except for Jace's voice in his helmet earphones, he was totally cut off from the real world.

"I can just see 'em all in court, saying they saw me kill you," Jace said. "Some big-deal eyewitnesses. Did you see a murder weapon? I'll ask 'em. No, the defendant did not have a weapon in his hands. What did the decedent die from? A massive cerebral hemorrhage. So how could the defendant have murdered the bum when he didn't have a weapon and the guy died of a friggin' stroke?"

"You know that's all a lie," said Dan, desperately stalling for time, hoping to find a way out of this endless cycle of killing.

"Prove it," Jace taunted. "Get the best friggin' lawyers in the world and they won't be able to prove it. Perry Mason couldn't pin a thing on me, pal! And besides, I've got the White House to protect me. Nobody's gonna lay a finger on me, Danno. I'll dance on your grave, buddy."

Before Dan could reply, the darkness began to shift. Grays and milky whites flowed softly before his eyes, slowly turning to colors, shifting, melding, blending into a wide billowing ocean. Dan felt a jolt of surprise; he had expected the western town, the O.K. Corral gunfight. But he found himself bobbing up and down in the middle of an endless sea, nothing but surging deep-blue waves no matter where he looked. No land, no ships, no birds in the air, an empty horizon beneath a cloudless sky of purest azure with a brazen hot sun blazing down.

Terrified, Dan tread water, flailing his arms and legs. His feet could not feel the bottom. His clothes sagged and pulled at him. Salt water splashed his face, stinging his eyes, sloshing into his gasping mouth.

I can't swim! I don't even know if I can float for long.

"This is *my* version of Neptune's Kingdom, pal," said Jace's voice out of nowhere.

Something touched Dan's leg. He twitched in sudden fear and thrashed about clumsily, swallowing more salt water, coughing, sputtering, desperately struggling to keep his head above water.

"Down you go, pal."

A tentacle wrapped itself around Dan's leg and pulled him under. He wanted to scream. It wasn't an octopus but a gigantic squid, platter-size round eyes staring. Dan tried to hold his breath, flailing and straining against the tentacle's strong grip, bubbles gurgling in his ears as the squid dragged him deeper and deeper.

Can't breathe!

And then it let go. The squid simply disappeared. Dan felt as if his lungs were bursting. *Can't breathe!* The sunlit surface of the ocean was miles above.

Sharks! Sleek, voracious killing machines gliding swiftly toward him. Three, five, a dozen, each of them huge and deadly, slicing through the water with terrifying ease. He wanted to scream. He wanted to get up into the air where he could breathe. Thrashing arms and legs pitifully, he tried to get away from the sharks.

But they were circling, circling, drawing closer while the pain seared Dan's chest and the fear thundered in his ears so loudly, he thought his heart would explode.

One of the sharks nudged him with its snout. He flailed out at it. Then he saw another rushing at him like a torpedo, its huge mouth opening wide, thousands of sharp white teeth like the gateway to hell rushing at him. Dan screamed as the shark bit him almost in two. Salt water filled his mouth, filled his lungs as the ocean reddened with his blood while the shark tugged and waggled back and forth, tearing off a chunk of meat, of Dan's body. Then the next shark hit. And the next.

Dan felt every tooth, every shuddering jerking motion as they tore his bloody body to shreds. He died, he knew he was dead, yet he still existed. Disembodied, disemboweled, deep beneath the surface of the ocean, he watched the sharks' frenzied feeding.

"I'm not dead," he marveled. He could feel nothing, but he was still alive, still conscious.

"Guess that wasn't painful enough," Jace muttered, sounding disappointed. "The body's first reaction is shock; that suppresses the pain."

Before Dan could reply, the undersea world disappeared and he was on solid ground again. Chained firmly to a stake with a pile of faggots heaped around his bare feet.

Jace stood before him in a brown monk's robe, the hood pulled up over his head, a blazing torch held high in his left hand.

"You have been found guilty of heresy, my son," Jace intoned sorrowfully. "The penance your body is about to suffer will be the salvation of your immortal soul."

Jesus Christ, he's going to burn me alive! Dan watched, terrified, as Jace touched the torch's flame to the kindling at his feet. Flames crackled all around him. It's only a simulation, he told himself. The pain may be real, but this isn't really happening, it isn't really—

The flames roasted his feet and ran up the legs of his baggy trousers. Dan felt his flesh blistering, roasting. "It's not real! It's not real!" he heard himself screaming.

Through the flames and smoke he could see Jace watching him, face wavering in the heat, peering at him intently from beneath the hood of his brown robe, studying him with narrowed eyes.

Somewhere in a far corner of his deepest being, Dan felt a hatred, a raging fury as hot as the flames that were consuming him. You bastard, Dan thought. You sadistic maniac. You want to kill me, torture me to death. I won't let you. I won't give in. Never! Never!

The pain was a crescendo of flaming agony as Dan screamed and cursed and finally lost consciousness.

"I should've mapped out your brain," he heard Jace grumbling, as if from a far, far distance. "I don't know where the exact pain centers are. Got to guess at it."

I'm still alive, Dan thought, the breath shuddering in his throat.

I'm still alive. Barely. He realized he was flat on his back, helmet still on and visor still down over his eyes. But he had survived. Every muscle in his body was shuddering, every nerve raw. How much more can I take? he asked himself.

A cold wind tore through him as he clung to the rocky face of the cliff. He was thousands of feet above the floor of the rocky gorge, the cliff's crest still far above him, lost in swirls of snow and cloud. He clung to the bare rock, tried to press his body against it while the whipping wind howled and tried to rip him away from his precarious perch.

I've got to climb all the way up there, he told himself. The top of the cliff seemed miles away, its face as sheer and smooth as a block of ice. Got to . . . get up there, Dan grunted silently as he reached up for a fresh handhold. The wind drove needles of ice into him, clawed at his pain-racked body, stung his face raw. One bleeding hand at a time, one booted foot searching for a fraction of an inch to grip, he edged his way higher.

It seemed like hours. Only once did he dare to look down, and the long drop made his senses reel.

Primal fears, he realized. Jace is playing on the primal fears. Drowning, sharks, fire—and now this. The fear of falling. It's wired deep down in our guts. It haunts our nightmares.

He could feel his strength draining away. His arms ached, his back was afire, his legs going numb from exertion. But he kept climbing, inch by agonizing inch, forced himself to keep moving, keep clawing toward the top while the bitter wind stung his face and tried to pluck him off the cliff.

"I'll beat you, Jace," he said to the shrieking wind. "I'll beat you."

"Guess again, Danno."

And the slim ledge beneath Dan's left boot crumbled away. His right foot slipped from its perch and he was dangling by his hands, the wind whipping at him, scrambling madly for another foothold. But his aching raw bleeding hands were too weak, his fingers were slipping from the smooth cold rock, he was going to fall, plunge all the way down to the sharp jutting rocks so far below.

"Are we having fun yet?" Jace's laconic voice called.

Hardly thinking about it, Dan planted both his boots against the rock face, let go with his hands, and pushed as hard as he could with his legs. He tumbled into the empty air, free of everything except gravity.

No sense of falling. No sensation at all except the wind fluttering at him and an exhilaration he had never known before. Dan was soaring free, arms and legs outstretched, sailing through the air like an eagle.

He looked up at the regal-blue sky and laughed. "I did it myself," he yelled into the wind. "I made the decision, Jace. Not you."

No response.

Dan pinwheeled through the empty air, laughing. "I've always wanted to try skydiving. Never had the nerve before."

Suddenly everything went black once more. Dan could feel a solid floor beneath his feet. He sensed he was back in the VR chamber.

"What's next, Jace?" he asked. "How much imagination do you have left?"

"Dan, can you hear me? It's Gary Chan."

"Keep your hands off the controls, Charlie!" Jace's voice roared. "Don't touch anything!"

Chan seemed to ignore Jace's warning. "Dan, I think I can figure out how to get you out of there. But it's going to take a little time to bypass—"

"Don't touch a friggin' thing!" Jace howled. "I'll zap him if you try it!"

"Gary," said Dan, holding his arms out in front of him like a blind man. "Leave everything alone. This is between Jace and me. Stay out of it until I tell you it's okay."

"Until *you* tell him?" Jace sounded amused, scornful.

Dan's legs felt shaky, his chest raw. But he answered, "That's right, Jace. You can't kill me. I'll take whatever you throw at me. I know this is just a sim. I'm not going to have a stroke. I've got a reason to survive, to get through all this."

The visor was still over his eyes, effectively blindfolding him. Dan felt as if he could move his arms now and take his helmet off. But he did not want to. Not now.

"What reason?" Jace growled.

"I'm going to beat you," said Dan. "I'm going to beat you at your own game. In your own world, Jace. You think you're the top dog, king of the hill. You think you're God? You're nothing but a scared kid who's never grown up. And I'm better than you are, Jace. Better and stronger."

"But, Dan," said Dr. Appleton, "you don't really feel that way, do you?"

Appleton stood before Dan, gray and rumpled in a tweed sports jacket, his everlasting pipe in his left hand.

"I mean, Dan," the Doc said softly, "you know that Jace is the most creative mind we've ever seen. You're his right-hand man, that's true, but you're not as good as Jace is. We both know that."

Appleton was walking slowly toward Dan, speaking earnestly, gesturing with his slim-stemmed pipe.

"After all," he went on, "I only hired you because Jace needed an assistant. And Muncrief only hired you because Jace liked having you around."

They were face-to-face, hardly a foot separating them. Dan caught a glint of light and saw that Doc's pipe had turned into a knife. Doc lunged, but Dan grabbed his wrist and held it. Doc's face melted, shifted. It was Dan's father now, angry and accusing:

"If you spent more time outside in the fresh air, you wouldn't get these goddamned asthma attacks!"

"It won't work, Jace. I'm not an impressionable twelve-year-old. All you're doing is making me madder than hell at you."

And he twisted Jace's wrist until he yelped and dropped the knife. Then Dan let go and pushed Jace away.

"Two mistakes, Jace," Dan told him. "Doc's right-handed. And when you mentioned Muncrief, you reminded me that he hired me because of Angie. All you're doing is pumping up my adrenaline. That's no way to induce an asthma attack, genius."

"Dan, Dan, come back to me."

He turned and saw Dorothy, wearing nothing but a filmy clinging negligee, smiling at him.

"We can be together now, Dan. Always. There's nothing to stop us; you can have me forever." Dorothy slipped the negligee's thin straps off her shoulders, let it fall to her hips, to the ground.

"I love you, Dan. I've always loved you."

"You're not real," Dan said to her. "I guess you never were."

"I can be as real as you want me to be," Dorothy pleaded. "I *need* you, Dan. Don't turn away from me."

But he did turn away. To find himself in a strange, narrow corridor of utterly blank walls that stretched off to infinity.

"I'm coming after you, Jace. You can't hide from me."

"Try and find me, Tonto!"

Dan swung a fist against the wall, and it shattered like a mirror. He stepped through into an even narrower corridor, dark and shadowy.

"What is this, the inside of your mind?"

"You'll find out."

Dan plodded forward. He tracked the length of the narrowing, twisting corridor, which turned into a dark cobblestoned street that slanted weirdly while a cold fog misted the night air and turned the tilting street lamps into feeble glows of yellowish light hanging disembodied and then it was a sewer knee-deep in fetid water, dark and foul, with the skittering screeching red-eyed rats hovering in the darkness.

"I'll find you, Jace, no matter where you try to hide. No matter how long it takes. You'll run out of these movie scenarios sooner or later and I'll still be here, coming at you."

A monster rose up out of the filthy water, its scarred face green with putrefaction, looming over Dan, stretching out its powerful arms toward him.

"I saw this movie when I was a kid, Jace." Dan made himself laugh. The monster reached out for him, but Dan kicked it in its shins and it yowled and disappeared.

"You can't scare me, Jace. I'm past all that. Cut the crap and let's get this over with."

"You'll never find me!"

And they were in a hall of mirrors, a hundred Jaces reflecting off the faceted glass, a hundred lean angular scarecrow figures capering and yowling at him.

Methodically Dan began smashing the mirrors. One by one he kicked them into shards of glass, punched them with his balled fists. "I'm coming for you, Jace," he called out. His fists were bloody, but Dan felt no pain at all. He smashed mirror after mirror until at last there was only one Jace standing before him, looking furious and frightened at the same time.

"All right," Jace said, his voice murderously low. "You think you're better than me? Prove it."

And the scene before Dan's eyes shifted again. Brilliant sunlight stabbed down at him, making him squint. It was the cartoonlike western town. It was what Dan had expected all along. Jace stood about a dozen paces in front of him, lean and lanky in his black gunfighter's outfit, a nasty scowl on his long face, a broad-brimmed black Stetson pulled low over his red-rimmed eyes.

"Is this the best you can do?" Dan taunted. "Are you all out of ideas, Jace?"

"This is all I need," Jace said. "This time I'm going to blow you away."

Despite himself, Dan felt a current of fear race along his nerves. But he fought it down and let the rage that smoldered inside drive him. Going to kill me, are you? Like hell you are!

"I'll give you a fair chance, Sheriff," Jace drawled. "I'll let you go for your gun first."

Wordlessly, stoking his fury, Dan stepped toward Jace. Toward the man who exposed his daughter to Muncrief. Toward the man who wanted to kill him. Toward the man who had ruined his career, his life, his dreams of using his knowledge to make the world better. Toward this friend who had turned into a murderous enemy.

"Hey," Jace said, backing away uneasily. "You're gettin' too close—"

Dan lunged at him and Jace pulled his gun at the same instant. Dan barged into Jace, knocking the gun to one side and driving the two of them into the dusty ground. The gun went off, but Dan barely heard it; he had one knee on Jace's thin chest and the other on his gun arm. He punched Jace's face with both fists.

"Going to kill me, huh? Going to help that sonofabitch rape my daughter? You stupid asshole piece of shit!"

Jace tried to twist away, tried to protect himself with his thin arms, but Dan held him pinned to the ground and pounded and pounded while the whole world went blood red with his rage.

And suddenly other arms were pulling him off Jace and everything went black and all he could feel was searing pain in both his hands and Susan calling, half sobbing, "Dan! Dan! Dan!"

CHAPTER 51

hen he woke up Dan found himself in a hospital bed, both his hands wrapped in bandages and an angry buzz in his ears. His eyes felt gummy; it took a few moments to focus them.

Susan was sitting beside the bed, half-asleep.

"What time is it?"

Her eyes flicked wide, then she smiled at her husband. "How do you feel?"

Dan shook his head tentatively. The room swayed. "Like I've got a hangover," he muttered.

"It must be the painkillers. You broke several knuckles punching Jace's helmet."

Dan looked down at his hands. The bandages were clean and white. They felt stiff, but he did not try to flex his fingers to test them.

"They'll be okay, the doctors said. It'll take a month or so, but they'll be all right."

"How long . . . ?"

Susan glanced at her wristwatch. "It's almost noon."

He thought a moment. "Tuesday?"

"Yes." Susan smiled at him. "They brought you here about three o'clock this morning. Gary Chan terminated the simulation after you knocked Jace unconscious."

Dan blinked, remembering. "Christ, I wanted to kill him."

Susan got up from her chair and came over to him. She sat on the edge of the bed.

"You saved Angie," she said.

"You found her."

"But you stopped Muncrief."

"Is he really dead?"

"Yes."

"It's a mess, isn't it?" he said.

"That doesn't matter. It's not important, Dan."

He reached up with his bandaged hands and pulled her to him. She kissed him, then broke into sobs. "I thought Jace was going to kill you!"

He held her tightly and patted her red hair gently. "It's all right, honey. I'm okay. Jace couldn't kill me."

"You beat him. We heard everything the two of you said. You told him you were going to beat him, and you did."

Susan pulled away slightly and dabbed at her eyes, and Dan saw a newfound admiration in her face. And the embers of stark fear.

"We heard Jace say he was going to kill you. I was so scared!"

Dan nodded. "Jace couldn't kill me. Even when he thought he wanted to, he couldn't go through with it. He just wanted to scare me. Cow me. Show me that he was better than me, stronger, smarter."

"But he's not," Susan said. "You're better than he is. You've always been."

"Maybe so." Dan sighed. "Maybe so." But I would've killed Jace, right there and then, he knew. I was mad enough to beat him to death.

Leaning on his elbows, Dan forced himself up to a sitting position. Susan cranked the bed up for him. He saw that they were in a private room.

"I hope the company's insurance covers this," he said.

"The government's paying for everything," Susan replied.

"Smith?"

"That's what Vickie told me. There are a couple of federal agents guarding the door. They don't want the media to know anything about this."

"How is Jace?"

Her eyes shifted away from him. "You broke his nose, and they think he's got a slight concussion."

Dan let his head sink back on the pillows. "What a mess. What a goddamned black hole of a mess."

"Angie's all right," Susan said. "You saved her."

He looked into his wife's eyes. Susan leaned over and kissed him again. "Nothing else matters, Dan. You saved our daughter from Muncrief."

He touched her cheek with his bandaged hand. "She's really okay?"

"Really. She's home right now with a psychologist from the school system baby-sitting. She's proud of her daddy. You rescued her."

"Yeah. But Muncrief's dead and the whole company's going to go down the tubes now. Unless—"

"You can get another job. A better job."

"What about Jace?"

He felt her body tense. "You don't need Jace."

"I know that. It's Smith I'm worried about. Him and his plans to put VR into the White House. Jace said Smith was going to protect him."

"Let him. What difference does it make?"

"VR shouldn't be used to manipulate people—especially the President of the United States."

"What's that got to do with us?"

"Honey, when they manipulate the President they manipulate us. All of us."

"But Smith—"

"Get him in here, will you, Sue? Find him, wherever he is, and get him in here. I've got to talk to him."

Susan gave Dan a strange look, then got up from the bed. With an odd little smile she said, "To hear is to obey, O master."

Dan lay back in the cranked-up bed, his mind whirling. So much had happened so fast. Got to call Doc and tell him about Jace and everything. Tell him the simulation's safe now. But Angie's okay. That's the most important part. Sue's right about that. Angie's okay. Got to build safeguards into the simulations. Got to make sure people can't tinker with them, corrupt them. But how? How?

He was still pondering when the door opened and Susan, Smith, and Vickie came in. Dan could see that there were two beefy men in dark suits standing guard out in the hallway.

"How are you feeling, Dan?" said Smith with a strained smile showing his perfect teeth.

"I'll be all right," Dan said.

Vickie looked like a woman who had just lost her boss and probably her job: tense, uncertain, fearful. The two of them came up to the bed, almost in step. Susan stayed back by the door.

"You said you wanted to see me," Smith said.

"Why is there a guard outside?"

Smith flicked a glance at Vickie, then answered, "For your own protection."

"Protection from what?"

"The media. We don't want any scare stories leaking out."

Dan puffed out a breath. "Some guy tried to kidnap me, my daughter was—"

"Kidnap you?"

"Last night. Said there were some people who wanted to pick my brain."

"Peterson," Vickie blurted. Turning to Smith, "You said you scared him off."

"Apparently not." He looked back to Dan. "When was this? Tell me exactly what happened."

"Later. I want you to tell me what you plan to do about Jace first."

"That doesn't concern you." Tightly.

"The hell it doesn't. He's killed three men. He tried to kill me."

"We'll take care of Jace," Smith said. Then he added, "Don't try to rock the boat, Santorini. You're dealing with the federal government here."

"Susan," Dan called. "Go home and look up the nastiest god-damned lawyer in Florida. I think we're going to need one."

"There's no call for that," Smith said.

"Be reasonable, Dan," said Vickie.

Pointing a bandaged hand at them, he accused, "You want to use a homicidal maniac to advise the President? And you want *me* to be reasonable?"

"Dan, it's not what you think. Not at all," Vickie said soothingly. "But we can't let the media get their hands on this; they'll distort it and ruin everything."

"Jace cannot be allowed to run your VR system," he said to Smith. "Under no circumstances whatsoever."

"I know that," Smith said. "But we're going to use VR anyway, Santorini. You can't stop it."

"Maybe I can't stop it, but I'll have to see to it that it's properly controlled."

"Controlled? By who?"

"By me," Dan snapped.

"You?" Vickie and Susan said it together.

"What happens to ParaReality with Kyle dead?" Dan asked Vickie.

She looked confused by the abrupt change of subject. "I don't know," she said. "This has happened so suddenly . . ."

"All right, then," Dan said, "I'll tell you. You're going to be the new president of ParaReality, Vickie."

"I am?"

"Who the hell else is there?"

"But I—"

"Do you want the company to go under?"

Vickie shook her head. "No. Of course not."

"Then you've got to convince Kyle's backers that you've been running the operation anyway. We'll open Cyber World on schedule and go on from there."

"But you said you're going to Washington."

Nodding, Dan said, "I'll handle the Washington contract. I assume we have a formal contract?"

"A letter of agreement," she said.

"I'll handle that end of it. Gary Chan can head up the technical staff, under my direction."

"You're taking over the company!"

"No, Vickie, the two of us are going to save the company. And save the jobs of the rest of the staff."

Vickie glanced at Susan, then turned back to Dan. "I didn't know what Kyle was doing, honestly I didn't. I wouldn't have let him hurt your daughter."

Dan saw Susan glaring at her. "Vickie, if there was somebody else—anybody else . . . But there isn't. I'm stuck with you, and you're stuck with me."

Smith gave him a studied stare. "What's going on in your head, Santorini? You think you're some kind of a saint or something?"

"A saint?" Dan laughed at him. "I'm just an ordinary citizen, Smitty. But I'm not going to let you or anybody else use VR systems without the proper safeguards."

"That's big talk."

"If you want a VR system set up in the White House," said Dan, "you're going to have to do it through me."

"There are other people," said Smith.

"Sure there are. But the more people you involve, the more leaks you're going to have. Technical people talk to each other, Smitty. How'd you like to have the *Washington Post* snooping around your operation?"

"We're not doing anything wrong!"

"VR is so new that nobody's made up the rules about what's right and wrong," Dan countered.

"And that's what you want to do," Susan realized. "Make up the rules."

"Somebody's got to," said Dan, "and I don't see anybody else volunteering for the job."

"You think it's so fucking easy?" Smith almost snarled. "Just like that: you waltz in and take control of everything we're trying to do."

Dan said, "I don't want to control anything. I just want to make certain that everybody involved with VR knows what they're getting into."

"The nation's conscience," Smith sneered.

Dan grinned at him. "That's what saints are supposed to do, isn't it? Act as a conscience."

"What about Jace?" Susan asked.

"Jace." All Dan's enthusiasm ebbed away. He's my friend, he thought. He tried to kill me, but he was like a kid high on drugs. All those years we worked together. Was Doc right? Is Jace incapable of real friendship? Is he missing a sense of morality altogether?

"You can't prosecute Lowrey," Smith said sternly. "Bringing him to trial would blow this whole story wide open. Besides—"

"I'm not certain that we shouldn't blow it wide open," Dan said.

"I can't permit that."

"You can't stop it. I don't care how many guards you put on my door, sooner or later the story's going to leak out. You know that, and there's nothing you can do about it. Sooner or later the media's going to find out about it, and the longer you try to keep it secret the bigger the explosion will be when the media does find out."

"Okay, then. We won't involve Lowrey in it. Will that satisfy you?" Smith asked.

"A court trial would be gonzo anyway," Dan muttered, thinking aloud. "He was right about that. Try proving that he killed people remotely. The legal system isn't ready to handle anything like this, not yet. The real evidence is inside his own head."

"We could track down his research," Susan said. She came up from the door toward the bed. "He must have copies of his programs stored in a computer somewhere. Maybe his home."

Dan nodded. "And the helmets he rewired for the biofeedback loops."

"I don't want this dragged into court," Smith insisted.

Dan looked at him. This could get very nasty, he told himself. Smith will do everything in his power to keep this mess quiet. I can't buck the whole Washington power structure. I've got to *use* his fear of exposure to get what I want.

"Jace has got to be kept under lock and key," Dan said. "The guy is brilliant, but you can't trust him in the real world. Keep him in his lab and let him work at the things he likes to do. Keep him happy. But somebody's got to watch over him like a surveillance camera."

"Don't worry about Jace."

"But I do worry about him," Dan said. "He was my friend. I can't turn my back on him."

Smith glanced at Vickie. Her eyes were wide, trying to digest everything that was flowing past her. Susan watched them both, as well as her husband.

It was Vickie who broke the silence. "Do you really think Toshimura and the others would accept me as president of the company?"

"I don't know. It's your job to convince them to. If you can't, then we'll have to find somebody who can."

"They'll want to sell out to Sony or Disney," Vickie said.

"Well, then, maybe you can get them to sell the company as a unit. Keep the staff together, that's the important thing."

She nodded, but she still looked terribly uncertain.

"And you," Dan said, pointing a bandaged hand at Smith, "you ought to get some of those guys you've got stashed out in the hall to track down this jerk who tried to kidnap me. And the people he's working for."

"We already know who he is," Smith said. "Attempted kidnapping is something we can nail him on."

"Okay, then, get on it. Vickie, maybe you ought to get a conference call going with the investors. Tell them that Kyle's dead and you're taking over the reins."

Vickie smiled at him. "You're a strange man, Damon Santorini." But she headed for the door.

Smith stared at him a moment longer, as if he was trying to make up his mind about something. Finally he turned wordlessly and followed Vickie to the door.

Dan called to him. "And I want to meet your boss, Smitty."

Smith turned back, frowning. "My boss? You know Quigley?"

"I mean the President."

"The President?" Smith's voice almost cracked.

"You owe me that. I want to tell him about virtual reality, face-to-face."

"What the hell have the medics pumped you up with, Santorini?"

Dan laughed. "You can introduce me to him. It'll be a feather in your cap."

Shaking his head, Smith opened the door and left the room, with Vickie close behind him.

Susan came over and sat on the edge of the bed. "My God, Dan, you take my breath away."

"Do you think I'm a strange man, too?"

She studied his face. "Not strange. But different."

"I learned something in the VR games with Jace. Something important."

"You've grown."

Looking down at his bandaged hands, Dan said, "I faced death, Sue. More than once. It was only a simulation . . . but I don't think I'll ever be afraid of anything again."

Susan reached out, touched his shoulder. "Do you really think you can control the way the government uses VR?"

"Not really. But somebody's got to. I've got to try. VR's too powerful to allow them to use it any way they like."

"I wouldn't trust Smith further than I could throw a horse," Susan said. "Or Vickie, either, for that matter."

"It's got to be done, Sue. We've got to do this. God knows what Smith is really up to. He needs a watchdog just as much as Jace does."

"But does it have to be you?"

"Until we can find somebody better," Dan said.

She kissed him gently on the lips. "I can't think of a better man for the job," Susan murmured.

"It's going to be a hell of a life for us."

She looked into his eyes and saw something new there, and something familiar: Dan's rock-steady sense of responsibility.

"I love you, Dan," she said.

He started to say he loved her, too. But instead, "Dorothy was in one of the sims Jace sprang on me."

"I thought so."

"I thought I loved her," Dan said. "But it wasn't real. You're my real world, Sue. I've loved you ever since I met you."

"And I've always loved you, Dan. I've always been proud of you. But now—now you're going to show the whole world the man I've always known you could be."

"You think so?"

"I know it."

Inwardly Dan wondered how either one of them was going to like the life he saw ahead. All the intrigues and power plays of Washington. He wondered if he could survive in that jungle. But he said nothing of that to his wife. He simply held her, knowing that no matter what the world threw at them, as long as they could be together they would be strong enough to face it. He clung to her, and she held him tightly.

After a long while, he said, "I guess I ought to see Jace."

Susan said nothing.

"He's here in the hospital, isn't he?"

"Yes," she answered. "But . . ."

"What is it?"

"You'd better see for yourself."

It took almost half an hour of cajoling nurses and calling in three different doctors and arguing with the federal agents guarding his door, but finally Dan was lifted into a wheelchair and allowed to go up to the top floor of the hospital where they were keeping Jace.

"I'm not an invalid," Dan grumbled to Susan, who walked beside him. "I can walk on my own two feet."

"Don't be difficult, dear," said Susan. One of the agents was pushing the wheelchair; the other walked ahead of them, like a big blocky football player in street clothes clearing their path.

Dan was still complaining when they wheeled him through the door of Jace's private room. "I still don't see why—"

Jace lay on the bed, uncovered, clothed in a green hospital gown, curled into a fetal ball, knees pulled up to his chin, skinny arms wrapped around his shins, eyes squeezed tightly shut. His nose was taped; an ugly bluish bruise spread across his forehead. A feeding tube was connected to one arm. Sensors were plastered to his chest and back, trailing thin wires to the monitoring equipment stacked on one side of the railed bed.

"Jesus Christ," Dan gasped.

"He's been like that since they pulled him out of the simulation chamber," Susan said.

"That's why Smith said I wouldn't have to worry about him," said Dan. "He's in a catatonic trance, for God's sake."

"The doctors said there's no telling how long he'll stay this way. No one's able to reach him."

"I can." Dan felt tears in his eyes. Looking up at Susan, he said, "Call Gary Chan. Tell him to get one of the minis up here. And a set of gloves and helmet."

Jace knew he had been bad and now they were going to punish him for it. But he had fooled them all and run far, far away where nobody could find him. It was lonely, though. There was nobody here, nothing at all except endless darkness.

"Can you hear me, Jace?"

That was Dan's voice. Jace froze like a rabbit caught in a car's headlights. Don't answer! Don't move! Don't even breathe. Stay quiet and he can't find you. Stay quiet and he'll go away.

"I'm putting on one of the programs we found at your bungalow, Jace." Dan sounded worried, concerned. But Jace knew it was a trap. *They're all against me. All of them, even Dan. There's nobody in the whole world who cares about me. Nobody in the whole universe.*

"I'm starting the program now, Jace. I hope it makes you happy. I hope you'll want to talk to me when it's finished."

Never, Jace answered silently. *I'm all alone in my own world, and it's a better world than the one outside. Lonely but better. Cold but better. Dark but—*

The darkness shifted, lightened. Jace squinted into the gray dawn and saw his old friends, the robots. And their evil masters, the slimy aliens who had enslaved them. He raised his right hand, and the purifying sword of energy glowed brightly.

The battle was long and hard, but at its end Jace was victorious. The slain enemy aliens lay in piles all around him. The robots bowed at his feet.

"This is only the first battle of many," Jace warned them. "The war will be long and hard. But we will win! Our victory is inevitable."

And then he saw the coldly beautiful queen standing before him. His mother stretched out her arms to him. His mother smiled at him, and Jace felt his heart break with happiness.

I'll never leave this world, he told himself. *I'll stay here always and always and ever.*

EPILOGUE

Dan coughed nervously as Susan straightened his tie. For the past two weeks, she had dressed him and undressed him, pulling his sleeves over his bandaged hands, tying his shoelaces, combing his hair. She would let no one else do it.

Dan felt like a helpless idiot, an invalid. He did not mind the undressing so much, though. Susan turned it into a sexy game.

But now he felt so tense that the first warning rasp of a wheeze scratched inside his chest.

Not now! he commanded himself. Relax.

Good advice, he said to himself as Susan patted at a cowlick.

"Stop fussing," he grumbled.

She inspected him from head to toe. Dan did the same for her.

"I think this is the first time you've worn a dress since we moved to Florida," he said, grinning at her.

It had been a wild two weeks. Dan was still not certain that Vickie could hold on as the new president of ParaReality, but so far the investors had not demanded her resignation. Gary Chan had taken the leadership of the technical staff; that side of the work was going ahead as smoothly as could be expected. But the rest of it—

Chuck Smith entered the room. He looked nervous.

"I hope you know what you're doing, Santorini," said Smith. Dan made a smile for him. "So do I."

The other door to the anteroom opened, and a secretary beckoned to them.

With Smith in the lead and Susan beside him, Damon Santorini stepped into the Oval Office.